"Seen enough?"

"I didn't mean to stare. I wa

"Curious?" Kellen demanded. "My leg might be mangled, but I can assure you everything else is in working order."

He'd expected Brigit to stomp out of the room in a huff. He should have known his dot-every-i and cross-every-t manager would do no such thing. Indeed, Brigit drew closer and came around the side of the bed.

"Now you expect me to apologize," he said.

"As a matter of fact..." She fisted her hands, settled them on her hips and sent him an arch look.

Nice hips. Neatly rounded and, along with her firm backside, just right. Given Kellen's position on the bed, the hips he was admiring were practically at eye level. His mouth watered and parts of his body that had been dormant for months began to stir back to life. Some of his frustration and anger dissipated, only to be replaced by feelings that were far more dangerous.

Even though he knew he was playing with fire, Kellen was helpless to keep his gaze from traveling up Brigit's slender frame and touching on all of the parts that interested him.

"Well?" she demanded.

Their gazes met—collided, really. He didn't see sparks fly, but he swore he felt them. They showered his skin.

The sensation was life-affirming. And he reveled in it.

THE HEIR'S UNEXPECTED RETURN

BY

JACKIE BRAUN

Published in Great Britain 2015
by Mills & Boon, an imprint of Harlequin (UK) Limited,
Eton House, 18-24 Paradise Road, Richmond, Surrey, TW9 1SR

ISBN: 978-0-263-25103-6

23-0115

Harlequin (UK) Limited's policy is to use papers that are natural, renewable and recyclable products and made from wood grown in sustainable forests. The logging and manufacturing processes conform to the legal environmental regulations of the country of origin.

Printed
by CPI,

Jackie Braun is the author of more than two dozen romance novels. She is a three-time RITA® Award finalist, a four-time National Readers' Choice Awards finalist, the winner of a Rising Star Award in traditional romantic fiction and was nominated for Series Storyteller of the Year by *RT Book Reviews* in 2008. She lives in Michigan with her husband and two sons, and can be reached through her website at www.jackiebraun.com.

For Mark, my real-life hero.

CHAPTER ONE

FAT THUNDERCLOUDS ROLLED overhead and spat rain like machine gun fire as wave after wave battered Hadley Island's sandy beachfront. As it was on one of the barrier islands off the South Carolina coast, the sixteen-mile-long stretch of pristine shoreline was used to the abuse. Mother Nature's fury, however, was no match for the emotions roiling inside Brigit Wright.

Unmindful of the worsening storm, she continued to walk. In the pocket of the yellow rain slicker she wore, she fisted her hand around the already-crumpled piece of paper. Printing out the email hadn't changed its content.

Miss Wright, I will be arriving home the day after tomorrow for an extended stay. Please have my quarters on the main floor ready.
—KF

Two curt sentences that still had her blood boiling.

Kellen Faust, heir to the Faust fortune, was returning coming "home" as he'd put it—to continue his recuperation after the skiing accident he'd suffered four months earlier in the Swiss Alps.

If the news reports she'd read about his fall were even remotely accurate, then Brigit supposed she should feel sorry for him. Along with a concussion, dislocated shoulder and broken wrist, he'd snapped his ankle, mangled his knee and shattered the femur in his right leg. Four months out and the man was still in the midst of a long and very painful recovery. Even so, she didn't want him here while he did his mending, potentially meddling in the day-to-day minutia of running the exclusive Faust Haven resort. Brigit preferred to work without interference.

Kellen's family had a large home outside Charleston, as well as an assortment of plush real estate holdings sprinkled around Europe. Why hadn't he picked one of those places to do his recuperating? Surely they would be more accommodating to Kellen's large entourage and the other assorted sycophants who enabled his Peter Pan–like existence.

Why choose Faust Haven? This wasn't his home. It was *hers*, dammit! Just as Faust Haven was *her* resort, the name on the deed notwithstanding. While he'd spent the past five years hotfooting around Europe, living off what had to be a sizable trust fund and enjoying the life of the idle rich, Brigit had been hard at work turning a tired and nearly forgotten old-money retreat into a fashionable, five-star accommodation that offered excellent service and amenities and, above all else, discretion, in addition to its panoramic views. As such it was booked solid not only for the current calendar year, but for the next three. Brigit had made that happen. And she'd done so without Kellen's help.

Now the heir was returning and he wanted his quarters readied. *His* quarters? During the time she'd managed the resort, Kellen had never set foot on the island. It was Brigit's understanding that he hadn't visited the island since he was a boy. So she'd made the owner's private apartment on the main floor her own, and had turned the manager's rooms into a luxury suite that commanded a handsome sum.

Where was she going to sleep now? She might go to bed after most of the guests were tucked in for the night and rise long before they awoke, but that didn't mean she wanted to bunk on one of the overstuffed couches in the lobby or the big leather recliner in the library, no matter how comfy she found it to be for reading.

Muttering an oath that was swallowed by the wind, she stopped walking and looked back in the direction she had come. The cedar-shingled resort stood three stories tall—four, really, given the pilings that raised it another twelve feet above sea level to protect it from flooding. Natural sand dunes dotted with clumps of gangly grass buffered the structure from the worst of the Atlantic's abuse.

Home.

Kellen might refer to it as such, but for Brigit that truly was the case. It was here she'd come after her nasty divorce. Pride battered, feeling like an epic failure. The sea air, the sense of purpose, both had played a key role in ushering her back from the brink of despair.

Her gaze skimmed the balconies that stretched out from every room to maximize the view. Even though it was early afternoon, the lights burned brightly in the windows, beacons of welcome to any guests who had braved the worsening weather and boarded the last ferry from the mainland before the storm halted service. Once travelers reached the island, of course, they would still have to navigate the winding roads over the hilly center of Hadley Island to the eastern shore where the resort was situated. But even accounting for the slow going, those guests would be arriving soon.

With a sigh, Brigit headed back. She had a job to do and she would do it. Right now, her priority was to see that all new arrivals were comfortably settled in their rooms. Once that task was accomplished, she would work on figuring out her own accommodations for the duration of Kellen's stay.

By the time she reached the resort, any part of her body not covered by the slicker was drenched. She had hoped to have enough time to change into dry clothes and do something with her hair before the first guests arrived, but a full-size black SUV was pulling up under the covered portico at the main entrance as she came around the dune.

The driver hopped out, as did another man, who came around from the vehicle's passenger side. Both were big and burly. Bodyguards? It wasn't a surprise. A lot of the inn's guests were important people—Hollywood A-listers, business magnates, politicians. Before either man could reach for the handle, however, the rear passenger door swung open.

Brigit covered her mouth, but a gasp still escaped.

Kellen Faust. The heir was early.

She'd never met Kellen in person. They exchanged emails and texts a couple times a month, and occasionally a phone call. But he'd never come for a visit. Now here he was. In the flesh. And he wasn't at all what Brigit had expected.

Every photograph she had seen of him—and the guy turned up in print and online media reports with as much regularity as the tide—showed a handsome young man with sun-lightened brown hair, deep-set hazel eyes, a carefree smile and a body honed to perfection under what had to be the capable tutelage of a well-paid personal trainer.

Meanwhile, the man trying to exit the SUV's rear seat was thin, borderline gaunt, muscles withered away from long hours spent still and sedated. The dark smudges under his eyes made it plain he hadn't been getting much sleep as of late. He remained good-looking, but if his rigid posture and pinched features were any indication, he was far from carefree.

Vital, healthy, fit? None of the descriptions she'd seen in press clippings applied to the man now.

"I'll get the wheelchair, Mr. Faust," said the man who'd come around from the front passenger side.

"No! I'll walk," he bit out in an angry rasp that carried to Brigit despite the howling wind.

"But, Mr. Faust—" the driver began, only to be shouted down.

"I said I'll walk, Lou! I'm *not* a freaking invalid!"

Kellen swung his left leg out the door without too much effort, but when it came to the right one, he had to use his hands to manipulate the limb over the threshold. Then, lowering himself to the running board first, he eased to the ground. He held a cane in one hand. He used the other hand to grip the door frame. Unfortunately, neither support was enough to save him. A mere second after both of his feet hit the driveway, his right knee buckled. The man he'd called Lou caught Kellen under his arms before he hit the pavement. Ripe cursing followed. The other man rushed forward, as did Brigit, determined to help.

"Who in the hell are you?" Kellen bellowed, shaking off the hand she placed on his arm.

She pushed back her hood and offered what she hoped was a professional smile. Wouldn't it just figure that she looked her absolute worst for the occasion? Despite the rain slicker's hood, her hair was damp, and the bangs that she was three months into growing out were plastered against her forehead. As for makeup, she doubted the little bit she'd applied that morning lingered on her eyelashes and cheeks now. Her feet were bare, her calves spattered with wet sand. It was hardly the professional image she'd planned to portray when she first made his acquaintance.

"I'm Brigit Wright." When he continued to stare as if she were something to be studied on a slide under a microscope, she added, "We've spoken on the phone and via email for, well, several years. I manage Faust Haven."

That news elicited not a polite smile, but a snort that bordered on derisive.

"Of course you do." His gaze flickered down in seeming dismissal. Although he said it half under his breath, she heard him well enough when he added, "I had you pegged right."

So, the man had preconceived notions of her, did he? That didn't come as much of a surprise. And to be fair, she entertained plenty of her own where he was concerned. Still, it irked her that, after a mere glance, he could so easily marginalize her—both professionally and, she didn't doubt, personally.

Brigit cleared her throat and drew herself up to her full height of five foot six. Since he was hunched over, it put them nearly at eye level. When their gazes connected she didn't so much as blink. Using her most practiced "boss" tone, she told him, "I wasn't expecting you. Your email, which I received only this morning, said you wouldn't arrive until the day after tomorrow."

"I changed my mind."

"Obviously."

"I was in Charleston visiting..." His words trailed off and his expression hardened. "I'm here now. I trust that's not a problem, Miss Wright."

"None whatsoever," she assured him with a stiff smile.

"I just wanted to explain that your *quarters,* well, they are not ready at the moment."

"Am I expected to wait out here until they are?" he demanded irritably.

Standing under the portico, they were protected from the worst of the rain, but the wind pushed enough of it sideways that it splattered them every now and again.

"Of course not," she replied as heat crept into her cheeks. What was she thinking, keeping a guest of his position, much less his current condition, out in the elements? She turned on her heel and marched toward the lobby entrance, calling over her shoulder, "Right this way, gentlemen."

Kellen didn't follow the ever-efficient Miss Wright inside to the elevator. Rather, he allowed Lou and Joe to half drag, half carry him in the direction of the door. He'd ticked her off but good. No surprise that, since he'd been so rude. Another time, he would have felt bad about the way he'd treated her. Unfortunately for her, both his usual good humor and his abundant charm had gone the way of his right leg. That was to say, fractured beyond repair. Or so the doctors claimed. They were wrong. They had to be. He couldn't spend the rest of his life like this... barely able to walk. A mere shadow of the healthy, active man he used to be.

The elevator doors opened after a bell dinged, announcing their arrival. The lobby looked different than he remembered from the last time he'd been to Faust Haven. Gone were the deep green, gold and maroon that had always struck him as more suited to a Rocky Mountains cabin than an ocean-side resort. Varying shades of blue and turquoise dominated the color scheme now, accentuated with weathered white and a pale yellow that reminded Kellen of sand. Overhead lights, along with the glow of table lamps, gave the lobby a warm, welcoming ambiance despite the storm that raged outside.

He exhaled slowly, and some of the tension left his shoulders. He remained a long way from relaxed, but he knew one thing for certain. He'd been right to come here.

He'd been second-guessing the decision to leave Switzerland ever since his plane touched down in Raleigh and the only one to greet him at the airport had been his mother's ancient butler holding a hand-lettered sign bearing Kellen's name. Orley hadn't changed much, but Kellen apparently had. The older man hadn't recognized him. Of course, it had been nearly a dozen years since Kellen had set foot in his boyhood home in Charleston.

And it had been longer than that since he'd been to the island.

He glanced around again. "This is…this is nice," he said to no one in particular.

"The remodeling was completed last fall. All of the guest rooms have been updated in a similar color scheme." She cleared her throat. Her tone was just this side of defensive when she added, "I emailed you numerous photographs."

He didn't remember the photos. He probably hadn't bothered to open the attachments. Too busy burning through his trust fund to care, he thought with a mental grimace. Well, he was done with that. In a way, the accident had forced his hand. He couldn't ignore his responsibilities any longer. It was time to put his degree to use and start earning his keep.

"They didn't do it justice," he murmured.

Nor, Kellen admitted, had the image he'd had in his head done her justice, despite what he'd just said about having her pegged.

For the past five years, he'd signed her paychecks, given the reports she'd dutifully sent on the first of each month a quick skim and approved her capital improvements—all while offering minimal input. This had been accomplished remotely. He'd never laid eyes on the woman to whom he'd entrusted what was now all that was left of to his birthright…until now.

She'd shed the old-man-and-the-sea rain slicker and stood in front of the reception desk wearing an aqua-blue polo shirt adorned with the inn's logo and a pair of white shorts that skimmed to mid-thigh. Nice legs—tanned, toned and surprisingly long for someone who probably topped out at five and a half feet. His gaze lifted to her waist, which was small, before rising to her breasts, which were just the right size to fill a man's hands.

He tore his gaze away, surprised to find himself ogling the woman—his employee no less—as if he were some sort of sex-crazed frat boy on spring break. At the same time, he was a bit relieved by his reaction, as base as it was. He'd felt dead for so long…

"I need to get off my feet, Miss Wright. Sooner rather than later, if you don't mind." Pain turned his tone surly.

"Of course." She gave a curt nod. "Follow me."

Pride demanded that he do so under his own steam, as slow as that would make the going. He took his cane from his driver before turning to Joe.

"Help Lou with the bags."

Officially, Joe was his physical therapist, but the younger man didn't mind pitching in as an extra pair of hands when needed. He was being paid well enough, and it wasn't as if he was kept particularly busy since Kellen regularly skipped his daily stretching and strengthening workouts.

He knew he needed to do them, of course. But knowing and doing were two different things. Hell, some days, Kellen was lucky to get out of bed at all, especially when specialist after specialist offered such a grim prognosis.

He shifted from his good leg to the bad one. Even using the cane to bear much of his weight, the pain was excruciating. He bit back a groan and wondered for the millionth time if it had been wise to swear off the narcotics his doctor prescribed, even if they had made him dizzy and brain-dead. Even if secretly he'd worried that the lure of oblivion might prove too much and he would wind up addicted.

His progress was slow, his gait uneven and lurching, although at least he was able to bear his weight. Brigit turned around once, concern obvious in her expression, but she didn't offer any assistance. Even when he stumbled before catching his balance, she kept her distance and said nothing. Apparently, his rude dismissal of her help outside had done the trick. He was glad for that. Kellen hated the way people were always rushing to his aid, opening doors, clearing a path for him. For the invalid. Hell, he was surprised they didn't try to wipe his mouth or other parts of his anatomy as if he were a damn baby.

Women had been among the worst offenders. That was one of the reasons he'd ditched the entourage of females that had routinely crashed at his chalet. As for his male friends, the number had dwindled to nil once it had become clear Kellen no longer would be throwing any of the parties for which he had become legend.

Users and hangers-on, every last one of them. What did it say about him, Kellen wondered, that the only loyalty he commanded was among people such as Joe and Lou and, yeah, Miss Wright, all of whom were on his payroll?

Behind the reception desk, a door led to a short hallway. To the left were the business office, supply room and laundry facility. Kellen remembered playing hide-and-seek in them as a boy during visits with his grandfather. The employee break room was new. He didn't ask about it, though. No doubt she'd told him about its addition in one of those emails he'd barely skimmed.

The owner's two-bedroom apartment was on the right. The door was closed, the word *private* stamped on a plaque affixed just below a peephole. After Brigit pulled a key from her pocket and opened it, Kellen stepped over the threshold, prepared to be assailed with memories of his grandfather, the one person in his life whose love had been complete and unconditional. But as in the lobby, nothing here was as he remembered. Given how emotional he already was feeling, he wasn't sure whether he was grateful for that or not.

The last time Kellen had been inside, the decor had been far more masculine. It wasn't only the pale, almost pastel shades of paint on the walls that made it seem feminine now. It was the furnishings: overstuffed white couch, patterned throw pillows, decorative lamps, fat candles in ornate holders, glass jars filled with an assortment of seashells that he'd bet Brigit had collected herself. The scent that lingered in the air was not that of his grandfather's pipe tobacco. Rather, it was light, fresh and pretty. Her scent. He inhaled deeply, finding it oddly comforting and arousing at the same time. He shoved the unsettling thought aside, only to have another take its place.

"You live here."

She frowned. "For the past few years, yes. Room and board are one of the perks of the job."

"I know that. But this was my grandfather's apartment. It's for the owner… I didn't realize."

"You didn't realize?" Her tone was as incredulous as her expression. "But I told you—"

He cut her off. "I thought there was an apartment on the other side of the lobby to accommodate the manager."

Brigit's mouth puckered at his response, drawing Kellen's attention to a pair of lush lips that needed no added color to make them appealing, despite the agitation reflected in her eyes.

"There is, or rather, there was. But since this apartment was just sitting empty all the time, I…that is, *we* decided it made more sense to turn the manager's apartment into a luxury suite that could accommodate four or more guests for an extended stay."

"*We* did?"

Color rose in her cheeks. He was surprised he couldn't see steam waft from her crown. "I sent you several reports listing the pros and cons. You said you agreed with the cost-benefit analysis that I supplied when I first made the suggestion."

"Right. I remember now." Kellen nodded, although he was damned if he could recall doing any such thing.

She'd taken excellent care of the inn. Every penny invested in capital improvements had paid off, he decided, thinking of the lobby. Whereas he had been reckless in the past, the risks Brigit took had been calculated and well thought out.

He might have approved her plans, but the decisions had been hers alone. Kellen had a business degree. One that he'd never earned a living from…although he planned to do so now. He'd be wise to pay attention, learn the ropes from what was obviously a very competent manager.

"It's been full ever since," she added.

Which meant it was full now.

Kellen appreciated her ability to turn previously unused space profitable, but it did make for a tricky situation. "Where are you going to sleep, Miss Wright?"

Where was she going to sleep?

Brigit gritted her teeth. That was the million-dollar question, but she shrugged and offered what she hoped passed for an unconcerned smile.

"I'll figure out something for the duration of your stay." As unspecified as that might be. And as short as she hoped it would turn out.

Kellen lumbered to the couch and dropped heavily onto the cushions, his face pinched with a grimace. Sheer will had kept him upright, of that much she was certain. She might have admired his tenacity if it weren't accompanied by such a surly disposition.

"Well, there must be at least one guest room available, right?" For the first time, he sounded more uncertain than he did irascible.

"No. Full means full. And we're full this week."

"And next?"

She exhaled slowly. "Actually, for the rest of the season barring any last-minute cancellations." When he just continued to gape at her, she added, "It's been an excellent summer so far. Revenues are up by—"

He cut her off with a ripe oath. "Well, you can't sleep in the damned lobby."

Brigit already had made the same determination, but her options were limited. The only alternative was…

Her gaze cut to the hallway and the spare bedroom, where she exercised when the weather prevented her from getting outside for a run. It had a futon that pulled out into what her older sister claimed was a pretty comfortable bed. Robbie and her son, Will, were the only overnight guests Brigit had ever entertained. On a sigh, she recalled their upcoming visit. She'd have to let them know plans had changed. Yet another disruption in her otherwise well-organized schedule.

"I'll have our bellboy set up a cot for me in the office," she said at last.

"The office we just passed?" He snorted. "It's barely big enough for the desk. You can't get a bed in there, even if it is a damn cot."

"It will be tight," she admitted. Not to mention that she would need to figure out where to shower and stow her belongings, but at least it would afford her more privacy than the inn's common areas.

"No."

She blinked. "No?"

"No." This time his tone made the single syllable sound even more final.

Brigit felt her blood pressure rise again. The man certainly knew how to push her buttons. She didn't like being told what to do. Since her divorce, no man had dared, nor would she have stood for it. After her fiasco of a marriage, during which she had all but disappeared behind her husband's overbearing and autocratic personality, she'd vowed never to become invisible or obsolete again. She had a brain and a voice. These days, she used both with impunity.

But just as she opened her mouth to protest, Kellen leaned his head back on the sofa and closed his eyes. Dressed in varying shades of gray and black—colors that mirrored his mood—she couldn't help but notice how out of place he looked amid the array of cheerful throw pillows. Still, she might have argued with his edict. Firmly but politely, of course, since he was her employer and tact was in order. But his expression stopped her. The taut line of his mouth and the way his brow furrowed made it plain that he was hurting.

"When was the last time you took a painkiller?" she asked. She kept her tone neutral, careful to keep any concern from leaking into it lest she knick his pride. From the way he'd shrugged off her assistance earlier, she gathered he didn't want any.

Men. It was all she could do not to roll her eyes. She'd thought she was done stroking their damned egos now that Scott was out of the picture. Well, apparently not.

"I quit those a few weeks ago," he muttered. Just when she started to think his decision was rooted in some sort of macho tough-guy bull, he added, "They make me a zombie. It's not all that unpleasant of a feeling, but the last thing I need is to wind up addicted to pain meds on top of everything else."

His reasoning was sound, even if it meant his pain was left unmanaged.

The two men who'd accompanied Kellen strode into the apartment then. The driver was hauling a pair of suitcases that were large enough to hold Brigit's entire wardrobe. The younger man pushed the wheelchair. A smaller piece of luggage was balanced on its seat with a garment bag draped over top of it. Brigit's stomach dropped. Kellen had brought a lot of baggage—in more ways than one. And none of it boded well for how long she would be displaced from her home.

"Where do you want your things, boss?" the driver asked.

Without opening his eyes, Kellen motioned with one hand in the direction of the hall. "Put them in the master bedroom, Lou."

"And mine?" the guy pushing the wheelchair asked.

Kellen did open his eyes now and he straightened in his seat. "Change of plans, Joe. Miss Wright will be bunking in the spare room. You'll be out here on the couch."

Brigit's mouth fell open. Just like that, he'd turned them all into roommates.

CHAPTER TWO

AGAIN, BRIGIT TRIED to protest. "That's not necessary. As I said, I can sleep on a cot in the office."

"And I say it is necessary." Kellen waved a hand. Then, "Not to be rude, but if you could move your belongings out of your room into the spare and be on your way, I'd appreciate it. I need to lie down."

He didn't wait for Brigit to respond. Rather, he returned his head to the cushion and closed his eyes once again.

She'd been dismissed like the hired help she was. Well, hired help or not, his dismissal made her blood boil. It took an effort, but she managed to swallow the pithy reply that likely would have seen her fired. Instead, as she followed the pair of burly men down the hall, she muttered half under her breath, "Sure, Mr. Faust. No problem, Mr. Faust. Happy to oblige."

Brigit kept a tidy home, even in the rooms that casual visitors normally didn't see. She was grateful for that fact now that strangers were invading her privacy.

Although the rooms were neat, she would have to change the sheets on her bed before Kellen used it. She'd planned to handle that chore in the morning, as well as gather up her clothes and toiletries in anticipation of his arrival. By showing up a day and a half early, and bringing another overnight guest, he'd left her scrambling and feeling…inadequate.

She swallowed the bile that threatened to inch up the back of her throat. The sentiment didn't sit well.

While the driver continued down the hall, Brigit stopped at the first doorway. Glancing around the spare room, she tapped a finger to her lips. The treadmill would need to be moved to the corner to make room to open the futon, which would need fresh linens. Ditto for the living room's pullout couch, where Kellen had assigned Joe to bunk.

As if reading her mind, Joe said from behind her, "Sorry for all of the inconvenience our stay is causing you."

She turned, taking in his sheepish smile. She guessed him to be a few years her junior, which would put him in his late twenties. Despite a hairline that was already receding halfway across his crown, his face was almost boyish. If he had to shave once a week, she would be surprised.

"It's no problem," she lied.

"I'm Joe Bosley, your other uninvited guest." He let go of one of the wheelchair handles so he could shake her hand. "I'm Mr. Faust's physical therapist."

"It's nice to meet you, Joe. I'm Brigit Wright. As you probably guessed, I manage Faust Haven."

Joe nodded. Then, "Hey, would it be okay if I stowed my stuff in here?"

Better in the spare room with her than taking up space in the main living area. Brigit nodded and then pointed across the room. "The drawers in that dresser are mostly empty. If you'd like, you can have a couple of them."

"Great. Thanks. I'll take the bottom two."

That left her with the top three. "And there's plenty

of room in the closet if you have anything you want to hang up."

"Nah." Joe wrinkled his pug-like nose and motioned to his hulking frame. "I'm a wash-and-wear kind of guy. Shorts, T-shirts and sweats mostly, although I do keep a pair of khaki pants and a few polo shirts on hand for anything that requires me to dress up."

She nearly smiled. Khakis and collared shirts were Joe's formal wear. Meanwhile, if all of the photographs she'd seen of Kellen over the years were any indication, the guy probably owned stock in Armani. *Not that Kellen didn't wear a tux well*, a traitorous voice whispered. She silenced it.

Joe's simple wardrobe explained why he had only one medium-size suitcase while his boss had brought a pair of ginormous ones as well as a garment bag. Whatever designer-label duds were stuffed inside of them really wasn't the issue. The sheer amount said he was planning a far more extended stay than she'd first assumed. Just her luck.

"This is a nightmare," she muttered, momentarily forgetting about her audience.

Not surprisingly, Joe misunderstood what she meant. "You'll hardly know we're here."

"I'm sorry. That was rude. I'm not usually rude," she said.

Uptight, unimaginative and colossally boring both in the bedroom and out, according to her ex, but even that jerk had never called Brigit's manners into question.

"It's okay." Joe sent her a reassuring smile. Then, motioning over his shoulder with one thumb, he added, "He's not so bad, you know."

"I'm sure." Her attempt at sounding convincing fell far short.

"Really," Joe insisted. "Mr. F is in a lot of pain right now."

She nodded. "He said he's not taking the meds the doctor prescribed. Said they give him brain fog."

She decided to keep to herself the part about him worrying about becoming addicted.

"They'd give an elephant brain fog." Joe leaned closer then and dropped his voice to barely above a whisper. "His pain isn't all physical, although I doubt he'd admit to that."

So, the accident had taken an emotional toll as well. Brigit supposed she shouldn't find that surprising. Even strong people could succumb to depression. God knew, she'd hovered at its dark door for a time just before finally calling it quits on her marriage.

"Mr. Faust's injury…how bad is it?"

"To be honest, it's one of the worst I've ever seen. His wrist and shoulder have healed pretty well, but his leg… he mangled it but good. Major tendon and ligament damage in addition to the bone fractures." Joe shook his head and exhaled. "You know, the doctors initially advised amputating just above the knee."

"My God!" Brigit gasped. "I had no idea."

"Yeah, well, he managed to keep that much from being leaked to the press. His *friends…*" Joe snorted, as if finding the word laughable. "They forwarded all sorts of information and even a few photographs snapped in Mr. F's hospital room to the tabloids. He wasn't happy about it."

"I'd say he needs a better class of friends."

Joe grunted at her assessment. "I can't say I was sorry when he announced we would be heading back to the States. Some of them probably haven't noticed he's gone, although they'll get the idea once the chalet sells."

Brigit's stomach dropped. "Sells?"

"He said he doesn't want to go back there. Of course, it might just be the depression talking."

One could hope. Because if he didn't go back there, she had the sickening feeling she knew where he might next call home.

"How's his therapy going?" she asked, hoping for good news.

That wasn't what she got.

"Slow." Joe sighed. "All of the scar tissue isn't helping, especially since most days he doesn't want to do his exercises."

"That must make your job difficult."

"It does. It also feeds his frustration, because depressed or not, he refuses to give up hope."

"Of walking without assistance, you mean?" she inquired.

Joe nodded. "Walking without assistance to start. Then running, skiing. He wants to be as good as new."

Despite a mangled leg that the doctors had wanted to amputate.

"That's not likely to happen, is it?" she asked softly.

Joe looked away and cleared his throat. "I really shouldn't be talking about Mr. F's case with anyone. I just wanted you to know that, well, he's not being a jerk right now just to be a jerk."

"Understood. Thank you."

But if Joe thought she was going to cut the irritable Kellen Faust some slack, he was wrong. Oh, she would tread lightly. She wasn't an idiot, and she loved this job. But letting people get away with being insufferable, even if they had a good reason for being that way, wasn't healthy for anyone. Besides, she was finished being anyone's verbal punching bag.

When Brigit reached the master bedroom, the driver

was waiting for her. Kellen's large suitcases were open on the bed.

"I'll need a few drawers in the bureau where I can put away his things. Hope that's okay?"

Where Kellen ordered, his employees asked. She appreciated their restraint.

"Sure." She grabbed a tote bag from the closet and started to fill it with socks and underwear from the top drawer. Over her shoulder she called, "I'll be out of your hair in a minute."

The man sported a shaved head, so her phrasing earned a wry look.

"No rush, Miss Wright."

"Call me Brigit."

He smiled, showing off a gold front tooth. "I'm Lou."

"So, Lou, where will you be staying? I assume you won't be bunking in here. Will you and Joe be flipping a coin to see who sleeps on the floor and who gets the pullout sofa?"

"Nah." Lou chuckled. "The kid gets the living room all to himself. I have family on the other side of the island not far from the ferry docks. I'll be staying there, although I'll be on call for the duration of Mr. Faust's stay." He grinned and sent her a wink. "Worried that you were going to have to make room for another unexpected boarder?"

"Not at all. The more the merrier," she said drily.

They both laughed.

While she finished filling her bag with clothes from the dresser drawers, Lou hung an assortment of shirts and pants in the closet. All of the garments screamed expensive and were far more formal than the nylon pants, T-shirt and track jacket Kellen had on now.

Did he plan to wear them? If so, when? Where? Once

again, she was left with the uneasy feeling that her employer was hunkering down for the long haul.

The man was accustomed to a robust social life, if the press accounts were to be believed. Well, he wouldn't find much of that on the island. Of course, since his accident, he'd lain low. In recent months, the only time his photograph had graced the newspapers, whether the legitimate press or the gossip rags, he'd been shown leaving a doctor's office or a hospital. No smiles for the cameras in those pictures. He'd worn the same pain-induced grimace she'd viewed firsthand. And his palms had been up, as if to ward off the swarming paparazzi.

Brigit finished clearing out the drawers and hastily grabbed a selection of outfits from the closet, which she took to the spare room. Joe had finished emptying his lone suitcase. Hands on his hips, he was glancing around.

"Can I help you with something?" she asked.

"I've got some equipment I need to bring in for Mr. F's sessions. Some of it is going to take up space. I don't think you're going to want it in the living room."

He was right about that. "The inn has a gym on the main floor. It's small, but there should be room for your equipment."

"Mr. F prefers privacy."

Brigit nodded. She couldn't blame him for that. She preferred privacy herself. Not that she would be getting much of it for the next who-knew-how-long.

"If I have my treadmill moved to storage, will that be enough space? The bookshelf under the window can go, too."

Joe squinted, as if visualizing the room sans the items she'd mentioned. "Yeah. I think that will do it."

"Great. I'll call the bellboy."

"No need. Lou and I can handle this."

"All right." That settled, she nodded toward the bag that was still on the wheelchair's seat. "Is that Mr. Faust's?"

"Yes."

"I can take that to the master bedroom, if you'd like. I still need to get my toiletries from the bath."

"Appreciate it." Joe handed it to her. Then, "Speaking of toiletries, I take it the two of us will be sharing the bathroom in the hall."

Brigit managed to squelch a groan. The invasion of her privacy was officially complete. Still, if she had to share a bathroom, she supposed she'd rather do so with an affable Joe rather than a sullen Kellen. The latter would be too…intimate.

Where had that thought come from?

She forced a smile and, striving for good humor, asked Joe, "So, are you neat?"

"I can be when the situation calls for it."

"Trust me. It does," she replied drily.

"Then I promise I'll do my best to remember to put the toilet seat down, too."

Brigit's laughter was cut short by a snort coming from the living room. Then Kellen yelled, "Can you two skip the chitchat and finish up? As I'm the one who signs both of your paychecks, I know you have better things to do with your time than flirt."

Flirt! Brigit felt her face flame, but it wasn't merely embarrassment that brought heat rushing into her cheeks. The nerve of the man accusing her of flirting, as if her spending a few minutes talking to a colleague meant she was some sort of slacker. And to think mere minutes earlier she'd started to feel sorry for him based on the extent of his injury. Every ounce of sympathy had evaporated now.

Joe pulled a face. "Sorry," he mouthed.

Brigit nodded, but she was too damned irritated to be sorry.

She delivered the bag to the master bedroom. While Lou and Joe moved the treadmill and bookshelf to storage to make room for the physical therapy equipment, she changed the sheets on the bed where Kellen would sleep. Afterward, she gathered up her toiletries from the attached bathroom and put out fresh hand and bath towels. Then, satisfied that everything was in order, she turned to leave only to do an about-face.

"Toothbrush," she muttered aloud.

She opened the medicine cabinet, planning to grab the item in question. When her gaze landed on the bottle of extra-strength ibuprofen, an idea formed. One that she couldn't resist. She fished the eyeliner pencil out of her makeup bag and, after jotting her message, grinned at her reflection in the mirror.

As Brigit entered the living room, she braced for an unpleasant exchange.

Be polite. Be professional. But hold to your principles.

She needn't have bothered with the internal pep talk. Kellen was fast asleep on her couch. He remained seated where he had been, but his bad leg was propped on the coffee table, one of her colorful pillows under the heel serving as a cushion. In sleep he appeared less formidable and intimidating than he had while glowering at her and barking out orders. But even in slumber he wore a grimace that pulled down the corners of his mouth. Pain. Add in a wheelchair and cane, and it should have made him seem vulnerable. Only none of that did.

Nor did it detract from his overall good looks. With his chiseled cheekbones and square jaw, the man was classically handsome. No getting around that, even in his diminished physical state. Nor was there any getting around his reputation as a freewheeling ladies' man. A lot of women probably thought his polished looks and well-padded bank account made him quite a catch. Especially if they were able to excuse his nasty disposition, she thought uncharitably.

Kellen's head was canted sideways in a position that was sure to leave his neck sore when he awoke. Even so, she didn't attempt to wake him. She had no desire to poke a sleeping bear. Instead, she tiptoed past him, eager to avoid further unpleasantness. At the door, she chanced a glance back. The less interaction Brigit had with her boss, the better.

Kellen woke to the sound of a door closing. He straightened on the couch and craned his neck to one side and then the other. In the short time he'd been asleep, a crick already had formed just below the base of his skull. He grunted. Yet another sore muscle for Joe to work on during their afternoon session. If Kellen went. Maybe he'd skip it again. What was the point, anyway?

It was this kind of thinking that made him angry, even as it also left him feeling defeated. He wanted to get better, but what if he never did? What if all of the medical experts were right?

Kellen rose unsteadily to his feet, bearing as much of his weight as possible on the cane. Damned thing. He hated using it. Hated that he *had* to use it. But most of all, he hated what it represented. It shouted to the world that Kellen Faust was no longer the man he used to be. He was injured, limited.

Useless.

The very thing his own mother had always accused him of being.

The conversation they'd had not long after he'd arrived at her home in Charleston sprang to mind.

"The only thing you're good at is spending money. You've all but drained your trust, living high on the hog in Europe. No cares, no responsibilities." She'd waved one of her bejeweled hands, the diamonds her second husband had given her winking under the lights. "Well, don't expect me to bail you out. You're just like your father. You've never planned for a rainy day."

They were estranged, had been since he was a boy, really. Since not long after his father's lengthy illness and death had left them nearly penniless. She'd come back stronger than ever thanks to remarrying well, but not before hocking almost everything of value to stay afloat. As his grandfather's sole heir, Kellen had been well provided for. In a way, that had only made her resent him, especially since he'd continued his father's free-spending ways. As a result, Kellen and his mother had never shared a close bond again. He'd been foolish to think things might have changed either because of his injury or his changing financial situation.

But he hadn't been wrong to come to Hadley Island. He'd come here to find a purpose, if not a vocation then an avocation. Something, *anything*, to give his life meaning if it turned out that all of the doctors, including the latest one in Charleston, were right.

The best memories of his childhood were rooted here. The place had been his sanctuary, both during his father's illness and after his father's death. Where his relationship with his mother had always been rocky, a young Kellen had been the apple of his grandfather's eye.

"You're bright, ambitious. You're going to be a fine man when you grow up, Kellen."

He wondered what his grandfather would think if he

could see Kellen now. The bum leg wouldn't be an issue. But what Kellen had made of his life to this point…that wouldn't sit well with the old man. Granddad had placed his trust in Kellen, left him his fortune and all of his real estate holdings, not the least of which was the resort. These days, most of what Kellen still owned of his grandfather's had been mortgaged to the hilt and would soon go on the auction block to pay off his mounting, post-accident debts. Except for the inn. Kellen had left that untouched.

"Everything I have will be yours someday." Kellen could hear his granddad's raspy voice, feel the hand he'd placed on his grandson's shoulder as he'd made the promise. "I know you'll take extra good care of the inn, because you love it as much as I do."

Guilt settled over Kellen now like a smothering fog. Yeah, he'd loved it so much that he hadn't been back in nearly a dozen years, and had rubber-stamped renovations without paying close attention to the plans. Thank God Brigit was so good at her job. The managers before her had been more than happy to stick with the status quo, shrugging their shoulders as the bottom line fell. She'd shored up the aging resort and had brought in record profits as well.

When all was said and done, Kellen would see to it that she was properly compensated.

"Do you need anything, Mr. F?" The question came from Joe, who, with Lou's help, was bringing in a portable table and the weight bench Kellen thought of as a personal torture device.

I'll take a new leg, some motivation and a renewed sense of purpose, he thought bitterly. But what he told the younger man was, "I'm going to lie down for a little while."

Joe frowned at him. "Do you think that's a good idea, Mr. F? Your muscles are probably stiff from the drive over, especially since we didn't get in a session this morning."

Joe was being diplomatic. His wording made it sound as if the omission of the a.m. therapy session had been an oversight rather than because Kellen had refused to cooperate. Hell, he'd refused to get out of bed. Well, at least Joe wasn't mentioning the evening before when Kellen had called it quits a mere five minutes into basic stretches using a tension band.

"I'm going to lie down," Kellen repeated, heading in the direction of the bedroom.

Joe lifted his shoulders as if to say suit yourself.

Lou cleared his throat. "As soon as we finish unloading this gear, I'm going to take off. That okay with you?"

Lou had been with Kellen for more than a decade, mainly working as his driver—more often designated than not. Sometimes he also stepped into the role of bouncer when party guests got out of control. There hadn't been much need for the latter services the past four months. Kellen's partying days were over. Truth be told, they'd lasted longer than they should have even before the accident.

"This mishap of yours might be for the best," his mother had said just that morning.

"Mishap?" He'd motioned with his cane. "I didn't fall down a couple stairs."

No, more like he'd tumbled head over skis down the side of an icy mountain.

"You know what I mean. You have to grow up sometime, Kellen. You need to start earning more than you spend and make sound investments for the future. Better to learn that now when you have no one counting on you for support. God knows, you father didn't figure that out until it was too late."

"I'd say you landed on your feet," he'd responded.

All these years later, her second husband remained a source of friction between them.

She'd pursed her lips at the remark, causing half a dozen fine lines to feather around her mouth. They marred her otherwise youthful complexion. At sixty-two, Bess Faust Mackenzie remained a beautiful woman thanks to good genes, enviable bone structure and the skills of an expensive plastic surgeon.

"I did what was necessary. Meanwhile, you are content to blow through what little remains of the sizable inheritance from your grandfather. I'm surprised you've held on to the inn. It's prime real estate. Even in this soft market, the money would keep you comfortable for… well, for a few years anyway."

Kellen blocked out his mother's parting shot as he took a couple halting steps. She was right about a lot of things, but he would never sell the inn. In fact, he planned to take a far more active role in its oversight.

"Boss?"

He stopped and glanced over his shoulder, realizing he'd never answered Lou.

"Fine. Cell service can be a little spotty on the island, so be sure to leave a landline number."

"Will do." Lou offered a jaunty salute. He always seemed to be in a good mood. Same for Joe. Kellen used to be like that, too. As much as his mobility, he missed his old disposition.

"And Miss Wright?" he asked. "I assume she cleared out her belongings."

It was Joe who answered this time. "Yep. Brigit moved her clothes to the spare room, and her toiletries are in the guest bath now. Lou and I got all your stuff put away."

Kellen barely heard the last part. Brigit. First-name basis. Hmm. For a reason he couldn't fathom, he didn't like Joe's familiarity. Just as Brigit's laughter with the younger man had grated on his nerves earlier.

"The last I saw her, she was on the phone in her office." Lou chuckled. "It sounded like she was giving someone a chewing-out over a delivery snafu."

Formidable. No-nonsense. Take charge.

All of those descriptions applied, as did intelligent and capable, which foolishly he'd taken to mean she was dowdy, her looks nondescript. In Kellen's social circles, attractive women were vacuous and helpless—or at least they pretended to be. Draped in frumpy yellow vinyl Brigit had fit his preconceived notion perfectly. But once she'd peeled it off and had shoved the damp hair back from her face, well, Brigit Wright wasn't at all what he'd expected.

Kellen found her attractive, which was a surprise in itself. She wasn't anything like the women who usually caught his attention: flashy women whose beauty relied on a lot of enhancement, from hair extensions and capped teeth to serious breast augmentation.

Brigit was pretty in an understated way. She'd worn no makeup that he could see, although her dark lashes hadn't needed much help to highlight her blue eyes. Her hair was as black as coal. It hung past her shoulders in a limp curtain, lacking any discernable style. Of course, she had just been out for a walk in the rain.

What would she look like with her hair coiffed, makeup accentuating her eyes and dressed up for a night out in something curve-hugging?

He silently answered himself with a second question. *What the hell does it matter?*

She was an employee. The same as Lou. The same as Joe. *Right.* Both his body and his mind mocked him.

He limped into the bedroom that had been his grandfather's during Kellen's childhood. It was decorated as differently as the lobby and the rest of the rooms. Bright, fresh, inviting even on this stormy afternoon. And more jars filled with shells on the bureau. The bedding had been turned down; the linens that peeked from beneath the comforter were creased in places, leaving little doubt that she had just changed the sheets for him.

He ran his fingers over the pillowcase. He would be sleeping in her bed.

And she would be in the room next door.

He swallowed hard and told himself the sudden uptick in his pulse rate was only because he was wondering how long the arrangement would have to continue. Weeks at least. Months? Possibly. She'd said the inn was booked, so it would be a while before a vacancy opened up.

Regardless, he had a lot to learn from the efficient Miss Wright if he hoped to run the resort as capably as she had been.

Eventually, that was his plan. He'd decided on it during his long stint in the hospital, when the shallowness of his life had been as impossible to ignore as his mounting debts. Kellen was done shirking all responsibility. Life as he'd known it was over in more ways than one.

In the meantime, he had an appointment with an orthopedic surgeon in Charleston the following week. He hoped to receive a better prognosis than the one the previous six had given him. *Hoped* being the operative word.

As if on cue, his leg muscles began to cramp and spasm. He leaned on the door frame to the bathroom to take the weight off his bad leg. When he glanced up, he spied the message. It was written in block letters on the mirror, and accompanied by an arrow that pointed to the bottle of over-the-counter painkillers on the counter.

"Non-habit-forming," he read aloud. "Take two and thank me later."

An odd sound echoed off the tile work as he studied his reflection. The hollowed-out eyes and gaunt cheeks no longer took him by surprise. But it came as a serious jolt to realize he was smiling. And that strange sound? It was his laughter.

CHAPTER THREE

A COUPLE HOURS LATER, Brigit was in the resort's commercial, galley-style kitchen helping the chef with dinner preparations when one of the swinging doors opened and her unwanted guest lumbered inside.

Sherry Crofton glanced up from the pot of sauce she was stirring on the cooktop.

"Sorry, but guests aren't allowed back here," the chef said politely, if firmly.

The kitchen was Sherry's domain, and she didn't care for outsiders breaching its door. To call her temperamental would be putting it mildly. She'd been known to shoo out the staff with a few choice words. One time, she'd even thrown a pot of blanched green beans at Danny's head when the young bellboy had had the audacity to filch a sugar cookie without asking.

But she was a damned fine chef, classically trained with twenty years of experience running some of the finest kitchens on the East Coast. Brigit considered it a major coup that she'd managed to get Sherry to sign on as the chef at a small resort tucked away on an equally small island, regardless of the inn's growing reputation.

Kellen's brows notched up in surprise. It was a good bet he wasn't used to being told where he could and could not go, especially on property he owned.

Hoping to ward off a battle of the egos, Brigit set aside her paring knife and wiped her hands on the bib apron she'd donned to protect her clothes.

"I think we can make an exception for this one since he signs our paychecks."

"Mr. Faust?" the chef began, her tone brimming with disbelief. Her gaze slid to his leg and then over to the cane. "I didn't recognize you. You look—"

Sherry was known for her innovative dishes, but not so much for her tact. Brigit decided to keep the older woman from digging herself into a deeper a hole.

"Mr. Faust, this is Sherry Crofton, the inn's chef. You're in for a treat at dinner tonight. She's making her specialty, pan-seared sea bass in an herbed butter sauce."

"Sounds excellent." He acknowledged the chef with a perfunctory nod, but his gaze strayed to Brigit and his eyes narrowed. "Why are you wearing an apron?"

"The sous chef is running late because of the storm. He lives on the mainland. I'm lending a hand with prep. Nothing that requires a culinary degree. Just chopping up vegetables for a steamed medley."

Eyes still narrowed, he asked, "Do you help out often?"

Since the question seemed rooted in genuine curiosity, she decided to answer truthfully. And, okay, she wanted him to be aware that she went above and beyond the call of duty when necessary.

"I wouldn't say often, but I pitch in when and where an extra pair of hands is needed, whether that's here in the kitchen or someplace else on the property."

Indeed, during her tenure, Brigit had changed soiled bedding, flipped mattresses, unclogged drains and performed dozens of other less-than-glamorous chores. Nothing was beneath her, despite her high rank in the staff's pecking order. Apparently all of her predecessors had had other ideas. They'd deemed themselves too good for menial labor. Brigit figured her willingness to roll up her shirtsleeves was why she had earned the staff's respect as well as their loyalty. Turnover was at an all-time low.

Kellen rubbed his chin. "I see."

Did he? Unfortunately, she couldn't tell from his expression whether he thought this was a good use of her time and managerial skills or not. Some of her old insecurities bubbled to the surface.

You're so stupid, Brigit.

She banished her ex's hurtful words. She refused to start second-guessing herself again. Those days were long over.

Squaring her shoulders, she asked, "Was there something you needed?"

"Needed? No. Just…taking a look around. I haven't been to the resort in years. A lot has changed."

From Kellen's tone, however, Brigit couldn't tell if he was happy about that or feeling nostalgic for the past.

His grandfather had owned the resort from the late 1950s on, which helped to explain why it was a virtual time capsule when she'd been hired. None of the managers before her had pressed for renovations to improve the business's bottom line. Perhaps they'd been as apathetic toward the place as their employer, seeing it as an easy paycheck rather than wanting to mine its potential. She'd gotten enough compliments from new guests as well as returning ones to know that the new look and amenities were a hit.

Speaking of changes, Kellen had undergone a bit of a transformation as well. His dark hair was wet as if he'd recently showered. He wore it slicked back from his forehead, although a few curls fell across his brow, giving him a rakish appeal. His face was freshly shaved, all shadow gone from its angular planes. But it wasn't the absence of stubble that caught her attention. It was the absence of a grimace.

"I see you took me up on the offer of some ibuprofen."

The barest hint of a smile lurked on his lips when he asked, "How do you know?"

"Well, for starters, you're no longer gritting your teeth."

"And?"

"You look…rested." The word *approachable* fit even better.

As did *handsome*. Despite his obvious weight loss, the man was definitely that. Instead of the workout attire he'd arrived wearing, he had on a crisp collared shirt that was tucked into a pair of beige dress pants. The carved wooden cane in his right hand added to his air of sophistication, although she was pretty sure he would take umbrage at her description.

"I got in a nap."

"And a workout?" Joe had mentioned something about that.

"No. I wasn't in the mood for more pain. Don't let Joe's baby face fool you. He can be ruthless."

Kellen's subtle attempt at humor came as a welcome surprise. She decided to return it.

"I would think that you'd pay him extra for that. No pain, no gain."

Just that quickly, his expression clouded. She gave an inaudible sigh. Apparently, she'd gone too far with the reminder of his slow recovery. While Brigit and Sherry traded covert shrugs, he looked away, breaking the silence a moment later when he asked, "New ovens, right?"

"Yes. The summer before last. And the cooktops were changed out at that time, too."

He glanced around, nodding.

Since it was so much easier to talk business than to try to exchange pleasantries, she continued. "The walk-in refrigerator just needed some repairs and it was good as new. Of course, your investment is almost fully paid back. Adding a meal package to the room rate has proved to be quite lucrative. And thanks to Sherry's talent we get quite a bit of non-guest traffic, too. The mayor stops by for Sunday brunch at least twice a month."

"Excellent." Kellen nodded, but she got the feeling he was only half listening to what she said.

Of course, she had sent him detailed reports every month. She'd like to think he'd read them.

"Are you hungry? Dinner service doesn't begin for another hour yet, but—"

"That's all right. Joe made me an omelet." He sent her a smile that bordered on sheepish. "We used up your eggs, by the way." He coughed. "And your bread. Joe was a little disappointed it wasn't whole wheat."

"Oh?" Brigit wasn't sure how she felt about strange men rummaging about in her cupboards. Every last inch of her private space had been invaded. But she kept her tone casual when she replied, "I'm sorry I don't keep more in my fridge and pantry. Sherry is such an excellent cook that I eat most of my meals here in the kitchen."

"In your office, you mean. The girl is a workhorse," Sherry told Kellen. Her expression turned shrewd when she added, "And probably due a raise."

Brigit smiled thinly. "Sherry and I will be heading to the mainland bright and early tomorrow for groceries and other supplies for the inn. We go the first and third

Fridays of each month. If you give me a list, I'm happy to pick up whatever you need."

"I'll have Joe put something together. If you can't find everything, don't worry about it." Kellen's lip curled. "He likes to make wheatgrass shakes and other…healthy concoctions."

"The body is a temple?" she asked.

He snorted. "Mine feels more like an ancient ruin, but, yes, that's his philosophy."

Kellen looked away and his scowl returned in force. She didn't think it was their lighthearted banter that had irritated him. But something had. She followed the line of his vision to the far side of the room. The only thing there was Sherry's oversize calendar with the days that had already passed marked off with red *X*s.

"Is something wrong?" she asked.

He shook his head and, without another word, turned and limped out of the kitchen.

"Real friendly sort, isn't he?" Sherry muttered sarcastically once Kellen was out of earshot.

For a moment, a very brief moment, he had been.

Brigit returned to the cutting board and picked up her knife. "Let's just do our best to stay out of his way, okay? As fast as this summer is going, he'll be gone before we know it and things will be back to normal."

At least Brigit hoped that would be the case.

Kellen wasn't sure why seeing the days marked off on the kitchen calendar had torpedoed his mood. He only knew that where a moment earlier he had been close to joking, being hit with the reality that four months had passed since his accident had yanked the rug out from beneath him. The ibuprofen Brigit had put out for him had taken the edge off his physical pain. His emotional pain, however, was another matter.

Nothing seemed to dampen that.

Kellen wished it were nicer outdoors so that he could sit on the raised deck and watch the waves rise and swell. When he was a boy, the ocean had always had a calming effect on his emotions. Even on days such as this one, when the waves beat ruthlessly against the shore, at least he'd known what to expect. Waves would crash, but the water always receded and eventually calmed. Soon enough, the sun would come out and chase away the gloom, and the beach would be the same as it had been before the storm.

Nothing about his life now was consistent…except for his limp and the pain that came with it.

Guests milled about in the lobby, which was to be expected, he supposed, on such a wet, gloomy day. In the library, a couple of well-dressed women sat reading books in the sand colored wing chairs that flanked the French doors leading to another section of decking, and a few preppy-looking college kids huddled around the coffee table playing poker.

Kellen remembered playing cards in this very room as a boy. Gin rummy with his grandfather and sometimes with Herman, the old groundskeeper. Kellen had rarely won. When he had, he suspected it was because his grandfather had let him. The memory had him smiling, even as it made him sad.

God, he missed the old man. Hayden Faust had been the only doting adult in Kellen's life from age eleven on. After his father's death, his mother had been too busy looking for a new husband to pay him much mind. Then she'd remarried and, once again, Kellen had been shunted aside.

Even now Kellen refused to consider how desperate she must have felt to find her financial footing kicked out from under her. His grandfather, however, had cut her some slack.

During Kellen's final visit to the island, as they'd sat in this very room, Hayden had told him, "I'm not condoning the way your mother has treated you since remarrying, but try to see things from her perspective."

"What do you mean?" he'd asked.

"You're so much like your father."

"You say that as if it's a bad thing." Kellen had laughed, not sure how else to respond.

His grandfather hadn't cracked so much as a smile as he'd laid his weathered hand on Kellen's shoulder.

"I loved my son dearly, but I'm not blind to his shortcomings. He made some poor choices over the years. Choices that your mother has paid for in more ways than one."

"What are you saying?"

"I'm saying, be sure you make better ones. Make me proud, Kellen."

A final request that Kellen had failed to honor. What would his grandfather think of the choices he'd made now? The likely answer had Kellen limping back to the privacy of his rooms.

"Mr. F?" Joe poked his head around the door.

Although Kellen was awake, he kept his eyes closed and feigned sleep. He'd been lying on the bed in his room for the past two hours thinking and trying to work out the details of his plan B. A plan that Brigit Wright wasn't going to like when he eventually told her about it.

His grandfather had left Kellen the inn with the hope he would actually run it, rather than merely sign checks and authorize improvements when he took a break from the ski slopes in Europe.

It was time to start making those better choices the older man had urged.

"Boss?" Joe called again.

Leave me alone! Kellen shouted the words in his head, but he didn't say them out loud. He was tired of being sullen and disagreeable, even as he felt powerless to change his mood. So he kept his eyes closed and his breathing deep and even. He expected that would be the end of it. Joe would go away and Kellen could continue to stew in silence.

But his physical therapist wasn't alone.

"He's sleeping soundly," Kellen heard Joe tell whoever was with him. "Just go in and grab what you need."

"I'd hate to disturb him." Brigit's voice.

She sounded indecisive. Once again Kellen found himself wanting to shout, *Leave!* His reason this time was embarrassment.

Could she see him? God, he hoped not. When he'd returned to the room, he'd shucked off his other clothes and now lay atop the comforter wearing a pair of black nylon gym shorts. Briefly, he'd pulled on a T-shirt whose neon green slogan was intended to inspire. Since it only served to mock him in his current condition, he'd tugged it off as well. He'd balled it up and tossed it. It was on the floor somewhere across the room. He'd never been embarrassed to go shirtless before, but these days he was a pale imitation of the physically fit man he'd been. Still, it would be the lesser of two evils if her gaze remained on his chest and didn't detour to the ugly web of scars on his mangled leg.

"Perhaps I'll come back later," she said.

"You'd rather see him when he's awake?" Joe's tone was wry and teasing.

Brigit chuckled and Kellen bristled inwardly. He didn't appreciate being the butt of their joke.

"You make a good point," she said. "Okay. I'm going in. I'll be quiet so as not to disturb him."

"I know you will." This time Joe chuckled. "Hey, I'm going to make wheatgrass smoothies. Stop by the kitchen on your way out. I'll make one for you."

"A wheatgrass smoothie?"

"They're delicious and good for you."

"Sure. Can't wait."

Liar, Kellen thought.

Footsteps sounded then. Joe leaving? Where was Brigit? Kellen strained his ears, listening for the creak of floorboards or the rustle of fabric—anything to announce that she was moving about inside the bedroom. Finally, on the opposite side of the room from the hallway, he heard a door squeak. The bathroom? The closet? He chanced opening his eyes. The room was dim thanks to the pulled shades. It wasn't quite dusk outside, although the weather certainly made it seem later. Brigit was in the walk-in closet, standing under the light. He studied her profile as she rose up on her toes and pulled down a basket from the one of the shelves.

She was slender and pretty in a way that left him to wonder if she purposefully downplayed her looks. After she gathered whatever it was that she'd come in to get, she turned. Through slit eyes, Kellen watched her switch off the light and gently close the closet.

She started to tiptoe toward the bedroom door, but then stopped at the foot of the bed. If she had looked at his face, she would have realized he was awake. His eyes were fully open now. But she wasn't looking at his face or any other part of his anatomy found above the waist. She was studying his bad leg, starting at the ankle. The break had healed, but the not the damage. The calf was noticeably smaller than its counterpart on his good leg. Joe attributed the disparity to muscle atrophy, although he couldn't guarantee Kellen that regular workouts would fix that.

Her gaze wandered up to his knee before skimming his thigh. It wasn't a pretty sight, to be sure. Nothing could be done to erase the scars from where jagged bone had ripped through his flesh or the multiple surgeries that had followed.

She didn't strike him as the squeamish sort, but she closed her eyes briefly. Did he disgust her? Did she pity him? He wasn't sure which reaction would be worse. He only knew he could tolerate no more of her thorough examination.

"Seen enough?"

She nearly dropped the belt she's retrieved from the closet.

"You startled me."

Spoiling for a fight, he levered up on one elbow. "You didn't answer my question."

"I didn't mean to stare. I was…I was just…"

"Curious?" he demanded.

She cleared her throat. Even in the dim light, he could tell she was flustered and probably blushing. Embarrassed? Definitely. But not turned on. Why would she be? He was an invalid, repulsive. Angry with them both, he spat out in a suggestive tone, "My leg might be mangled, but I can assure you, everything else is in working order."

She did drop the belt now, and her hand flew to her chest. "Excuse me?"

"I think you heard me."

At that, he expected her to stomp out of the room in a huff. He should have known his dot-every-i and cross-every-t manager would do no such thing. Indeed, Brigit drew closer and came around the side of the bed.

"I heard you. I was trying to give you the benefit of the doubt."

"And now you expect me to apologize," he said, keeping his tone insolent.

"As a matter of fact..." She fisted her hands, settled them on her hips and sent him an arched look.

Nice hips. Not too wide, not too narrow. Neatly rounded, and along with her firm backside, just right. Given Kellen's position on the bed, the hips he was admiring were practically at eye level. His mouth watered and parts of his body that had been dormant for months began to stir back to life. Some of his frustration and anger dissipated, only to be replaced by feelings that were far more dangerous.

Even though he knew he was playing with fire, Kellen was helpless to keep his gaze from traveling up Brigit's slender frame and touching on all of the parts that interested him.

"Well?" she demanded.

Their gazes met, collided really. He didn't see sparks fly, but he swore he felt them. They showered his skin. The sensation was life-affirming. He reveled in it.

Common sense took a backseat to desire, and he taunted, "You first."

"What?"

"You apologize first."

"You expect *me* to apologize to you?"

Her tone hovered between incredulous and royally ticked off. Perversely, he found it a turn-on. As he did her narrowed eyes and pinched lips.

"That's right."

"What am I to apologize for?" she demanded.

"Well, for starters, you're trespassing. You're in my bedroom…uninvited." *A small matter that could be remedied easily enough*, his libido whispered before he could quiet it.

"This is…well, until this afternoon, it was my bedroom. I'm hardly trespassing."

He held up a finger. "Technically, as the resort's owner—"

She'd worked up a good head of steam and talked over his clarification of the bedroom's ownership.

"Look, I just came in to get a belt from the closet. I would have asked *permission*—" her lips twisted on the word "—but you were sleeping and I didn't want to disturb you. The fact is, I wasn't given much time to gather up my belongings before you moved in. If you want an apology for that, fine. I'm *so sorry* for the inconvenience."

She didn't sound sorry. She sounded aggrieved, irritated and ready to combust. Kellen knew he should quit provoking her, but he couldn't help himself. He pressed.

"You got your belt, yet here you stand, Miss Wright. Er, Brigit. Under the circumstances I think we should be on a first-name basis. Don't you?"

"I…I…" she sputtered, glaring at him as if he'd grown a second head.

"You're standing at my bedside. And you were staring at me."

"I wasn't staring—"

"You were. Or maybe I should say gawking. The way one does at a train wreck."

Kellen pushed all the way to a sitting position. The instant he did so, excruciating pain radiated out from his knee, shooting down to his ankle and up to his hip. He wasn't able to bite back his yelp. Apparently, the ibuprofen had worn off.

"Mr. Faust?" She started forward.

"It's Kellen, dammit. Kellen!" he spat, still angry with both of them. Indeed, in that instant, he was back to being angry with everyone and everything. His new status quo. "Just go."

"Do you need—"

"Do you really want to know what I need, Brigit?" When she stood there eyeing him, he prompted, "Well, do you?"

"I know what you need." She said it softly, a hint of a smile playing on her lips.

Despite his anger and the raw pain he was experiencing, that Mona Lisa smile tugged at places inside him.

"Tell me."

"A wheatgrass smoothie. I'll have Joe bring one in. I hear they're delicious and good for you." She turned on her heel and walked out with her shoulders squared, her chin up.

Kellen flopped back on the bed. Anger dissipated along with the worst of the pain. Shame and embarrassment settled in their place. He wondered what it said about him that the most alive he'd felt in months had been while provoking an employee.

Brigit was right about one thing. He was the one who owed her an apology.

CHAPTER FOUR

BRIGIT WAS FUMING. Molars grinding, she stomped out of the apartment without saying a word to Joe. The blender was on high, making it easier to just wave and go. Anger carried her all the way to the resort's kitchen. Although dinner service was over, she asked Sherry, "Got anything for me to chop into very small pieces?"

The cook eyed her knowingly. "Something tells me it would be a bad idea to hand you a sharp knife right now. What's got you so upset, anyway?"

"Not what. Who."

Kellen Faust.

Who did the man think he was, demanding that Brigit apologize for being in her own bedroom? She didn't give a damn if he owned the resort. The room, the entire apartment, was hers or it had been until just that morning. The man was acting like an inconsiderate tyrant.

One with a faulty memory to boot.

He'd agreed with her plan to turn the old manager's quarters into a luxury suite for high-end guests. He'd agreed to let her move into the unused owner's apartment. She had saved their written correspondence to that effect. Maybe she should remind him. Maybe she should pull out her contract, which clearly stated that she was entitled to on-site accommodations as part of her compensation, and return to the bedroom and confront him.

She swallowed, thinking of the sight of the man lying on her bed. Okay, so she'd glanced at him on her way back to the door. Maybe she'd stared for a couple seconds longer than was polite. Fine, she'd outright ogled him, which definitely was not her style. But Kellen Faust sans shirt and wearing shorts, well, he'd certainly caught her attention. And since she'd thought he was asleep, she'd figured it wouldn't hurt to satisfy her curiosity and snatch a closer look.

She'd gotten an eyeful, all right. The accident had taken a toll on his once-fit body. Even allowing for the fact that photographs added weight, Kellen was definitely thinner now, even more so than he'd initially appeared when fully dressed. He wasn't skinny exactly. Lean, wiry—those descriptions would be more accurate. Regardless, he was all male, and seeing his bare limbs, scarred or not, spread out on her comforter had had an unsettling effect on her breathing.

Brigit tried to recall how long had it been since she'd felt the air back up in her lungs where a man was concerned. Or that tightening sensation low in her belly. She couldn't. Within the first year of her marriage, things had gone from acceptable to bad. From there, they'd made the leap to god-awful. In all, four years of her life wasted. It still shamed her to admit that she'd allowed herself to be a doormat for that length of time.

In the immediate aftermath of her ugly divorce, she'd been too shell-shocked even to think of dating again. Once she'd landed the job at the resort, she'd been happy to focus on her career. It wasn't that she didn't have time for men. She didn't *make* time. While staring at Kellen, Brigit had begun to have second thoughts.

Stupid, stupid, stupid. Standing in the kitchen now, she rubbed her temples.

"I think I can guess who you mean," Sherry said, pulling Brigit from her introspection.

Be that as it may, a good manager didn't gossip, much less talk disrespectfully about the boss, so Brigit shook her head and worked up what she hoped passed for a smile.

"I'm just frustrated with one of our suppliers," she lied. "He keeps trying to jack up the prices we've already agreed to."

"Supplier, hmm?" Sherry didn't look fooled.

Brigit cleared her throat. "Thanks for letting me vent. I'll just get out of your way."

It was after eleven o'clock when Brigit finally returned to the apartment that night. Joe was sitting on the couch watching television. Kellen, thankfully, was nowhere to be seen. She let out a breath she hadn't been aware she was holding and smiled at the physical therapist.

"I hope you weren't waiting up on my account." She grimaced then. "I never got your bedding."

"That's okay." Joe cocked his head sideways. "Everything all right?"

"Fine." She shrugged. "Why do you ask?"

"You left in a hurry earlier, and you've been gone ever since. I thought maybe Mr. F had woken up while you were in the room and said something to upset you."

Oh, Kellen had said something, all right. Something off-color and out of line. Something that had made her blood boil, but not only with temper. As such, she wasn't going to share the details with Joe. So she waved a hand.

"I had some work to finish up."

She swore her bogus explanation received the same

knowing look from Joe that her earlier fabrication about supplier trouble had received from Sherry. Brigit went to grab bedding and an extra pillow from the linen closet. When she returned, Joe had turned off the television and was moving the coffee table so he could pull out the sofa bed.

"I got this," he said when she tried to help him. Then he went on as if she'd asked about their mutual employer. "Mr. F was in a lousy mood tonight."

"Oh?"

The bed unfolded, the mattress flopping down on the frame with an unceremonious *plop*. Her thoughts were on another mattress. Another man.

Joe said, "He complained about his leg bothering him."

"The ibuprofen probably wore off. He needs to take two tablets every four to six hours, according to the dosage instructions on the bottle."

Joe pulled the fitted bottom sheet around the top corner of the mattress. "He brought some of the pain on himself. He spent too much time today sitting or lying down. He blew off our afternoon therapy session. He needs to keep moving, despite the pain. The scar tissue needs to be stretched along with his tendons. The longer he stays stationary, the stiffer his muscles become."

His muscles weren't the only part of his anatomy that had become rigid. Brigit swallowed and focused her attention on securing her ends of the fitted sheet.

Kellen slept poorly, tossing and turning—and then groaning in pain—for the better part of the night. His conscience bothered him as much as his leg. Maybe even more since he'd grown used to the nagging physical ache.

He'd heard Brigit come into the apartment the previous night. She'd talked with Joe for a bit, although he hadn't been able to hear the actual words of their conversation. Afterward, her steps had been light in the hallway before she'd entered the spare room. He'd pictured her curled up on the uncomfortable futon, and his conscience had nipped at him again, not because he'd displaced her from her bed, but because his imagination had worked overtime on what she'd been wearing.

He tossed back the covers now. He needed to apologize. He'd leave out his wayward imagination, though, and concentrate on his rude behavior from the day before.

He found her on the private deck off the living room. She was seated in one of the lounge chairs, her fingers busily clicking over the keys of a laptop computer. A mug of something hot was on a small table next to her. Joe was at the rail drinking an unsightly green concoction through a straw. He spied Kellen through the sliding glass door and rushed over to open it.

"Good morning, Mr. F!" he said with his usual good cheer. "You're up early. Brigit and I were just out here enjoying the sunrise. It's going to be a great day."

The man's enthusiasm should have been contagious. Kellen glanced at Brigit, who looked as unmotivated as he felt.

"Want a wheatgrass smoothie?"

What Kellen wanted was a cup of high-octane coffee and a couple extra-strength ibuprofen. But he needed a few minutes alone with Brigit, and Joe had just provided him the perfect excuse.

"Yes."

Kellen's response not only had Joe's eyes widening; Brigit turned from her typing to look at him.

"Really?" Joe said.

"You're always touting their health benefits."

"I didn't think you were listening," the younger man replied with comical honestly.

"I'll also take a couple painkillers and some coffee when you get a chance."

Joe grinned. "Coming right up. Anything for you, Brigit?"

She shook her head. "I'm good."

Once they were alone, Kellen moved to the lounge chair next to hers. Its low height would make sitting down difficult. Bearing his weight on the cane, he tried to lower himself slowly, but his leg gave out halfway down and he landed on the seat with a *plop*. Getting up without assistance would be impossible. He decided not to think about that now and tucked the cane under the chair.

"I'd offer to help, but I know you don't want it," she remarked as he struggled to get both of his legs up on the footrest.

He grunted and surprised them both by admitting, "It's damned depressing to need assistance to perform something as simple as taking a seat."

She studied him a moment before nodding. Then she went back to her typing.

He tried again. "It's a nice morning. The calm after the storm."

She nodded again, this time without looking up from her laptop. A spreadsheet was open in one of the windows on the screen. Some sort of chart that compared the previous year's energy costs to this one's. In another window was an article on solar panels, to which she was adding notes. It was not even 6:00 a.m. and Brigit was already showered, dressed and on the clock. Most of the women he knew would have been a few hours into their beauty sleep after a late night out partying.

He cleared his throat, but the words still stuck a little

before finally coming out. "I…I wanted to talk to you, Brigit."

"Brigit, is it? We're sitting on the deck. Should we still be on a first-name basis?" she asked nonchalantly.

Meanwhile—*tap-tap-tap*—the fingers on the keyboard never slowed.

Kellen scratched a hand over the stubble on his jaw. He deserved that. "I owe you an apology for what I said and for how I acted yesterday."

Tap-tap-tap. "Yes. You do." Her tone was matter-of-fact.

"Could you…could you maybe stop typing for a minute and look at me?"

She hit a few more keys, exhaled slowly and then closed the laptop. Turning in her seat, she gave him her full attention. He almost wished she hadn't. Bright blue eyes fringed with amazingly long black lashes left him feeling laid bare.

"I am sorry. The way I acted…the things I said…I was out of line."

"Apology accepted. Thank you." She lifted a hand and her fingers caught in the ends of her dark hair, twirling some of it in a gesture that struck him as almost tentative. "I should have waited to get my belt."

"You left it on the floor, by the way."

"I know."

He reached into the pocket of his track pants and pulled out the slim length of leather, which he'd wound into a tight coil. "Here."

A smile tugged at her lips. "Thanks."

"We got off on the wrong foot." He snorted at his unintentionally apropos phrasing. Since humbling himself wasn't as difficult as he'd presumed it to be, he continued, "I should have realized that my early arrival here would cause some…upheaval."

Early or otherwise, it had and then some, especially for the woman sitting beside him.

"Can I ask you something?" she said after a moment.

"Sure. What?"

"Did you even read the monthly reports I've been sending for the past five years?"

The woman certainly didn't pull any punches. He decided he owed her the truth. "No. I glanced at them. Well, some of them, but…no. I didn't give any a thorough reading."

"So when you approved my ideas and gave the green light to my renovation plans, you did so blindly?"

Her tone held a note of censure. Or was it disappointment? His stomach took a surprising roll. It had been a long time since Kellen had cared what someone thought of him. Not since his grandfather.

"My schedule was pretty busy." He laughed without humor and came clean. "All those parties, you know."

"I wouldn't know. I work for living, even on the weekends."

Oh, yeah. Definitely censure.

"I should have read them." A responsible business owner would have, he admitted to himself. "But I did and I still do trust your judgment. Besides, we graduated from the same business school."

"*You* have a degree from the University of Connecticut?"

The shock on her face was unmistakable and reflected in the disbelief in her tone. Kellen's battered ego took another blow.

"I haven't put it to much use, but yes, I have a degree from UConn, earned a few years before you would have started classes. When I interviewed you for the job—" which he'd done by phone and email between runs down the slopes in the alpine town of Grindelwald "—I was impressed by your credentials, even if you didn't have much practical experience."

Her expression turned oddly guarded and she glanced away.

"I got married right after graduation." She paused. "My husband didn't think I needed to work."

"You're married?" That came as a surprise. An unpleasant one based on the way his stomach somersaulted. Why would it matter if she was taken? Kellen rallied as quickly as he could, hoping that none of his dismay showed in his expression. He was her employer. As such, her marital status was none of his business, legally or otherwise. That was why it hadn't come up during the interview process or any of their other dealings.

"Happily divorced," she corrected. Her jaw clenched after she said it and she reached for her coffee cup.

It wasn't relief he felt, he told himself. That would be inappropriate. Still, he couldn't help but be intrigued. Not only about what had happened to end Brigit's marriage, but what kind of man this quietly attractive and obviously smart woman would have wed in the first place. But he kept his questions to himself. Business, he reminded himself. That was the basis of their relationship. And when it came to business, in spite of the degree he'd earned more than a decade earlier, Kellen had a lot to learn.

Thinking of that, he noted, "None of the three managers before you thought to implement any capital improvements."

More damning, Kellen had never thought to implement any either. The inn was his inheritance, yet he'd all but left it to rot while he'd done his damnedest to confirm his mother's low of opinion of him as a wastrel.

Brigit was no longer clenching her jaw. In fact, he

heard excitement bubble in her voice and saw it spark in her eyes as she told him, "I saw so much potential for change the first time I toured the property. This location is amazing. The oceanfront view...." She motioned to the horizon where the sun blazed gold and orange before blurring into pastel shades of pink and blue.

"It should have been packed year-round. Yet it had vacancies during the peak tourist season. And the internet reviews were dismal. People want amenities. When they go on vacation, they are willing to pay for six-hundred-thread-count sheets, complimentary turndown service complete with mints on their pillows, satellite television and wireless internet. Give them the option of superb dining on-site and they will not only book a weekend, they'll come back again and recommend us to their friends."

"Your changes have made sure of that. I may not have read every line of your reports and correspondence, but that much I figured out."

The compliment had her blinking, but she said dryly, "I would imagine the bottom line speaks for itself."

He nodded. "It speaks volumes. Revenues are up—what?—two, two hundred and fifty percent from five years ago?"

"Three hundred," she amended after a discreet cough. Though her expression remained neutral, he saw pride spark in her eyes. And no wonder.

She'd tripled his income. At this rate, the money he'd invested in upgrades would be repaid in no time. His future was secure, financially at least.

And he owed it all to her.

Guilt throbbed like a bad tooth since his newly worked out plan ultimately would see her displaced from her job. After all, he doubted someone of Brigit's caliber would want to stay on in a reduced capacity, basically sharing managerial duties with him once Kellen was sufficiently healed and up to speed. He'd offer her the option, of course. He wasn't a fool. As much as he wanted to take over, he didn't plan to work around the clock like she apparently did.

If she left—more likely when—he would see to it that she was fairly compensated. He made a mental note to meet with his lawyer to draft a generous severance package when he went into Charleston for his doctor appointment.

"Thank you. For everything," he told her now.

Then he reached over and laid one of his hands over hers. The gesture was intended to be companionable, but the way his body responded to the benign contact was far baser in nature. Her skin was soft, warm.

She pulled her hand away, using it to tuck a few stray strands of dark hair behind her ear. Her cheeks had turned a becoming shade of pink, and he couldn't help wondering if it was the contact that had thrown her or his gratitude.

Finally, she replied, "The Christmas bonus I received was thanks enough." She picked up her coffee cup then and focused her attention on its contents. "I like living here. On the island, at the resort. And I like this job. I'm *good* at it."

He found the comment odd. She seemed to be trying to convince him of her competence. If so, she needn't have bothered.

While he covertly studied Brigit's profile, wondering what beyond job satisfaction drove her to labor for such long hours, she sipped her coffee and scanned the horizon. She had a nice profile. He took in the slope of her cheek, slight lift of her nose, delicate jaw that ended in a blunt chin. All of it stirred him up in a way he found both compelling and concerning. The squawk of gulls and slap of waves on sand were the only sounds to break the silence until the door opened and Joe stepped out onto the deck. He carried a tray that held a mug of coffee and a glass filled with a sickly looking green concoction that had Kellen's taste buds staging a revolt.

"Here you go, Mr. F. One wheatgrass smoothie as requested. I took the liberty of adding half a banana." The young man grinned. "They're an excellent source of potassium."

"Mmm." Kellen grimaced and his gag reflex threatened to kick in. He hated bananas almost as much as he hated wheatgrass.

"Well, I need to get ready to meet Sherry to go shopping on the mainland. I have your list," Brigit told Joe. Then she rose to her feet, laptop in hand, her gaze on Kellen. "Enjoy your smoothie."

Was it his imagination or was she biting back a grin?

CHAPTER FIVE

KELLEN WOKE EARLY the following Wednesday morning. Even earlier than he had been waking for the past several days. He used to sleep till noon. Even after his accident, he hadn't become an early riser, rousing by ten o'clock but only because that was when Joe scheduled his first session.

Since his arrival at Faust Haven the week before, however, he'd been up each day by dawn. Being on Hadley Island seemed to have reset his internal clock. He didn't mind. He'd felt more rested the past few days than he had during the past several months.

This morning, however, he couldn't claim to feel the same. That was because today was *the* day. His doctor appointment loomed at one o'clock. Kellen had slept fitfully when he'd slept at all. What would the specialist in Charleston say?

He didn't want to believe that nothing more could be done, that his current physical condition, with its accompanying limp and many limitations, was the best he could hope for when it came to his recovery. But it was a very good possibility that this doctor would tell him the same thing all of the other doctors had. The same suffocating sense of defeat that had defined his life for the past four months settled over him.

After lying in bed for an hour, his mind racing as much as it wandered, he finally threw back the covers, rolled to his side and struggled out of bed. His leg was stiff, sore. It always was first thing in the morning. He performed a few of the stretching exercises Joe recommended and got dressed in his usual outfit of loose-fitting track pants and a lightweight T-shirt.

Dawn had chased the darkness from the apartment by the time he stepped into the hallway. As he passed the guest room, he noticed that the door was ajar. He glanced inside, doubting even as he did so that he would find Brigit there.

At this hour, she would be out on the deck, a mug of coffee on the table at her side and the computer booted up and open on her lap. It was how she started her days, a routine that she apparently followed seven mornings a week unless the weather was bad. So, for the past week, coffee on the deck was how Kellen had started his as well.

He couldn't tell if his presence bothered her, although if it did, he suspected she would have found a different spot. The resort had other decks, although none quite as private as the one off the owner's apartment.

They sat, sipping their coffee and watching the sunrise. She'd pay bills or perform some other task related to the resort. All the while he would ask questions, the kind with answers a conscientious owner already would know.

Kellen hadn't been a conscientious owner. Both he and Brigit knew that. He gave her credit for refraining from saying so. Still, he'd caught her questioning expression whenever he made an inquiry. As patient as she was in answering, he figured she also had to be annoyed.

What did it say about him, Kellen wondered, that he found the furrow that formed between her amazing eyes whenever she was confused or agitated to be so sexy?

Movement inside the room caught his notice. Not only was Brigit there, she was…undressing. He should look away. He should go away. But he stood rooted in place, gaze glued to her slim figure. Her back was to him, but he caught a glimpse of sky-blue lace stretched across the pale skin of her spine as she pulled off the shirt she'd been wearing and traded it for another. Her movements were practical and precise, hardly the sort choreographed to seduce. Still, the sight of smooth ivory skin and lean contours had his mouth going dry, and for one ridiculous moment Kellen found it difficult to breathe.

He managed to inhale, and a familiar and all too pleasing smell filled his nose. Clean and crisp with a hint of citrus. It was the same fragrance that teased him at night while he lay in her bed. The sheets might have been fresh, but her scent was all around him. Making him yearn. Making him burn. That heat enveloped him now, threatened to incinerate what remained of his manners. He took a couple of halting steps backward and cleared his throat noisily in an effort to announce his presence. When he drew even with the door a second time, Brigit was pulling it fully open.

"Good morning," she said.

"Good morning."

She'd exchanged the blue shirt she usually wore for a turquoise version in a similar cut. Both had the inn's logo embroidered on the chest and…he was staring at her breasts. He ripped his gaze away only to have it settle on the tangle of sheets that littered the futon behind her. He frowned.

"That doesn't look very comfortable," he murmured.

Brigit glanced over her shoulder. "Not as comfortable as the queen-size pillow top you're sleeping on," she agreed. "But it's not so bad."

"No?" He thought it looked like a medieval torture device.

He grimaced. "I've never apologized for the inconvenience my stay has caused you."

Her eyes widened fractionally, but that was the only sign his words surprised her. "No, you haven't."

"I am sorry, Brigit."

She nodded. "It's all right."

But it wasn't. His thoughtlessness made him ashamed. "I should take the guest room. I can have Joe move my things in here today, and you can have your room back."

"I appreciate the offer, but it really is *your* room. Besides, you wouldn't be comfortable on the futon." She motioned over her shoulder at the piece of furniture under discussion. "It sits too low to the ground."

It was like the lounge chair on the deck in that regard. And they both knew how much effort it took for Kellen to get up from it.

Brigit was saying, "My back will survive the inconvenience. It's not like it's forever."

No, indeed. It wouldn't be forever. Eventually, their living arrangements, along with their business arrangement, would be decided. But only one of them knew that at the moment. He changed the subject. "I thought you'd already be out on the deck. It's after six."

"I was, but I spilled some coffee on my shirt."

"So, that's why you changed it." He realized his faux pas even before her eyes narrowed. "I mean, so you came into change it."

"How long have you been up?" she asked.

"Up or awake?" He shrugged and surprised himself by admitting, "I didn't get much sleep last night."

"You have a doctor's appointment today, right? Joe mentioned it."

Her gaze lowered momentarily to the cane gripped in his hand. It was what everyone saw when they looked at him, part and parcel of that all-important first impression.

"Right." And an appointment with his attorney, Kellen added silently.

As much as he would prefer Brigit stay on in some capacity, he doubted someone as adept in making decisions and giving orders in the day-to-day running of the resort, would be willing to follow his. He would ask her to stay, but he also would offer her a generous severance package and glowing letter of recommendation to help with her job search in the more likely event that she decided to go.

"I'll have my fingers crossed for you."

"Thanks." He frowned at the cane. "I'm hoping for a more promising prognosis." Again, his admission surprised him. What was it about Brigit that made it so easy to bare his soul?

"And if you don't get it? What then?"

Kellen squinted at her. "You know, you're the first person who's asked me that."

He didn't count his mother. After all, she hadn't asked. She'd told Kellen what he needed to do: grow up.

Brigit glanced away. "I'm sorry. I shouldn't have—"

"No. I appreciate your bluntness in this case." He took a deep breath and exhaled slowly. "To be honest, I don't know what I'll do. This is the sixth specialist. At what point do I just…"

Give up. His fingers tightened on the cane's handle until his knuckles turned white. He was unable to go on.

"Joe says you don't always do your exercises. You can't expect to recover fully if you don't put in the effort."

"Recover fully." He made a scoffing noise.

She wasn't deterred. "All right. Recover more of your lost mobility. That is the reason behind rehab, isn't it?"

No one else had dared to say such things to him.

Even Joe trod lightly when it came to admonishing Kellen for his lack of effort. Instead of making him want to tell her to go to hell, her straightforward nature compelled him to reply with similar honesty. "Yes, that is the reason behind rehab, but…but some days it's all I can do to get out of bed. Some days everything seems so…so… damned pointless."

The admission hung between them, suspended in the ensuing silence. Something flickered in her eyes. Understanding? Empathy?

"That's depression talking. It makes every obstacle seem insurmountable," she said after a moment. Her tone was filled with compassion, which only made it worse.

Depression? As if he weren't already feeling helpless and emasculated. Pride had him snapping, "What, are you a shrink now?"

She appeared to take his irritable tone in stride. "No. I just know that when a person is at his or her lowest point, it's not always easy to grab the nearest rope, even when it's well within reach."

"The voice of experience?"

She eyed him for a moment before speaking again.

"I'm heading back out to the deck. I have a few more emails to send before I get to work. Are you coming?"

Her switch in topics made it clear she knew something about how difficult it was to climb one's way back up after hitting rock bottom. Her divorce? That seemed the obvious culprit, but he let the matter drop.

"Can I get a cup of coffee?" he asked.

"Sure. I'll even carry it outside for you," she offered

with a smile that seemed more friendly than merely polite. He decided to think of that as progress.

Kellen followed her. His pace was slow and measured compared to her brisk one, and far less graceful. The view was worth it, though. Well worth it, he thought, as his gaze dipped south to watch her hips swing side to side. Although her movements were economical, that didn't keep them from being sexy. His interest was piqued again.

When they reached the living room, he glanced toward the sofa. The bed had been folded back up, cushions and throw pillows returned to their original positions.

"Is Joe out on the deck already?"

"No. He went for a run. He left about forty minutes ago, so he should be back within the hour. I'm sure he'll be happy to whip up one of his smoothies for you then."

Kellen groaned. "That's what I'm afraid of."

She stopped at the granite-topped island that separated the kitchen from the living room and poured their coffee before starting for the door that led to the deck.

It was breezier this morning than it had been on previous days. The wind caught at her hair and pushed several ribbons of it across her face. She finger-combed them back into place after depositing their coffee on a table and settling onto her lounge chair. His fingers itched to do the task for her, itched to touch her hair. He wouldn't find it sticky with gels or sprays. But soft, silky…

He concentrated on getting onto his chair. He'd gotten better at it over the past week, but it still required more effort than it should. As for getting up, well, he couldn't do that unless he positioned the lounge chair next to the deck's railing, which he used to haul himself to his feet.

By the time Kellen had his legs stretched out in front

of him, Brigit was already tapping away on the computer's keyboard.

Emails, she'd said. He assumed they were business-related, since, from what he could tell, the woman was on the clock 24/7.

What drove her? While he appreciated her above-and-beyond approach to her duties, it wasn't expected. Nor was it particularly healthy. He nearly chuckled aloud at that. As if he had any right to judge another person's lifestyle.

He glanced idly at the computer screen, expecting to see her confirming reservations or responding to guests' suggestions on the internet comment board. Too late, he realized the message she was writing was personal.

"Do you always read other people's correspondence?" she inquired blandly

Despite his embarrassment, he marveled again at how appealing he found her bluntness.

"No. Sorry. I just assumed that whatever you were working on was business-related."

"I do have a life." She glanced over at him in seeming challenge.

Not as much of one as she should, but he kept the opinion to himself. He did ask, "Who's Will?"

Her former husband? A current lover? Kellen found neither possibility palatable.

She closed the laptop and gave him her full attention, blue eyes blazing bright with an emotion he couldn't pinpoint. He didn't expect her to answer, but she said, "He's my nephew."

"Lucky you." When she frowned, he added, "I'm an only child. No siblings, no nieces or nephews. Just…me."

With his father and his grandfather gone and his mother estranged, that was truly the case.

"I have a sister. Robbie. Short for Roberta. She's older by eighteen months." Her expression softened, and the hint of a smile lurked around the corners of her mouth.

"You're close."

"Yes." Now she frowned again. "We don't see each other as often as we'd like. She lives in Pennsylvania."

"Does Will have siblings?"

"No. My sister wanted more children, but Mitchell, my brother-in-law, he…he was a Marine."

Was. Her use of the past tense had his stomach dropping. "God, I'm sorry. Iraq?"

"Afghanistan. A roadside bomb took out half his patrol. Will was a toddler at the time. He doesn't have any real memories of his dad."

"Sorry," Kellen said again, although the word seemed grossly inadequate under the circumstances. Her family had lost someone to the violence of war. In some ways, it made Kellen's own struggles seem minor, especially since his accident had been the result of foolish hot-dogging to meet a dare rather than something as honorable as serving his country. It was a humbling realization.

She was saying, "Will is eight now. For the past couple of summers, he and my sister have come out to Hadley Island over the Fourth of July for a visit. There's always a big fireworks display in Charleston that's visible from the western shore. We spread out a blanket, bring a basket of snacks and watch it."

"So they'll be coming this summer?" he asked, oddly envious of the picture of domestic bliss her words had helped conjure up.

"They stay with me, Kellen," she replied.

Despite the pointed look that accompanied her words, it took him a moment to realize what she meant.

Then, "Ah. Got it. No room at the inn and no room in your apartment. I'm s—"

"Don't apologize. What's done is done. I've promised Will that he and his mom can come another time later in the year, maybe during Christmas break."

The assumption being that Kellen wouldn't be at Faust Haven then. He swallowed. He wasn't planning on going anywhere. But would Brigit still be on his payroll at Christmas? Or would she have moved on to manage another resort?

While she went back to her typing, he scanned their surroundings. White-capped waves danced on the horizon before crashing to shore. Down the beach, he caught a glimpse of Joe. For a physically fit young man, he looked winded and pained. Still, Kellen envied him.

"I used to run every day," he remarked almost to himself.

Brigit looked up from the computer screen. "You're a runner?"

Was. But he nodded without bothering to correct her, and said, "I ran five miles every other day when I was skiing. Every day when I wasn't." He pointed in the direction of his physical therapist. "I'd like to think I didn't look as miserable as Joe does right now."

Brigit laughed. The wind carried the sound away too soon for his liking.

"That's exactly why I don't run. No one looks happy while they're doing it. And it's hard on the knees. I walk. Besides, you see more of your surroundings that way, and the health benefits are just as good if you keep your pace brisk."

Kellen couldn't manage brisk at this point, but he was intrigued. "Where do you walk?"

"When it's too nasty to be outside, I use a treadmill."

"The one that's been moved to storage?"

"That would be the one." She wrinkled her nose. For the first time he noticed the freckles sprinkled across its slim bridge. "It's not a big deal. The weather has been nice lately. Besides, I like to walk on the beach. I'm a seashell addict."

He recalled the assortment of jars filled with shells spread around the house. Some people paid a decorator to bring in such touches. Brigit had collected them herself.

"Do they have a twelve-step program for that?"

She blinked. "Was that an actual joke you just made?"

"I used to have a good sense of humor."

"Did you break that in the accident, too?"

He laughed aloud, a rusty sound that scraped his throat as it came out, and sounded as foreign as it had that day he'd read the message she'd penned on the bathroom mirror.

"Funny. So, how often do you walk?"

"I try to carve out an hour every evening."

Every evening? Her toned legs and trim waist spoke of regular exercise. Still, he'd had no idea. He and Brigit were living under the same roof, but beyond sharing a cup of morning coffee on the deck, they had spent little time together. Part of the reason for that was her crazy work schedule. While he appreciated her dedication, since he benefited directly from it, once again he found himself wanting to know what drove her.

"Why do you do it?" he asked.

He was referring to the long hours she put in at the resort. Brigit, of course, assumed he was speaking about her evening walks.

"It's a good way to regroup mentally. And more obviously, it's a good way to work off calories so I can keep off the pounds."

She didn't look as if she had a problem with her weight. If anything she leaned toward too thin. He said as much.

"I used to be heavier."

Kellen worked hard to mask his surprise. He needn't have bothered. She wasn't looking at him. Her tone sounded far away when she added, "It was a long time ago. A lifetime ago. During an unhappy time in my life."

She closed her computer and rose to her feet just as Joe jogged up the steps that led from the sand. When the physical therapist reached the top, he stopped and bent at the waist, breathing heavily.

"Enjoy your run?" Brigit asked. She sent Kellen a wink.

"Y-yeah. Gr-great…morning…for it. The breeze…" He took one hand off his knees and motioned vaguely. "Kept me cool. It's…it's gonna be…a hot one."

"The humidity is expected to climb, too. The beach will be crowded. A lot of day-trippers come over from the mainland hoping to cool off on days such as this."

"Lou won't be fighting traffic at least," Joe remarked, having fully caught his breath, before he retreated inside.

Joe's comment brought back his worry about seeing the specialist in Charleston.

And his attorney.

Kellen rubbed his thigh. The daily regimen of ibuprofen he'd begun had dulled the worst of the pain, but nothing was successful in taking it away completely.

"Are you nervous?" Brigit asked.

He shook his head, but the words that came out of his mouth were, "A little. Okay, a lot."

He swung his legs over the side of the lounge chair, determined to stand. He didn't like being forced to look up at her, especially for a conversation in which he already had admitted vulnerability. He grabbed the railing and, using his upper body strength, levered to his feet. Brigit didn't offer any help. She merely waited until he was standing and steady on his feet to speak.

"I used to play this game with myself before…well, before I left my husband and took control of my life again. I'd ask myself, 'What's the worst thing that can happen?' Once I'd faced that fear, I knew I could handle anything."

The breeze kicked up, whipping several ribbons of dark hair across her face. This time, Kellen gave in to impulse and tucked it behind her ear before she could. It was as soft as silk, just as he'd suspected. Afterward, his hand lingered next to her cheek, his palm so close he could feel the heat from her skin.

He watched her eyes widen. In surprise? Interest? He needed to believe it was the latter. He needed to believe that he was still desirable. *Liar.* He needed to believe *she* found him desirable. He caressed her jaw before resting his palm against the curve of her cheek. Soft, so soft. Her lips parted ever so slightly, and Kellen leaned in and kissed her. When she didn't pull away, he went back for seconds.

He settled his mouth firmly over hers this time. Their noses bumped. She rose on tiptoe and tilted her head to one side. Problem solved. Now it was their bodies that brushed together. Or would have if the damned laptop she held hadn't been in the way. She remedied that issue, too. Without breaking off their kiss, she dropped the computer onto the lounge chair's cushions. Both of her hands were free now, and she brought them up to his shoulders.

Passion, the raw and unfettered kind, coursed through Kellen's veins. He welcomed it. Hell, he reveled in it. For the first time in months, he felt alive again. He felt… whole.

His left hand remained on the rail. He needed it there

for support. But something told him that even if both of his legs had been working just fine, his knees would have felt weak. The kiss was that potent.

She pulled back slowly, blinking up at him as if in disbelief while she returned the heels of her feet to the deck's varnished boards. Although her hands remained on his shoulders, the moment was ending. Soon, all too soon, they would be back to the roles of business owner and employee. But Kellen didn't want this intriguing spell to be broken. Not yet.

He traced her bottom lip with the pad of his thumb and felt her shiver.

"Kellen. I don't think..." Her voice was barely a whisper. He leaned closer to hear her, but she shook her head. Whatever else she'd been about to say was snatched away by the wind.

"That game that you mentioned," he began. "What was your worst fear, Brigit?"

She didn't respond. Instead, she dropped her arms to her sides and backed up a step. Then, without another word, she turned and hurried inside, leaving him alone on the deck with far more questions left unanswered than the one he'd just asked.

CHAPTER SIX

"SORRY ABOUT THE change in plans," Brigit told her sister when they spoke on the phone later that same day.

"Don't worry about it." Brigit pictured her easygoing older sibling waving a hand in dismissal. They couldn't be more opposite. Brigit envied Robbie's roll-with-the-punches outlook. "We can come another time. As you wrote in your email, maybe we can plan a visit over Christmas break."

"Yes. Is Will upset?"

"He was looking forward to it," Robbie averred.

Brigit pictured her nephew's wide-set brown eyes, mop of reddish-brown hair and blunt chin. With every birthday he looked more like her late brother-in-law.

"I saw Scott in town."

This news had Brigit sitting up straighter in her office chair, a chill passing down her spine. Even all these years later the mere mention of his name caused the old fears to coalesce. She swallowed, beat them back and let nonchalance take their place.

"What did he want?"

"He didn't *want* anything. In fact, we didn't speak. I just saw him while I standing in the supermarket checkout. He was a couple lanes down unloading groceries. He waved. I pretended I didn't see him."

"Did he…come any closer?"

"No. He's pretty careful to honor the restraining order."

Not only had Brigit taken out one against her insistent ex. So had her mother and her sister after he'd started showing up at their homes and places of work unannounced.

Brigit let out a silent sigh of relief. Nonetheless, she said, "I wish things could be different. I wish Scott could be different. I mean, he is Will's godfather." And with Mitch gone, he could have served as a much-needed father figure if he had been a better man.

"Don't remind me. But even if he had professed to have changed, I wouldn't let that…that…*bully* near my son after the way he treated you. Some things are unforgivable." On this her easy-breezy sister's tone had turned implacable.

"I just hate making things harder for you and Mom in Arlis." Nearly everybody in the small southern Pennsylvania town thought Scott Wellington walked on water.

That was one of the reasons Brigit had changed her name back to Wright and decided to move after their divorce was finalized. Scott had made sure she'd been portrayed as the bad guy. She hadn't been able to prove it, but she was certain he'd been behind the rumors about an affair that had started just prior to their reaching a settlement. By that point she'd been happy to give him whatever he'd wanted just to get away.

Of course, he'd wanted Brigit. He'd wanted to continue to control her, to make her bend to his will and live her life according to his rules. She hadn't been about to let that happen. Not any longer.

So she'd signed over their house and all of its furnishings. She'd even let him keep the china that had been a wedding gift from her late grandmother. Whatever it had taken to get out from under his thumb, she'd done. She regretted giving him so much now. So many people in town had viewed her wholesale retreat as an affirmation of her guilt. Since her sister, nephew and mother still lived in Arlis, they were the ones who had to put up with the gossip mill. And five years later, it was still churning out tall tales.

"Mitch thought of Scott as a brother," Robbie said now. Indeed, Scott had served as best man at her wedding. "If he had known how controlling—"

But Mitch hadn't. No one had. After they'd wed, and Scott's rigid expectations had become intolerable, Brigit had kept quiet. She'd thought of her bad marriage as her own problem, her own private shame. And now she was determined that it all stay in the past.

Returning to the reason for her call, she told Robbie, "I hate having to disappoint Will."

"He'll be fine. And now he'll look forward to Christmas break all the more." Robbie cleared her throat and her tone turned sly when she asked, "So, what's Kellen Faust like in person? Do the photos I've seen of him shirtless on a beach in the Mediterranean do him justice?"

Almost all of the photos splashed over the internet and in the tabloids had been snapped pre-accident. His physique had been buff then, his skin tanned, toned and vital. Every inch of him had screamed fun-loving, hard-bodied stud. Now…

"He looks different," Brigit replied truthfully.

"Different good or different bad? Is it true that he can't walk?"

Even with her sister, Brigit didn't feel comfortable discussing the particulars of Kellen's condition. "You know how the entertainment media love to blow things out of proportion."

"So, he can walk?"

"He uses a cane, but, yes, he can walk."

"A cane, huh?"

"It makes him look sophisticated and…and sexy," she said in his defense, as if her sister were the sort of person who judged on appearances alone. "Sorry. It's just that he's very sensitive about it."

A long pause followed. So long a pause that Brigit thought the connection might have been lost. "Robbie? Are you still there?"

"Yep. Still here. So…sexy, huh?" Her sister made a humming noise. "That's an interesting description coming from you."

Brigit recalled the earlier kiss on the deck. It had awakened long-dormant desire, resurrected almost-forgotten needs. Rusty though she might have been when it came to intimacy, she recognized passion when she felt it, and she knew it had flowed both ways. Kellen had wanted her as badly as she'd wanted him. But the fact remained…

"He's my boss." She said it flatly. It served as a reminder to herself as well as an answer for her sister. "So, I think he's sexy. Big deal. I think the guy who plays Thor is sexy, too. It doesn't mean anything, Rob." She swallowed hard and forced herself to say it a second time. "It doesn't mean a thing."

Kellen wanted to break something. He wanted to hurl his damned cane across the examination room or punch a hole in the wall. He was even tempted to plow his fist into the doctor's face, as if it were the man's fault that Kellen's leg was shattered beyond repair.

He'd been foolish to come here. Foolish to hope for a better prognosis from this specialist when five of the guy's highly recommended peers already had told Kellen the same thing.

"You need to accept that your life has changed," the doctor was saying. "You can still live a full and active life, but it won't be the same active life you used to live. You need to find new hobbies, Mr. Faust. You need to figure out a new lifestyle. Other people in your position have. If you'd like, I can put you in touch with some of them."

"That's all right," he bit out.

The doctor cleared his throat. "I also recommend therapy."

"I'm in therapy," Kellen replied, pointing to Joe, who sat on a stool in the corner jotting down notes.

"I'm not talking about *physical* therapy, Mr. Faust," the doctor said. His expression was patient, kind…condescending. Kellen nearly did punch him in the face then.

To prevent that from happening, he balled his hands into fists in his lap as he sat on the exam table. He stayed that way for the remainder of the appointment.

"Sorry, Mr. F," Joe began as they left the doctor's office. "I know you were hoping for better news."

Kellen didn't answer. Once they were in the SUV, he barked an address at Lou. At least the attorney wouldn't be able to contradict Kellen's plans for his future.

More than ever, he needed to take over the helm at the resort. Be the one calling the shots. With so much else beyond his control, he needed to feel in charge of something. And the resort, the haven of his childhood, was all he had left.

After calling her sister, Brigit remained at the desk in her small office for most of the day on the pretext of catching up on paperwork. Hiding out was more like it. She was embarrassed, mortified, confused. What had come over her? She'd kissed her boss!

Technically, of course, Kellen had been the one to initiate contact. He'd tucked the hair back from her face, caressed her cheek and then… She hadn't seen it coming until that very moment. Still, he'd given her a chance to break it off and back away. Instead, what had she done? She'd put her arms around his shoulders, held on tight and kissed him right back. She'd even set down her laptop so she could do so. Set it down? She'd all but tossed it aside.

She pinched her eyes closed, dropped her head into her hands and groaned. The only thing more damning than that was the fact that she'd enjoyed it. Every blessed second and stroke of his tongue. It had been pure heaven.

Brigit wasn't sure she liked the man, even if she found him too attractive for her peacc of mind. Over the past week, thanks in large part to those quiet mornings on the deck, they had developed a cordial relationship, one that still fell safely within the boundaries of being professional. She wouldn't pretend to understand him or what he'd been going through since his accident, but there seemed to be more to Kellen than the spoiled, apathetic heir she'd first assumed. She'd spied unexpected depths to go along with whatever demons it was that he fought.

But *cordial* didn't describe that kiss. Nothing about it had been friendly or casual. It had lit her up on the inside like a string of Christmas tree lights, and she swore they were still blinking maniacally, which just plain ticked her off.

She'd sworn off men after her divorce, eager to stand on her own two feet, determined to prove to herself that she'd never again let herself become spineless, worthless, invisible. She hadn't missed men, either.

Until now.

Damn Kellen! And damn her own foolishness!

Now what was she supposed to do? How was she supposed to act around him? Did she demand an apology? Or did she owe him one? What if he was expecting a repeat? She shivered even thinking of it, and loathed herself all the more when anticipation was the emotion that bubbled closest to the surface.

An hour later, she was still mentally berating herself when she heard two pairs of footsteps in the hall outside her office. One set was heavy, uneven and accompanied by the distinctive click of a cane on tile. The other was more measured. Kellen and Joe. They had returned from the mainland.

Act natural, casual, unaffected. Above all else, be professional. She exhaled through her mouth, rose to her feet. On her way to the door, she smoothed down her top and schooled her expression into one of polite interest.

"How did—?"

That was all she got out before Joe shook his head.

Kellen, meanwhile, never even glanced her way. He glared straight ahead with his jaw clenched, his sandy eyebrows pulled low over his eyes in a scowl reminiscent of the expression he'd been wearing during their first meeting.

Whatever news he'd received, it hadn't been good. Her heart sank. This, she knew, was Kellen's worst fear.

He took dinner in his room. Not just in the apartment, but in his bedroom. Brigit took the tray herself. Joe was at the apartment's kitchen peninsula, creating some kind of smoothie. He glanced up and smiled.

"Hey, Brigit. You're a gem. Just leave the tray on the counter. I'll take it in when I finish with this," he said as he added fresh banana slices to the blender.

That sounded good to her. The less interaction with Kellen the better. For both of them.

"Is that for Kellen?" She nodded to the blender.

"Are you kidding?" The physical therapist's laughter was subdued. "In his current mood Mr. F would probably chuck it at my head."

Brigit's anxiety over how to act around Kellen after their kiss was forgotten. She glanced down the hallway and lowered her voice to just above a whisper. "So, bad news today?"

"Not necessarily bad. Just not the news he wanted to hear." Joe stopped what he was doing, leaned his elbows on the counter and sighed. "This specialist basically told Mr. F the same thing all the other ones have. He won't be hot-dogging down the slopes again. For that matter, he's never going to walk without a limp and a cane. The faster he comes to accept that and move on with his life, the better off he's going to be."

Joe straightened and resumed what it was he'd been doing. Soon the blender blades whirled, making conversation impossible.

Her heart ached. Poor Kellen. He must be devastated, she thought as she left the apartment.

Brigit stopped feeling sorry for him when, nearly a week later, he remained holed up in his bedroom with the curtains drawn. Joe had been the only visitor allowed to breach the threshold, and then only to bring Kellen his meals.

At first, she'd been almost relieved that Kellen hadn't joined her on the deck in the mornings. After that amazing kiss they'd shared, things between them were bound to be awkward and strained. But now, five days after his return from the doctor, she was out of both sympathy and patience.

The man had been dealt a bitter blow. No doubt about that. But brooding wouldn't change anything. Brigit knew firsthand that self-pity got a person nowhere. He needed to concentrate on what was possible rather than on what wasn't.

Really, Kellen should be thanking his lucky stars. He could have suffered a massive head injury or broken his neck in the fall and become a quadriplegic. Despite his injuries, he was healthy overall. He had all of his mental faculties. He was still handsome, sexy, virile. Her body began to hum as she recalled their kiss. Oh, yeah. The accident had done nothing to diminish his sexual appeal. She swallowed, regrouped.

He was physically capable of working, even if he was wealthy enough that he didn't have to. Yes, he would have a limp and be required to use a cane for the rest of his life. But it wasn't the end of the world. He could trade in the ski slopes, his Swiss chalet and his sycophantic friends in Europe for a tropical island hideaway. There he could lie on a beach, surround himself with equally vacuous toadies and live comfortably off his inheritance, she thought uncharitably.

How many people could afford such a choice? Brigit certainly hadn't been given many options when her life had crumbled into pieces before, and immediately after, her divorce. Putting those pieces back together had taken a Herculean effort. But she'd managed it. She was happy. Well, maybe not happy, but content.

Although lately… No. She shook off the thought that the solo, work-centric life she had planned might no longer be enough to satisfy her.

This wasn't about her. It was about Kellen and his future. And he could find contentment, too. First, however, he had to want it and put in the effort to attain it.

Joe was perched on the edge of the couch cushions watching a baseball game when she arrived with the evening's meal tray.

"You didn't have to bring Mr. F's dinner," the young man admonished as he rose to his feet. "I was heading to the dining room to eat after this inning and would have brought one back for him."

"That's all right. I was on my way here to change my clothes."

He consulted his watch. "It's a little early for your evening walk. It hasn't even started to cool off outside yet."

Indeed, the mercury was still pushing ninety, which was why she usually waited until just before nightfall to comb the beach. With the exception of a handful of committed anglers, it was largely empty by then, even the most hard-core sunbathers having packed up for the day. Any shells that had washed ashore would be picked over, but she took a bag with her. Just in case. The beach always seemed to give up tiny treasures. Even after five years on Hadley Island, she wasn't able to resist collecting them.

"I know, but it's been a slow day. No new guests and the dinner crowd was light because of the music festival happening on the other side of the island." She set the tray on the kitchen counter and nodded toward the television. "So what's the score?"

Joe originally hailed from Florida, so he was grinning when he replied, "Tampa Bay is up by three runs in the top of the fourth."

"Go, Rays," she said without inflection. As expected,

Joe laughed. Then she inclined her head toward the hallway. "Has he been out of his room at all today?"

"Nope. Never even got out of bed. He kept the shades pulled again, too." Joe shook his head. "It's like a tomb in there."

"That makes how many days now since his last physical therapy session?"

"Six. He's going to be extra sore once he finally decides to rejoin the land of the living."

She pursed her lips and shook her head.

"I know what you're thinking," Joe said.

"That he's so busy feeling sorry for himself he's sabotaging his recovery?" When Joe said nothing, Brigit tipped her head to the side. "Well, am I wrong?" she demanded.

"Not in the least."

This came from Kellen. He was in the hallway, standing just outside the door to the master bedroom. Despite the distance, he'd heard every word.

She swallowed and felt her face heat. "I'm sorry."

"Oh, please. Don't ruin your forthrightness with an apology," he told Brigit as he lumbered toward her. "Your honesty is one of the qualities I like best about you."

He was spoiling for a fight, and Brigit decided not to disappoint him. She notched up her chin. "All right. I'm not sorry. What I am is…disappointed."

Kellen's sandy brows lifted in surprise at that and he repeated, "Disappointed?"

Brigit settled her hands on her hips. "That's what I said. Disappointed."

Joe picked that moment to mumble something about going to dinner and wisely retreated. Kellen waited until the apartment door latched behind his physical therapist to continue.

"Yeah, well, get in line. I'm sure there's a spot open right behind my mother. I've never been able to do anything right in her opinion either." He shook his head. Some of the bluster went out of him. "She's right, of course. No one to blame for that but myself."

The comment momentarily threw Brigit. What the heck did his mother have to do with this? What was the woman right about? Another time, she might have asked him. But not right now. Right now, she remained focused on the issue at hand: his reaction to this latest setback. She chose not to dwell on why it was so important to her that Kellen not give up.

Taking a step toward him, she demanded, "How can you expect to improve your condition if all you do is lie around and wallow in self-pity all day long?"

"Didn't Joe tell you? There's no improvement to be had. This is it, Brigit! What you see is what you get!"

Kellen's voice thundered through the apartment and he lifted his cane for emphasis. The mocking smile he sent her vanished when he lost his balance. He was able to catch himself on one of the island's stools before he crashed to the ground, but he had to let go of the cane to do so. The gold-tipped walking stick clattered to the floor, and a round of vicious cursing followed. Brigit allowed him to vent his frustration, waiting until he was done to continue speaking in a moderate tone.

"You're not going to be able to tackle the steep slopes in Europe again. You're not going to be able to run a marathon or a half marathon or even the island's annual two-block tyke trot. And it looks like competitive ballroom dancing will be a no-go, too."

"I don't need you to list all the things I can no longer do!" he shouted. Veins pulsed at his temples and his jaw clenched afterward.

She retrieved the cane and held it out to him. He snatched it away. If fire could have shot out from his eyes just then, Brigit figured her skin would have been charred. He was furious, but she took his rage in stride. After Scott, she'd vowed never to back down when she knew she was right. And she *was* right in this instance. She needed to make Kellen use his rage to his advantage. Channeled correctly, it could be beneficial. God knew, she'd used her own anger as a catalyst for change. She was proud of all she had accomplished since then, proud of the way she'd taken the bull by the proverbial horns and reinvented herself rather than succumbing to despair.

So she ignored his temper and went on. "All right. I'll tell you what you *can* do. Based on your current physical condition and attitude, you can continue to be an embittered invalid."

She expected her words to get a rise out of him. To her consternation, the fight went out of Kellen. His voice lost its steely edge and he stated flatly, "I *am* an invalid, Brigit, bitter or otherwise."

"Joe thinks you could get stronger if you followed his advice to the letter rather than skipping days at a time and then putting in minimal effort when you finally do show up."

"So you and Joe are discussing my therapy? I wasn't aware I was a topic of conversation between the two of you."

He was trying to make her feel bad, but she wouldn't let him. "You know what your problem is, Kellen?"

He blew out a breath. "I'm sure you're only too happy to tell me."

"As a matter of fact..." She smiled sweetly and went on. "Your problem, Kellen, is that you're expecting someone to wave a magic wand and hand you back your good health."

"Bull—"

"I'm not finished," she interrupted.

And Brigit sincerely hoped that she wasn't, career-wise especially. Her bluntness could wind up costing her big-time, but the fact remained that the man needed a swift kick in the seat of his designer-label track pants. Since no one else seemed inclined to do it, she would do the honors. The faster he was back on his feet—literally as well as figuratively—the faster he would leave and things could get back to normal at the resort.

Brigit ignored the twinge of regret the thought of his leaving caused. She ignored the small voice that whispered she would miss him. Instead, she plowed ahead, intentionally discarding any effort to employ tact. Politeness would only get in the way at this point. Kellen needed to hear the unvarnished truth.

"You have the power to change your circumstances. You may not be able to return to what you used to be. But being happy, carving out a fulfilling future, those things are up to you."

"Is that what you did, Brigit?"

The question caught her off guard. "What do you mean?"

"After your divorce. You tucked yourself away on Hadley Island, threw yourself into your work.

"You don't know anything about my marriage or my divorce."

"Easily remedied," he murmured, eyebrows lifted. Even if she had been tempted, the offer to spill her secrets was hardly sincere.

"We aren't talking about me."

"Handy." He cocked his head to one side. "Are you happy, Brigit? Are you *fulfilled*?"

The way he said it, the way he looked at her had needs she'd nearly forgotten bubbling to the surface. She chose to ignore both his question and her dormant desires and took a breath. "We're talking about you. Ask yourself, Kellen, is this how you want to spend the rest of your life? Being angry and unpleasant and acting defeated? If it is, then I hope you will find somewhere else to do it."

His mouth fell open for a moment before he asked in disbelief, "Are you telling me to leave my own resort?"

"No."

"Really? Because that's sure as hell what it sounded like to me, Brigit."

"What I'm saying is that no one wants to be around someone who is irritable and angry all of the time."

"Yourself included? You don't want to be around me? You didn't seem all that adverse the other day on the deck." His tone was suggestive; his gaze slid down her body slowly before returning to her mouth.

"Don't."

"Don't what?" he challenged, his tone retaining all of its redolence.

"Don't be a jerk. Don't treat me like one of the brainless ski bunnies who hang out at your chalet."

"Because you're better than that?" he asked snidely.

She blinked, regrouped. After only a moment's hesitation she replied. "You're damned right I am. But actually, what I was thinking is that *you're* better than that."

She'd hoped to snap him out of his funk, but her words only seemed to make him angrier.

"This is me, Brigit. Don't like it, then get the hell out. I can replace you in a heartbeat."

Something inside of her went cold. For one panicky second, old insecurities threatened to overwhelm her. They battered her self-esteem the way waves battered the coast during a Category 5 hurricane.

You're so helpless, Brigit.

You're so incompetent.

How stupid can a person be?

You should be thanking your lucky stars every day that someone like me wanted to marry someone as naive and backward as you.

She mentally swatted away Scott's belittling remarks, angry with herself for letting them back in for even a moment. At least with Kellen, she understood why he was lashing out. Scott had sought to hurt and demean her for the pure sport of it. That kind of cruelty was incomprehensible to her.

Kellen was saying, "Faust Haven is mine. My grandfather left it to me. So I'll stay here as long as I damned well please. That is my right!"

The heir had spoken. A couple of weeks ago, she might have believed his imperious act. But she'd glimpsed the man behind the curtain, knew him to be vulnerable, lost.

"That is your right," she agreed calmly, even though her pulse was still pinging on high. "And I'm sure finding another manager would be easy. You found a few before me."

She loved her job. She loved the island. She would be devastated to be forced to leave and start over. Where would she go? How would she land another position with a black mark such as being fired for insubordination on her résumé? And how could she leave Kellen?

The last question caught her by surprise. Nothing was going on between them. A kiss and some friendly banter did not make a relationship. And then there was the fact that he was her boss.

"But?" he pressed as she puzzled over her feelings.

Briefly, she wondered if she should cut her losses and apologize. In his current mood, he might very well fire her. Brigit swallowed and backed up a step, but she didn't retreat. She couldn't. She wasn't done having her say and, if her joke of a marriage to Scott had taught her nothing else, it had taught her to hold her ground, because never again would she allow herself to be turned into a self-effacing coward afraid to voice her opinion.

"But they won't be as good as I am." She swallowed and added, "At my job."

"Is that all?"

Her palms were damp. She ignored the telltale moisture as she gripped them together. "No. That's not all. The point I am trying to make, Kellen, is that whether you stay on Hadley Island or go back to Europe or—" she motioned with one hand "—park your rear end at the North Pole, no one wants to be around a person who is determined to wallow in his misery."

"Do you think I enjoy being miserable?" he asked, sounding incredulous.

"No, but you've accepted it. Heck, you've embraced it."

There was no backing down now. She'd opened this particular can of worms and she would see it through. But, God, she hoped the walls were thick enough to prevent the resort's guests from overhearing their heated exchange.

"I've done the damned exercises. They don't help. Nothing helps!"

"Please," she spat with a shake of her head. "You only get out of physical therapy what you are willing to put into it. Can you honestly say that you've done the exercises faithfully?" When he glanced away, she knew she had him and so she pressed on. "You have the money to hire a personal physical therapist. He's at your disposal 24/7. He lives under the same roof as you do, for heaven's sake. Do you have any idea how many other people recovering from serious accidents would love to be in your position?"

"I know I'm fortunate, but you make it sound so easy."

She moderated her tone and dropped the volume. "That's not my intent. I know it's hard and painful and the odds may be stacked against you. But at least you have options, Kellen. And you have a lot to be grateful for." She place a hand on his arm. "You walked away from an accident that could have left you confined to a wheelchair for the rest of your life. If you can't work up a little gratitude for that alone, then maybe you injured your head in the fall, too."

He closed his eyes momentarily, and she thought she might have gotten through to him, but then he demanded, "Are you done?"

"I…I guess I am," she replied, exasperated with both of them. Why did it matter to her what he did? She wasn't his keeper.

"Good." He pointed to the tray of food that sat forgotten on the countertop. "I'd like to eat on the deck tonight."

He turned and started for the door. Apparently, he expected her to carry the tray outside for him. He was back to his heir act. And she his dutiful underling. She picked it up. The cheery yellow daisy in the bud vase mocked her. She might be his employee, but she damned well wouldn't be his enabler. Even if it cost Brigit her job, she'd be damned if she would allow herself to be marginalized. Not again. *Never* again. She returned the tray to the countertop with enough force to cause the dishes to rattle and the iced tea to slosh over the rim of its glass.

"You carry it," she told him.

He glared back at her. "What?"

"You heard me."

He snorted. "Very funny. I can't and you know it."

"That's right. So, you know that that means?" She didn't wait for him to respond, but held up a finger. "A, you need to be nicer to the people who are helping you, whether they are paid or not." Holding up a second finger, she added, "And B, you need put more effort in to improve your situation."

"Do you think this is what I want?" His voice had turned soft, but she wasn't fooled by the muted tone. He was every bit as angry as he had been moments ago. Maybe even more so based on the way his face now flushed scarlet. That anger wasn't directed at her, at least not intentionally, and once again she found herself thinking how, channeled correctly, his intense emotions could prove a benefit rather than a hindrance to his recovery.

"I think—"

That was as far as she got before he cut her off.

"Do you think this is how I want to live? Having people help me stand and sit and carry my plate? I hate this! I. Hate. This!" He brought the cane down on the edge of the granite countertop with such force that it snapped in two. One half flew into the living room. The other flipped end over end before striking Brigit just under her chin. The jagged wood pierced her flesh. Pain mingled with surprise as she clapped her hand over the wound. Her fingers came away bright red.

The color drained from Kellen's face.

"My God! Brigit, I never meant..."

He reached for her, but she batted his fingers away with her bloody hand.

More frustrated than anything, she turned and rushed out of the apartment, passing a wide-eyed Joe as she sought the refuge of her office.

CHAPTER SEVEN

KELLEN WAS DISGUSTED with himself. What kind of a monster had he become? Of course he hadn't intended for the cane to snap and strike Brigit, but the fact remained—that was exactly what had occurred. His rage had caused her injury. And all she'd been trying to do was help him.

He rubbed a hand over his face as he slid down the wall to the floor. Never had he hated himself more. Brigit was right. He had a lot to be grateful for. Self-pity would get him nowhere. Hell, his mother was right. He needed to grow up, take responsibility for his life, be the man his grandfather had believed Kellen could be.

He'd thought he'd been doing that by coming to the island, determined to learn the ropes and eventually take over the day-to-day management of the inn. But he'd been fooling himself. He'd come here to hide not to heal. He'd been so stuck in the past that living the present, much less having dreams for the future, had been impossible.

He was still seated on the floor when Joe rushed in several minutes later.

"Mr. F?" The young man's eyes were rounded with concern. "Brigit's in her office and… Wh-what happened? Are you all right?"

Kellen wasn't sure how to respond. He wasn't all right,

but it had nothing to do with his leg. So, instead of replying, he asked, "Can you help me up? Please."

"Sure thing."

With Joe's assistance, Kellen was soon on his feet with his back braced against the wall.

"What happened to your cane?" Joe retrieved one of the pieces from the floor.

Kellen's gut clenched on a potent mixture of embarrassment and shame. "If you don't mind, I'd rather not talk about it right now."

"Okay. Sure. No problem." The therapist bobbed his head in affirmation.

That was Joe, eager to please, unable to call his boss on the carpet for either his actions or his attitude. Unlike Brigit, who'd given Kellen a piece of her mind even though it meant having to step into the line of fire. Literally. Kellen pictured her bloodied chin again and a fresh wave of shame swamped him. He wasn't fit company.

"I'd like to return to my room. I want to…" To what? *Hide* was the word that taunted him, but he said, "I want to go lie down."

"Right now, Mr. F?" Joe frowned. "But you only just got up."

"I know, Joe. My room," he repeated. "Therapy tomorrow, I promise, but right now I have a lot to think about."

The therapist pointed to the tray. "I can have your dinner warmed up, if you want. The chicken was excellent tonight, and a good source of protein."

Kellen shook his head.

Given the way his stomach was churning, he doubted he would be able to keep down anything.

The following morning, Kellen made his way out to the deck even before the sun was fully up. Without his cane, he'd had to call on Joe for assistance. He'd hoped to see Brigit sitting in her usual spot, drinking coffee, the computer open on her lap. God knew, he needed to apologize, to beg her for forgiveness if need be. He'd acted abominably. But the deck was empty.

"Looks like I beat Brigit out here today," he said in what he hoped sounded like a conversational tone rather than that of a man desperate to make amends.

Joe helped him into one of the lounge chairs, waiting until he was settled to say, "I'd imagine she's going to sleep late today."

"Oh? Why do you say that?" Kellen asked.

"She didn't get back from the emergency room on the mainland until after three this morning."

"Emergency room?" And Kellen had thought he couldn't feel any worse than he already did.

"I called Lou and asked him to take her. She didn't want to go, but that gash on her chin was pretty bad."

Swallowing hard, Kellen asked, "How bad?"

"Bad enough that it needed to be closed with stitches." Joe studied Kellen without blinking. Questions brewed in the other man's eyes, but all he said was, "It's too bad about her slipping on the floor and hitting her chin on the island."

"Is that what she said happened?"

"Yep." Joe nodded. "That's what she said, all right."

For the first time since Kellen had known Joe, the man's affable smile and easygoing nature were nowhere to be found. He couldn't blame the guy for being suspicious, and while Kellen didn't owe his employee any explanations, he felt the need to clear the air and own up to his responsibilities.

"It was my fault," he said.

Joe's gaze turned as cold as a tombstone. In the instant before Kellen went on, he knew that the seemingly friendly giant of a man was fully capable of violence should the situation call for it. Even though that violence would have been directed at Kellen, he found a new respect for the guy.

"I struck the counter with my cane. It broke and the halves went flying. One of them struck Brigit on the chin." He swallowed hard, but the sour taste remained in his mouth.

"So it was an accident," Joe said, some of the tension ebbing from his broad shoulders.

Kellen nodded. "But it was still entirely my fault and I feel sick about it. She was only trying to be helpful."

But it was time he helped himself.

That was the realization he'd come to last night, as he'd sat alone in his room replaying not only his conversation with Brigit, but reviewing how he'd spent the four months since his accident. Hell, how he'd spent his adulthood. He been dealt some hard knocks, but that was no excuse for his behavior.

It had taken a blunt-spoken employee to finally make him see the light. He pictured Brigit, and amended, a pretty, blunt-spoken woman with dark-lashed blue eyes who saw through his bluster to the man beneath.

Suddenly, it was vitally important that she like what she saw.

Brigit changed the bandage on her chin in the small restroom off her office. In the three days since her visit to the ER, the flesh surrounding the gash had turned from deep purple to mottled red to an unsightly bluish-green. She had a feeling it would turn a couple more unattractive colors yet before finally fading. As for the wound itself, it was going to scar. No way around that, as the ER doctor had confirmed. But it was low enough on her chin that it wouldn't be very visible. No one was likely to see it unless they stooped down in front of her and then looked up.

Well, it was her own damned fault. She'd pushed Kellen too far. He'd passed his breaking point as surely as his cane had when it had met the granite countertop's edge. For the past few days she'd tried unsuccessfully to get his guilt-stricken expression out of her head. Indeed, she'd done her best not only to avoid thinking about it, but to avoid him. That meant coming into the apartment late at night and leaving before it was light the following day. She missed her early mornings on the deck, watching the sun scatter muted gold rays across the horizon. She missed Kellen and his quiet presence. But she took her coffee at her desk and kept the door closed while she was in there. Not surprisingly, she was able to find plenty to do to keep her busy.

Are you happy, Brigit? Are you fulfilled?

She did her best to forget his questions. They were irrelevant, she assured herself.

As for Kellen, it was none of her business if he wanted to forgo his physical therapy and sit around feeling sorry for himself. None at all, even if she could admit she was attracted to him. Why then, she wondered, did she still feel the need to do something to help him?

She blamed the kiss, even as she sought to discount it. So, they'd locked lips in one of the most amazing kisses of her life. Big deal. That didn't make her his keeper. It didn't make her *anything* to Kellen. They were adults. Two lonely people looking for…nothing.

Brigit wasn't looking for anything. She had a job she loved, one that she wanted to continue doing well into the future. To ensure that she got that chance, she needed to stay out of his personal business. Sooner or later, despite his familial attachment to Faust Haven, he would get bored and leave. Then her life would get back to normal. And their relationship would return to one marked by intermittent professional correspondence via the internet. She ignored the hollowed out feeling in her gut. That was what she wanted. Okay, maybe not what she wanted, but it was all she could expect.

That evening while she finished logging in a couple of Sherry's last-minute changes to the week's dinner menu an email dropped into her inbox.

She knew the sender well. *FunLuver17,* a moniker that could be taken a couple of ways. Ambivalent, just like the man.

The subject line read: Need your assistance, please

Please? Hmm, the bow to manners was a new twist. As was his admitting to needing some help. Curiosity got the better of her and she clicked on the email.

Dear Miss Wright, it began.

So, they were back to courtesy titles. She should have been pleased. In the absence of physical distance, emotional distance would be for the best. But disappointed was what Brigit felt. Irritated with herself, she shrugged it off and continued reading.

Joe has the night off.

She knew that, of course. Lou had come to collect him. The two men were heading to Little John's Crab Shack a couple miles up the beach for a late dinner and some live entertainment. Joe had stopped by the office on his way out to tell her that Kellen was in bed—whether again or still, she hadn't asked—and not likely to need anything. Well, apparently, Joe had been wrong.

Could you bring a dinner tray?

Many thanks, KF

She closed the email and sighed. He had used *please* and *thanks*. So much for her efforts to avoid him.

The apartment was quiet when she entered holding the tray. Quiet and dark. The shades were drawn even though sunlight stole in around the edges. No wonder Joe had been eager for a night out. It was depressing in here.

"Hello?" she called.

As tempted as she was just to leave the tray on the kitchen counter and leave, she had to be sure Kellen could get to it. He still didn't have a cane, but Joe had mentioned finding a piece of driftwood on the beach during one of his morning runs. He'd trimmed off a couple knobby outcroppings and had cut it down to the proper size. According to Joe, it would do until the new one Kellen had ordered arrived.

"In here."

His bedroom. Of course.

The last thing she wanted to do was confront the lion in his den, but she swallowed, notched up her bandaged chin and breezed in holding the tray aloft.

A lamp burned at his bedside. The base was clear glass, which she'd filled with shells. She nudged a book out of the way so that she could set the tray on the nightstand.

Kellen sat on the bed with his back against the upholstered headboard. His good leg was bent at the knee, foot planted squarely on the mattress. He wore his usual nylon track pants and cotton T-shirt, this one with a quarter-size designer logo embroidered on the breast.

That was as far as she allowed her gaze to stray. She didn't make eye contact.

"Here you go," she told him in lieu of a greeting. "I think you'll enjoy it. Sherry's stuffed pork tenderloin always gets rave reviews from our guests. The portion size is smaller than what we serve in the dining room, but Joe insisted on no more than a playing card–size portion and double the amount of veggies."

With that she turned to leave. She made it almost to the door before Kellen said, "I think I will eat on the deck tonight."

Her back was still to him, so she could grimace and mutter a curse under her breath without him seeing. Then she turned, a forced smile curving her mouth while she returned for the tray.

As tempting as she found it to dump the sliced pork, red-skinned potatoes and steamed asparagus tips over his head, she resisted. The chef had worked too hard on the meal to treat it with such disrespect, and besides, Brigit would be the one who would have to clean it up.

"Certainly, Mr. Faust," she said in her most dutiful tone.

"I prefer you call me Kellen," he told her as he maneuvered to the edge of the bed.

"I thought since your email referred to me as Miss Wright…" She let her words trail off and shrugged.

"I did that out of respect," he told her quietly as he struggled to stand.

Out of respect? Hmm. What to make of that?

Even though she was confused, she replied, "I see."

For the first time since entering the room, she glanced at his face. He looked like hell. The dark smudges under his eyes made it look as if he'd gone a few rounds in the ring with a prizefighter, and from the prickly growth on his jaw it was clear he hadn't shaved in days. His hair was unkempt, tufts going this way and that on his crown. Despite all the time he'd spent in bed, he hardly appeared rested.

"May I…may I call you Brigit?" he asked quietly. His gaze was on her bandaged chin, and an emotion she'd never seen before glazed his eyes.

Where he had been irritable and bitter at their last meeting, this time he appeared subdued, humbled. Rather than making demands and hurling out edicts, he was asking for permission to call her by her given name.

Her heart warmed, melted in a way that spelled danger. Still, how could she say no?

"I…I…" She recalled their kiss, the passion it had ignited. Under the circumstances it seemed ridiculous not to be on a first-name basis. "That's fine."

He nodded and reached for the walking stick tucked next to the nightstand. Sand and water had worn off the bark, leaving the grayish-brown wood smooth. The top curved just enough to make the perfect handle.

"Joe told me about the piece of driftwood he found."

"It does the job," Kellen agreed.

She collected the tray. Before she could turn to go, he said quietly, "Brigit?"

"Yes?"

"How…how is your chin?"

"It's fine."

"Joe said you had to go to the emergency room for stitches."

"Actually, they used glue. The wonders of modern medicine. No needles and no stitches to be removed later. I just need to keep the area clean and dry." She forced a laugh.

His expression remained sober. "Did they say if it would scar?"

"Probably." She shrugged.

"God!" He bit off an oath, and reassured her, "I'll pay for you to see a plastic surgeon. The best money can buy."

"That won't be necessary. I'm not a vain woman, and even if I was, it's not in an obvious place."

She watched his throat work. When he spoke, his voice was hoarse. "I'm sorry, Brigit. You have to believe me. I never meant for—"

"It was an accident, Kellen."

"Still, it was my fault that you got hurt."

Angry and bitter, Kellen had been easier to resist. But standing in front of her looking tortured and acting humbled and contrite? Her heart kicked out a couple extra beats and that was before his eyes locked with hers. Under his current scrutiny she felt more self-conscious than she had when his gaze had first homed in on her chin.

"Apology accepted," she mumbled.

Then, tray in hand, Brigit hurried from the room.

She took his dinner outside, bypassing the lounge chairs and setting the tray on the wrought-iron bistro table tucked into the corner of the deck. By the time she returned inside, he had reached the French doors. She held one open for him. Their bodies brushed innocently as he stepped outside. He stopped and held her gaze. The fingers of his free hand grazed her cheek. She remembered that light touch. Helpless to do otherwise, she pressed her cheek against his outstretched palm.

"I want…I would like…" He pinched his eyes closed and exhaled slowly. Then, "Will you stay? With me? Please."

"I just assumed you would want to be alone."

He took a seat on one of the heavy wrought iron chairs she'd pulled out for him. Rueful laughter followed.

"I don't know what I want anymore. Well, except that I'd like you to keep me company. If you have the time. Please."

Her breath hitched as he stared up at her. This was not the entitled heir who had arrived at the resort mere weeks earlier. Nor was it the bitter man who'd neglected his therapy sessions despite desperately wanting to get better. And it certainly wasn't the angry and frustrated man who'd vented his ire just the night before. The man before her was contrite. Open in a way she'd never seen him before.

She swallowed. This was the kind of man who could make her believe in the happily ever after Scott's abusive ways had destroyed.

Her head told her to politely decline Kellen's invitation, but it was her battered heart she heeded as she slid on to the chair opposite his and adjusted the angle so that she could look out at the ocean. While he ate, she took in the scenery beyond the waving grass that topped the sand dune. She'd always loved this view and the privacy of the deck, which was bounded on either side by vine-covered trellises whose blooms scented the sea air.

It was a hot evening, the humidity almost oppressive. People who were not used to it often complained and preferred the air-conditioning of the dining hall to eating alfresco. In truth, she was surprised that Kellen had wanted to come outdoors, but after holing up in his room for a few days, maybe he'd felt the need for a change of scenery regardless of the heat that accompanied it.

"Hot night," he said, almost as if he could read her mind.

"Humid, too," she replied just to make conversation. What topic could be safer than the weather? So she went on. "I heard on the news tonight that temperatures are expected to hover in the nineties until the weekend."

"Beach will be crowded."

She made a humming noise that passed for agreement.

Kellen set his fork aside with a clatter. "You must think I'm the biggest jerk in the world."

Brigit blinked, caught off guard by his blunt statement. "Actually, I reserve that title for my ex. Besides, it's not my place to make judgments."

"Because I'm your boss."

She could have agreed and left it at that. Perhaps she should have. But it wasn't the truth and even though she couldn't figure out why, she felt that she owed him that much.

"I did things I wasn't proud of when I…when I was going through a rough patch in my life."

"Your divorce, you mean?"

It wasn't something she talked about often. Even with her sister and mother, Brigit had been stingy with the details. She'd found them too painful to recount, too humiliating to admit to. But she nodded.

"When it came right down to it, I had a choice to make. I could stay and accept my life as it had become, which was pretty bad, or I could leave. It sounds simple—" she sent him a wry smile "—unless you're the one taking the big leap and not at all sure where you're going to land." She reached across the table and laid her hand over his. She meant it to be friendly, but she also wanted to touch him. To connect. "Change is never easy, Kellen."

He grunted. "I admire you, Brigit."

"Me?" She blinked in surprise.

"Yes, you. And I respect you. I may sign your paycheck, but you're not afraid to speak your mind, even if it's to tell me that I'm being an ass."

"I don't remember using that exact word," she mumbled.

"The sentiment was the same." Humor lurked in his tone, but then he went on. "It may not seem like it, especially after the way I acted the other night, but I do value your opinion, and not just on matters that pertain to the resort. I guess what I'm trying to say is..." He looked away and she watched his Adam's apple bob. "I need you, Brigit."

A lump formed in her own throat. She'd never been needed before, not by a man. Especially not by a man she'd criticized, even if that criticism was warranted and intended to be constructive. She didn't know what to say.

"Speechless, I see," he said after a long silence.

"More like flattered."

He shifted in his chair, grimaced.

"What did the doctor say about pain?" Brigit asked.

"It's to be expected, but should lessen over time." Kellen picked up his knife and fork and cut off another bite of pork. "Sometimes I think I should have let them amputate my damned leg. At least I'd be in less pain," he muttered before popping the meat into his mouth.

"That's defeat talking."

Kellen bobbed his head. "But I'm not giving up."

"Good."

"You'll appreciate this. He offered to give me something in the interim."

"And you turned him down," she guessed.

"Actually, I asked him for a non-narcotic alternative. He prescribed a high-potency ibuprofen." His wry laughter floated away on the breeze. After a few minutes of silence, Kellen asked, "So, do you think this doctor could be wrong?"

"Wrong is a strong word," Brigit said slowly. The last

thing she wanted was to give Kellen false hope. But… "You might be able to improve the prognosis."

"If I put in more effort, you mean."

She nodded. "I'm not saying you'll ever be one hundred percent, Kellen. That's not going to happen and you need to accept that. But accepting isn't the same as admitting defeat. There's no reason to embrace your current condition."

She expected an argument, but he nodded.

He picked up his glass and took a sip. His grimace was comical. "I've been meaning to tell you, this stuff is awful."

"It's tea. Iced tea," she added unnecessarily, given the cubes that tinkled against the sides of the glass.

"But it's not sweet. This is the South, Brigit. We take our iced tea with lots of sugar down here."

She wondered if he was aware that as he spoke his tone took on a noticeable drawl.

"Yes, well, not all of the guests who stay at Faust Haven are from the South. In fact, a good number of them hail from points north, especially in the winter. We keep packets of sugar on the tables in the dining room so guests can sweeten their own drinks. I must have forgotten to put some on the tray for you. If you'd like, I can go get you some."

She was already rising when he said, "I'd rather have wine. How about if you bring a bottle of red?" When she hesitated, he added, "I'm not driving."

Nor, as he'd just explained, was he taking any medications that would restrict alcohol consumption.

"All right."

As she started for the door, he stopped her with a new request. "And bring two glasses." The corners of his mouth lifted. "One for you."

"Oh, no wine for me. I'm on the clock." She winked. "What would my boss say?"

"He'd say, you're no longer on the clock. I'm giving you the night off. Have Danny cover for you."

"He's nineteen and the bellboy!" she exclaimed. "Besides, he's already gone home for the night."

"Someone else then."

"Kellen—"

His gaze had been on the horizon, where the waves were capped briefly in white before they churned to shore. Now his eyes shifted to her.

"Have a drink with me, Brigit? Please."

She'd been attracted to the man who'd issued commands and barked orders. To the one who now asked politely and extended invitations, she was putty. That should have made her nervous. But she suspected the butterflies flitting about in her stomach had a far different origin. "One bottle of red and two glasses coming up."

CHAPTER EIGHT

BRIGIT RETURNED FIFTEEN minutes later.

Holding the neck of an opened bottle of merlot in one hand and the stems of a pair of wine goblets in the other. Her movements were deft, economical and sexy despite that.

A sigh whispered out before he could prevent it, and the smile he sent her was genuine. He'd meant what he'd said about needing her. But at that moment, it wasn't Brigit's frankness he was admiring.

"Louise is at the reception desk, in case you were wondering," she said.

Kellen mentally shifted gears. "Louise?" he asked, trying to picture the employee in question. He'd met most of the staff over the past few weeks, but only in passing. That would have to change, of course. He needed to know who was responsible for what.

Birgit was saying, "She works in housekeeping, but I've been training her to work the desk. She's young, but capable. And she knows where to find me if anything comes up that she can't handle on her own." Merlot poured, she set the bottle aside and slipped into her seat. "Thank you, by the way."

"For?"

"The wine. Although, now that I think about it, I

should have picked one of the pricier labels. We stock a couple vintages that I can't afford on my salary."

"Maybe you're due a raise then."

"Maybe I am." She sent him a sideways smile as she lifted her glass and tapped it against his.

After the quasi toast, they both took a sip.

"This is good," he said, turning the bottle so he could read the label. His brows shot up in surprise. "Medallion Winery?"

"It's a vineyard in Northern Michigan," she said.

"Yes, I've heard of it. I met the owner, Zack Holland, a couple of years ago when I accepted a friend's invitation to ski the slopes in Aspen for a couple weeks. He was on vacation with his new wife, Jane. No, Jaye. Very outspoken woman." He smiled. "You remind me of her."

"I'll take that as a compliment," Brigit said.

"Good, because I intended it as one." Kellen studied the contents of his glass. "They talked up their wine and some of the awards it had won, but I wasn't expecting..."

"They had an excellent year in 2007. In fact, this vintage earned a couple of prestigious awards, which is why Sherry asked me to order a few cases to serve at the inn. According to her, it pairs well with her stuffed pork tenderloin."

Kellen spared a glance at his forgotten meal and nodded thoughtfully before agreeing, "It does."

They both took another sip.

"Are you a connoisseur?" he asked.

"I wouldn't say that." She wrinkled her nose and laughed. He liked the sound. "I just do a little research, even if I also rely on the experts when ordering for the inn. You probably know more about wine than I do."

"Not really. I just know what I like." He realized his gaze was on the woman rather than his wine, so he held up his glass and studied the deep red liquid in the waning light. "Dry and medium-bodied. I've never been able to pick up the aromas of this and notes of that the experts talk about."

"Same here."

She chuckled again and settled back in her chair, almost as if she were becoming relaxed. Kellen knew he was. His shoulder muscles, which were always so tense, had started to loosen. And while his leg still ached, the throbbing had subsided, so much so that he was able to ignore it.

Which reminded him. "Don't tell Joe."

"About the wine?"

"He doesn't want me drinking during my recovery."

"But you aren't taking any medications that require abstinence," she replied. "A glass of wine shouldn't hurt."

"I know, but he has this very holistic approach to my rehabilitation, including diet and nutrition."

"His smoothies?"

"For starters."

"And you've followed his advice religiously," she replied drolly.

"He can be a tyrant."

"Joe?"

He nodded. "At first, he tried to ban all caffeine unless it came in the form of green tea. I can't live without my morning coffee."

"Yes, and I'm sure you were very diplomatic when you explained that to him."

Kellen had bellowed his protest in blistering fashion. Brigit's wry expression told him she'd guessed as much.

"I made him see reason."

She sipped her wine. "Green tea is very good for you. Antioxidants and such."

"Do you drink it?"

"I've tried it," she said slowly.

"Then you know that it tastes like steeped grass clippings."

"Having never tasted steeped grass clippings, I will defer to your judgment."

"Come on. Just admit that you don't like it," he coaxed.

Her eyes held as much amusement as challenge when she replied, "It's not my favorite beverage, but then I don't care for black tea either. Satisfied?"

Satisfied? At the moment, Kellen was far from it. But he grunted out an affirmation anyway, since the source of his dissatisfaction was difficult to determine. All he knew was that suddenly worries about his busted-up leg and concerns for his future—the two things that had dominated his life—had been replaced by other thoughts.

He and Brigit didn't speak for the next several minutes. The sound of the waves and the chatter and squawk of seabirds hunting for their evening meal occasionally broke the silence. As did snippets of conversation from beachcombers or guests on the inn's public decks.

"I love this place." He didn't realize he'd spoken the words aloud until she glanced over, her expression making it clear that she was waiting for him to go on. He usually didn't talk about his childhood, not even the good parts. But he did now. "I came here almost every summer when I was a boy."

"Sounds like heaven," she murmured. "I spent my summers at YMCA day camps until I was old enough to take care of myself. My mom worked."

"And your father?"

"Gone."

"I'm sorry. My father died when I was a kid, too. Cancer." His grandfather had tried to shield Kellen from as much of the disease's cruelty as possible, but the image of his father's gaunt frame and sunken eyes remained burned into Kellen's memory to this day. It was just another reason he considered the resort such a sanctuary. He had good memories here. Happy ones. The kind every kid, rich or poor, should have.

Brigit snapped him out of his reverie by saying, "My dad didn't die. Shortly after I was born, he simply opted out of fatherhood. He wasn't part of either my life or my older sister's."

There was no *simple* about it, regardless of her matter-of-fact tone. Kellen asked, "But he supported you, right?"

"Financially, you mean?" At his nod, she shook her head. "My mother said he wasn't the sort who could hold a job for long."

Kellen tried to digest that. Money had never been an issue in his household, or so he'd thought at the time. After his father's death, his mother had been faced with a lot of bills and not a lot left in her savings once she'd paid them. The experience had left her angry with her late husband and estranged from the son who reminded her so much of him.

For better or worse, he and Brigit each had been shaped by their upbringings. The nuggets of information he had mined from Brigit over the past few weeks offered an interesting glimpse into what had created her self-sufficient and direct personality. She didn't need men. The ones who had been in her life—father and husband—had disappointed her. Or worse? He wondered.

"Sorry," Kellen offered a second time.

She shook her head. "I'm not. It's hard to miss something you never had. Besides, my mom more than made up for his absence. She is smart, capable, determined and very independent."

And the apple hadn't fallen far from the tree, he thought. "Then I'd say you're lucky."

"What's your mom like?"

The question was innocuous and in keeping with the conversation. Still, it caught him off guard. He offered the first description that came to mind. "Hard."

"Hard?"

"Hard to please. Hard to live with. Hard to love. We don't have much of a relationship. Haven't since my dad died when I was eleven. I'm just like him, apparently." Even as he said it, Kellen held on to his grandfather's explanation that it wasn't actual resentment she felt toward Kellen, but a manifestation of her grief since Kellen looked so much like his late father, and shared so many of his personality traits.

"I'm sorry. That must have hurt. It must still hurt."

He swallowed, amazed at how perceptive Brigit was. Indeed, even as a thirty-six-year-old man, he was still hurt by his mother's distance, even if he could admit he'd helped push her away by doing everything in his power to confirm her low opinion of him.

Brigit was saying, "Surely since your accident, she's been supportive of you."

Pain, deep and unexpected, lanced his chest. "She's been…busy."

So busy doing whatever it was she did that she hadn't been able to fly to Switzerland to be by his side at the hospital after his accident. Or after any of his many operations. Or at the chalet as he'd begun the grueling process of rehabilitation. She'd been so busy that, even after he made the long, transatlantic flight, she hadn't been able to come to the airport to welcome him home.

He sipped his wine, which seemed to sour in his mouth.

"I'm sorry."

He glanced over at Brigit. “For?”

“It took me a long time to figure out that my father’s shortcomings have nothing to do with me.”

“I’ve given her reasons—”

“No,” Brigit said, that one syllable brooking no argument. “Regardless of what you’ve done and how you’ve acted, your mother should have been there for you, Kellen.”

They sat in silence as the sun began to set. Words weren’t necessary. He liked that about her. Most of the women he knew would have become agitated, feeling ignored. Brigit merely sipped her wine, seeming to appreciate the view and the calming sound of the ocean as much as he did.

The inn’s long shadow crept steadily over the beach as the sun began its descent. Kellen had drunk two glasses of wine. The alcohol hadn’t calmed him as much as Brigit’s company had. Just under half a bottle remained, but he knew it was pointless to ask her to stay for another round. The day was ending.

So, before she could say it, he announced, “It’s time to call it a night.”

“I was thinking the same thing,” she replied, rising to her feet. She touched his shoulder. “But this…this was nice.”

This as in the wine? Or was she referring to the evening off? Or spending time with him? He wanted to pin her down, but stopped himself from asking what she meant.

She had loaded up the tray and disappeared inside even before he managed to stand. By the time he reached the door, however, she was back. His muscles were stiff from sitting. His recent inactivity certainly hadn’t helped. As a result, his leg was uncooperative, disobeying his brain’s commands. He didn’t bother trying to camouflage his discomfort or ungainliness as he moved inside. It was what it was.

"Own it and move forward," he murmured. His new mantra.

He hadn't intended the words to be loud enough for her to hear. Her brows drew together.

"What did you say?"

"Giving myself a pep talk." Half his mouth rose in a smile. "Someone recently told me something similar."

"She sounds smart," Brigit said lightly, stepping close and putting one of her arms around his waist for support.

Her fingers grazed his side before settling on his hip. He swore their heat radiated through the nylon fabric of his track pants. But what really grabbed his libido's attention was the way the side of her breast pressed against his ribs. Firm but surprisingly soft at the same time, much like the woman herself.

"She is," he murmured, dipping his head to whisper the words against her ear. "And she knows it."

Brigit was a relatively small woman, but her large-and-in-charge personality made it impossible to consider her delicate. It was her power that appealed to him even more than the curve of her cheekbones or her dark-lashed blue eyes.

The air in the apartment was cool and humidity-free. But Kellen felt hot. He burned with sudden awareness. Long-dormant needs were now fully revived. Did she feel it, too? He recalled the kiss they'd shared on the deck just a week earlier. He'd forced it from his mind, told himself that he'd imagined the passion that had flared between them. What would a woman want with someone like him? *Fool*, he berated himself. But there was no escaping the truth. It burned inside him now—stronger, bolder, hotter. His breath hitched.

"Are you okay?" she asked.

He'd been hoping to work his way in that direction, but with her staring up at him, he was lost.

"No. I'm not okay."

"Maybe the wine wasn't such a good idea. Let's get you off your feet."

"Yes, let's," he murmured, although he doubted they had in mind the same idea for how to accomplish that.

His ardor cooled substantially when he spotted Joe sitting on the couch in the living room. The other man was watching television, a bottle of water in one hand and a bowl of popcorn in his lap. He glanced up as Kellen and Brigit staggered into view.

"Everything okay?" He set the bowl aside and wiped his hands on his T-shirt as he rose to his feet.

"What are you doing here?" Kellen asked.

"Lou ate some oysters that didn't agree with him, so we decided to call it a night."

"That's too bad," Brigit said. "For both of you."

Joe shrugged. "I didn't mind. The band sucked. Let me give you a hand." He started forward, but Brigit waved him off.

"I've got him. He's just a little stiff."

Indeed he was, though not how she meant.

She whispered to Kellen, "We wouldn't want him smelling wine on your breath."

Kellen nearly chuckled at that, but managed to keep a straight face.

"How's the leg tonight, Mr. F? Is it spasming again?"

"A little." He grunted before admitting, "It's my own damned fault."

Joe's brows shot up in surprise at his admission. Kellen glanced at Brigit, expecting to find a similar expression on her face. But she looked—what?—satisfied, pleased.

Taking total responsibility, he added, "I'm paying the price for all of my laziness. You've been doing your damnedest to help me, Joe. I haven't been a very good patient. That's going to change."

"Physical therapy at the usual time tomorrow?" Joe asked, his expression hopeful.

"No. First thing in the morning. Maybe we can add a second therapy session in the afternoon." Kellen swallowed, his gaze shifting to Brigit. "I'm not going to give up."

CHAPTER NINE

BRIGIT SLIPPED FROM bed even before her alarm went off the following morning. She hadn't slept well. Even though she'd dropped off not long after her head hit the pillow, she'd startled awake just after two and hadn't been able to fall back to sleep.

She wanted to blame the wine. But she knew it was the man. Kellen had her tied in knots.

It wasn't merely physical attraction causing her concern. That she could deal with, however inconvenient she might find it given their current living arrangement. Her ex had been Hollywood handsome with a former marine's hard body to match. It still galled her to admit that his good looks had blinded her to his controlling personality until after their wedding. What she had written off as overzealous courtesy while they were dating became rigid perimeters that had defined daily life. If she'd needed something from the store, Scott had insisted on going out for it. If a package needed to be mailed, he had been the one who took it to the post office. On and on it had gone, until her life had been reduced to what went on inside her home. And even there, she'd had no say. Everything from the paint colors to the style of curtains to the cleaning products used—Scott had decided them all.

My way or the highway.

Scott actually had told her that once, before their marriage, when they'd been settling a disagreement over their choice of reception venues. Foolishly, she'd thought he'd been kidding.

Kellen had a similar hard edge to him. He could be stubborn. But he also could admit when he was wrong.

Just when she'd been ready to write him off as shallow and self-pitying, he'd surprised her. The man wasn't as superficial as she'd assumed. In addition to being sexually attracted to him, Brigit had actually begun to like him.

She thought of the glimpses into his private life that he'd allowed her the previous evening. Apparently, even before the accident his world hadn't been perfect. God knew, it was easier to think of him as spoiled, pampered and self-indulgent, but after what he'd told her, it was clear the silver spoon he'd been born with had tarnished over time.

Like Brigit, he'd grown up without a father. Worse, at least to her way of thinking, he had known and loved his father, only to have illness snatch him away. Meanwhile, Kellen's mother hadn't been there for him.

Hard to please. Hard to live with. Hard to love.

Brigit found Kellen's blunt description of his relationship with his only surviving parent sad. If someone were to ask Brigit to describe her mom, the words on the tip of her tongue would be loving, devoted and dependable. Delia Wright always had made Brigit feel safe. Even as an adult, Brigit knew she could rely on her mother, which was why when she'd finally left Scott that was where she'd gone. Home to her mom, where she'd been welcomed with open arms and gently chastised for not coming sooner.

Kellen had come home to…a resort.

Outside her room, Brigit could hear someone moving around. She figured it would be Joe, getting ready to start his day. She wondered when Kellen would rise. He'd claimed he wanted to start his physical therapy first thing. His resoluteness the night before had seemed sincere, but would he?

She was still wearing her favorite UConn T-shirt and pair of plaid boxer shorts when a light tap sounded at the door. Joe probably needed some of his things from the dresser they were sharing.

"Just a sec," she called. While her outfit was hardly provocative, she wasn't wearing a bra and the shorts barely covered the tops of her thighs. She pulled on a robe and loosely belted it for modesty's sake.

It wasn't Joe who stood in the hallway, but Kellen. Her heart executed a funny tuck and roll at the sight of him. Some of his hair stuck up on his crown and his jaw was shadowed in stubble. If she had to guess, she'd say he'd just gotten out of bed. Her heart somersaulted a second time as she pictured him there, tucked amid the blankets wearing…

"Good morning." His voice was roughened by sleep, but his gaze was alert as it did a quick view of her body.

Brigit shivered even as her blood heated.

"Good morning. You're up early," she told him.

"I couldn't sleep."

Oh? What had kept him awake? She felt like an idiot for briefly hoping it had been thoughts of her.

"Eager to get to work with Joe?"

He eyed her for a moment. "Sure."

Kellen tucked his hands into the pockets of his track pants. They were black with a trio of white stripes down the sides of both legs. But what snagged her attention was his T-shirt. She was wearing its twin.

"Nice shirt."

He glanced down, then back at her. "Thanks."

At his confused expression, she pulled the lapels of her robe open to show him her tee. The view provided far more than mere clarity, however. Her taut nipples strained against the fabric beneath the university's logo.

"UConn never looked so good," he murmured.

The loosened belt rode low on her hips. Kellen hooked his finger over the spot where it tied. His fingertip gently scored her belly through the thin cotton of her shorts. A gentle tug was all it took to release the tie completely. The sash fell to the floor, taking common sense with it. When his gaze detoured to her bare legs, she felt her flesh once again prickle with desire.

Brigit hadn't been with a man since her divorce. For that matter, she'd been on only a couple dates in all that time, both set up by her well-meaning big sister. On the island, which was largely populated with tourists for much of the year, it was easy to dodge any sort of intimacy. Her job kept her busy for most of her waking hours, and any men she met were either guests at the resort, which put them off-limits, or guests at another resort, and as such in town for only a brief time.

When it came to Kellen, she was playing with fire, and the look in his eyes told her he was only too happy to provide the kindling. Well, one of them needed to be smart and act like an adult rather than a sex-crazed teen. Brigit figured that role fell to her.

She had the most to lose, after all. He owned the resort. He was her boss. He wasn't going to stay on the island any longer than it took him to recover. Meanwhile, this was her career, her livelihood, her home. It was her heart, a soft voice whispered.

She swallowed and pushed that thought aside. Her heart was in no danger, she told herself. Besides, Kellen needed her. He'd told her so the previous night. And what he needed—what they *both* needed—was for her to remain level-headed. So she tugged the robe's lapels together and folded her arms over her breasts.

"Is there something you needed from me?"

She intended the question to be polite rather than provocative, but given the interest that flared in his eyes, she had a pretty good idea in which direction his mind had veered. God help them, hers wanted to follow.

Be professional, she reminded herself. *Be sensible.*

Apparently he had conducted a similar internal pep talk, because he glanced away and replied, "I just wanted to let you know that I'm going to skip morning coffee on the deck."

Disappointment settled like a barbell in her stomach. It was silly to look forward to that hour or so while they sat together watching the sun rise. Half the time, they didn't even speak.

Half "Oh?"

"I decided to get the torture over first thing." A rueful grin accompanied the words.

"Ah. And here I thought maybe you had decided to heed his advice and take up green tea," she quipped, keeping their banter light and friendly.

"Let's not get carried away."

Joe picked that moment to amble down the hall. He was dressed in the same clothes he'd been wearing the day before, although his hair was damp from a shower. He held a half-eaten apple in one hand.

"I see I don't need to wake up either of you." He studied Kellen then. "Ready to be pushed, Mr. F?"

Kellen sobered, his expression just this side of fierce when he replied, "Bring it on."

"That's the attitude I was hoping for. I thought we'd start with some basic stretching exercises before moving on to the strengthening ones." Joe's gaze slid to Brigit then. "We can start in the living room with some tension bands and the medicine ball, but eventually we'll require some of the equipment in here."

"Of course. Not a problem. Give me twenty minutes to shower, dress and grab my things, and the room is all yours." She sent Kellen what she hoped was an encouraging smile. "Good luck."

Later that day, Kellen sat alone at a table in the dining room. He was tired, sore, sleepy even, given his restless night. But he'd resisted the urge to lie down. Not only because he'd promised to turn over a new leaf, but because Brigit had claimed she would join him for lunch.

Unfortunately, she had yet to come and sit down. He'd eaten half of his Joe-approved Waldorf salad when he heard a familiar voice call his name.

"Kellen Faust, as I live and breathe."

He turned to find Jennifer Cherville crossing to his table. At one time the two of them had been an item. They'd dated throughout college. Not surprisingly, after graduation, Jennifer had expected an engagement ring. Kellen, meanwhile, had purchased a new pair of skis and booked a flight to Switzerland. Where she'd wanted to settle down, preferably in Charleston, and start producing little Kellens, he'd wanted to defy death on the slopes. How differently his life might be now if she'd gotten her way. Even so, he had no regrets.

She wasn't the sort of woman he wanted to wake up to every morning. A fiercely determined black-haired beauty came to mind.

When Jennifer reached his table, he tried to rise.

"No, no. You poor thing. Don't get up." She pressed her hand to his shoulder and then leaned down to air-kiss his cheeks. "I heard you were back. Courtney—you remember Courtney Dobson?" Before he could even nod, Jennifer was saying, "She and I stopped at the club the other night for dinner and ran into your mother and father."

"Stepfather," he corrected thinly.

"Anyway, she mentioned you were home." Jennifer tipped her head sideways and her tone turned syrupy with sympathy. "How are you?"

"I'm fine."

"Aww, Kellen. So brave."

She offered a patronizing smile while he gritted his teeth. Just a week earlier, he would have asked if she had come to the island to gawk at the invalid. He would have treated her rudely and been insufferable. Unlike Brigit, who had called him on the carpet for his bad behavior, Jennifer would have reacted with teary eyes and run away.

"Did you get the flowers I sent?" she asked.

"Flowers?"

"Stargazer lilies," she added, as if that would mean something to him. He didn't know a daisy from a tulip. "I had them delivered to the hospital after your accident."

He recalled the assortment of bouquets, plants and get-well cards that had lined the surfaces in his room, although who had sent what escaped him now. But he nodded anyway.

"Thank you." His manners had been rusty, but the

more he used them, the easier it became. So, he added, "That was kind of you."

"It was the least I could do. I was very worried about you. I'm still very worried about you, Kellen. If there's anything I can do to help. *Anything.* Just ask."

What to say to that? He settled on repeating, "That's kind of you."

She leaned closer and said, "You know, I've never quite gotten over you."

"Jen—"

"All these years, and I still find myself hoping…"

He'd never made any promises, but after four years of dating, it was understandable that she'd made assumptions. He regretted that.

And he regretted that, just as Jen made her provocative admission, Brigit showed up at their table. Her gaze slid from Kellen to Jennifer and back, one brow arched. But he'd be damned if he could tell what she was thinking.

"Should I bring over another chair?" she asked politely.

Jennifer glanced at her, apparently noted the logo on the shirt and, before Kellen could say anything, replied, "There's no need for that. The table already has two chairs."

"Yes, but the free one is taken."

"By whom?" Jennifer asked, her tone affronted. She straightened. In heels, she was as tall as Kellen, and so she towered over Brigit, making it all the easier to look down her surgically improved nose. Kellen knew her parents had given her rhinoplasty for her twenty-first birthday.

"Me." Brigit dropped into it, making a show of folding the cloth napkin over her lap.

Jennifer transferred her outraged glare from Brigit to Kellen. Not sure what else to do, he made introductions.

"Brigit Wright, this is Jennifer Cherville. Jen, Brigit."

"Brigit, hmm. I see that you work here." Jennifer pointed to the logo on Brigit's shirt.

"That's right. I've managed Faust Haven for the past five years."

"That's nice." Jen's tone was condescending. "Kellen and I go back more than a decade. We were college sweethearts."

"That's nice," Brigit parroted, using the same mocking tone.

Kellen did his best to keep a straight face. Meanwhile, Jen's eyes narrowed.

"Do you mind? Kellen and I were having a private conversation."

"Shall I leave you alone?" Brigit asked him.

"No. We had a lunch date." He shifted his gaze to Jennifer. "Look, Jen. I appreciate your concern, but there's no need for it. I may not be fine, but I am getting better."

"Yes, about that. Your mother told me you were back in Charleston to see another specialist. She also mentioned all of the other medical opinions you've already received."

"Then I'm sure you know my dancing days are over," he replied lightly, surprised by the absence of bitterness. As Brigit had noted when making her point mere days earlier, he wasn't likely to take up the tango or cha-cha or any number of ballroom staples. Surprisingly, he was okay with that. More of the gratitude he should have been feeling all along for simply being alive made an appearance.

Jennifer, however, wailed, "Oh, Kellen! Don't say such things. Don't even think them!"

"Shall I leave you alone?" Brigit asked again. Her dry tone told him exactly what she thought of the other woman's theatrics.

"There's no need. Jen won't be staying." He transferred his gaze back to the statuesque blonde. "I appreciate your concern, but it's not necessary. Really."

She pursed her lips and nodded. He could tell she didn't quite believe him. "If you change your mind, Daddy knows an orthopedic surgeon at Johns Hopkins. Dr. Taft is relatively young, but Daddy says he's excellent at what he does. A true visionary when it comes to trying new treatment protocols. A lot of professional athletes seek him out after they suffer what are considered career-ending injuries. He can perform miracles."

For a second time, she leaned over to kiss his cheek. This time, however, her lips made contact. After shooting a pointed look at Brigit, she left.

"So, are you going to call him?"

"Who?" Kellen asked before taking a sip of his ice water.

"The miracle worker your girlfriend mentioned."

He nearly spat out the water.

"First, Jen is not my girlfriend. We dated. Past tense. It was a long time ago."

Brigit shrugged. "And second?"

"Second, no, I'm not going to call him. No more doctors, no more opinions."

"Oh?"

"The diagnosis would be the same. My prognosis, however, well, that's up to me."

"Yes, it is."

Brigit smiled. She looked satisfied, smug. Something about her was different. He studied her closely trying to figure out exactly what it was. Her attire was the same, a uniform top that wasn't intended to draw attention to her figure. Her hair was the same, black curls pulled back in their usual ponytail, which swung like a pendulum between her shoulder blades whenever she walked. Her makeup was minimal, just the barest hint of mascara on her long lashes and no kind of foundation, or whatever it was called, to cover up her freckles.

Some people might call her looks average. Pretty, but certainly not stunning. Kellen might have been one of them if he hadn't glimpsed the determination and steel beneath her relatively nondescript facade. To him, Brigit was beautiful, and growing more so with each new thing he learned about her.

"Why are you looking at me that way?"

"No reason," he lied, even as the truth buzzed around inside him like an out-of-control bee.

For the first time in his life, he was in danger of falling in love.

CHAPTER TEN

BRIGIT FOUND THE cane while she was down in the storage area rummaging around for a vase to hold more seashells. It was black with a curved and ornately carved handle inlaid with mother-of-pearl.

She brought the handle closer to study the figure carved into it. Was that a seahorse? The tail seemed wrong. Wider and scaly, shaped more like a snake's with a fish's fin at the end. Regardless, she knew who it had belonged to: Kellen's grandfather.

As such, she knew he would welcome its return, the timing of which was perfect since other than the piece of driftwood, he still didn't have a replacement for the one that had broken.

She waited until dinnertime to give it to him. It wasn't exactly a gift, since technically it already belonged to him. But she wrapped it up anyway—as best as one could wrap a cane—and was excited to see his reaction when he opened it.

Instead of eating in the dining room, she suggested they dine on the sprawling deck just outside it. Diners were sparse outdoors this evening. Not only was it hot, but the sky had turned gray. A storm was forecast—thunder, lightning and the works—for later in the evening.

“Are you sure you want to eat out here?” Kellen asked a second time after a gust of wind whipped the napkin right off her lap.

“If the breeze picks up any more we can move inside, but I prefer it out here.” The draft rustled his hair and she was tempted to reach across the table and smooth it down. Instead, she turned her attention to the ocean, where frothy waves churned to shore. “Mother Nature’s going to be putting on quite the show later.”

“That’s one way to put it,” he replied. “You sound like you’re looking forward to it.”

“I like storms,” she admitted. “Especially when I’m indoors, safe and dry. I always have, except when—”

“Except when?” he prompted.

“For a brief time in my twenties,” she hedged. While married to Scott, a sense of security had eluded her no matter what the weather.

“Why then?” he asked. “What about that time made you dislike storms?”

She shook her head.

“You would have been married then.” His brows rose. “Right?”

“What about you? How do you feel about storms?” she diverted.

To her surprise, he snapped his fingers and shook his head. “I thought I had you.”

“What do you mean?”

“I thought you’d open up a little, maybe even tell me some of your deep, dark secrets.”

“I have no secrets to tell,” she lied. “Deep, dark or otherwise.”

He made a humming sound. “If you did, would you share them with me?”

The question had her swallowing. Something was

happening between them, growing stronger just like the wind. A storm was brewing in more ways than one. It left her with that same feeling of anticipation rather than fear.

"I'd have to be able to trust you," she said slowly.

"And you don't now?"

"I'm starting to."

It was an honest answer, but she thought he might object to it. He was a man accustomed to having his wants and needs met instantly. Or at least he had been. Once again, he proved to be changing, improving more than physically.

"I'll work harder then."

He shifted in his seat and the driftwood cane slid along the table's edge before falling to the deck.

"That reminds me," she told him as she bent to retrieve it. "I have something for you."

"Like a gift."

"Like a surprise."

"Even better," he replied on a grin.

Their hands touched as she handed back the walking stick. A simple brush of skin that had the same effect as a lighted match dropped on kindling. His gaze lingered on her mouth. She forced herself to break contact and reach for her cellphone.

"I just need to make a quick call."

"Now? After you got me all worked up?" He grinned. "Over a surprise, I mean."

"The call relates to the surprise."

She tapped Danny's number into her cell. The young bellman answered immediately since he'd been expecting her call.

"Ready." That was all Brigit said before hanging up.

"Very cryptic," Kellen murmured. "You have me intrigued."

He changed his tune as soon as Danny came onto the deck carrying the wrapped cane.

"Gee. I wonder what it could be," he said dryly as he took the item from the bellboy, who returned inside.

"Looks can be deceiving."

"Isn't that the truth," he replied with feeling. "Should I open it now?"

"Unless you want to continue the suspense."

He ripped off the paper, which Brigit then balled up in a wad so it wouldn't be whisked off by the wind.

"A cane! Who knew?"

"Not just any cane. This one belonged to your grandfather."

Kellen's grin faltered and his gaze lowered to the item in his hands. He turned it over, his expression became reverent. "I remember this thing. Granddad didn't need a cane to walk, but a friend of his had traveled to Greece and brought it back for him."

"So that creature carved on the handle, it's part of Greek mythology?"

Kellen nodded. "A hippocampus. Where did you find it?"

"In the storage room. I was looking for a vase earlier today when I stumbled across it. There might be other personal effects of his in there if you want to have a look sometime."

"I will." He glanced over at her then. "Thank you."

Kellen rested his head against the side of the tub and let the pulsating water soothe his screaming muscles. After a full three weeks of relentless torture, he'd thought Joe might give him the weekend off, or at least ease up on the grueling routine. But he hadn't. If anything, Saturday's sessions had been more intense than ever. And the one this morning? Nothing short of merciless.

"Let me know if you can't handle it," Joe had said mildly before cranking up the resistance on the stationary bike.

Kellen swore the therapist had only made the offer to appeal to his boss's stubborn streak. Regardless, the trick had worked. Whatever Joe had dished out, Kellen had taken and then come back for seconds. He was paying for his pride now.

Still, he thought he was making headway. As sore as they were, the muscles in his thigh and calf didn't seem quite so rigid or as hard to control when he walked. He still leaned heavily on his cane, but his leg was starting to feel more stable. When he walked, he no longer worried that his mangled knee would give out or lock up and cause him to fall. All this after less than a month.

He berated himself for not applying himself with such vigor earlier. Who knew what progress he might have made by now if he had?

Or if he'd come to the island sooner, to Faust Haven. He gave the place some of the credit for the turnaround in his condition. And Brigit, of course. No, Brigit most of all. She'd offered him just the kick in the pants he'd needed to start living again rather than merely existing. He wasn't sure how to repay her. But repay her he would.

He recalled the severance papers he'd had his lawyer draw up. They ensured that Brigit would be well-compensated for not only her years of service, but her assistance with his recovery. But they weren't the repayment he had in mind. Indeed, Kellen hadn't thought of the papers in weeks. Nor did he want to think of them now, much less to think of Brigit leaving the resort. Leaving him. More so than any other time in his life, his life seemed in flux, his future far from determined.

Things Kellen had thought he'd wanted no longer mattered. Things he'd never thought would appeal to him suddenly did. He wasn't sure how, but Brigit figured into the chaos. Somehow, she figured into his future.

Twenty minutes later, he sat up in the tub and turned off the jets. The water had grown cool and Kellen wanted to get out. Unfortunately, that wasn't a feat he could manage without some assistance. He hollered for Joe three times before he finally heard footsteps outside the door.

"Get in here, already," he shouted. "I'm turning into a prune."

But it wasn't the physical therapist who answered. It was Brigit.

Her tone was tentative when she told him, "Um, Joe isn't here."

"What do you mean, Joe isn't here? Where did he go?"

"I'm not sure, but he's not in the apartment. I just stopped in to grab a yogurt when I heard you calling. I can go look for him, if you'd like?" she offered.

Who knew how long that would take? In the meantime, Kellen wanted out of the tub.

"That's all right. I can…I can do this," he said and reached to unplug the stopper. Water began to glug down the drain.

"Do what?" She sounded alarmed. "What are you going to do, Kellen?"

"I'm going to get out of the tub."

"I think you should wait for Joe." The door muffled her reply, but he still heard the concern in her tone.

Meanwhile, the water was down from the middle of his chest to his belly. Gooseflesh prickled his skin. He wasn't going to wait. "I'll be careful," he promised.

Standing up was going to be difficult, but the real challenge would be swinging his leg over the side of the tub. One way or another, he would have to balance momentarily on his bad leg. After weeks of strengthening exercises, would his knee hold?

Only one way to find out. Kellen grabbed the side of the tub, rolled onto one side and wedged his good knee beneath his body. The water that remained in the tub sloshed around his hips.

"Kellen!" Brigit shouted. "What are you doing?"

"Trying to stand."

"No! Absolutely not. Do you hear me? You need to sit back down and wait for Joe."

The same pride that had pushed him these past few weeks during his physical therapy sessions reasserted itself. Kellen wasn't going to sit down. He wasn't going to wait. He was going to get up and get out of the tub under his own steam.

With both arms over the side of the tub, he pushed to his knees. Barely six inches of water remained in the tub. He watched as a funnel formed over the drain, and debated the wisdom of waiting until the rest of it was gone.

"Kellen!"

"I'm fine. I can do this," he told her, hoping to convince them both.

Brigit wasn't buying it. "Cover up because I'm coming in," she called a moment before he heard the doorknob jiggle.

What the…? She wouldn't. But she would. And she did. He had just enough time to yank the towel off the bar before she barged in with her eyes pinched closed and one hand out in front of her, apparently to ensure she didn't run into anything.

"Are you decent?" she asked. "Can I open my eyes?"

He was resting on the heels of his feet with the towel thrown over his lap. The ends on either side floated in the remaining few inches of water. Even though he was sufficiently covered, he still felt exposed. He was stronger, heavier than he'd been when she'd seen him shirtless that first day at the resort, but he was a long way from his once-chiseled physique.

He answered honestly. "I'd rather you didn't see me like this, Brigit."

Her eyes opened, her gaze focused on his face. "See you like what, Kellen?" Even though she hadn't looked down, she said, "You're sufficiently covered."

"That's not what I mean. I used to be…a lot more physically fit than this."

"You look pretty good to me, especially for someone on the mend."

Her tone was matter-of-fact, but a blush crept up her cheeks.

The sight of her flushed face assuaged his ego.

"Yeah?"

She nodded.

"You look better than pretty good to me," he said softly. "You're beautiful, Brigit. Inside and out. So strong."

"Not many men appreciate strength in a woman," she said quietly.

"Well, I do."

The last of the water gurgled down the drain, breaking the spell.

"Can you grab my bathrobe from the hook?"

He pointed to where it hung and she handed it to him. While she turned her back to him, he pushed the soggy towel aside, shrugged into the robe and secured its belt.

"I'm ready," he told her as he got back up on his knees,

distributing more of his weight to the good one to lessen the pain.

She turned around and studied him for a moment, tapping one finger against her lips. Nothing about her pose was provocative, nor were her words when she told him, "I think I need to get in there with you."

That didn't stop his libido from firing to life. Even as he was trying to wrestle his desire into submission, she was toeing off her shoes and stepping into the tub.

"Let me just get behind you," she said, slipping around so that she was all but straddling his back.

He swallowed thickly, wishing their positions were reversed. Wishing she wasn't fully clothed, but naked like he was under the robe, her skin slick and slippery from soap and water.

He groaned.

"Are you in pain?" she asked.

Oh, he was in pain all right. But Kellen shook his head. "Let's get this over with."

"So impatient," she muttered.

"You have no idea," he muttered back.

She bent over and slipped her hands under his arms. She wasn't wearing her usual ponytail so some of her hair fell forward and tickled the side of his face. He inhaled deeply as her scent enveloped him.

"Let's get you into a standing position. On the count of three, okay?"

"Mm-hmm." He inhaled again.

"One…two…three."

Her grip was surprisingly strong. Added to his effort, he managed to push up so that one foot was planted firmly on the bottom of the tub. He braced both of his hands on his thigh. With her help, he was able to get his bad leg to cooperate. Finally, he was standing.

Brigit's hands were no longer under Kellen's arms. Now, they were resting on his waist just above the robe's sash. It would be so easy for her to unfasten it and reach beneath it, where she would find his body eager and more than ready. Despite his best efforts to stop it, a fantasy formed of her doing just that. He found himself almost wishing for the cool water that had been drained from the tub. Anything to shock him back to his senses.

"Okay, now I want you to sit on the edge of the tub. I'm going to get out. Then I'll help you swing your legs over the side." She stepped over the edge as he lowered onto it. "Ready?" she asked.

He offered a jerky nod and dutifully followed her instructions, hoping the robe would hide his arousal as she helped him lift his legs over the side. He needed to think of something else. One of his elementary school history teachers had made Kellen write out the preamble to the US Constitution forty times for talking in class. As such he had it committed to memory. He began to recite it in his head. Anything to get his mind off sex.

We the people of the United States, in order to form a more perfect union...

Once his feet were planted on the tile floor, she offered him her hands. Standing in front of him, her breasts were at mouth level. Kellen swallowed.

...establish justice, insure domestic tranquility, provide for the common defense...

"Okay, now stand."

He started to straighten, shifting most of his weight to his good leg. Brigit gripped his hands and smiled encouragement. How was it possible for this woman to tie him in knots and unravel his worries at the same time?

...promote the general welfare...

"You did it."

"With your help," he amended.

"We make a good team."

He nodded and leaned closer, lured by her scent. Distracted, it took him a moment to realize that she was backing up.

"Come on."

He took a step. Some water must have been on the floor, because his foot started to slip. The harder Kellen fought to maintain his balance, the more precarious his footing became on the slick tile. Brigit's eyes widened with concern and she wrapped her arms around him just as he started to go down.

The fall seemed to take place in slow motion. He didn't go down with a crash as much as he slumped and wound up cushioned on her body. He stared down into a pair of blue eyes that looked as surprised as he felt.

"Are you okay?" he asked, shifting his weight so that his hip and good leg were on the floor. His bad leg, however, remained draped across both of hers, and his hands were braced on either side of her shoulders.

Brigit's lips twitched with a smile. "I think that's supposed to be my line."

If she could joke at a time like this, then surely she couldn't be injured. He commanded his jackhammering heart to slow, but it picked up speed as he became aware not only of how lovely she looked with her dark hair fanned out over the crisp white tile, but of their rather intimate pose. His chest was mere inches from the tips of her breasts, and his erection was pressed against her hip, growing harder by the minute. Even if he were still so inclined, there was no way to hide his desire now.

The preamble. The damned preamble. What came next? Something about blessings.

...And secure the blessings of liberty to ourselves and our posterity...

Brigit was no longer smiling. Her expression had switched to solemn, and the crystal-blue eyes that were regarding him had turned almost opaque. Was she feeling it, too? All of that pent-up need that was just begging to be satisfied?

He was fighting a losing battle, and he knew it.

...do ordain and establish this Constitution for the United States of America.

He finished the words in a rush in his head. Aloud, he muttered, "To hell with it."

Watching her closely to gauge her mood, he lowered his head. He saw no protest, felt no resistance. When their lips met, her lids drifted closed and he felt her arms come up around his shoulders.

In the instant before he deepened the kiss, a sound—half sigh, half moan—vibrated from her throat. Oh, yeah. She was every bit as turned on as he was.

Unfortunately, it was becoming clear he couldn't continue to brace himself above her for much longer. As it was, his arms were beginning to shake from the strain. Any minute now, they were going to give out on him. Even though he was still fifteen pounds shy of his usual weight, Kellen still worried that if he lowered his torso to hers he would be too heavy, especially since the tile floor beneath her offered none of the give a mattress would.

He was just getting ready to suggest they take their business elsewhere when he heard the shuffling of feet. They broke off the kiss and both glanced toward the door. Joe stood at the threshold with his hands on his hips, doing his best to tuck away a grin.

"I see you didn't need my help getting out of the tub after all, Mr. F."

CHAPTER ELEVEN

"GOING FOR YOUR WALK?" Kellen asked the following evening as Brigit laced up her shoes.

She had changed into shorts and he took a moment to admire her toned legs.

She glanced over. "That's right. I won't be gone long. I'll challenge you and Joe to a game of gin rummy when I get back."

It wasn't exactly what he wanted to hear. Since their encounter in the bathroom the day before, Kellen hadn't had a moment alone with her. Whether on the deck in the morning or sitting in the living room just now, Joe was always with them. Three had definitely become a crowd.

"Mind if I go with you?"

Brigit blinked in surprise. "For a walk?"

"That's right."

"On the beach," she said slowly.

"That's where you usually walk, isn't it?"

She looked at Joe, who was in the kitchen making God only knew what with kale.

In exasperation, Kellen asked, "What? Do I need his permission?"

"No, I just… The sand is hard to walk on."

"I'm up for the challenge. Unless you'd rather go by yourself," he said.

"No. I don't mind the company." She smiled, glanced away, her expression oddly shy. "I just wanted to be sure Joe thought it was a good idea."

The physical therapist grinned. "It'll be more work walking through sand than on a boardwalk. You had a pretty intense workout tonight, Mr. F. Sure you're feeling up to it?"

The only thing Kellen was certain of was that he wanted some time alone with Brigit. But he smiled and nodded. "I'm sure."

His cane wasn't much support since it kept sinking into the ground. But Brigit walked close by his side as they made their way to the beach. The going was slow and difficult. They used a well-worn path between the dunes that was free of vegetation. Once they were on the beach proper, she pointed to the spot just shy of where the surf churned at the shore.

"It will be easier to walk down there. The sand is flat and hard. Of course, your feet might get a little wet from time to time."

"I'll chance it."

Once they reached the compacted, damp sand, walking was indeed much easier. Brigit danced out of range to avoid rogue waves that lapped ashore in their path. Kellen, however, had neither the agility nor the coordination to do so, which meant his feet, shoes and all, were soon drenched. He didn't care. Other than for his doctor appointment, this was the first time he'd been outside the resort since his arrival. He didn't count sitting on the deck, where he'd been a spectator more than a participant.

"You're doing well," she commented.

"Thanks. I'm trying not to embarrass myself in front of you after yesterday's bathtub fiasco."

She pushed dark hair away from her face. Her smile

was secretive, borderline sly, when she told him, "I don't know, I thought that turned out okay, all things considered."

"It ended before it began."

"That's not quite how I remember it."

"Yeah?" He recalled their kiss, the way their bodies had fitted together on the floor. She had a point. "Well, Joe's timing still sucks."

"I have to agree with you on that." She chuckled.

"In addition to being my physical therapist, he's starting to seem like a chaperone."

"Do I need one?"

For what seemed like the millionth time, Kellen found himself wondering where things would have led had he and Brigit not been interrupted. He knew where he'd *wanted* things to go.

"You might." He snagged her hand and stopped walking, forcing her to as well. "This is where, as your boss, I should apologize for my…forward behavior."

"Forward, hmm? Seemed horizontal to me."

Her lips quirked and he was tempted to kiss away the humor he spied there. But he had something to say, something important.

"I know the kind of reputation I have."

She was serious now as well. "I know it, too. I read the stories, Kellen. Long before you arrived on the island. In fact, before I ever took the job here, I did some internet searches. I was curious about the man I was going to work for."

"And?" he prompted.

"I'd like to say that I withheld judgment and gave you the benefit of the doubt. After all, the tabloids are notorious for making mountains out of molehills or out of no hills, for that matter." She scrunched up her nose. "But I did make some assumptions."

"Where there's smoke there's fire?" he asked, his tone wry.

She nodded.

A five-alarm blaze in his case, Kellen thought. He'd lived carelessly, living up to—or was that down to?—his mother's low opinion of him.

"Let me guess," he began. "You thought I was a slacker, living off my trust fund instead of earning a living. That I partied seven days a week, surrounded by people as aimless, unambitious and self-involved as I was."

As he spoke, a wave splashed over their feet. Brigit didn't try to avoid it this time. Even as the water frothed around their ankles before receding, she seemed not to notice. He had her complete attention. The hems of his track pants were soaked and clinging to his ankles. Some of the sand under his feet slipped away. But that wasn't why he felt off balance as he watched Brigit closely and tried to gauge her reaction. What she thought of him… it mattered. More than it had ever mattered with anyone else before.

"Was I wrong?" she asked slowly.

"No. Not in the least." It was a hard thing to admit, especially to this woman, for whom he was starting to develop such serious feelings. Yet the admission was cathartic at the same time. "I'm not proud of it, but I was all those things and more."

"Was." She nodded and squeezed his hand. "I like the sound of that."

"Do you?"

"Yes."

"I like the sound of it, too. I have changed, Brigit. I want to be sure you know that. It's important to me."

She studied him, wide blue eyes unblinking. "Why? Why is that so important?"

His emotions were churning as forcefully as the surf. "It just is. Your opinion matters to me. I've never met anyone quite like you."

"I'm…flattered."

His heart sank. It wasn't exactly what he'd hoped to hear.

He lowered his head, his tone beseeching as he pressed, "Is that all you are? I could have sworn you felt…something more the other day."

"You're my boss, Kellen. I work for you."

"What if you didn't?" He wasn't thinking about the severance package, although he needed to tell her about it at some point. But now wasn't the time. Besides, he rationalized, maybe there would continue to be a position for her at Faust Haven. So much was in flux, not the least of which were his emotions. But the resort's management wasn't the point of this conversation anyway. So he changed tactics. "Tell me you're not attracted to me."

She issued a strangled laugh. "You know that I am."

"But?"

"I'm not in the market for a relationship."

Kellen wasn't sure he was either. Other than with Jennifer, he'd never maintained a serious, long-term bond with a woman. He suspected her reasons were not quite as shallow as his. "Your ex-husband really did a number on you."

"He did." The words came out so softly that even though he was bending close, Kellen was barely able to hear them.

"Want to talk about it?" he asked. Brigit's eyes widened. She wasn't able to camouflage her astonishment. He chuckled drily. "I'm as surprised as you are, but over the past few weeks, I think I've become a better listener."

And wasn't that the truth, he marveled. The evolution of Kellen Faust continued, and the woman standing next to him had played a huge role in his personal growth.

"It's not something I like to remember, much less talk about."

"I get it. No problem." Disappointed, he nodded anyway. The few snippets of information she'd told Kellen about her ex, the more curious he became. Still, he knew better than to press.

They started to walk again. Their fingers were still loosely knit together. She broke the contact to bend down and pick up a shell. Realizing it was broken, she tossed it back into the ocean. Then she reached for Kellen's hand again.

"Scott was a marine. And a good friend of my sister's husband's. That's how we met. Scott was the best man at Mitch and Robbie's wedding, and I was the maid of honor. We had a whirlwind courtship and, six months later…" She held up one hand. "We got married. My mom thought it was too soon. I was just finishing up college. She wanted me to experience a little more of life before I settled down. I think she worried I was looking for a father figure, since my dad had never been in the picture."

Kellen could see her mother's point. But he held his tongue and waited for Brigit to continue.

"While we were dating he was the perfect gentleman. He opened doors for me. If I was cold, he gave me his coat. When we went out to eat at a restaurant, he insisted on ordering my meals. When we went to the movies, he picked the feature. Now I see those last couple things as red flags, but back then?" Her shoulders lifted. "I thought of them as old-fashioned chivalry. I thought I was marrying the man of my dreams," she said quietly. "Boy, was I wrong."

"What happened?"

"You know, I've asked myself that same thing a million times." Brigit frowned. "I mean, how come I didn't see it coming? All I know is that the solicitous guy I dated and the controlling man I married were like Dr. Jekyll and Mr. Hyde."

Kellen gripped the walking stick with almost painful force. "Did he…did he hurt you?"

"Physically? No, not really. I mean, he grabbed me by the shoulders a few times and gave me a shake, but he never punched me or anything like that. But emotionally…"

It took her a moment to go on. In that time Kellen's blood ran cold.

"Everything in our house had to be just so. Canned goods had to be lined up, but not touching, with labels facing out. Towels were folded a specific way and then placed in the linen closet so that you could see rolled edge rather than the individual layers. Anything that was placed in the dishwasher had to be thoroughly rinsed first. The smallest smudge of food and I was in for a lecture. I know what you're thinking."

"I doubt it."

"A lecture. What's the big deal? But after a while his words were like drips of water on stone. They wore away at me. I began to doubt myself."

She picked up another shell. Discarded it as well. Hand in hand they continued to walk. And she went on with what he knew had to be a painful recitation of her past.

"The obsessive behavior was annoying and a little freaky, but then he started to get paranoid. He took away my cell phone, and I had to ask permission to use the landline. It was for my own good, he told me. He said

I was too naive. I failed to see other people's true motives." Her laughter was harsh. "He had a point. I mean, I didn't see him for what he was until we were legally bound together."

Kellen was hardly an expert on matrimony, but what Brigit was describing was a prison sentence, not a marriage. Her husband had been her jailer. Kellen recalled what she'd said earlier about her ex not wanting her to work. No wonder. It was easier to control someone who had no money of her own, no outside contacts. He squeezed her fingers. "That wasn't your fault."

"I know. Now."

She didn't hesitate with her response, which told Kellen that in the five years since her divorce, she had meticulously sorted through her baggage and lightened the load considerably. He admired her for that.

"But at the time you weren't so sure."

"No. And so, yeah, I did blame myself. All those drips of water, you know. When Scott got mad or upset, it was always because of something I'd done or had failed to do."

"Which made his bad mood your problem." The assessment hit a littlc too close to home for Kellen, since he'd lashed out at everyone around him after his accident. Still, he wanted to believe his behavior had never bordered on abusive.

"Don't," she said softly.

"What?"

"Don't compare yourself to him. You're not the least bit similar."

"I appreciate the reassurance, believe me, but I know I was a jerk to be around."

"Oh, totally," she agreed without compunction. "But you were still nothing like Scott. You never waged psychological warfare on me or the other people around you. That was his tactic, his specialty. He blamed me for his foul moods so often that I started to believe it myself." A groove had formed between her eyebrows. "It didn't hurt that Scott was a master at making me feel worthless and useless and, worst of all, helpless."

Kellen had never done that. Even at his most obnoxious, he'd never made the people around him feel inferior. As much as he regretted the way he'd been acting, at least he had that in his favor.

"What did your family say?"

"They didn't say anything because they didn't know."

"You didn't go to them?" He couldn't hide his surprise. From everything she'd told him about her mother and sister, it had seemed a safe assumption that she would turn to them in her time of need.

But Brigit was saying, "How could I tell my mom that she had been right about Scott, when she was telling me how happy she was that I hadn't listened to her?" She shook her head. "He was on his best behavior around her. He was on his best behavior around my sister and brother-in-law. I was the only one who saw the real Scott. And he had me half convinced I was imagining things."

"But you got out."

"It took me four years to do it, but yes. I got out. By then my brother-in-law had been killed and my sister really needed me. I stayed with Robbie and little Will until my divorce was final, then…then I came here."

She sent him a smile, but he was still puzzling over the time line. She seemed to have left out a lot of parts. In particular, he found it odd that she would leave her Pennsylvania hometown for a secluded island off the South Carolina coast. He told her as much.

Brigit nodded, but she didn't answer right away. Instead, stooped down to collect another shell, wiping away sand from its edges as she straightened. This one was dark gray with deep ridges fanning out from its base. Nothing about the shell would have prompted Kellen to give it a second look, much less pick it up, but apparently Brigit deemed it a keeper because she tucked it into the pocket of her shorts. They walked a little farther and she stopped for another shell, going through the same process before depositing it, too, in her pocket.

All the while, he waited, giving her time to fill in the blanks as she saw fit.

Finally, she did.

"I couldn't stay in my hometown."

"Too many bad memories," he guessed.

"Bad ones, yes, but good ones too, since that was where I grew up. But that wasn't why I left. Even after the divorce papers were signed and our marriage was officially over, Scott was still trying to control me.

"He started by begging me to come back. He told me I had misunderstood him. That if he was guilty of anything it was loving me too much. He wanted another chance to prove he had changed. I just wanted to move on. But everywhere I went, he would turn up. If I dropped off a dress at the dry cleaners, I'd walk out and find him in the parking lot. If I had a dentist appointment, he would be sitting in the waiting room. He started showing up at my mother's house unannounced, bringing her flowers and acting concerned for my well-being. She knew enough by that point that she could see through his act, but the rest of the town?" Brigit shook her head and sighed. "He'd used every angle he could think of to manipulate me and when none of them worked, he switched to manipulating public opinion."

"What do you mean?"

"Rumors started swirling around town that I had had an affair and that was why I'd left him and sought to end our marriage. He painted me as coldhearted and conniving. He even made me out to be anti-American."

"Anti-American?"

"Because he was a veteran. Trust me, the guy worked every angle he could think. He's still working them."

"Sounds as if you could write a book," Kellen said, trying to keep his reaction light even as he wanted to wrap his hands around the other man's throat and give it a good squeeze.

"Yeah. *I Was Married to a Sociopathic Stalker.* Not sure whether it would be shelved in the nonfiction section of the library or with the horror titles. It was a nightmare."

"But you survived. And from what I can tell, you're stronger than ever."

She tilted up her chin. "I am."

"That must tick him off but good."

"I'm sure it does." She smiled. Not at Kellen, but at some unseen point in the distance. She was proud of herself, as well she should be.

Something occurred to Kellen then. Icy fingers danced up his spine as he asked, "Does your ex know where to find you?"

"I'm not in hiding," she replied somewhat indignantly. "I had to leave my hometown, but I'll be damned if he'll turn me into some kind of recluse. Besides, he never resorted to physical abuse."

Kellen nodded, all the while thinking that it was only a short hop from controlling someone with words to controlling them using force.

"Have you considered a restraining order?" he asked.

"Considered it and did it." She sent him a droll look.

"I'm not an idiot. My mother and sister took out restraining orders against him as well."

"Good."

"They still run into him from time to time, but at least he's stopped showing up at their homes. And I gave his photograph to all the ferry operators. They let me know whenever he's on his way over."

Despite the heat, those icy fingers were back. "Wait. Did you say *when*? He's been here?"

"He doesn't come as often as he used to, but yes. When I first took the job, he would show up once or twice a month. Now it's maybe once a season."

"So much for that damned restraining order," Kellen murmured.

"Oh, Scott honors it. He can't come within five hundred feet of the inn. One inch beyond that? He spreads out a blanket on the beach and settles in for the day, binoculars trained on the resort." She shrugged, although Kellen saw through the casual gesture to the nerves below.

"I don't like it," he muttered.

"Neither do I, but since he's honoring the letter of the law, there's not much I can do about it."

Kellen disagreed. Sometimes a bully just needed to be bullied by someone else to finally get the picture. He might not be in any condition to pose a physical threat, but Lou cut an imposing figure. Maybe Kellen would ask his driver-slash-bodyguard to have a "chat" with Brigit's ex the next time the guy ventured onto Hadley Island.

Beside him, Brigit expelled a deep breath. "Anyway, that's my story. Are you sorry you asked?"

"No." And he wasn't. He used to avoid backstory where the women in his life were concerned, but he couldn't seem to learn enough about Brigit. "If I'm sorry about anything, it's that you had to go through all that."

They both had suffered devastating injuries, Kellen realized, albeit in different ways. Hers had been inflicted on her psyche. Since his were physical, they were more obvious, but that didn't make them more debilitating.

"Ready to turn back?" she asked.

Kellen was tired, but Brigit's sheer nerve had inspired him. Faced with adversity, she could have given up. She could have gone into hiding, living her life in seclusion to avoid being stalked. But she had done neither.

"Not quite yet," he told her. "Let's walk a little farther."

More than ever, he felt as if he had something to prove. To both of them.

CHAPTER TWELVE

BRIGIT SAT AT the desk in her cozy office. She'd set aside paperwork for something more soothing: a craft project involving the shells she'd been collecting. She added the first layer to the bottom of a cylindrical vase she'd picked up at a flea market after having no success in the store-room. All of the shells were in varying shades of gray and, as such, not particularly pretty. Which was why she planned to alternate with layers of pale blue glass pebbles. When she finished half an hour later, she studied the final product in satisfaction. Alone, the cheap vase, seashells and colored glass hadn't been much to look at, but put together as they were, they had been transformed into something attractive and interesting.

Thinking of transformations, Kellen certainly had undergone one since his arrival on Hadley Island more than two months earlier. It was well into August now, the heat outside almost intolerable even with the ocean's breeze. But he hadn't used that as an excuse to ease up on his rehabilitation efforts. Each evening he walked on the beach with Brigit. This despite his grueling daily workouts with Joe.

For the past several weeks, he'd pushed himself to the absolute limit, following his physical therapist's advice to the letter. His range of motion had improved vastly. His leg was stronger, more stable. Muscle tone had returned. Best of all, he claimed his pain level had moved to the tolerable range. He still needed a cane to get around, but he didn't complain.

Indeed, even more than his physical transformation was his emotional one. He seemed at peace with his situation even as he was still working hard to improve it. He appeared to have discovered a sense of purpose. It seemed like a lifetime ago that he'd last closeted himself in his room. In fact, he rarely stayed in the apartment for more than his workouts. Otherwise, he could be found out and about in the resort, greeting guests, fraternizing with his employees. He'd won over Sherry easily enough with regular compliments for her evening dinner specials.

And he'd won over Brigit, even though she'd meant what she'd told him about not being in the market for a relationship.

In the market or not, how could she keep from falling for a man who appreciated her strength? Who viewed it as attractive? Who saw it not as a flaw to be exorcised, but a trait to be emulated?

But what the future held for the two of them was unclear. Kellen was healing, getting stronger by the day. That was the outcome she'd often wished for when he'd first arrived, because she'd been eager to see him leave. Now? Of course she was happy he'd improved so much in so short a period of time. But part of her couldn't help wondering what would happen when he felt he had recuperated enough. He loved the island, seemed to feel as connected to the resort as she did. But would he stay? And if he did, what would their relationship be then?

She fussed with the top layer of shells.

"That's pretty. You have a good eye."

She glanced up to find Kellen standing in the doorway.

She hadn't heard his approach, another example of how much he had improved. His limp remained pronounced, but he no longer staggered and dragged his foot.

"Thanks."

"Where will you put this one?"

She made a humming sound. "I haven't decided yet. One of the guest rooms, most likely."

"Maybe I should start paying you a decorating fee."

A lopsided grin accompanied his words. His face was tanned from time spent outdoors and the corners of his mouth no longer turned down with pain. He was ridiculously handsome, even with his long hair. He hadn't had it cut since his arrival and the ends reached his collar. It gave him a dangerous vibe.

"I'll settle for dinner. Are you buying tonight?" She intended it as a joke. They often ate together in the inn's dining room.

"Actually, I am. I'd like to take you into Charleston for a meal."

"Charleston?"

"Unless you'd prefer someplace else."

"You want to take me out to dinner in Charleston," she repeated slowly.

"I do. But you can say no." He sobered. "This isn't business-related, Brigit. I'm asking you out. On a date."

A date.

Her heart took a flying leap off the high board before diving straight to her toes. This was a scary step. although not completely out of the blue. Something had been brewing between them since that first kiss. But it had been easier to marginalize those feelings within the context of their professional relationship. They were spending a lot of time together. In fact, they were living together, albeit innocently enough.

Now he was making it clear he wanted something else…something more? As a professional, she urged herself to decline. Dating the boss was never a good idea.

But she also was a woman. A woman who found Kellen attractive and interesting and enjoyed spending time with him.

"I'd love to."

Brigit had almost forgotten what it was like to get dressed up for a night out. It had been more than a year since she'd last clocked out at the resort for a Saturday night. Her sister and nephew had been visiting then, and, since it had been the Fourth of July, the three of them had driven over to the opposite side of the island to watch the fireworks sprout up over Charleston. She dabbed a little perfume in her cleavage, wondering what kind of fireworks she might be in for this night.

She'd gone with a dress and actual heels. Both were several years old. She could only hope they were still in style. It was that or her no-nonsense navy business suit and rounded-toe pumps. Her sister called as Brigit studied her reflection in the mirrored closet door of the guest room.

"I can't talk now," she told Robbie almost immediately, because once her sister got going it was hard to get a word in edgewise.

"It's a Saturday night, Brig. You really need to knock off and kick up your heels once in a while. Put your boss on. I'll make him see reason."

Brigit had been purposely stingy with the details of her and Kellen's relationship. In part because she hadn't been sure where it was heading. But also because she was afraid what her family would think. Scott had enjoyed a solid reputation in their community, and he'd still turned out to be a total jerk behind closed doors. Meanwhile, Kellen's picture was probably in the dictionary beside the word *womanizer.*

Still, she valued her sister's opinion. needed her advice. And so Brigit let out the truth in a rush of words: "I'm going on a date with Kellen tonight."

"What? Slow down and say that again."

Brigit took a deep breath and exhaled. "Kellen and I are heading over to Charleston for dinner in a little while. I'm getting ready right now."

"And it's a date?"

"Uh-huh." She glanced at her reflection, took in the sleeveless pale blue sheath and strappy sandals. "I'm wearing the dress I bought for Will's christening. I don't have anything else in my closet that's fancy enough. Do you think it still works?"

"It's a timeless piece. And the color is perfect for you. It brings out your eyes."

"Thanks."

Brigit examined the eyes under discussion. She'd added more liner than she usually went with. Same went for the mascara. Her eyes were her best feature.

"Are you…nervous?" her sister asked.

"A little. I mean, it's a date, and I haven't had one of those in a long time." Actually, it wasn't the date that had her nervous as much as what might come afterward. It had been even longer since she'd had sex. And lately, it was all she thought about.

"It will be fine. Relax and enjoy yourself. I guess I'm just a little surprised."

"Kellen and I have been spending a lot of time together, so it's not as if this came out of the blue."

"Yet you've barely breathed a word of it to me, even

when I've asked you about him," Robbie shot back. Her tone told Brigit she wasn't angry, but maybe a little hurt.

"I know. And I'm sorry. I just wanted to keep this to myself for a while longer. I'm not sure what my feelings are, or his, so I wasn't ready to examine them."

"And you're ready now?"

She fussed with her hair, which she had left down for the occasion. No, she definitely was not. Here goes nothing, she thought.

"Well, I'm not looking for a fairy tale." She'd gone that route once already and had lived to regret it. Her eyes were wide open this time. "I'm looking for a little… fun."

"That doesn't sound like you."

Brigit pictured her older sister frowning and had little doubt Robbie would be on the phone with their mother as soon as they hung up.

Secretly, Brigit had to agree. A casual relationship wasn't her style. But keeping things light and noncommittal seemed for the best. At least until she was certain of Kellen's intentions.

So she told Robbie, "Whatever happens between Kellen and me, I'm not going to romanticize it."

"What do you mean by that?"

"Well, I know it won't lead to wedding bells." His track record with women told her so. As much as he'd changed in the past several weeks, surely he wasn't willing to give up his flashy lifestyle to hang around Faust Haven forever, even if the resort had been bequeathed to him by the grandfather he'd adored. "I'm not even sure that's where I would want it to lead anyway."

"Aw, honey. Don't let your experience with Scott sour you on marriage."

Brigit shot back, "You're one to talk. It's not as if

you're out dating, and it's been how many years now since Mitch died?" She regretted the words as soon as they left her mouth. "I'm sorry, Robbie. That came out wrong. You know I just want you to be happy. As happy as you were with Mitch."

"I know. And I appreciate that. But our situations aren't the same. And not just because I'm a widow. I have Will to think about. Fair or not, I'm a package deal. A lot of the guys who might be interested in me aren't interested in a ready-made family."

"Then they're stupid."

"Totally," Robbie agreed without hesitation. "And as such they aren't good enough to be Will's stepdaddy. Now, back to you. You say you're not sure you're interested in a serious relationship. Okay, Brigit. I guess I can understand that after all you've gone through. But what is it you *do* want?"

Needs. Wants. She'd been thinking about both a lot lately. And she still hadn't reached any firm conclusions. She wanted to be happy. She wanted to be needed. Right now she was both. Could that be enough?

From the hallway, she heard the *tap-tap* of Kellen's cane. He was coming to collect her for their date. Excitement, not all of it sexual, bubbled to the surface, breaking her outward calm.

"What I'd love is a new dress," she told Robbie, even though she knew that wasn't what her sister wanted to hear.

"Oh, come on!" Robbie complained. She was gearing up for what surely would have been an inquisition when Brigit cut her off.

"I'm sorry, but I've got to go. We'll talk about this another time."

"Do you promise?"

"Yes."

Then Brigit opened the door and, despite all her talk about not romanticizing her relationship with Kellen, one look at his handsome face and elegant form and she knew she was lost.

Brigit stood framed in the doorway, a vision in pale blue silk that hugged her delicate curves. Although his gaze hadn't yet made it to her feet he knew she was wearing heels, because her mouth was now level with his chin. Kellen's heart executed the same dizzying flip it used to perform whenever he'd stood at the top of a ski slope gazing down the run he was preparing to tackle.

This was better. And, at the same time, a hell of a lot scarier. Things were changing between them. He was changing. And it wasn't just his recovery.

"You look amazing," he told her. What other women spent hours trying to perfect, she'd achieved in barely one. He knew this because the shower in the hall bathroom had been running when he'd passed it to go take his own.

"Thanks." She smiled and fussed with the ends of her hair, looking uncertain, a description he never thought he would ascribe to her. "You look pretty amazing, too."

He glanced at the dress pants, tie and button-down oxford. "I forgot what it was like to put on something other than a T-shirts and track pants. I'm lucky I remembered how to tie a tie."

The Windsor knot at his throat suddenly felt too tight, and that was before she laughed and tugged playfully at the strip of silk.

"I remember wondering where you'd wear all the clothes that Lou hung in my closet that first day."

"I'm not sure why I packed them. Habit, I guess. But

I'm glad I did now so I have something suitable to wear for our dinner."

"I wouldn't care if you were in track pants and we were going to split a pizza on the beach," she told him.

Yes, Brigit would be fine with that. He had no doubt. But more than with any other woman he'd known, Kellen wanted to impress her. He wanted to show her a good time. Dazzle her a little, even. If that made him shallow, so be it. But he thought a woman who'd been through what she had deserved a night to remember.

"I've got something better in mind than pizza. Do you like steak?"

She glanced over Kellen's shoulder. "Is Joe within earshot?"

He chuckled, realizing as he did so that he'd laughed more in the past few weeks than he had in the several months preceding them.

"No. He mentioned something about going to the kitchen to talk to Sherry about ways to lower the fat and sodium count in her recipes without sacrificing flavor. He took a notebook."

"Brave man," she murmured.

"Brave or stupid. But he should be okay. I think Sherry has a soft spot for him."

Brigit nodded. "It's impossible not to like Joe. He's a giant teddy bear."

"I'll tell you a secret. When I first got here and the two of you were all chatty and giggly—"

"Chatty and giggly? I think I'm offended," she inserted. But the flash of her smile contradicted her words.

"As I was saying, the two of you hit it off so quickly that I felt a little left out."

"I seem to remember you accusing me of flirting with Joe."

"I did." Kellen nodded. "I was…jealous."

"You were not!" Her laughter rang out. She thought he was joking.

"I didn't fully realize it at the time, but I was. Jealous of the easy banter. Jealous of the instant friendship. Wondering if maybe…" He ran his fingers down one of her arms. Her expression sobered and she shivered.

Kellen stepped forward, bringing him fully into the spare room. Behind her, the futon was folded up, but he could picture Brigit on it, all of that glorious black hair spread over her pillowcase like spilled ink.

Only one wall separated the two of them at night. For weeks now he'd lain awake, his mind taunting him with fantasies of the pair of them together…at last. Other than stolen kisses and hand-holding during walks, their relationship had remained as chaste as could be. He marveled at his restraint, knowing that not all of it could be blamed on his bum leg. He was proceeding with caution. Brigit wasn't one of his dalliances. Everything about her was different…special.

"I want you," he said softly. "More than I can ever remember wanting anyone."

He watched her eyes widen at his bold statement. He should have known it wouldn't throw her. Hell, he should have expected that she wouldn't be outdone.

"I feel the same way."

Kellen waited, expecting a "but" to enter the conversation, given their talk on the beach when she'd made it clear she wasn't ready to plow ahead with any sort of relationship. Instead, she settled a hand on one slim hip and notched up her chin. One edge of the scar was visible. Overall, the cut had healed nicely, but it had yet to fade from red to white. She didn't try to camouflage it. Hell, she didn't seem bothered by it at all. Just as she accepted Kellen despite his scars and disability. Or maybe even because of them.

She really was a most extraordinary woman.

He had plans for their evening. They included a sumptuous meal at one of the area's newest and most popular steakhouses. And a champagne toast to the beginning of what he hoped would be a long relationship, because despite all he'd learned about Brigit over the past couple months, he knew he'd only scratched the surface. He wanted to know more. To know everything. And even then he doubted he would ever grow bored. At thirty-six, he'd finally grown up.

Hell, he might even be up for some dancing during their evening out, as long as it was slow and didn't involve too much movement. Finally, he'd planned to cap it off with a late-night stroll on the beach, so that they could be alone. He intended to take a blanket, spread it out on the sand, sit with her and count the stars. Then, maybe…

"We have…reservations," he managed.

"Do we? I have no reservations."

"No?"

He watched her swallow. With nerves? Or with need?

"None whatsoever."

His plans were forgotten the instant their lips met. Even then, Kellen might have been able to summon up some willpower if she hadn't wrapped his tie around her hand and drawn him farther into the room. With their mouths still fused, she kicked the door closed behind him. The *snick* of the lock opened the floodgates. A tidal wave of pent-up need flowed out.

No words were necessary as she walked backward toward the futon, pulling Kellen along by his tie. He didn't mind being led. Vaguely, he was aware of his cane falling to the floor, the clatter of wood meeting wood all but lost to the blood roaring in his ears. His hands were locked on her waist, not merely for support, but to let her take the lead. She needed to be in control. He got that. And he was happy to accommodate her.

Brigit let go of the end of his tie, but only so she could free it from its knot. She yanked the length of silk from around his neck with a flourish, triumph gleaming in her blue eyes as she sent it sailing through the air. Then she tugged the shirt from his pants and started in on the placket of buttons with what he considered maddening slowness. Left to him, Kellen simply would have rent the fabric and sent the buttons flying. She was much more practical…and patient.

What seemed like an eternity later, she finally finished. The heat of her hands singed his skin as she spread open the shirt and pushed it off his shoulders. He had to lower his arms so that it could drop to the floor, joining his discarded cane and tie on the hardwood. Her fingertips trailed over the bare skin of his chest and she kissed the shoulder that had been dislocated in his accident. It hadn't bothered Kellen in months, but he groaned now, suffering an exquisite form of pain as her mouth trailed along his collarbone and then cruised south to his nipple. She passed her tongue around it before meeting his gaze.

"How are you holding up?" she asked softly.

"Ready to combust," he admitted.

She smiled slyly. "I meant your leg. You've been standing unsupported for a few minutes now."

"I wouldn't mind lying down." His smile was every bit as cunning.

"Let's get you out of those pants first."

The breath backed up in his throat, but he finally managed to exhale. He fingered the soft silk of her dress. "What about you?"

"We'll get to me in a moment. Right now, I'm undressing you. Is that a problem?"

"Not at all."

"Good." And she reached for his belt.

Never had Brigit been this forward, acted this boldly. Of course, she had little practice with seduction. Other than Scott, she'd only been intimate with one other man. A boy really, since the act had occurred after her high school prom. All of her experiences with sex had been, well, disappointing.

She was positive that was about to end. Kellen wasn't a boy. He was all man. And eager, if the erection straining against his fly was any indication. But unlike her ex, he wasn't telling her what he wanted from her or how she was supposed to act or criticizing her for doing something wrong. Kellen was allowing her to be in the driver's seat, and she planned to enjoy every second of the ride.

She slipped the pants down his legs and sat on the edge of the futon so that she could help him step out of them. Another time, she would have taken a moment to fold them to prevent the fabric from wrinkling. But just as she had with his shirt and tie, she left them where they were. Other matters were taking precedence. Namely, getting out of her dress.

Kellen's hands found the zipper in the back. He lowered it to between her shoulder blades, but couldn't continue without leaning over, a feat complicated by his bad leg. She corrected the matter by standing.

A moment later, they were both naked, their breaths coming in heavy gasps as, bodies pressed tight, they strained to get closer still.

"I think we'd better get you off your feet," she told him. The words came out between panting breaths.

"I think so, too."

Together they lowered onto the futon.

CHAPTER THIRTEEN

JOE WAS SITTING in the living room when they emerged from Brigit's bedroom forty minutes later. Lou was next to him on the couch. Both men were drinking iced tea while they watched a baseball game. Other than offering a greeting when she and Kellen entered the living room, neither of the men said a word.

Brigit, however, took one look at Kellen's wrinkled clothes and satisfied expression and knew it had to be obvious what the pair of them had been up to.

She wanted to be embarrassed. It wasn't like her to behave so…so what? The possible answers seemed endless. She narrowed it down to three—spontaneously, wantonly and recklessly—and couldn't stop a smile from turning up the corners of her lips.

"Keep grinning like that, sweetheart, and everyone will know what we've been up to," Kellen whispered in her ear.

"Yes, and they'll be envious. *Really, really* envious," she whispered back. To which he chuckled.

Lou pushed to his feet. "Ready to go now, boss?"

"Yes."

The driver nodded. "I'll bring the Escalade around and meet you at the main door."

Joe rose as well and pulled a slip of paper from his pants pocket. "I took the liberty of calling the restaurant,

Mr. F, and jotted down a few of the menu's healthiest selections." He handed the note to Kellen while adding, "I'd stick with fish. The grilled salmon in particular sounds excellent. And it has all of those healthy omega-threes. Just don't let them douse it in any kind of sauce."

"Salmon?" Kellen's mouth puckered on the word as if he were sucking on a sourball. "It's a steakhouse, Joe."

"You know how I feel about red meat."

"I do."

"And haven't you gotten healthier and stronger following my regimen?"

"I have."

Joe nodded, as if the matter was resolved. "None of the selections I wrote down contain monosodium glutamate, but I'd ask the server to hold it anyway, just to be on the safe side."

"Hold the MSG. Got it," Kellen replied in a dutiful tone that didn't fool Brigit one bit. This was merely the path of least resistance.

"And remember, baked potato instead of fries, and watch the dressing for your salad. Lots of hidden fat there, not to mention sodium. I suggest requesting vinegar and olive oil, and go light on the oil."

Kellen still had about a dozen pounds to gain back to put him at his optimum weight, but Joe remained adamant that he wanted him to do it the healthy way.

"Fish, no sauce. Salad, no dressing. Potatoes baked not fried. Can't wait to dig in," he muttered.

Kellen tucked the paper in his pants pocket, where Brigit was fairly certain it would stay for the remainder of the evening.

Sebastian's Steakhouse was located in a renovated three-story building on Broad Street in Charleston's historic downtown. They were late for their reservation, but a fifty-dollar bill slipped to the maître d' apparently smoothed over any problem.

The first two stories of the restaurant were open to all diners. The third, which was where they were seated, was reserved for A-list guests only. Brigit had never eaten at Sebastian's, regardless of the floor. And it was no wonder, she decided as she studied the à la carte menu. The prices were well beyond her budget.

No sooner had they sat down at their table than a black-vested server arrived with a tray carrying two champagne flutes and bottle of Dom in a silver ice bucket.

"Shall I pour?" he asked Kellen.

"Please."

This was Kellen's lifestyle, she realized. As dazzled by it as she felt, it also represented a world she knew little about. A world to which he would be returning at some point in the not-so-distant future. The thought threatened to tarnish the luster of the evening, so she shoved it away.

"Enjoy," the waiter said before leaving.

Once they were alone again, Kellen said, "I had plans to sweep you off your feet tonight. An amazing meal, maybe even a little dancing."

"Really?" The latter came as a surprise. A welcome one, since it showed how far he'd come.

"Really. Instead, I'm the one who's been swept off my feet." He raised his glass. "By you."

She clinked the rim of her champagne flute against his. "I'd say it was mutual."

They caught one of the last ferries back to Hadley Island. Lou had the radio on a jazz station. Brigit sat snuggled up to Kellen's side in the backseat. The Escalade's high beams illuminated the surroundings as they returned to the resort. Their night out was ending.

Joe was asleep on the sofa bed in the living room, snoring softly as they made their way past him to the hallway. At her bedroom door, Brigit stopped.

"I guess this is where we say good-night." She smiled.

Kellen's expression remained serious. "Does it have to be?"

It was exactly what she'd been hoping to hear, although her previous boldness had ebbed, preventing her from saying as much.

She took the hand he offered. Together they walked to the bedroom at the end of the hall. As they stepped over the threshold she knew that much more than their sleeping arrangements for the night had changed.

CHAPTER FOURTEEN

ONLY A WEEK of the official summer season remained. Once Labor Day passed, children would head back to school and parents would start hoarding their vacation days to use on their kids' breaks.

The island would be quieter without all of the families, life a little slower until the snowbirds started arriving in November, eager to leave the cold weather of the north behind for a couple weeks or even months.

Brigit would be happy for the break. She was looking forward to taking a little time off. In particular, she wanted to spend it with Kellen doing whatever they wanted to do.

The past couple weeks had been a lovely blur of stolen moments during the day and unbridled passion at night. The depth of her feelings amazed her. Falling for her boss hadn't been her intention, but that was what had happened. She'd tumbled headlong into love.

It terrified her, but she couldn't deny she was happy. Happier than she'd been in years. Even though he hadn't said so, she was certain Kellen felt the same. His every glance, touch and expression told her so. When they made love, it was perfect. A union of souls as much as bodies. She smiled as she laid on the bed that had been hers, then his and now was theirs. The two of them had been sharing it since the night of their dinner in Charleston.

It was only six o'clock, but Kellen was already awake and up. He'd told her to wait for him in bed and he would be back in a few minutes with a surprise.

Just as she'd learned to be spontaneous and go with the flow, Brigit had learned to appreciate surprises. Especially Kellen's. The other day he had surprised her with a bouquet of roses, a good two dozen of the long-stemmed red variety. They were in a vase on the nightstand, their fragrance perfuming the air even as their velvety petals had begun to wilt.

And just the day before, he'd had his mother and stepfather out to the island to dinner. Brigit had assumed the invitation was to begin restoring their relationship and she'd been proud of him for extending an olive branch. Pride had changed to shock when he'd insisted that Brigit dine with them. And shock had morphed into an emotion too huge to name when he'd introduced her as his girlfriend rather than as the inn's manager. She smiled at the memory and, growing impatient for his return, called out, "What's taking you so long?"

"Perfection takes time," came his reply from down the hall.

"I don't need perfection. What I need, all I want, is you!"

She threw her arms wide as she made the declaration, only to have her hand connect with the roses. The flowers, vase and all, tumbled to the floor, water soaking a portion of the area rug before sloshing over the hardwood. "Shoot!"

She opened the drawer in the nightstand, where she kept a box of tissues. Grabbing a handful, she sopped up what she could. Afterward, she straightened, intending to throw the sodden mess in the garbage. The manila envelope caught her eye. Her name was printed on the outside. Where had it come from? She certainly hadn't put it there. Which could only mean that Kellen had. But why? What was it? She reached for it and opened the flap. The soggy tissues were forgotten as she looked over the document she'd pulled from inside.

She swallowed in disbelief as the words registered and her heart broke. No! No! This couldn't be right. But it was all there in black and white, Kellen's plan to dismiss her.

It was mere minutes later, although it felt like a lifetime, when Kellen filled the doorframe and called, "Surprise! Breakfast in bed."

He held a tray laden with two plates of Belgian waffles, sliced fresh strawberries and a pair of coffee cups. A small bouquet of daisies spilled from a squat square vase. As distraught as she was, it barely registered that he was standing unsupported, cane nowhere to be found. At the moment, the only thing Brigit was aware of was the terrible ache in her chest.

Surprise, indeed.

He'd planned to let her go. All this time she'd been trying not to worry about whether he would leave again or where their burgeoning relationship was heading. It had never occurred to her he might stay and she would be the one packing her bags.

Give him the benefit of the doubt, her head argued. But the busted up heart that had only recently healed, had her holding up the document and asking coolly, "When were you going to spring this surprise on me?"

He blinked in confusion for a moment. Was that proof that he didn't know what she was talking about? Or proof that he was just like Scott? A first-class liar and manipulator. His face paled and a guilty grimace replaced his easy smile. She took that as her answer, and wondered how else he had deceived her.

"Where did you get that?" he asked.

"It was in the nightstand. You'll forgive me for opening it. After all, the envelope was addressed to me."

"Brigit, it's not what it looks like." He limped into the room. Coffee sloshed over the rim of the cups on the tray as he set it down on the bed, where just that morning they'd made love.

How original, she thought. And how utterly untrue. "It looks like a severance package. Are you going to tell me I'm wrong about that?"

"No. You're not wrong. That's what it is. When I first came back, my thought was eventually to take over running the resort myself. I didn't think you'd want to stay on given that your duties would be reduced, but I'd planned to ask."

"How nice of you to give me the option," she drawled.

"I sounds bad, I know, but things changed. You have to believe me, I had it drawn up months ago. Long before you and I—"

"Had sex," she stated flatly, even though the words left her feeling sick.

"Don't say it like that. Please."

"How should I say it, Kellen?" she demanded. "That's what it was, right? Sex. With my boss."

"It was more than that. It *is* more than that!" he insisted.

"You lied to me. Are you going to deny that?"

"If I lied to anyone, Brigit, it was myself. When our relationship began to change, I didn't trust my feelings for you."

But she wouldn't hear it. She couldn't believe it. "It all comes down to this, Kellen. Once you had your fun, you planned to let me go." Her eyes blurred again as she studied the document. "You're very generous, by the way. I've been well compensated for my...service."

Her stomach threatened to heave on the last word. All of the beauty she'd found in their lovemaking became sordid. Used, that was how she felt now. And stupid, because all of her internal lectures about keeping things casual and enjoying the moment had been a load of baloney. She'd fallen in the love with Kellen. She should have known better.

She ran from the room, not stopping when he called her name. She couldn't stay. Couldn't bear to hear more lies. She was at the apartment door, fingers curled around the handle when she heard a crash followed by an oath. That alone wouldn't have stopped her. But the ensuing sob that prevented Brigit from opening the door.

She tiptoed back through the living room and peeked down the hallway. Kellen was sprawled face down on the floor just outside the spare room. He wasn't trying to get up. His face was pressed into his crossed arms, shoulders shaking. He was crying.

"Kellen?"

He raised his head. His face was damp, eyes red. "I thought you were gone."

"I was worried you'd hurt yourself," she lied. "Are you okay?"

He pushed up until he was able to bring his legs around into a sitting position with his back against the wall. "No. I'm not okay, Brigit."

"I'll get Joe."

Before she could turn, however, Kellen held out his hand. "I need you."

She swallowed. He'd told her that before. "But you're letting me go."

Arm still outstretched, he replied, "Never! I know it looks that way from the document, but I had it made up months ago, the day of my disastrous appointment with the specialist in Charleston."

She recalled the interest he'd shown in the daily operations. His interactions with the staff. "You wanted to run it with me out of the picture."

"If you wouldn't stay." He nodded. "Yes. When my grandfather left me this place that was his wish. But Brigit—"

She continued to ignore his outstretched hand, and instead demanded, "When were you going to tell me about your plans?"

Kellen closed his eyes and let his hand drop to his side. "I didn't have a firm date in mind. Then, I just… forgot about it."

"We're talking about my future. How could you *forget* something as big as this?" she demanded, shaking the sheaf of papers in front of her.

"You," Kellen stated simply. Half of his mouth rose and some of her pain lifted with it. "You made me forget a lot of things, Brigit. Like how to be bitter and angry and hopeless. And you taught me a lot, too."

"Like how to manage a resort?" she asked, though the question carried no heat.

"Like how to believe in myself. Like how not only to accept my life as it was, but how to dream new dreams. And I have. I'm dreaming of a different future. Here at the resort." He paused. "With you. I love you."

Love. The word threatened to snatch her breath away. "You didn't say anything," she said slowly, cautiously.

"That's because I've never been in love before. I've used the word with other women, but I never felt like this. I wanted to be sure, and I am. But—"

"But what?"

"Well, you had been in love before. So much so you got married. Your ex-husband used the word, but mangled its meaning. He hurt you so badly, made you doubt yourself… I didn't think you'd trust the word alone, so I've been trying to show you how I felt instead."

Brigit swallowed. He was right, of course. She wouldn't have trusted the mere word, as potent as she found it to be now. But actions spoke clearly and left no room for second-guessing.

And so Kellen had been showing her, revealing his true feelings to her in gestures big and small.

How different this man was from the brooding and broken self-involved heir who'd first darkened her door and had turned her life upside down with his edicts and demands.

"You love me." She whispered the words, hugged them close as she dropped down beside him on thc floor.

"More each day," he replied, reaching for her. "Tell me you'll stay. I want you with me always. I want Faust Haven to be our home. This resort to be ours to run together. I don't want a future that doesn't include you. Please, tell me you won't leave."

Brigit framed his face with her hands, kissed his damp cheeks. The last pieces of her broken heart fitted together and fused, leaving it whole. Finally.

"I won't leave, Kellen. Ever. I love you, too." Just before their mouths met, she whispered. "You are my future."

* * * * *

It shouldn't matter to me.

He sawed through the wood with the handsaw he preferred to an electric version. Thinking about her like that was selfish and thickheaded. The only thing that should matter was whether or not she could be convinced to let him spend time with his daughter.

He'd thought it would be easier somehow—that perhaps if Shiloh was being cared for by someone with a family of her own, that the help of a parent might be, if not wholly welcome, then possibly some relief, financial or otherwise. He hadn't considered that she'd be living with an incredibly dedicated and, admittedly, alluring young woman whose presence had an intense, unwelcome effect on him.

Sam put the saw down to measure another piece of wood, working as fast as he could while maintaining precision. Soon enough he'd be done cutting the lumber, and he could begin to pound nails into boards. Maybe the sweat and hard work in the Texas spring sun would remind him of the potential storm ahead, brought on by his own actions, and he'd forget the way his heart raced at the mere sight of Lucy Monroe.

FINDING HIS LONE STAR LOVE

BY

AMY WOODS

Published in Great Britain 2015
by Mills & Boon, an imprint of Harlequin (UK) Limited,
Eton House, 18-24 Paradise Road, Richmond, Surrey, TW9 1SR

ISBN: 978-0-263-25103-6

23-0115

Harlequin (UK) Limited's policy is to use papers that are natural, renewable and recyclable products and made from wood grown in sustainable forests. The logging and manufacturing processes conform to the legal environmental regulations of the country of origin.

Printed and bound in Spain
by CPI, Barcelona

Amy Woods took the scenic route to becoming an author. She's been a bookkeeper, a high school English teacher, and a claims specialist, but now that she makes up stories for a living, she's never giving it up. She grew up in Austin, Texas, USA, and lives there with her wonderfully goofy, supportive husband and a spoiled rescue dog. Amy can be reached on Facebook, Twitter and her website, www.amywoodsbooks.com.

For Grandma and Grandpa Bruce,
who would have been proud.

Chapter One

There was no less-qualified cook in the town of Peach Leaf, Texas—okay, possibly the whole world—than Lucy Monroe, and she would be the first to admit it.

So then, to Lucy, given the way things had been going lately, it wasn't really all that surprising that she was responsible for preparing lunch for the hungry kids on a field trip, who now crowded the Lonestar Observatory's small café. Thirty or so second graders, and their already-worn-out teachers and parent-chaperones, who must be standing staring at the still-swinging kitchen door, thinly veiled impatience clouding their features as they wondered what on earth was keeping their solo waitress. Not that Lucy was much of a server, either, for that matter. Lord help her, Lucy needed a break.

Or a miracle.

She was short on both.

Full order pad in hand, she grabbed an apron, tying it quickly over her lemon-colored pencil skirt and white button-down shirt. Lucy rushed to the prep table to start slicing cheese and bread for sandwiches, and to check on the caramel apple pies she'd had the foresight to put in the oven earlier between her regular duties. The pie recipe was her grandma's—an old favorite—and the only thing she really knew how to get right in the kitchen.

Unlike Nana, Lucy was as out of her element in a kitchen as a hog in a chicken coop, which was exactly why she'd hired the best chef she could find to handle the observatory's little café. A very skilled, highly trained, seemingly intelligent chef, who, at that very moment, was on a plane to Las Vegas with the fiancée he'd met only a week ago.

Damn that Axel.

Lucy pulled out a knife and began slicing a loaf from the day before, pushing the utensil through the soft bread perhaps a little harder than was necessary.

Surely he could have given more than a day's notice before he skipped town. But then, Axel had probably made his rash decision with something other than his brain. He'd called and woken Lucy late the evening before to give his resignation. She'd bitten her tongue to prevent her true thoughts from escaping her mouth when Axel had said he *would* be sorry to cut out on her on such short notice, except for the fact he'd found the love of his life and therefore was the happiest man on the planet and didn't have a sorry bone in his body.

Lucy had more than enough sorry bones for the both of them. He'd left her high and dry for a red-eye to Vegas, and she hadn't had a single second to hire someone to take his place. Her regular tasks as the observatory's manager would have to wait. Finding a suitable new chef was first on her agenda—that is, after she'd appeased the ravenous throng waiting on the other side of the kitchen wall.

Her thoughts were interrupted when the door swung open and her coworker and best friend, Tessa McAdams, burst in, quickly closing the door behind her as she stared wide-eyed at Lucy.

"There's an angry mob out there, Lu," Tessa said, turning back to the door and standing on tiptoes to stare out the small round window. She ducked back down, fast. "They're closing in. I think they might come in after us if you don't get some grub in their bellies soon."

"Damn that Axel," Lucy said, out loud this time. She lowered the bread knife into the loaf once more and continued to saw, but when she looked up again a strange expression crossed Tessa's face, causing Lucy to pause midslice. Tessa crossed her arms and her lips formed a straight line, her dark eyes sparkling with mischief, nose wrinkling up like a rabbit in the same way she'd had since they were kids, whenever Tessa was on the verge of revealing a secret or in the process of calculating a naughty plan.

"Whatever it is, out with it. Now," Lucy demanded, sparing only a second to toss a serious look at her friend before getting back to work.

"Tell me straight, Lu. I know it's been a while since you had a decent date, but starting fires just to get a hot firefighter out here is no way to go about catching a man."

For a second, Lucy had no clue what Tessa was talking about, but then the unmistakable scent of scorched flour and butter hit her nostrils with full force.

"Oh my gosh, Tess!" Lucy said, tossing aside the bread and knife and making her way to the stacked ovens on the other side of the kitchen, as if her life depended on it. The way things were going, it might indeed. "My pies!"

For a second she froze, unable to do more than stand still, shocked, afraid to open the oven and face the inevitable pastry carnage. Thankfully, adrenaline took over.

Her previous impishness wiped away, Tessa rushed over to join her friend. Lucy tossed a set of oven mitts at her. "Here, put these on," Lucy said, cloaking her own hands in another pair. "You pull out the rack and I'll grab the pies. We might be able to rescue the ones on the top shelf if we're quick."

Tessa took the mitts and followed Lucy's instructions, but Lucy saw doubt crease her forehead as she pulled out pie after pie, the crust of each more burned than the one before. "Lu," Tessa said, shaking her head in defeat, "I know less about cooking than you—and that's saying something—and I hate to mention it, but...I really don't think these are salvageable."

The last pie retrieved from the oven of doom, Lucy pulled her hands out of the mitts and grabbed the bread knife. She began cutting off the charred pieces of crust and singed chunks of her special oatmeal-pecan topping, ignoring Tessa's words. She had to save the pies. Otherwise, there would only be plain sandwiches to serve her guests, and there was no way she could let all those kids and their parents and teachers return to their schools in Austin, thinking that the Lonestar Café had such poor service. The place was in enough financial trouble already.

The Lonestar Observatory had much higher standards in serving guests. In particular, its café was known for delicious, home-cooked Southern comfort food, just the way it had been when Lucy's dad was in charge of everything. He had ensured that everything in the facility was top-notch, from providing the latest stargazing equipment available, to seeing that the café served only the best cuisine. Her dad had received his PhD in astronomy with high recommendations and, instead of becoming a professor as all of his instructors expected, he, along with her mom, had accepted the local university's offer to head the small observatory, just a few months before Lucy was born.

Her dad had died the day after her twenty-fifth birthday. Lucy convinced the university to let her take over managing the observatory, on the condition that she hired a properly credentialed expert in the field to stand in as official director. Despite not finishing formal training in astronomy, Lucy knew the observatory better than any of the scientists interviewed for her father's job before the university admitted she was best for the position. She'd learned everything she needed to know from her dad, first toddling along as he checked the telescopes each day, all the way through high school and her first semesters of college, when she'd begun her own research projects to advance the field. And the director, sweet Dr. Blake, who looked and behaved more like Santa Claus than a scientist—which described the rest of the observatory's employees—respected Lucy enough to let her have her way in running the place. It wasn't the same as being a true scientist, but it would have to do. She'd wanted to be an astronomer since she was a little girl, learning constellations and galaxies at her father's side, and if she had a spare second, she might admit that she regretted not being able to finish school.

But Lucy didn't have time for regrets.

Everything aside, more than her job and her life and the means by which she was able to take care of her niece, Shiloh, the Lonestar was Lucy's home. It was where she'd been raised and where she'd learned to look up when things in her own world weren't going well. It was the only place on the planet where she felt whole and centered; she would do anything to keep it running like a well-oiled machine, even when funding was low or when struggles with Shiloh tested her patience. Or when love-struck chefs quit at the last minute.

So this was about more than burned pies.

It was about letting down her dad—the only man she'd ever been able to trust.

Tessa had come to her side and was attempting to pry the knife out of Lucy's hands. Finally, warm tears pooling behind her eyes, Lucy let her friend take the utensil as she sank to the floor, settling her face in her hands. "Dad would be so disappointed if he saw what a disaster this is," Lucy said as she fought against the tears that threatened to escape. "He would never have let this kind of thing happen to this place." She raised her head and peered at Tessa through her bangs, which stuck out all over and clung to her glasses, frizzy and wild from the chaos of the past half hour.

"Shhh," Tessa soothed, setting down the knife and crouching beside her friend. She brushed aside Lucy's frazzled hair. "You know that's not true, hon. You're just having a rough time lately, and you're stressed. Your daddy loved you more than he loved the stars. And that's saying something." Tessa lifted Lucy's chin with her finger and stared into Lucy's eyes, a mischievous smirk behind her own. "But one thing I do know—he would not have let you set foot in this kitchen without supervision, not even to make a few pies. That's for damn sure." Tessa smiled and Lucy felt her chest relax, ever so slightly. She reached up and wiped at her eyes, then made a fist and softly brushed Tessa's chin in a mock punch. Tessa laughed and the melodious sound of it was almost enough to coax a smile out of Lucy.

Almost—but not quite.

She'd made such a mess of things today. And, even though her best friend had a way of making her feel better, the world still awaited her, and something had to be done about the hungry crowd waiting outside the door. And there were afternoon tours scheduled back-to-back, quarterly tax forms to review and Shiloh to meet at the bus stop. Lucy closed her eyes and sighed, concentrating all her effort on taking one deep breath after the other. This wasn't the first time she'd had more responsibility than any one person could possibly handle, and it was highly unlikely that it would be the last. She would just have to buck up, make the sandwiches and tackle the rest later, then find some way to deal with the fact that, for today, her beloved place— her home—had poorer pickings than a fast-food joint.

Sam Haynes had bitten off more than he could chew. He'd assumed the drive to Peach Leaf would be a piece of cake after making the trip to Austin from Houston when his plane had landed that morning, but clearly he'd underestimated the distance. The Texas road stretched on forever and looked much the same the whole way, save for a few tiny towns along the route, and not a Starbucks in sight. Hills with clusters of trees here and there, but mostly dust, dust— and more dust. And real tumbleweeds, which Sam had only seen in his grandfather's beloved old black-and-white Westerns. It was true what they said— everything was bigger here—including, unfortunately, the highways.

Luckily, he'd seen the sign for Peach Leaf about a mile-and-a-half back, shining like an oasis in the desert, and there couldn't be that much farther left to go—he hoped. A native New Yorker, Sam wasn't used to driving this much, and he'd got to the point where he'd do just about anything this side of the law to get a decent meal and a bed for the night. And he'd *die* for a strong cup of coffee.

His journey had been long in more ways than one. He'd received a phone call about his daughter's whereabouts from the PI he'd hired a few weeks prior, just when he'd been about ready to jump out of his skin from the wait. The guy seemed sure this time—he'd really found her. Sam had thought such a feat near impossible, given how little he had to go on, but the investigator had come with high recommendations from a friend mindful enough not to ask pressing questions, and sure enough, the guy had accomplished the task. After taking a few days off to process the news and make some plans, Sam had notified the chefs at the three restaurants he owned that he would be available only by email until further notice, and he'd booked a plane out of New York City, with a room waiting for him at The Frederickson Bed-and-Breakfast in Peach Leaf.

Now here he was, in the middle of nowhere in West Texas, looking for a girl he'd never even met. A girl who, until fairly recently, he hadn't even known existed.

A few of his closest friends had pronounced Sam's plan crazy for picking up and leaving without any real explanation, but he knew enough to know that sometimes, the crazy thing was the right thing.

His heart swelled at the thought of seeing her for the first time. Would she look like him? Would she have Sam's brown eyes and hair? Or would she have Jennifer's green eyes and wavy, reddish hair, with freckles dotting a button nose? Would she have his love of books and music, or would she be more like her mysterious mother, whom Sam had barely known?

It was only meant to be a one-night stand—no strings attached. Jennifer had been hesitant to even offer up her first name, though Sam insisted. He'd been young, a frat boy in college, and she was just another coed notch on his bedpost before he'd wised-up and straightened out his life. When he'd got the call from Jennifer a month ago, saying she was sorry, but she just *had* to tell him something she'd been keeping to herself for years, he'd been expecting anything but the news she gave him. Before she'd spoken the words that forever changed his life in an instant, he had thought that maybe she needed help, or maybe she just wanted to get together for a drink after all those years—hell, maybe she needed money. Anything was possible. But instead, the strawberry-haired girl from a reckless one-night stand whose last name he'd never known gave him the most life-altering news a man could hear.

They had a daughter.

He had a daughter.

As Jennifer explained everything to him, Sam had been so confused and angry he could barely breathe. It turned out she had given their baby to her younger sister long ago when she'd been broke, unemployed, "lost"—whatever that meant, Sam didn't want to know—and couldn't handle having a kid. A recent hospitalization for mental illness, it seemed, had prompted Jennifer to think long and hard about some of her choices. She had decided that, even if their daughter didn't have a mom, she should have a chance to know her father. The girl's name was Shiloh, and Jennifer's sister had adopted her when she was an infant. Jennifer said she'd been back to visit only once, but never again. Even when pressed, she wouldn't say why. She would only reveal that it had been a mistake to go back that one time, and she would never do it again. She'd also said that she wasn't sure if her sister and child even lived in the same place anymore—she had called a few times but the old number was dead, and she hadn't tried any harder than that, preferring to leave them alone.

Sam's heart had fallen straight to the bottom of his shoes at the news. It had taken a weekend of pacing his town house, racking his brain to figure out what needed to be done. Maybe Jennifer had abandoned the girl, but Sam, now that he knew of her, had no intention of doing the same. He'd been irresponsible and foolish as a young man, but he'd done his best to change his ways, and he wouldn't turn away from this obligation. He couldn't even if he'd wanted to.

Moreover, how could Jennifer have kept this from him? How stubborn must she have been to handle the news on her own? Sure, he was young and foolish back then, but he would have been there for Jennifer and their daughter. He would have done everything he could have to help raise their child. He would never have given up on his own kid.

The road began to narrow and Sam's thoughts dissipated. This had to be it. The Lonestar Observatory. He had no real idea what his daughter was doing there. Her location was all the PI had been able to find so far, and he'd assured Sam that the records he'd been able to locate regarding Sam's daughter pointed to the observatory. It looked, he'd said, as if she might even live there, though the reason for that, like so much else, was still unknown. But in his mind, all Sam could think about was: what could a twelve-year-old be doing spending so much time at a science center? The whole thing was a mystery he'd just begun to unfold. Who knew what other secrets would turn up?

He had to find out all he could about her, regardless of what that might involve.

He turned his rental truck into the winding road that marked the way to his destination. He could see large white objects almost the size of buildings spotting the green land, though he assumed given where he was that they had to be telescopes. Even in his haste, and despite his fatigue from driving so far, Sam sensed a quiet beauty about the place. Clusters of trees blanketed acre upon acre with the white stargazers dotting the landscape here and there, like some kind of industrial flower. Sam didn't know anything about astronomy, but if that's what his daughter was interested in, he would find a way to be interested, too.

He would do just about anything to get to know her, but he'd also have to be careful. He couldn't let her, or anyone who knew her, find out his relationship to her before he was ready—before *she* was ready. He'd give himself just a week to check on her, even if only from a distance; he'd make sure she was doing okay and getting along well, that she was safe and healthy and cared for, and then he would head home and decide how to proceed. He'd researched his legal rights, but he wasn't going to do anything to hurt his daughter. If his child didn't want anything to do with him, he supposed he'd somehow have to make his peace with that, but he was hoping against hope that he wouldn't have to face such a thing.

The trees thinned as he reached what must have been the main building, and Sam pulled into a space in the parking lot out front next to a couple of school buses. His heart climbed into his throat and breathing was suddenly difficult.

Despite the hours spent planning, going over what he would say and how he would explain his abrupt arrival, his mouth went dry as reality closed in. Maybe his friends were right—maybe he was some kind of crazy for jumping into this headfirst. He'd had plenty of miles now to think about how he'd chosen to handle things. Patience had never been his strong suit, and even Sam had to admit that maybe this wasn't the most intelligent move. But what if… What if he'd had a phone number and called instead—and been refused? Sam swallowed at the painful idea. At least this way he could see her, and give her a chance to choose whether or not she wanted him to be a part of her life.

Regardless of whether he was allowed to be a dad, Sam was a father now, and he'd followed his instincts—for that he would make no apology. If he had any say in the matter, he would make sure that his daughter didn't grow up without a dad. At least not any longer.

He'd made his choice and he wasn't going back, and he'd start by getting out of the truck. Then he would walk to the front door. One step at a time, he'd make his way into his daughter's life, and hope that she'd eventually allow him to stick around.

"Well," said Santa Claus, or, as the nameplate on his cherrywood desk indicated, Dr. Edward Blake, "I'm the official director of the observatory, but if you want more information, you're gonna want to talk to Ms. Lucy Monroe. She's the real brains around here."

Brains, huh? If Edward Blake, PhD, a man who, by the multitude of plaques and degrees decorating the wall must be a very successful and accomplished astronomer, wasn't the brains of the place, then Ms. Monroe must be a damn genius.

"All right, then, point the way," Sam said, working to keep his anxiety from saturating his voice.

Dr. Blake eyed Sam up and down, assessing him more like a suspicious father before his teenage daughter's first date than the director of a research institution.

"I'm not so sure that's a good idea just now." Dr. Blake crossed his arms over his ample abdomen. Geez, the man couldn't look more like good old Saint Nick if he'd been wearing a red suit. Sam could hardly help the smile that threatened to spread across his face. This guy was a dead ringer for the Christmas character.

"And why is that, Mr. Clau—Dr. Blake?" Sam was not a patient man, but he could appear that way when he wanted to. And even though his patience was being tested at the moment, he would do nothing to ruin his chance of getting to meet his daughter.

"Well," Dr. Blake said, leaning across the desk to stare straight into Sam's eyes. Now Sam felt as if he really was on trial. His pulse quickened and he sucked in a breath, letting the air out slowly as he gathered his thoughts. "Because you still haven't given me a good answer to my question. What exactly is it that you're doing here, Mr. Haynes?"

Sam leaned back, putting a foot or two of distance between himself and the doc. He could feel his heart rate returning to something resembling normal as he took a few more deep breaths.

"Look, Dr. Blake, I just need some information, that's all. I'm here on business, and I really need to talk with someone who knows the place inside and out. Since, as you said, that person is Ms. Monroe, I'd just like to have a moment with her. I will explain everything, and then I'll get out of your hair."

The doctor leaned back, looking slightly satisfied with Sam's answer. He offered Sam a small smile, and damned if Sam didn't feel as if the man was about to reach under his desk and pull out a present from a great red sack. This guy really needed to consider a job playing the man in the big red suit, if he hadn't already.

"All right, Mr. Haynes, I'll take you to her. And I apologize if I'm being a little overly cautious." Dr. Blake folded his hands on the desk and a look of sincere concern brushed over his features. "It's just that, well, Lucy's special. She's indispensable here, and she's had a hard go of things. It's important to me that I look out for her, is all. I'm probably saying too much. I just needed to know you didn't have anything shady up your suit sleeve there."

The doctor pointed a finger in Sam's direction and Sam looked down at his expensive Italian suit. He supposed he was a tad overdressed. People seemed to go a little more on the casual side out here in the country. He'd have to keep that in mind and maybe stop for some different clothes if he ended up sticking around. He reminded himself not to get ahead of the game. There was still a considerable chance that the girl would want nothing to do with him.

And of course, now he'd have to get past Lucy first, provided she knew anything about his daughter. The PI had said that someone resembling an older version of the child in the picture Jennifer had provided had been seen more than once at the observatory. In hindsight, it wasn't much to go on, and arguably not near enough to warrant the steps he'd already taken. Then again, you didn't have to be an astronomer to figure out that his situation was fraught with difficulty at all ends. There wouldn't come a better time to face whatever his future as a father might hold.

Best to just jump in and then learn how to swim.

It was all he could do, and he could only hope that following his instincts would prove the right course of action.

"Nothing at all up my sleeve, Dr. Blake," Sam said, cautiously calculating his next words as he revised his original plan. "You see, I'm in the restaurant business, and I'm interested in the observatory's café for market research purposes, is all. Nothing more."

Sam feigned a glance at his watch for an excuse to look away from the doctor's eyes to avoid choking on his own lie. He wasn't in the habit of stretching the truth, not even to strangers, and it made him a little sick in his stomach to start things out this way, regardless of whether the doctor would have anything to do with him after that moment.

So he needed the people of Peach Leaf on his side, and he'd need all the support he could get if he ran into any problems. If his child did have any interest in a relationship with her dad, Sam was fully prepared to rearrange his life to meet her needs—flexibility was a luxury his career afforded, and he would use it if necessary. He wouldn't do anything to upset the girl's world, but he would do anything in his power to be as much a part of her life as she'd allow. If she wanted him around, Sam would do what he could to make it happen, and in a small town, that would almost certainly involve getting acquainted with thc locals.

"Well, then, if that's all," Dr. Blake said, rolling back his desk chair and lifting his considerable bulk to make his way around to the front, "let me show you to Lucy's office."

The doctor held out an arm and Sam walked ahead and opened the door, holding it for Dr. Blake. As they walked, he couldn't help humoring himself, to quell the anxiety that had taken up permanent residence inside him the past few days. "Have you ever thought about dressing up as Santa Claus at Christmastime? I would venture I'm not the first to tell you that you have the perfect beard for it. Kids would love you," Sam suggested, grinning, doing his best to lighten the tension.

Dr. Blake stopped midstep and turned to stare wide-eyed at Sam, as if he'd never heard anything more ridiculous in his life.

"Now, why on earth would I do that, Mr. Haynes?"

Sam choked on his words and tried to keep the surprise from his expression. A very uncomfortable few seconds passed before a huge grin stretched across the doctor's face, and a deep, rumbling chuckle escaped.

"I'm just messing with you, kid. Of course I've considered it. In fact, the observatory puts up a giant Christmas tree out on the café's porch each year, and we do a big ceremony of lighting the thing. I dress up like the big guy from the North Pole and we make a thing of it. It's a lot of fun. You see," Dr. Blake said, his voice more serious, "this is more than just a place for science research and learning. It's a big part of the community. That's why it's so important that we keep it alive. Tell you what—after you meet with Ms. Monroe, why don't you come back by my office and I'll set you up with one of the interns? You should check the place out while you're here. And of course," he said, nudging Sam with an elbow, "the museum always welcomes donations."

Dr. Blake smiled wide at Sam, who was fairly certain the old man winked. Sam had never believed in Santa even as a child, and he hadn't had many pleasant holiday seasons growing up. With a single mom who'd had to work so much, there hadn't always been much time for celebration. But if he'd ever put his cards on a miracle, he supposed now was the time. He could use all the help he could get.

After searching for Ms. Monroe all over the museum, Dr. Blake suggested they try the observatory's café.

"Here we are," the man said, as they rounded a hallway corner and Sam saw a sign for the Lonestar Café. "It's the only other place she could be, though between you and me, I can't imagine what she'd be doing in the kitchen, unless she's having a snack. She's in charge of the staff and in all the years I've worked here, I've never once seen that woman take a break during the business week. Besides, anyone who knows her can tell you that Lucy Monroe sure as shoot does not belong near a kitchen."

The doctor chuckled and Sam felt as if he'd missed out on some sort of inside joke. Being in the small Texas town, even for a short while, would take some getting used to. Not that people weren't friendly where he came from—it's just that the pace was different. He was used to the city and the constant bustle of people moving from one thing to the next, but here, the director of a significant institution seemed to have all the time and patience in the world to chat with Sam and show him around. He would have to be careful in this environment, where people were more likely to notice him, and Lord knows he must stick out like a sore thumb.

Sam and Dr. Blake walked through a small, but comfortable, dining area with beautifully handcrafted wooden tables and chairs, and Sam wished he had a moment to stop and admire the work; he had a fondness for carpentry and had taken a few classes. He had developed some skill and he'd made a few pieces here and there, mostly for friends, but he'd never had the luxury of taking on a real project. Maybe he would finally be able to carve out some time to do so.

As they got closer to the back of the café, a terrible scent bit at Sam's nose. As a trained chef, there was one thing he loathed the smell of more than anything in his kitchen, and that was the exact odor permeating the air as he inhaled. A thin cloud of smoke lent a gray haze to the area, and Sam and Dr. Blake had to force their way through a crowd, some of whom were peering through the kitchen door. They all probably had the same question. What in the hell was burning? Sam sniffed the air again and had the answer in an instant: butter and flour. Someone on the other side of that door was ruining pastry. Maybe he'd be of use here in more ways that he had anticipated.

"It's hotter than a hog's behind in here" were the first words Sam heard the second he opened the door.

"Well, thanks for the welcome," Sam joked.

The owner of the voice, a woman with olive skin

and short, spiky black hair, stood near a prep counter, smiling at him, and was joined a second later by the cutest girl Sam had ever laid eyes on. She was petite with gorgeous curves, reminiscent of 1940s pinup beauties and comic book heroines, though, sadly, the clothes she wore did much to hide what he guessed was an incredible figure. Curls the color of autumn-red leaves brushed her shoulders. Huge green eyes, filled with what looked like disappointment and traces of tears, maybe from the smoke Sam could see billowing out of the oven in great clouds, peered at him curiously from behind large purple glasses.

"Hi, there. Looks like you could use a hand."

Dr. Blake said he'd see them all later and disappeared as fast as he could. Sam couldn't blame the doc, but there was no chance of escape for him now, as he'd walked straight into a war zone.

Sam rushed over to join the two women, grabbing oven mitts from a counter along the way, and began taking the pies from them and dumping the offending confections into the nearest large trash can.

"Oh my gosh! What do you think you're doing?" the lovely, green-eyed girl shrieked, actually pulling a pie from Sam's hands and holding it to her chest as if he'd just snatched a baby from her, the momentum causing what remained of the pie's less thoroughly burned contents to spill on her shirt. Sam stared at her, alarmed at her reaction.

"I'm saving whatever disaster of a dessert you've got going here, is what I'm doing," he said, gently taking back the pie. He had to peel the woman's fingers from the edges, and as he did, chunks of blackened crust hit the ground, causing her cheeks to redden until she had no choice but to let Sam slip it out of her hands.

"Who are you? And what on earth are you doing in my kitchen?" she asked. Sam had the feeling she meant to sound stern, but her voice came out thin and defeated.

"I'm Sam. Sam Haynes," he said, in as soothing a voice as he could. From the look of things, the woman had had a hard day, and he could understand her frustration at a stranger showing up, but he had the strong idea she could use his help.

"This is your kitchen?" He raised an eyebrow, suspicious. It didn't line up with what Dr. Blake had mentioned, but if the kitchen were indeed hers, clearly he'd arrived right in the nick of time.

"Well. For now it is. My chef quit and—" she glared at Sam and placed both hands on her hips "—what difference is it to you anyway? Why are you here?"

"Actually, if you're Ms. Monroe," Sam said, glancing at the apple filling–splattered name tag on her lapel that read Lucy, "I'd really like to speak to you in private."

"Regarding?"

"Well, it's complicated," Sam said, weighing his words carefully. He cursed himself for not thinking this through all the way. Then he had an idea. He squared his shoulders. "Actually, I'm in the restaurant business and I have some experience. It's clear you're in need of a chef, and it appears I've come at a good time."

"You're really a chef?" she asked, eyeing him up and down as she took in his choice of outfit.

"Straight from heaven, it would seem," said the other woman, moving forward and offering Sam her hand. "Hi, I'm Tessa. Forgive my bestie here. We've had a rough morning, if you hadn't figured that out already. The chef really did just up and quit, so it's true that you are just in time if, in fact, you're really a chef, Mr. Haynes."

Still holding his hand after shaking it, Tessa batted her eyelashes at Sam. The woman he'd assumed was Ms. Monroe tossed her an irritated look.

"What?" Tessa asked, innocence sugaring her words as she finally released Sam's hand.

"Never mind her," Lucy interrupted, waving a hand at her friend. "Where did you train, Mr. Haynes?"

"Call me Sam. Please."

"Okay, Sam. Where did you train? And where are you from? And what—"

"Hang on now. Let's tackle one thing at a time, if that's all right with you."

She seemed to back down and lower her defenses, just a little, enough so that Sam had a moment to figure out where to go next. The fact that he was an experienced chef was the definite truth. From there, he'd have to be careful. He wouldn't outright lie to her, but he couldn't come out with the full reason for his presence there, either. He would figure out a way to bring up his daughter, but for now, he seized the opportunity before him.

He had a way in, and it might be a good approach to find out more about his kid. He'd have to take his chances. He could always quit and head out of town if things didn't work out, or if the PI's info had somehow been wrong. But he knew when a bone had been thrown in his direction, and he wasn't about to toss it aside.

"I have no formal training, but I assure you, I'm qualified. I know my way around a kitchen and I own a few restaurants here and there. I can get paperwork to you soon enough, but if you don't mind my saying so, it looks like you've got a little emergency here that needs taking care of before we talk official documents. I'll help you out now, free of charge, and if you like my cooking, and if the customers leave satisfied with the food, then maybe you'll consider giving me the job on a more permanent basis." Sam held out his hand, offering a deal that could benefit them both.

Lucy narrowed her eyes, staring him up and down. Skepticism—and he didn't blame her for it—was written all over her face, but she accepted his hand. Warmth rushed through his skin at her touch as though he'd jumped into a sunbaked river. Sam saw a flash of something in her eyes, and he knew she'd felt it too, but it passed just as quickly.

"I don't think I've said yet, but I'm Lucy. Lucy Monroe."

Sam gently took back his hand and crossed his fingers that she'd buy in to his offer. He knew he could prove himself in the kitchen, and doing so was a start to proving himself to the town, where he hoped to find his daughter.

"All right. You fix this mess and we'll talk," she said, glancing nervously toward the door as she pushed her glasses farther onto her nose.

The motion was endearing, and, even though he'd never dated a girl like her, Lucy was undeniably adorable in her giant, grape-colored glasses. Still, he couldn't keep himself from wondering what she would look like if he took them off.

"Great," Sam said, a sigh of relief escaping his lungs as he pushed away the scene he'd begun to imagine against his will. He was surprised at how good her mild approval felt, but he didn't have time to dwell on that now. He had a lot of work ahead of him if he was going to convince her to let him stay.

"Don't get carried away yet, Sam," Lucy said, holding up her palm. "I make no promises. Just… cook the lunch," she said, waving him away, "and we'll go from there."

Sam nodded and took off his suit jacket to begin rolling up his sleeves. Lucy showed him where the aprons were, observing him suspiciously the whole time as if already regretting her decision. He could tell she wouldn't be easy to win over. Something about her indicated it would take a lot of hard work and dedication to get her to trust him. And, though Lucy's last name was the same as Jennifer's, he still didn't know Lucy's exact relationship to his daughter. He still had a lot to figure out. But he'd been given a lucky shot, and he planned on taking it.

Tessa and Lucy watched in amazement as Sam prepared turkey and provolone sandwiches, faster than either of them could believe. But they weren't just any turkey and cheese stacks. He scoured the pantry as if he belonged in that kitchen, pulling out items as if he'd worked there his entire life, and chucked pine nuts, olive oil and basil into the food processor to whip up a pesto sauce to spread on the bread. It looked and smelled amazing. Lucy ate in the café often since it was convenient and inexpensive, and Axel's dishes had been delightful in a comforting sort of way, but Sam's style was more adventurous and a little more daring than anyone the Lonestar had ever hired before.

Lucy wondered if maybe he would prove to be a good change.

Ticket and tour sales were suffering lately. It seemed families and schools weren't spending as much on educational vacations and field trips, at least not to the observatory. Despite some steady funding from the university, which had seen some scary cutbacks in the past few years, they needed the revenue from tourists to cover employee salaries and up-to-date equipment. Lucy and Dr. Blake had already spent agonizing hours, scaling down as much as they could without actually letting anyone go, which was something Lucy all but outright refused to do. If she didn't have Shiloh to provide for, she would give up her job before making anyone redundant. She feared that would become necessary at some point, but she kept hoping she could push that day further and further into the future until things got better and she could just forget about it altogether. Maybe hiring someone like Sam was a good idea. At least they could give him a try and see how visitors responded. Maybe they could keep some of the old favorites on the menu and add some new dishes to test things out.

"Do you think he's legit?" Lucy asked Tessa, who had cleaned up several pie pans while Sam worked, and had come to stand at Lucy's side, blatantly enjoying the sight of their new company.

"What?" Tessa asked, forcing her eyes away from the new guy with concentrated effort.

Lucy rolled her eyes.

"I said, do you think he's legit? Do you think he's really a chef?"

"I just think he's pretty," Tessa said, resting her elbows on the table with her chin in her hands.

Lucy jabbed her friend in the side, but stopped short of disagreeing. She wasn't blind, after all.

"Come on. I just let a total stranger take over the kitchen, which I'm indirectly responsible for thanks to Axel the ass, and all you can think about is how he looks in that suit." Even as she spoke, Lucy knew she was just voicing her own thoughts. Apparently Tess caught on.

"Hey, sister. I said nothing about that suit. I'm just appreciating the scenery. It's nice to see a man dressed up, rather than the rest of the scientists in their twenty-year-old khakis and plaid." Her eyes gleamed. Tessa teased them, but Lucy knew her best friend loved the geniuses just as much as she did. "Besides, you should have seen the way he was ogling you earlier. That man couldn't pull his eyes away, and, you know I love you and all, but you're a mess today, so he must have some real interest."

Lucy shook her head, used to her friend's playfulness, and it was Tessa's turn to roll her eyes before pointing a thumb in Sam's direction.

"Anyway, what's the worst that could happen? We've been watching him the whole time. The dude washed his hands. And maybe he'll be able to calm the starving masses outside the door. As far as I can see, he looks like he's got everything under control."

"What do you reckon he's doing here, though? He's a little too timely, don't you think?"

"Maybe applying for Axel's job, like he said. He's a handsome stranger in Peach Leaf, Luce. We could use a little mystery around here, so don't be so quick to kill it."

"But I didn't post the position yet. I haven't had time," Lucy said.

Tessa raised her palms in exasperation.

"I don't know what you want me to tell you, sweetheart. Maybe he's an angel dropped right out of the dadgum sky," Tessa said, her face filled with more conviction than Lucy was comfortable with, considering the woman's ridiculous suggestion.

Lucy didn't believe in angels, or miracles, or chance, or luck. She believed in what she knew, in what she could see and touch and quantify. She believed in hard data and facts. Although something inside her told her that Sam Haynes was okay. He didn't seem like an ax murderer, and he dressed decently and had showered at least. Not that Lucy was an expert on appearances, but he seemed all right. And there were those sandwiches and cookies. So far, she had no valid reason not to give him a shot.

She would consider this an experiment, and, if it didn't work out, she'd start with a posting in the *Peach Leaf Gazette.* Jobs were in short supply in their small town, and there were a lot of folks looking for work. If she couldn't find a trained chef to take over full-time, she was sure someone could be taught to manage breakfast, at least.

But then, who would teach that person?

Lucy hung her head.

She really didn't have much of a choice at the moment. Sam looked better and better for the job as she weighed her limited alternatives and came up with a whole load of nothing.

Tessa was right. Not that Lucy would voice as much.

"I suppose he deserves a chance. But, if this plan doesn't work out, I'm coming at you first."

"The only reason you'll come to me is to thank me," Tessa said, crossing her arms with an air of confidence and giving Lucy a fake angry look, complete with her tongue stuck out.

Sometimes it was as if not a moment had passed, and they were still in second grade, with shy, bookish Lucy holding up walls at school dances while Tessa partied the nights away, both of them carrying bruises inside that no one else could see.

With the exception of a few minor details, not much had altered. It was just one of the many ups and downs of living the whole of one's life in the same small town.

Chapter Two

Lucy was rarely wrong, and when she was, she hated the feeling more than almost any other. But boy, was she this time.

"All right, so this worked out," Lucy said, a couple of hours after Sam had arrived, as she and Tessa rested in the dining room while he finished up in the kitchen. "That doesn't mean he's sticking around. It could just be beginner's luck."

"Come on, Luce, I know you don't believe in luck any more than you believe in love," Tessa said.

Not this conversation again, Lucy thought.

"I believe in *love*," she said, emphasizing the word, "just not *romance*. There's a huge difference." She continued quickly before Tessa could bring up her usual objections to Lucy's theory. "Anyway, sometimes experiments have false positives, and that just tells me we need to figure out what's going on here. We need more data before we'll be able to draw any authentic conclusions."

"Lu, honey, Sam is not one of your science experiments. He's a real person. And I don't need to point out that he's an especially attractive one."

Tessa raised her eyebrows up and down several times and Lucy couldn't help but giggle. To some extent, Tessa was right. But Lucy trusted only one thing in life, and that was science.

Sure, Sam had shown up at the exact moment they'd needed him—that *she'd* needed him—and sure, he'd cooked gorgeous sandwiches and had somehow pulled a delicious cookie recipe out of thin air and brought it to life. Sure, the salad he'd made her and Tess for lunch after they'd served all the visitors was possibly the most delicious thing she'd ever eaten—despite her general hatred of salads—but that didn't mean he was the right man for the job. Although, at the moment, she was having a really hard time coming up with reasons to support the contrary conclusion.

"I guess he did sort of save my butt, huh?" Lucy said, glad she'd made the wrong call. Tessa made no effort to hide her victory.

"He did way more than that. He saved the observatory money," Tessa added. "Can you imagine what would have happened if all of those people went back to Austin and told everyone they knew that the Lone-star Café had no food?"

Lucy didn't need to answer. They were both aware of the exponential damage that could be caused by a single customer's bad experience.

"I guess he can stick around for another day or so. We'll see how well he does planning a menu for tomorrow, and if he doesn't run off with the company credit card when I send him for groceries, maybe we can let him stay."

Tessa nodded in agreement.

Sam finished washing his hands and came out of the propped-open kitchen door to join them at their table in the dining room. His hair stuck out all over and he was covered in various food messes, but still, the man was gorgeous.

"So," he said, searching Lucy's face with what looked like a mix of hopefulness and apprehension, "do I get the job?"

"Not so fast, Mr. Haynes," Lucy answered. "I still know nothing about you. And I'll need some form of ID to give to Human Resources if you're staying." Lucy held up an authoritative forefinger. "Notice I said *if*."

Sam grinned and something stirred deep in Lucy's chest. He really was beyond appealing, scientifically speaking. His face was symmetrical with a perfectly proportioned nose and a strong, angular jaw. His eyes were the soft golden shade of fresh caramel, and his collar-skimming sandy hair picked up the late-afternoon sunlight streaming through the windows of the café. He stretched long arms across the table easily, as if he was completely comfortable here, despite his very recent arrival, and Lucy couldn't help but notice the shoulder muscles flexing under his crisp white dress shirt.

Since when did she notice things like that about a man?

She was Lucy Monroe, quiet, hardworking wallflower, just as she had always been.

She was happy here at the observatory, but she'd long ago given up on any thoughts of romance, or men in general. The guys at the observatory were much too absorbed in their work, and the married ones, well, Lucy sometimes had difficulty figuring out how they'd got that way in the first place, as clueless as some of them were about the opposite sex. They certainly never noticed her for anything other than her interest in the field of astronomy. Even though she hadn't finished school, she loved to hear their theories and any updates in their research. In a way, she lived vicariously through them—they were a connection to what she might have been.

But dating any of those guys? No way, and part of her liked it that way. The status quo kept her from having to admit to herself that she was afraid of anything resembling a relationship. She had become involved with a few guys in the past, and things with Jeremy had been serious. When that part of her life hadn't worked out, she'd finally paid due attention to the glaring signals that she just wasn't cut out for romance, and she'd given up trying.

Besides, she didn't have time for that sort of thing. She had her management work—more than any one human could possibly ever finish—and she had Shiloh, whom she loved more than anything else in the world, but who required more time and attention than other kids her age, or at least Lucy thought so.

Though lately, Shiloh had been resisting anything to do with her aunt, pushing Lucy away whenever she tried to talk to the girl she considered her own daughter. It was hurtful sometimes, Lucy had to admit, but she only wanted what was best for her niece; she'd dedicated her life to making a decent living and to providing the best she could for the girl. Parenting was sometimes a thankless job, and it didn't matter that Lucy hadn't chosen the position for herself. She was the only true parent Shiloh had, and Shiloh was Lucy's whole world now. She would do anything to make her niece happy—a wish that sometimes seemed as far off as the moon.

"Got it. *If* I'm hired," Sam said, breaking the silence and raising his hands in surrender, his thick voice teasing. His smile widened and small creases formed near his brown eyes. Lucy felt her face warm and she had to look away, uncomfortable with his attention. She knew he only wanted the job, and was probably just trying to charm his way into it, but all the same she felt as if she was the only girl in the room when he looked at her across the table.

Usually, when Tessa was in the room, it was pretty hard to feel that way. Her friend had been a cheerleader in school, and even though she was gorgeous, she'd latched on to Lucy the first day of second grade and had never let go, despite the differences in their social statuses. It was only one of the many things Lucy loved about her sweet best friend. But sometimes, she had to admit, being around pretty Tess brought her straight back to their school days, when Lucy felt inadequate despite her history of perfect grades and the commendations she'd received before she'd been forced to give up her scholarship at the university to take care of Shiloh.

Shiloh. Lucy checked her watch and stood up from the table. She needed to meet her niece at the bus stop soon.

"I'm sorry to cut this short, Mr. Haynes—Sam—but I have to head out and meet my niece. Would it be possible for you to meet me here in the morning? I can get James to show you the ropes for breakfast. He's the dishwasher for the early shift, but he usually puts out a small spread for morning visitors and for the volunteer docents and other employees—nothing fancy or complicated. Muffins and fruit and coffee—that sort of thing. Then, later, if you decide you'd like to stick around a bit, we can talk about working out a menu and deal with the shopping. I hate to do it, but we may have to close the café if we can't work something out. And I can't thank you enough for your help today." Lucy met Sam's eyes and noticed their hazelnut color for the hundredth time since they'd met only a short while earlier. It was silly, really, how much trouble she had focusing with him around.

"Don't mention it again," Sam said, that warm smile causing both his face, and Lucy's heart, to light up. "I'm glad I could help. And of course, I'd be happy to help with breakfast in the morning. Should I arrive at seven? I noticed the café opens at nine."

It was almost too good to be true. Lucy didn't trust those kinds of things, but did she really have another choice at this point?

The answer was obvious. "Seven is good," she said, running a hand through her bangs, which likely only caused further frizzy disarray.

"Let me walk you to wherever you're heading, Ms. Monroe. I'd really like to see the grounds if you don't mind. Get more comfortable with the place."

Lucy hesitated. Shiloh would be happy to see she'd brought someone along with her; it seemed the nascent social butterfly was friendly with just about anyone but Lucy lately.

"All right, that's fine," she said, checking her watch again. "I've got a few minutes."

Sam held the back door open for her, and Lucy followed him out of the café, locking up behind her. Tessa mouthed goodbye from inside the window with a wave and a sneaky smile, which Lucy promptly ignored. Her friend headed back to the front desk, where she supposedly worked once in a while when she wasn't busy pestering Lucy.

She and Sam walked a few areas of the grounds, Lucy naming the telescopes for him. Bless him; he didn't seem bored by her explanations of the different mirror and dome sizes and how the giant instruments deciphered light from distant stars.

She stopped talking and looked at Sam, embarrassed. "I'm sorry if I'm going on and on. I just love this place. And I like to see other people show interest in space. We have so much to learn from the galaxies out there. There's a whole world beyond our own, and I just need to know as much as I can about it. I can't get enough."

Sam stopped and turned toward her, searching her eyes. For what, she didn't know.

"Am I rambling too much?" she asked, heat rising to her cheeks.

"Absolutely not," he said, his eyes reassuring. He seemed to be telling the truth from what Lucy could tell, which she admitted wasn't much. She wasn't used to interacting one-on-one with men who weren't employees at the observatory. And, though she loved the scientists, they were a different breed altogether—one she understood, at least, thanks to her dad. "It's nice to see a woman who's passionate about her work. I feel the same way about my own."

Lucy grinned, his compliment holding more weight than it should. "Did you always like to cook?" she asked, hoping to guide the conversation away from herself. She wasn't sure she could take much more of Sam's intense gaze on her. It felt as if he could see straight through her skin and bones and right down to her rapidly beating heart.

An emotion that Lucy couldn't identify crossed Sam's face, before passing just as quickly as he looked away, and she found herself wanting to ask him what he'd just been thinking of. She reminded herself that she barely knew him. She didn't trust the way she was able to talk to him so openly, and the way she felt almost as if they'd known each other for ages.

She needed to focus on the facts.

Guys like Sam didn't go for girls like Lucy.

It was that way in high school, and that way still. Some things in life didn't change. She'd learned to live with that and most of the time she was pretty happy with the way things were—or at least...comfortable. She refused to get her hopes up just to have them smashed back down.

"Yes, I came to love cooking, once I figured it out," Sam answered.

"What do you mean?"

"Well, growing up, I always thought that you had

to have a recipe, and that's just not my style. I got a job as a sous-chef, by chance really, and once I started practicing and playing with food, so to speak, I realized that it's more of an art than a science, and I was able to put my own spin on things. I started creating my own dishes and experimenting with different ingredients just to see what I could come up with. That's when I realized that cooking is actually a lot of fun. It can be a way to express yourself just like any other art form," Sam said, his eyes lighting up as he talked about his work.

Lucy understood what he meant about experimenting with things, but expressing herself was another animal altogether, for which she shared no familiarity.

"So did you start the job straight out of high school?"

"Actually, no. I worked in restaurants while I went to college. I studied anthropology, of all things. Mostly because I couldn't decide what else to concentrate on and, well, what's more interesting than people? So I settled on that."

Lucy could list many things more interesting to her than people. She preferred her stars and planets. Their mathematically calculable rules and patterns made more sense to her than those of human beings, but she decided to keep that to herself. The last thing she wanted to do was offend Sam.

"Did you enjoy it?"

Sam laughed and shook his head.

"The school part, no, not really. I was more of a goof-off. I didn't spend a whole lot of time in class."

"Ah, I know the type," Lucy said. She'd known plenty of guys like him, had been made fun of by more than a few, and she'd formed an opinion of them early on.

"What do you mean?"

"You know, I just mean, well, it's just that—" Lucy tugged at her glasses, suddenly nervous and tongue-tied "—guys like you…" She stopped talking before she said something off-putting.

"Guys like me?" Sam abruptly stopped walking and faced her. "I just met you, Ms. Monroe, and, forgive me, but you don't know enough about me to be able to size me up and categorize me with other men you've known."

He was right, and Lucy blushed at his surprisingly blunt correction. She didn't know what to say so she kept silent and just kept walking.

Sam caught up to her but he was quiet, and when she stole a glance his way, his brows were knitted and he seemed lost in his own thoughts. Lucy was surprised at how strong the urge was for her to ask what he was thinking, but she reminded herself that it wasn't any of her business. Still, the intensity she saw in the set of his jaw made her strangely sad, and she found herself wishing for something that would break the spell she'd unintentionally cast.

Thankfully, they had covered most of the grounds and were at the front entrance, where Shiloh's bus would drop her off. They were lucky the bus came all the way to the observatory, several miles from the outskirts of town. The school had made a special arrangement for Shiloh since Lucy was her only guardian and couldn't drive into town each day to pick up her niece. The bus driver was a sweet lady, who loved Shiloh, and Lucy was grateful she had someone she could trust to drive Shiloh home every day in her place. Shiloh hated the special treatment, as she hated all such things, and she didn't like being the last one off the bus when everyone else, even the kids who lived farther out of Peach Leaf, was already off by the time they reached her stop.

Sometimes Lucy didn't know what to do to please the child. She was twelve now—spunky—and had a mind of her own, and a mouth to go along with it; there were some days when Lucy wished her niece would return to being the kind darling she had been as a little girl. But she loved her so much and couldn't be angry with her for anything for very long. Lucy just hoped Shiloh's habit of shutting out her aunt was a phase she'd get through soon.

Dust billowed around them as the bus lumbered to a stop. Lucy waved at Mrs. Stevens and waited for the driver to unfasten Shiloh's wheelchair and lift her down. She turned and saw Sam's face as he realized that Shiloh wasn't going to walk out of the bus on her own two legs.

Lucy was accustomed to people catching themselves staring when they saw a child in a wheelchair. It wasn't that they meant any harm—it was just a human reaction to someone who was different than most. But there was something odd and unusually powerful about the way Sam's mouth straightened, and his eyes clouded. Surely the man had seen a kid with a disability like Shiloh's before.

"Is something wrong?" Lucy asked. She hoped Sam would be honest. People usually tried to skirt around the subject, but she'd found she preferred if they asked questions or talked about what they felt, rather than try to ignore what anyone could see with their own two eyes.

"No, no, nothing at all," Sam said, shaking his head. He turned to grin at her and the strange, concentrated expression she'd seen a moment ago was gone. "It's just that I didn't know that your niece used a wheelchair to get around. You didn't say anything about it."

Lucy searched his eyes.

"Of course, you didn't have reason to," Sam said, understanding the question in her features. He turned and smiled as Mrs. Stevens pushed the lever to lower Shiloh down from the bus. Shiloh raised both hands as though she were on a roller coaster and Lucy melted at the old inside joke they shared, glad there was a trace of the sweet little girl in there somewhere.

"Who's this dude?" Shiloh asked, sizing up Sam.

Shiloh had a knack for saying exactly what she was thinking, just like her mom, Jennifer—Lucy's sister. People had always joked that neither mom nor daughter had been born with a filter.

"Well, hello to you, too, sweetheart," Lucy said, brushing a strand of hair out of Shiloh's eyes, before her hand was promptly swatted away, just as she'd suspected it would be.

"Shiloh, meet Sam, our new…trial chef."

Shiloh stared up at Sam, hooding her eyes with her hand. "Hi, Sam," Shiloh said, her tone completely unreadable.

Sometimes Lucy understood her niece, and other times she couldn't remember ever having been as nonchalant about everything as Shiloh was, though she knew most of that was just Shiloh trying to hide any kind of emotion, like a normal teenager.

"Hi, there." He grinned and held out a hand, not in the slightest fazed by her lack of care at his presence. "I have to say, that's a pretty sweet ride."

Shiloh cracked a genuine smile, the first Lucy had seen in a long time. It was a nice sight. Maybe Sam would earn his place after all.

"So," Sam continued. "How long have you had it?"

Shiloh stared at him, skepticism suddenly taking over.

Lucy bristled, bracing herself for whatever words might come out of her niece, though she was glad that Shiloh spoke her mind most of the time. Lucy had spent plenty of her own time keeping her words to herself at Shiloh's age, and it hadn't necessarily served her well. She would have loved to have Shiloh's confidence when she'd been young—heck, she could use a dose of it now.

A fierce need to protect Shiloh from the world was in her blood, despite the fact she hadn't brought her niece into the world herself. Lucy loved Shiloh as though she had carried her in her own womb, and part of that love—that parental love—she guessed, was constant worry.

Sam's heart fell to the bottom of his stomach with such force that he was surprised he couldn't actually hear a thud. He kept his expression as neutral as possible as he tried to process everything in front of him.

There was no mistaking that this girl, Shiloh, was his daughter.

She didn't look like him at all. She took after her mother and Lucy. The same copper hair, except wavy rather than curly, the same eyes, and the same freckles, like fairy dust across the bridge of her nose and cheeks. But all the same, he knew she was his as sure as he knew his own name.

Shiloh looked at Lucy, her expression insecure, and then back to Sam.

"Do you mean how long have I had this specific chair? Or how long have I been…like this?" She pointed at her legs.

Sam swallowed. He wasn't sure which he meant, actually. He wanted to know every single thing about her down to the tiniest detail, and it didn't matter where she started—as long as she did.

"Both," he said, deciding that the best way to navigate the new waters he found himself in was to just be honest.

Shiloh studied him and shrugged her shoulders, seeming to decide that this was okay with her.

"Well, I got this chair last year from Dr. Blake for Christmas," she said, pointing out the bumper stickers with the names of popular bands she had stuck all over the back. "But, I've been like this—" she pointed down at her legs again "—for a long time."

Shiloh tossed her long strawberry hair over her shoulder. Sam was impressed at her openness, and, though he knew he had no right to be, he was proud of her confidence and straightforward answer. "Ever since the accident," she continued, before Lucy interrupted.

"So how was school today, Shi?" Lucy asked, obviously eager to change the subject.

Shiloh looked up at Sam as though he and she were in cahoots.

"She means, how was the math test?" she said,

narrowing her eyes at Sam and tossing up her hands. “Math isn’t so good to me.”

“She can do anything she wants,” Lucy interjected, crossing her arms. “She just doesn’t apply herself in math because she doesn’t like it. But sometimes in life, we have to work hard at things, even if we don’t like them. Right, Shi?”

Shiloh rolled her eyes and tossed her head back with much dramatic flair, causing Sam to giggle. “Right, right, right,” she said, drawing out the words as though to illustrate her boredom with the whole concept.

“So you’re terrible at it, then?” Sam asked, smiling at Shiloh. Lucy’s mouth shot open and she lowered her eyebrows, as if offended on behalf of her niece, but Shiloh just laughed.

“He’s not wrong, Aunt Lu,” she said.

Lucy moved behind her niece’s wheelchair to push her home, but Shiloh’s fingers moved quickly over the controls and she zoomed over to Sam’s side, leaving Lucy behind in the cloud of dust in her wake.

“Just like me,” Sam said, grinning down at her.

Just like her father.

A million thoughts rushed through his mind, so he concentrated on the simple act of putting one foot in front of the other, to keep the surge of emotion from drowning him.

His daughter was beautiful, as her mother had

been the last time he'd seen her all those years ago. And like her aunt.

He made a mental note to call the PI later, thank the man for his services and close out their contract. Sam had all the information he needed to take things from here. He would let his head New York chef, Jack, know that he wouldn't be returning to the restaurant for a while, and to call if anything major came up. The other restaurants in LA and Seattle were doing great, and Sam needed only to fly in for occasional visits. He trusted his assistant could manage the rest with no trouble, freeing Sam to move to Peach Leaf temporarily.

He watched as his little girl drove ahead of him and Lucy, making figure eights in the dust, seemingly unfazed by her limitations.

He had questions, of course—thousands of them. But to his surprise, he was only mildly interested to know more about the accident she'd mentioned, the event she'd endured without him by her side. Instead of rage at the unknown entity responsible for her pain, Sam wanted to know more about Shiloh as she was now. He knew she wasn't a fan of math, so then what was her favorite subject at school? What did she love to do in her spare time? What hopes and dreams filled her young mind as she slept through the night?

Did she know anything about her absent father? Did she want to? Or was her life more peaceful without an explanation for the missing man?

It would kill him if she thought she wasn't wanted.

No.

Even though it would complicate her world, the girl deserved to know that her dad cared for her, that he hadn't purposefully abandoned her and that he would do anything in the world for her now that he knew she existed.

Once she had that knowledge, it would be up to her to decide what to do with it. He would take whatever chance he had to spend time with both Shiloh and her aunt, and when the right moment came—and he hoped he would recognize it—he would speak to Lucy.

It was astounding to think how his world had turned upside down with the few words Jennifer had spoken to him over the scratchy phone connection a month ago, though he regretted nothing. He had never planned on becoming a father, but with the way he'd behaved as a young man, he shouldn't be surprised that it was a possibility. When Jennifer had called, he'd vaguely recalled a broken condom incident that he had dismissed in the heat of the moment. He'd realized after how stupid he had been and had never made the same mistake again.

But the result of what he'd considered a mistake at the time, though tremendous and frightening, was… perfect, and the onslaught of new, pure love coursing through his veins at the sight of his daughter was proof that he'd done the right thing by taking a risk in coming to find her.

The road ahead would most certainly be bumpy, but there was nothing more important than her left for Sam back in New York. Now there was only here. Only his Shiloh.

Chapter Three

Thor was snoozing on the porch when Lucy and Shiloh got home that afternoon. At the sound of the gate opening at the end of the short driveway, the mutt dashed across the lawn toward them, ears flopping, barking joyfully the whole way. He bounded into Shiloh's lap and she let out a happy squeal as he began to sniff her face. Despite many sessions with a trainer since he'd wandered onto their property as a skinny puppy, about six years before, their dog repeated the same routine day after day, unable to contain his joy when he saw his girl. Lucy laughed and rubbed behind his ears. He tossed her a quick lick before turning back to his true love, and they all made their way into the small home where Lucy had been raised.

The house had been part of the deal when her dad agreed to run the observatory. When her mother had left, and after her father died, Lucy hadn't been able to part with it. The little red brick home had grown shabby with age and it needed some work, but the fact that she didn't have a mortgage made it possible for Lucy to stretch her salary further than it would otherwise. And even though, once her parents' marriage had started to fall apart, many of her childhood years there had been less than pleasant, for some reason she couldn't let go. The house wasn't the reason her parents had fallen out of love, and it wasn't the reason her mother had left the three of them so long ago.

When the observatory board had offered it to Lucy in her dad's place, she had done the best she could with what she had to make it her own, adding pretty curtains and paint, and now she couldn't imagine living anywhere else. There were things, though, that she would have to address sooner rather than later. Like the aging boards of Shiloh's wheelchair ramp. Tessa's brother, Andy, had built the ramp shortly after the accident, with more heart than skill, and Lucy didn't have it in her to tell Andy about its increasingly decrepit state; she'd made Tess promise to keep mum about it as well, despite her friend's protest. It was Lucy's responsibility. She'd made a few calls to find a carpenter, but the quotes offered had all been too expensive.

There always seemed to be something pressing on her time though, and right now that thing was Shiloh's sudden burning desire to try out for the Peach Leaf Junior High basketball team, which terrified and thrilled Lucy in equal parts.

She stopped at the bottom of the stone steps leading to the front porch and bent to lift her niece out of the chair. It was a routine they'd grown used to in the absence of a functioning ramp, but which lately had begun to embarrass Shiloh. And Lucy had to admit that it wouldn't be long before her little girl would grow into a young woman, with a need for more independence, and there wouldn't always be someone to carry her inside if she got home and Lucy wasn't there.

"All right, sweet girl. Let's try to get that homework out of the way before dinner."

Shiloh groaned in the melodramatic way that only preteens and teens could master. Lucy just shook her head. Shiloh would complain the whole time, but she would do her homework, and for that, Lucy was thankful. She didn't know what she would do if she'd been responsible for a wild child like Jennifer. Shiloh had her faults like any other person, and she certainly knew how to put up a fuss, but thank the stars, she was a good kid. Her mother had always struggled with the idea of being responsible for a child, and Jennifer had never opened up to Lucy about who the father was. It was a detail—like so many others—that Jennifer had chosen not to share with her sister. Much to Lucy's disappointment, the two of them hadn't got along past middle school, and when Jennifer left for college and dropped out halfway through her freshman year, no one in town had been surprised. Lucy was the only one who'd ever believed Jennifer was capable of much more, but now those hopes and dreams belonged to Shiloh.

They went inside and Shiloh headed toward the living room. Before she even heard the TV click on, Lucy reminded Shiloh that she had to finish her homework first before she could watch television.

"I wasn't going to watch TV," Shiloh shouted, but Lucy wasn't buying it.

"Don't lie to me, kiddo," Lucy said, and Shiloh let out a dramatic sigh.

"All right," she yelled back, returning to the kitchen where Lucy was standing in front of the refrigerator, trying to decide what to make for dinner. It was a daily battle to figure out what to feed the two of them every evening, and Lucy knew she should erase the overused Peach Leaf Pizza number from her speed dial. They were a few miles out of town, but it was hard to resist ordering something quick when she'd had a long day at work.

She mulled over the sad-looking contents of the freezer, ticking off an ambitious grocery list in her head, and suddenly thought of Sam. How awesome would it be to have someone like him living in her home?

Lucy looked up at the ceiling, remembering the incredible taste of the sandwiches he'd whipped up at the last minute. She was surrounded on a daily basis by men with genius IQs, but she doubted a single one of them could make a meal like the one she'd had for lunch. What kind of man knew how to cook that way, and also looked like *that*? If Sam turned out to also be a decent guy, Lucy would have to stick him to see if real blood ran through his veins.

She closed the fridge and tried the pantry instead, sighing to herself. She had no business thinking about Sam Haynes, mystery man, who currently occupied her office at the museum. She shook her head. How stupid it had been of her to allow Tessa to offer him her office couch for the night when he found out the B and B wouldn't have his room available until the next morning. Tessa thought it probably had something to do with Mrs. Frederickson's increasingly unreliable memory. The sweet elderly woman had recently begun leaving her home in little more than her underwear, and her neighbors had got used to quietly returning her home. But truth be told, Lucy was sort of relieved—she'd been more than a little worried that if Sam left the grounds, he wouldn't come back, on account of the craziness he'd walked into at the kitchen earlier.

After Sam had parted from her and Shiloh to head back to his truck, Lucy had called Tessa to see if Sam had left. Tessa said he'd returned to the front desk and told her the situation, and Tess had listened in as he'd made call after call on his cell to other B and Bs and inns in town, and not a single one of them had an available room—not really surprising for spring in Peach Leaf. She'd asked Tessa for advice on what to do and her friend had suggested that Lucy offer him the extra room in her house.

Not a chance.

Aside from her lapse in judgment that day, she wasn't stupid, and she had a child to look after. After all, Sam had popped into town out of the blue, and so far had not really adequately explained his reason for doing so, which Lucy made a mental note to force from him tomorrow.

So her office had seemed like the only choice until the room he booked was ready. He'd grabbed his bag and taken a quick shower in the staff locker room, and was ready to call it a night. There was a cozy old plaid couch in Lucy's office, left over from the nights her father had spent there when he'd been neck-deep in his research, or, as Lucy had suspected in later years, when he and her mother had been unable to remain in the same house.

Shiloh turned the corner and joined Lucy in the kitchen.

"Nothing good to eat, huh, Aunt Lu?"

Lucy turned to Shiloh. "Are you surprised?"

"What do you think?"

"I'm sorry, love. You know I hate making this decision every day."

"And I hate that no matter what you pick, I always have to eat vegetables and you don't."

"That is so not true! I eat vegetables…sometimes."

Shiloh stared at Lucy as her aunt's blatant lie hovered in the air.

"Once a week. Okay. Once a month," Lucy admitted. "I eat vegetables at least once a month. Besides, I drink plenty of V8 and I take multivitamins."

"Ha. That's more like it," Shiloh blurted out, pointing an accusatory finger. "I'm surprised you don't have scurvy."

They both burst into giggles and Thor rushed over to see what in the world had got into them, before they settled back down. In the quiet moment that followed, Lucy noticed Shiloh nibbling on her nails—a habit she shared with Jennifer, and which made Lucy's skin crawl, thinking about the insane amount of germs Shiloh was absentmindedly shoveling into her mouth.

"Stop, honey. That's gross," Lucy said, swatting at Shiloh's hand. "What's bothering you anyway? Did something happen at school?"

Shiloh took her nail out of her mouth.

"Well, yeah, Aunt Lu. Lots of things happened at school."

"Come on, Shi, you know what I mean. What's wrong?"

Shiloh hesitated before speaking, and Lucy tried not to dwell on the idea that her niece might be deciding what she should and should not reveal to her aunt, but Lucy forced herself not to push too hard. Experience had shown that Shiloh would be more open if Lucy didn't press her, and she desperately wanted to know if something was bothering the girl.

"Nothing, really. It's just that there's this thing coming up, and I'm trying to figure out if I should go or not," Shiloh said, studying a ragged fingernail.

"What kind of thing?" Lucy asked, treading lightly. She had a feeling she knew what was coming, and she wasn't sure what help she was possibly qualified to offer.

She drew in a steadying breath. Lucy would not project her own past, her own experiences, on Shiloh. She wouldn't.

"It's a dance, isn't it?" Lucy asked, hoping she'd injected enough positivity into her tone for her niece not to notice the true sentiment underneath her words. But Shiloh's face fell, and Lucy knew she'd failed.

"I know it's not something you care about," Shiloh said, scratching at an invisible spot on her jeans, not meeting Lucy's eyes. The girl picked up on her aunt's emotions as if she could sense them. So much like her mother.

Lucy and Jennifer had been close once, as kids. Jennifer, one year her sister's senior, had let Lucy climb into her bed on rare stormy nights when they were both little and told her stories. She would drag Lucy away from her books when Jennifer claimed the reading had gone on long enough. They'd blasted music and she'd forced Lucy to dance with her until they both collapsed to the floor from laughter and exhaustion. She'd brought out another part of Lucy—the one that wasn't afraid of what other people thought. With Jennifer by her side, she'd forgotten her biggest fears. The pressure from her dad to get perfect grades, countered by her mother's insistence that she get contacts, change her hair and get out more, so she could be more popular.

Like Jennifer.

Lucy had sworn—since that day Jennifer had shown up on the porch where they'd grown up, tiny wriggling bundle in her arms, to say that she was sorry but she just couldn't do it—that Shiloh would never feel compelled to be anyone other than herself.

Guilt balled up in her stomach, thinking back to the conversation she'd had with her niece earlier about the math quiz, and Lucy made a mental note to leave well enough alone next time. Shiloh was passing all of her classes, and maybe that should be enough. Parenting was just a challenge—a constant series of actions, results and reassessment for the next time. Just like her work, in many ways, but with infinitely higher stakes.

"If it's something you care about, then I care about it, too," Lucy said, measuring her words carefully.

Shiloh looked down again and scratched under Thor's chin. The dog's eyes closed and Lucy smiled at his un-self-conscious adoration. If only she could find a guy as loyal and loving as their four-legged man of the house.

Lucy pulled cereal out of the pantry, along with two bowls and spoons, and set everything on the table. She would cook a real dinner, complete with meat, healthy carbs, and yes, the obligatory vegetable.

Tomorrow.

Shiloh didn't say anything about the meal. They both knew how to pick their battles.

"So," Lucy said, as casually as she could muster, "what's bothering you about the dance, then?"

Shiloh raised her eyes to meet Lucy's, and then moved to the table. Lucy poured milk for her niece and joined her to eat. Shiloh took a bite and chewed for a long moment, a mix of emotions battling in her eyes.

"I'm not sure if I should go or not."

Lucy didn't respond, only nodded and took a bite of her own cereal.

She swallowed. "Well, do you want to go or not?"

she asked, hoping she'd successfully masked the apprehension she felt.

"Yeah. I think so," Shiloh said slowly, drawing out the words as if working to finalize her decision. "Yeah, I do." Her answer was firmer this time, and her eyes flashed with barely guarded excitement. She took a bite of cereal, covering her budding smile.

"Then what's the problem? If you want to go… then, go."

Shiloh put down the spoon and swallowed, her expression completely flat, the joy from only seconds ago mysteriously vanished.

Lucy knew that look, and she knew instinctively that she was at fault for putting it there, though she couldn't say how. She quickly retraced her steps, coming up blank, and looked helplessly at her niece. Shiloh only shook her head with exasperation.

"God, Aunt Lu," she said through clenched teeth. "You're so dense sometimes, it's unbelievable."

"It was a simple question," Lucy said, putting down her spoon as her temper rose. She hated feeling so adrift and out of control amidst the tossing sea of Shiloh's preteen emotions.

"It's not simple at all, and you know it." Shiloh was on the verge of shouting now, and Lucy fought to keep from matching her volume.

"Shiloh, hon'," Lucy begged, eyes closed to calm herself. "Just tell me what's bugging you and we'll talk about it."

Shiloh's lips tightened into a thin line and she pushed her wheelchair back from the table. "Never mind," she grumbled, heading down the hallway to her room.

Just like that, Lucy had lost her again, her niece's approval as elusive and unpredictable as Texas rain. She'd learned a long time ago that it was best to wait to follow Shiloh, who needed time alone to cool off when she got upset. Later, Lucy would knock on the door and make sure homework had been done, teeth brushed, that her niece wasn't hungry and that she got into bed safely.

Lucy concentrated on what she understood and could control—scrubbing the dishes and opening the stack of mail she'd neglected for several days. As she flipped mindlessly through a catalog, she stopped on a page advertising men's shirts. She ran a finger along the sleeves in one of the pictures, imagining what it would be like to have a partner in all of this—someone to talk to and bounce ideas off when she couldn't figure out how to solve a problem—someone to carry a share of the burden alongside her.

There had been a time when she'd believed that such a man might exist, and she'd even given two years of her life to Jeremy, convinced he was that man. In the aftermath, when she realized what a colossal mistake she had made, she'd given up the notion that such dreams would ever be a reality for her. She'd dated a few times since then, mostly when

Tessa or other well-meaning but misguided neighbors and coworkers set her up with a string of brothers, cousins and nephews. Eventually she'd tired of the same old painfully awkward scenario. She'd chosen to leave the merry-go-round for good the last time one of those guys had taken a single look at Shiloh and suddenly decided that they weren't really ready to jump back into the dating pool, saying that it wasn't her, it was him.

She no longer believed that romantic love had a place in her life. She had learned to be content with the fact that she had a job, though a challenging one; she had a comfortable home she loved to return to at the end of each day; and she had her beautiful, smart, strong-willed girl. Even if she did sometimes long for more, it wasn't likely to show up on her doorstep. And that was just fine.

Lucy grinned and reached down to rub Thor's scruffy neck. Even he'd stayed behind with his second choice, intuiting that Shiloh needed her space.

"Smart boy," Lucy said. Thor thumped his tail against the floor and raised a paw, happy to have pleased someone.

Yep, Lucy thought. *Better to stick with a dog.*

Sam was restless and desperate for something to occupy his hands. He'd gone a little overboard on the breakfast spread the past two mornings, having shopped the day after he'd arrived for fresh fruit and ingredients for lemon-raspberry muffins, along with coffee from a little shop he'd found on Main Street. He'd scanned the pantry and noticed the shop's name on a near-empty bag, delighted at the discovery that the Lonestar purchased goods from a local place. The list of things he liked about the woman who managed it all grew longer each moment he spent near her.

He would have to watch that.

That list couldn't get any longer or he'd have a problem on his hands.

He'd come to Peach Leaf with one purpose, and he wouldn't allow anything to distract from it. And he especially would not get involved with the one person who might stand in the way of any chance of his building a relationship with his daughter. If he let himself get caught up in Lucy and it didn't work out, his daughter would be the one to suffer, and he would not allow that.

He'd expected the sister Jennifer spoke of to be married, with her own children perhaps. Certainly not the sunny-haired, evidently single beauty he'd discovered instead. He'd seen already that she was hardworking, fiercely independent, and very clearly adored her niece. Keeping the truth from such a woman—especially a woman whose physical beauty was such a distraction—would not be an easy task.

He shoved the grim thought aside and grinned, recalling that morning.

Lucy had taken one bite of a muffin and, crumbs

sticking to her cute, dimpled chin, had pronounced Sam hired. He had presented her with his driver's license and Social Security card, and the woman had seemed mostly satisfied that he hadn't yet killed anyone or stolen anything. They had made plans for him to go shopping the next day for supplies that weren't delivered on a preset weekly basis, but with the restaurant and museum closed early that afternoon for maintenance, Sam found himself with nothing to do. The restlessness had begun to bother him.

He'd had an idea that he ran by Tessa, and, without thinking any further on the subject, he'd made a decision and headed into town to pick up lumber and tools from the hardware store. The little town and its shop owners had charmed him, and he'd got a kick out of the fact that everything a local might require could be found with minimal effort on Main Street. Its appeal aside, a solution would have to be found for the town's disturbing lack of dining choices, should he end up staying. A person could only handle so much bratwurst, burgers and beer.

Sam pulled his rental truck up to the road just outside Lucy and Shiloh's gate, at the bottom of the hill Tessa had described. When he opened the unlocked latch, a large dog bounded up and sniffed Sam's hand before letting out several happy barks. His tail wagged ninety miles an hour.

"Some guard dog you are," Sam said, scratching behind the dog's ears, which earned him a permanent friend. Once he'd propped the gate wide, he opened his truck door and the dog jumped right in, settling his furry butt in the passenger seat as if he owned the place.

"Well, make yourself at home," Sam said, laughing as he buckled the seat belt over the dog's chest before snapping on his own.

He drove his new buddy up to the house and got out, letting the dog loose. Glad no one appeared to be home, Sam unloaded the boards and supplies he'd bought and set to work. Tessa had said Lucy would be in the office all afternoon, catching up, and Shiloh had gone to help out with a friend's children, so he planned on finishing before they returned.

He didn't want any resistance. The project was necessary and long past due. It was that simple. He knew he was stepping outside of his bounds since he'd only just met his daughter and her aunt, but he'd seen the two of them from the road the day before on his way into town, and he knew the finished product would be accepted on Shiloh's behalf.

Whether it should have or not, his heart had broken as he'd stood there watching Lucy lift his daughter out of her wheelchair to carry her inside, the girl's slim arms wrapped around the woman's neck. Lucy's body language had spoken her unbridled love and serenity in the action, and Sam had melted.

It should have been him carrying his daughter.

Regardless, even if she was annoyed at first, he was certain Lucy would appreciate the repairs.

Lucy.

The woman couldn't be over thirty and yet she had the inner soft nature of someone far older, as though she had experienced every brand of pain and hardship the world had to offer and resigned herself to it. What he couldn't tell, and what tugged at him as he began measuring the wood, making marks with his carpenter pencil where to cut, was whether Lucy had experienced enough joy.

It shouldn't matter to me.

He sawed through the wood with the handsaw he preferred to an electric version. Thinking about her like that was selfish and thickheaded. The only thing that should matter was whether or not she could be convinced to let him spend time with his daughter.

He'd thought it would be easier somehow—that perhaps if Shiloh was being cared for by someone with a family of her own, that the help of a real parent might be, if not wholly welcome, then possibly some relief, financial or otherwise. He hadn't considered that she'd be living with an incredibly dedicated and, admittedly, alluring young woman whose presence had an intense, unwelcome effect on him.

Sam put the saw down to measure another piece of wood, working as fast as he could while maintaining precision. Soon enough he'd be done cutting the lumber, and he could begin to pound nails into boards.

Maybe the sweat and hard work in the Texas spring sun would remind him of the potential storm ahead, brought on by his sudden appearance in his daughter's life, and he'd forget the way his heart raced at the mere sight of Lucy Monroe.

Chapter Four

"What in the— "

Lucy pulled to a stop and grabbed her purse before stepping out of the car, squinting against the sun as a man she recognized as Sam set down a hammer and stood up, taking a few steps forward to greet her. His white T-shirt was damp with sweat and clung tightly to his skin as he stretched out his solid arms, temporarily distracting her from her surprise at his presence. Thor bounded up and licked at her hands with abandon until she gave in and knelt to pet him.

"I should have asked first, I know, but I got a little carried away," Sam said, running a hand through his hair in such a nervous way that Lucy had the bizarre urge to comfort *him*, even though he was the one who'd startled the tar out of *her*. He moved aside and pointed a thumb behind him and for the first time since pulling into the drive, she understood exactly what he'd done to her house.

Lucy scanned the new, fresh wood, the carpentry skill evident even from several feet away. She walked straight past Sam toward the front porch, unable to take her eyes off the sight before her. As she dropped her purse and bent to run her hands over the smooth, expertly polished wood, tears, sudden and wild, sprang to her eyes and she was powerless to stop them.

Oh my goodness.

"You built this?" she asked, turning back to Sam, forgetting to care that the emotion on her face must be as obvious as the Milky Way on a clear night.

"I did," he said, his voice warmer than the afternoon sun as he met her eyes. "I didn't mean to scare you, though. I planned to finish before you got home from work, but your dog here decided to help me, and well, things took a little more time than I thought they would." Sam held open palms out to his sides. "I hope you're not upset. I hope this is okay," he said, a hint of apprehension tingeing his words, even as he held her gaze with confidence.

Lucy choked out a laugh around the meteor lodged in her throat. "Yeah, Thor tends to involve himself in any project that goes on around here, whether his assistance is needed or not," she answered, suddenly embarrassed as she wiped at her tears with shaky hands and struggled for composure. Sam nodded, picking up the hammer, and Lucy watched, enchanted, as he drove in a couple of more nails and finished up by wiping away a few traces of sawdust.

Sunlight baked the wood's freshly sanded surface as Lucy studied Shiloh's beautiful new wheelchair ramp. She could have searched the entirety of Peach Leaf's Yellow Pages and not found a better carpenter—not to mention the materials and labor would have cost a small fortune. But when she turned around to thank him, instead of beaming with pride or waiting for praise, the craftsman responsible was loading tools into his truck as if nothing significant had happened. As if he hadn't just made Lucy's life a hundred times easier.

She retrieved her purse and slid it onto her shoulder, Thor following close as she picked up Sam's saw and a few stray rags, joining him at his truck. Sam took the supplies from her and deposited them in the bed of his truck. He jumped up to sit on the gate for a break and wiped his hands on his jeans, reaching down a hand to help Lucy do the same. She set her purse down and took the offered hand, the warmth from Sam's touch melting over her skin like hot maple syrup. It was like being a kid again, sitting in the back of a truck, swinging her legs over the edge. Sam leaned back, resting on his elbows, and they sat like that for several minutes, enjoying the end of a workday, the silence sweet and comfortable between them.

Lucy tucked her knees against her chest and studied the dirty green Chuck Taylor sneakers she'd traded her heels for after the observatory had closed for the day. When she finally turned, she found Sam contemplating her, his eyes calm but curious, as if trying to discern her thoughts. Lucy realized with sudden horror that she hadn't even thanked the man. His presence was so tranquil, so relaxing that she'd lost track of anything that had previously cluttered her mind. She hadn't felt any pressure to fill the air with words as she usually did when she met new people. In an odd way, it seemed as if she'd known Sam far longer than she had in reality.

"Thank you," she said quietly. A smile glowed in his eyes before it spread to his lips.

"You're very welcome. Do you like it?" he asked, his smile fading a little as he waited for her response.

Lucy coughed. "Do I like it?" she repeated. "I can't even—" she raised her palms up "—I don't even know how to…yes. Yes, I like it. Very much. It's amazing, but—" She paused.

"But…"

"But why did you do this for me—I mean, for Shiloh? You hardly know us."

His eyebrows folded together, turning his expression serious. His shoulders lifted up and then dropped. "I had the time and the tools and it needed to be done." Sam moved to sit up, his knee briefly grazing Lucy's thigh as he moved closer to the edge of the truck bed; she felt the warmth of his skin all the way up into her belly. The quick, innocent touch, combined with the intensity of his hazelnut eyes, made her turn her attention to Thor, who was curled up under her feet.

It wasn't as though Lucy was a stranger to kindness. When she'd gained custody of Shiloh, and then again when she lost her father, the whole town had rallied around her, filling her fridge with endless casseroles and taking care of all sorts of chores that would have otherwise piled up and overwhelmed her, things she'd been in too much pain to notice until later, when she'd finally written and hand-delivered thank-you notes that couldn't begin to express her gratitude. But that was different; those people were her friends and she'd known them her entire life. Sam Haynes was a complete stranger, yet he'd spent hours building her something that would serve her and Shiloh for years to come. Did he have any idea what that meant to her?

The question was…why?

Maybe she should be experiencing something other than appreciation, like suspicion. But the thing was…she didn't. Maybe it was his gentle nature each time he'd spoken to her when she'd stopped by the café for a quick breakfast the past few days, and the kind, open friendliness he showed the other employees. Maybe it was the way he seemed to dote on Shiloh, giving her his full attention where other new people often chose to ignore her as a result of their own discomfort.

Or maybe it was just that Sam seemed to expect nothing in return for his simple act of kindness.

Lucy mined her brain for some way to express how much the project meant to her and came up short by a mile. But then she had an idea. Her culinary skills were pitiful at best, but the Southern hospitality ingrained in her from birth meant she couldn't let the man leave without at least offering him something to drink.

"Sam," she said, and he trained those gorgeous melted-caramel eyes on her again, "I can't begin to thank you enough for what you've done, but…would you like to stay for dinner?"

A mischievous grin tickled the corners of his mouth and he crossed his arms over his chest as he scrutinized her. "That depends," he said.

"On what?"

"On who's cooking."

Lucy laughed, grateful for the distraction from Sam's attractiveness, which she noticed more and more by the minute. "It's not going to be me."

Sam raised his chin. "Can I get that in writing?"

Lucy feigned a pouty face and shoved him gently with her elbow. "Hey now," she said. "I'm not *that* bad."

He raised his eyebrows, challenging her faulty statement.

"Okay, fine," she said, her tone mocking. "I promise not to cook for you if you promise not to perform any more miracles on my house."

Sam sat back, resting his hands on his thighs. Lucy's eyes were drawn where they landed, and she couldn't pull away as she watched his fingers spread over taut, generous muscles under the worn denim of his jeans.

What was wrong with her?

She hadn't noticed a man's physicality in ages. She just needed to remind herself that her response to Sam was purely biological. It was natural for a woman to feel some physical attraction to a man who looked like Sam—those clear eyes, that perfect smile with the charming dimples, those handfuls of sandy brown hair—so it didn't make sense to chide herself for feeling drawn to him. But just because her body reacted to his in such a way did not mean she had to act on it. That was what separated humans from animals, wasn't it? She could make a conscious decision to ignore what her body wanted.

Even though she'd never finished her degree, Lucy had gone through plenty of scientific training, so she knew that the best course of action would be to follow through on her original plan. She'd sworn off the opposite sex completely after her last failed foray into dating, and her decision was best for both her and Shiloh. She had more than one heart to look after, and she would not waste time on another guy when she knew the probable outcome in advance.

Still, there he was, looking delectable in the afternoon sun, teasing her in a way that made her feel special…wanted.

"I don't think I can make that promise." His response brought back Lucy's attention and she glanced up at his face, which was maybe not the best idea, because his mouth was just as diverting as his thighs.

Geez. Fabulous idea, Luce, inviting him for dinner.

Right—dinner.

"Guess I'll have to accept that for now," she said, "but, to save us both, I'll stick to my end of the deal and not cook."

Sam smiled and jumped down from the truck bed. He stood planted in front of her and there was no way to get out except to hop down right where he was standing. She didn't have much time to plan an alternate exit, though, because Sam wrapped his hands around her waist and lifted her onto the ground, leaving very little space between them. There was the slightest twinkle of humor in his eyes as he stared down at her, but the tight line of his lips and the clench of his jaw made her feel an urge to do something she would regret. Lucy's mouth was suddenly dry as the dust beneath her sneakers and she couldn't move her feet.

"I'll, um...I'll just order pizza," she said, squeezing her body out from between Sam's and the truck's gate. Thor looked up from his perch and thumped his tail against the dirt, and she was almost sure the darn dog was laughing at her. She couldn't work up the nerve to glance back at Sam, so she just headed toward the house, desperate for a cool drink of water to chase away some of the heat coursing through her body.

Sam finally picked up his leaden feet and followed Lucy into her home, where she instructed him to sit on the couch and handed him the best glass of sweet tea he'd ever tasted. It was a Southern favorite, he'd quickly learned over the past few days in the small Texas town, and he was happy to accept every ounce offered his way. But Lucy's was amazing—dark, strong, with just the right amount of honeyed sweetness and a subtle hint of peaches. Sam could expertly analyze a good merlot or sauvignon blanc, but never in his wildest dreams would he have imagined himself discerning flavors in a simple glass of iced tea.

He grinned at the unexpected turn his life had taken, landing him in the cozy living room of this odd, beautiful woman who was doing a fine job on her own of raising the daughter he'd never known he helped create.

An itchy feeling stuck in his chest like a burr. He'd been in Peach Leaf for three whole days and had yet to say anything about who he really was. He knew he needed to tell Lucy soon—the longer he waited, the worse it would make him seem when he opened up about being her niece's father. If he didn't speak up, his omission would look more like an intentional lie than careful timing, and he would lose any credibility he'd built. So why was it so hard to just open up his mouth and let the words spill out?

The doorbell rang. "I'll get it," Lucy called out from the kitchen a few feet away. She smiled at him as she passed and Sam's chest closed tight around his heart.

He'd almost kissed her back at the truck. Just recalling her body lodged between his and the warm metal gate was enough to set off a pleasant but unwelcome chain of thoughts.

There had been a spark of something between them, and the way Lucy had rushed away let him know he wasn't the only one who'd felt it. He was glad she'd got out of there though, and saved him from doing something he shouldn't. But how long could he keep it up? He'd come to Peach Leaf with a single purpose—he couldn't possibly have anticipated being blindsided by a sweet, redheaded beauty—but there wasn't room for any distraction from getting to know his daughter. Somewhere inside, though, he knew the two were a package deal, and he had no intention of coming between them. He just wanted to fit in there somewhere, too.

Sam was just going to have to face the challenge of becoming a dad to Shiloh while ignoring his attraction to Lucy. He would never have one without the other, so he might as well learn to manage by pushing aside Lucy's increasing appeal.

He would start by keeping her curves a safe distance away from him, and his lips to himself.

Easier said than done, of course.

He jumped up from the couch and hurried to get the door before Lucy. There was no way she was going to pay him for installing the new ramp for Shiloh with dinner. It was a pathetically minuscule act when he thought about the years Lucy had spent caring for a child who wasn't even her own—how many sacrifices must she have made for *his* daughter? There was nothing in the world he could ever do to repay her selflessness, so pizza was definitely off the table.

He made it just in time, tugging a few bills from his pocket and shoving them into the delivery girl's hand before Lucy had a chance to object. He thanked the teenager and as soon as the girl turned to walk away, he practically slammed the door behind him.

"What was that about?" Lucy asked when he spun around. Her eyes were huge and full of confusion.

"What?"

"That," she said, crossing her arms. "You nearly ran me over to beat me to the door. At least let me pay you back." Her nose wrinkled in a cute way and

Sam couldn't tell if she was more angry or amused, but he hoped the latter.

"I'm not letting you buy me dinner," he said, waving his free hand as she opened her wallet.

"Why not?" she asked, following him down the hall to her kitchen.

Sam situated the pizza in the center of the table, noticing that Lucy had set out napkins and more of that obscenely delicious tea. He turned to face her and, no thanks to the size of the tiny dining room attached to her galley kitchen, there she was again, only inches away.

"Just call me old-fashioned," he answered, though the thoughts running through his mind were anything but.

"How very gentlemanly of you," she said, rolling her eyes.

The images flashing behind his eyes—of his mouth on hers, the pizza forgotten, her green eyes filled with a desire to match the level mounting in him—were pretty damn ungentlemanly. Good thing she couldn't read his mind or she'd kick him right out the door and he'd lose any chance of accomplishing what he'd come here to do.

"But, no. Not a chance." She moved around him and opened the pizza box, grabbing two slices and plating them. She set the plate next to the napkin in front of him and pointed to it. "Sit. Eat. And tell me why on earth you won't let me buy you a few slices of pizza after building that stunning new ramp for my niece."

Sam saw little choice but to obey, so he did as he was told and sat down, taking a long sip of the tea before speaking. "I already told you. I had the time and the know-how, and it needed doing." He took a bite. So maybe Peach Leafers owned iced tea, but this wasn't a New York pie by any stretch of the imagination.

Lucy sat across from him but didn't make a move to serve herself. She scrutinized his face, her emerald eyes narrow and stern. There were flecks of gold in them, like the stars he'd looked up at in the clear country sky last night—more stars in one night than he'd seen in years of city life. Odd to think that they'd always been there, masked into invisibility—just like his daughter.

Lucy didn't seem convinced. She formed a teepee with her fingers on the table in front of her and focused her eyes on her hands. "It can't be that simple."

Sam swallowed and took another sip of tea. "Why not?"

"It just can't be," she said, still staring at her fingers. "Men just don't do things like that for…for me. For Shiloh."

He put down his glass, bristling at the thought of any man dating Lucy and brushing off his daughter. He didn't say anything for a few long seconds. "Well, she's a great kid. Anyone who can't see that is a damn fool and doesn't deserve to be around her anyway."

Lucy looked up and smiled, her eyes glistening. She unfolded her hands to finally grab a slice. "I agree. One thousand percent." She bit into her pizza and chewed, her forehead creasing as she swallowed. "But it's still weird that you just rolled into town and did this amazing thing for us." She took a sip of her tea. "I may not be a psychology guru, but I know enough to know that a man has a motive when he does something that selfless for someone he knows, much less someone he just met." Lucy set her glass down. "So, stranger. What's yours?"

Chapter Five

Sam grinned, oddly thankful that the woman responsible for his daughter was bright enough to suspect him of ulterior aims. His gut twisted, and it wasn't because of the pizza.

She had good reason to be guarded, after all. He couldn't tell her the truth—not yet. It wasn't the time or place. He didn't want to bring up something so big in her own home, which would no doubt upset her—to what degree he couldn't yet fathom. Regardless of what happened before he left town, he and Lucy were knit together by Shiloh; he and Lucy would have a relationship no matter what, and he wanted it to be a good one…for his daughter's sake. He didn't know when he would tell Lucy the truth, but his intuition told him it shouldn't be now.

But he couldn't lie to her, either. He refused to lie to her.

"I had a single mom growing up," he said, before finishing his first slice of pizza in one big bite. He'd worked up an appetite that afternoon, so, New York style or not, the food was welcome. He swallowed. "She and my dad got pregnant young and Mom left college to raise me. She'd been a stay-at-home mom and when he cut out on us, she did what work she could find. Mostly minimum-wage stuff."

Lucy's face was filled with empathy—he knew she could relate to his mom's situation, and he couldn't help but feel he had a lot to do with that fact. Yeah, Jennifer had kept their daughter a secret, but still, he hadn't been around—an absent father just like his own. Did the reason really matter?

"I started doing dishes in restaurants as soon as I was old enough, and with both of our jobs combined, we made ends meet. Most of the time." He recalled those long nights, catching the bus from his neighborhood public school to a nicer section of Brooklyn, where he'd worked in the kitchen of an upscale bistro until early morning, riding back home to catch a few hours' sleep before starting the whole gig all over again. "But it was hard on Mom. There were times when she could have really used a helping hand, even if it came from a stranger."

Lucy nodded in understanding. What he'd said was true. He wouldn't have ended up sitting in her kitchen if it wasn't for his daughter, but if the opportunity had come up to build a ramp for someone else's kid who needed it, he would have done the same. He loved making things with his hands, loved spinning beautiful, useful things from wood that would outlast anything from a machine in a factory. "I should really be thanking you instead," he said. His statement caused lines to form between Lucy's brows.

"What could you possibly have to thank me for?"

"I don't get to build things back in New York. I don't have the space for equipment, or the time. It's been a while since I've had a chance to practice." Without thinking, he reached over and tapped Lucy's hand with his knuckles. The fleeting contact with her skin sent a rush through his nerves, and the way she startled just a tiny bit indicated he wasn't alone. "So, thanks."

A small, quiet sound like a cough came from Lucy and she quickly got up from the table and headed toward the sink, taking her unfinished food with her. "Would you like some more tea?" she asked, her voice higher than he'd ever heard it before.

If she was as rattled inside as he was about how it felt when they were in the same room together, then they were in serious trouble.

"No, thanks. It's wonderful, Lucy, truly, but if

I have any more, I'll be up until dawn." He stood, taking his empty plate to the sink, where he hovered behind her. "That stuff is stronger than any coffee I've ever had."

She wasn't facing him, but he could see the corners of her pretty mouth curl in a grin and his heart kicked up its rhythm. "Thanks for dinner," she said, lowering the plate and turning toward him.

When her eyes hit his, they were wide and sparkling, their green intensified, and the temperature in the room seemed to bump up a few degrees.

The words were right there on the edge of his tongue, but he couldn't let go of them, knowing they would alter the atmosphere. He'd come here for Shiloh, but each minute that passed had him wanting to get to know Lucy, as well. His restaurants kept him busy, leaving little time for dating, and for the most part, Sam liked it that way. He'd never been one to turn down an evening—or night—with an attractive woman, but he was careful not to ever let it extend much beyond that. What he felt for Lucy was different somehow; he wasn't just interested in the distraction of a warm female body.

Lucy came with risks he wasn't willing to gamble on. When he told her who he was, he would need her support and cooperation. He knew his rights to see Shiloh, and he'd spoken with his lawyer to get the details, but it would be so much easier on everyone involved if Lucy simply agreed to let him be a part of his daughter's life. He wanted to kick his own ass for deciding to handle this the way he had and, at the very least, he didn't want to stir up any more dust than he had on his way into town.

If only he could convince his body, which was getting warmer and warmer by the second in Lucy's proximity. What was it about her that made him want to forget all the rules he should follow and just take her in his arms?

"Are you okay?" she asked, bringing his head back into reality. She had a funny look on her face and Sam guessed she might have a faint inclination of what he was thinking.

"Of course," he answered, his voice coming out just a touch too rough.

She shook her head as if to dismiss the awkwardness. "Listen, I was thinking I could show you around the rest of the observatory grounds. We missed some of my favorite spots on your first day—I mean, if you don't have plans or anything. You're new in town and you work here now, so I thought you might like a tour while the place isn't filled with visitors."

She tilted her head to one side and twined her fingers together as she had at the table. He was learning that nervous habit of hers, but he wanted to know more. He wanted to know everything about Lucy. He should just say "no, thank you" and head back to the B and B where he'd comfortably spent the past few nights after the owner, a sweet elderly woman, had sorted out his room mix-up and offered him a massive discount. Of course he'd refused, touched that righting a simple, understandable mistake meant so much to the lady.

"Yes, I'd like that," he answered, ignoring his own advice like a total idiot.

"Great," Lucy said, clasping her hands together in front of her in a way that sent a thrill up his spine. She brushed past him and stopped where her purse sat on the edge of the short bar that extended from the kitchen's counter. "I'll just text Shiloh and tell her to meet us up there when Paige drops her off." Lucy pulled her mobile phone out and started moving her fingers across the screen.

Excitement flooded Sam at the thought of spending a few hours with the two of them. He waited, enjoying her chatter while she finished typing and dropped the phone back into her bag, exchanging it for a set of keys.

"Paige is Lucy's favorite teacher from elementary school. She was a principal for a while, but now she's teaching part-time at the middle school and sometimes Shiloh babysits for Paige's son and daughter. Today Shiloh's helping with the littlest one's birthday party."

Lucy's eyes were bright and full of joy as she talked about her niece, and a bittersweet sense of pride lodged in his heart. His daughter was wonderful…and he had nothing to do with that fact. He hadn't contributed a single speck of anything that made her who she was—unique, bright, lovely and brave. And it wasn't that he wanted to take credit for the person she'd become—he just wondered if he had anything to offer that she didn't already have.

What if she was better off without him? What if he'd made a mistake in coming—in thinking he deserved a place in her life?

"Ready?" Lucy asked after a few moments.

"Ready," he answered, regretting the lie. He was anything but.

"All right, city boy. Almost there," Lucy said, checking back over her shoulder to make sure Sam hadn't fallen behind.

"Watch it, girl," he said from only a few inches behind her. "I may not have a regular habit of traipsing through the boonies, but in my town we walk everywhere, so I'm no stranger to traveling on my feet."

Lucy laughed. She enjoyed teasing him, but she was actually quite impressed with his stamina, as they'd hiked up a steep hill to visit her favorite telescope. The path was relatively smooth—a pretty, paved trail, dotted with bluebonnets and Indian paintbrushes this time of year, that extended over much of the property so that visitors could tour the grounds, but it wasn't flat by any means. She and Shiloh often covered the three-mile track on weekends for exercise—Lucy had the leg muscles and Shi the arms to prove it, but she hadn't expected a New York City chef to be able to keep up.

He was stronger than she'd expected—more talented than she could have imagined and, when she admitted it, far sexier, too.

The thought came before Lucy could stop it, but it was true. She'd noticed his good looks that first day he'd walked into the café and prevented an epic disaster, but it was only this afternoon that she'd realized the full extent of his appeal. How could she not, when he'd been standing in her front yard in those snug dark jeans and T-shirt, having just presented her with the kindest, most generous gift she'd ever received? He reminded her that she was still a woman in her own right. Most of the time, she felt as if her identity was just that of Shiloh's caregiver, and she didn't resent the role for a minute, but she'd almost forgotten why she had ever bothered with the whole dating game in the first place before giving it up.

She should be annoyed with Sam, actually, for stirring up that piece of her again. No matter how much she wanted to, though, she couldn't feel anything other than pure attraction to him, especially since he seemed genuinely interested in both Lucy and her niece. Maybe he was exactly what she saw—a nice, handsome guy with an abnormally good heart. That was possible, right?

She turned around again when they reached the top of the hill. Sam was standing there taking in the view, only the slightest hint of moisture on his brow, whereas she was sweating like crazy, causing her to become suddenly self-conscious.

Lucy rested for a minute, admiring the azure sky before pulling her keys out of her back pocket and heading to a gate a few yards away. Sam came to stand behind her and she was much too aware of his nearness as she unlocked the latch. Her breathing was heavy and she wasn't sure if it was his proximity or the exercise, but she was glad for the distraction when they finally reached their destination and she could show him her favorite telescope. Talking about it would take her mind off Sam, at least until Shiloh joined them.

"Here's my second favorite girl," Lucy said, standing back so Sam could admire the telescope.

Sam laughed. "It's made of metal. How can you be certain she's a girl?" he asked, and it was Lucy's turn to chuckle.

"I just am," she answered.

"Wow," Sam said, his eyes wide as he circled the instrument's perimeter. Lucy's heart did a little jig, pleased that he was impressed by something she adored so much.

"Beautiful, isn't she?" Lucy asked, not giving Sam any time to answer. "She's the smallest telescope on the property, but that doesn't make her any less special. She actually came to exist because of one of the larger telescopes. I like to think of them as kind of like family in that way," Lucy said, grinning to herself.

Sam followed eagerly as she opened the door to the control room and led him inside. Lucy was so excited to give him a private tour into her world that she couldn't seem to stop once she got started.

"The mirror is actually the center of one of our bigger ones. When my dad bought the fused silica for our largest telescope all those years ago, they cut a circle in the middle to allow light to reach the instruments. They cut the leftover glass in half and used one piece to make this one. She's not as precise as some of the other equipment, but the scientists use her for search and survey projects in scanning a large area—her specialty. Each of our pieces has its own unique purpose, and they're all vital to the research, but this one's my favorite."

"Like people," Sam said, and Lucy pondered his statement for a moment.

Her eyes bounced up to his face, but he was busy studying one of several computers responsible for gathering and interpreting the telescope's data.

"Exactly," she agreed, touched that he'd expressed a sentiment she had always carried around, but never shared with anyone. None of the few guys she'd dated had ever shown more than fleeting interest in the work that went on at the observatory, but it was a vital part of Lucy's soul. Not having a degree had never stopped her from keeping up with the scientists' latest finds, and they were always happy to share with her when she dropped by to talk on one of her less-hurried days. She imagined they welcomed talking to a nonacademic whose eyes didn't glaze over at their technical language.

She stood still, watching as Sam paced around the tiny room, immersed in the fabric of metal, plastic and glass that comprised the remarkable instrument.

"To tell you the truth, I've always been overwhelmed by the night sky." He still faced away, running a hand a few centimeters over the telescope, not quite touching the material, but his voice, soft and sincere, carried to where Lucy stood. "In a way, I prefer the city, where it's impossible to see how—" he paused as if searching for the proper word "—infinite it is."

"That's a normal feeling," Lucy said. "It's human nature to fear things that are out of our grasp…what we can't completely understand."

Like you.

Her thoughts turned from Sam to the first time she'd looked through one of her father's telescopes and seen Saturn's rings. That rush of raw amazement had been almost too much to bear, setting off her fight-or-flight instinct, and she'd run all the way from her dad's office back to their house to hide under her covers, unable to express in language what she'd just experienced. It wasn't until her father found her and held her and explained, without teasing Lucy about her reaction, that the enigmatic beauty of those rings consisted merely of particles of ice, dust and rocks gathered from passing meteorites and comets that the planet's gravity pulled in and collected. Then it all made sense, and became a little less scary.

That was the moment Lucy decided she wanted to be a scientist, so she could find reason in all the things about life that confused her. Like why her mother left them when she was little, and why her dad didn't try harder to make Lucy's mom stay. Science had rarely failed her, but some facts were easier to swallow than others.

Lucy was glad Sam was preoccupied with the equipment so he couldn't see any evidence of the sadness that might have escaped into her features. "All I see when I look up there is beauty and endless possibility," she said.

Something strange and unidentifiable passed through Sam's eyes at her words, but it was gone almost as fast. "Did you ever consider going?" he asked.

"Going where?"

He aimed a forefinger up into the sky.

"Up there?" Lucy nearly choked as the words sputtered out.

Only every other minute.

"No, not really." Sometimes a little white lie was

simply easier to handle than the truth, or at least less painful.

"Huh," Sam mused, his tone revealing that he'd managed to delve further into her psyche than he was permitted. "I don't buy that for a second."

He stepped closer to her, filling the remaining few feet between them with electric charge. His inexplicable ability to read her without really knowing her was startling, but somehow also refreshing and thrilling. Maybe he wasn't aware, or maybe he was just being kind, but he'd expressed more interest in her innermost dreams and aspirations with only a few words than anyone else ever had, besides her father—but then, he'd shared her fascination with the cosmos. Sam didn't. But he cared that she loved it.

She wanted to let herself unravel, to sink into the way he made her feel, like jumping into a still-cool lake on the first long evening of summer. But things were rarely as simple as they seemed, and she wasn't yet sure if she could take Sam at face value. Sometimes the people she'd trusted most had kept things hidden from her, things that had unleashed mind-blowing surprises and altered her entire life in the span of a few minutes. She wasn't willing to go through that again, so she was right to guard her heart. It was the wise thing to do...but definitely not always the easiest.

"It may have crossed my mind a time or two," she admitted, her voice thin. She seemed unable to shut him out. Sam was so easy to be around, so free of expectations or assumptions about her. He made her want to be herself.

"Can I ask you something, then?" Sam turned from the telescope to gaze at her, his eyes molten in the thin sliver of light that sneaked into the control room. Lucy realized suddenly that she hadn't bothered to flip on the main switch. Noticing the dimness sent a shiver up her spine. She'd never thought of the place as an aphrodisiac—awesome, yes, but never romantic. But with the few stray rays of sunlight casting a haze over Sam's amber-colored eyes, the thick, warm air surrounding them, and the room's modest size an unexpected intrusion, Lucy's heart doubled its pace.

"Sure," she said, hoping her voice sounded convincing, when what she really felt was apprehension. It was almost impossible to keep her true feelings from him. Every time she opened her mouth in response they came spilling out, as though set free from a flooded dam.

"Obviously, this—" he gestured at the room "—is your passion. It's clearly what you love. You're intelligent, strong and hardworking, so if you wanted to go to space, what stopped you?"

Lucy concentrated on his question. It was something she'd thought long and hard about many, many times before and the answer had always seemed obvious—because of Shiloh. But coming from Sam, who didn't know her history, was like hearing it anew, and the answer was no longer quite so clear. When Jennifer dropped Shiloh off on Lucy's doorstep all those years ago, Lucy's life had screeched to a halt. One day she was a bright, promising college student studying to become an astronomer, and the next she was a new mom, having missed the crucial step of deciding to become one. But was that really the reason she hadn't fulfilled her dream? Or would she have given in to fear if the opportunity had come up?

She would never know. She would never, ever know what might have been if Jennifer hadn't made a series of choices that ended up changing Lucy's future. Somehow that was far worse than getting to make her own choices—right or wrong.

Lucy looked up at Sam, studying the sincerity in his features. She hesitated for a beat, still uncertain why he wanted to know so much about her past. Finally she decided she'd had enough. She wasn't going to try to second-guess every single sentence that came out of his mouth anymore. Even though he'd only been in her life for a few days, she had no reason yet to doubt anything that he might say, or to believe that he had any motive other than what he'd indicated, which is that he left his own past behind and was looking for a new life in a small town. If things went any further between them, if they did become friends or perhaps more, if she allowed him to get to know her in a deeper way, then she would ask. She would give him space to share what his life had been like, what had happened to make him decide to start over again. But there would be time for that. For now, she would give him the courtesy of being honest. It hadn't worked for her before, but this time felt different. Sam was different. There was no real reason to compare him to the dating failures of her past.

"All sorts of reasons really, the most important of which, of course, is Shiloh. When she came into my life, there was never a question of whether or not I would take care of her. She's family. But if I'm honest, sometimes I do wish that I could go back and start over, but that would involve Jennifer starting over, as well. She made some choices that I wouldn't have made myself, but they intersected with my life in a way that didn't allow me to turn away from them. And at the end of the day, even though things turned out differently than I had planned, I wouldn't trade it for anything in the world. Shiloh is my entire life, and she's wonderful. I've never thought of her as anything other than my own child."

Sam stood watching her intently, his brow furrowed in concentration. He didn't interrupt, but stood there patiently waiting for her to say more if that was what she wanted. She liked that so much about him, that she could be completely open and herself, but that there was no pressure to offer any more than she wanted to. Rather, his openness about her gave her space to speak, to be authentic, and already she was getting used to his presence, inching closer to a dangerous line—wishing he would stay.

"Sometimes we don't get to choose our own path. Sometimes life just gives us circumstances and we have to make the best of them. And Shiloh's taught me so much about what's important in life. She's the bravest person I've ever known. And if Jennifer had not decided to give her to me, to trust me with her care all those years ago, then I wouldn't have had the blessing of raising such a special kid."

Sam looked down at his feet, a grin tracing dimples near his mouth. "She is pretty special, isn't she?"

"Yeah, she is."

Sam glanced back up at Lucy, his features guarded so that she couldn't tell what he was thinking. "I know it's not…really any of my business, and I know it made you uncomfortable when I asked before, but…what happened to Shiloh? I mean, how did she end up with her disability?"

Lucy's heart raced. "You're right—it does make me uncomfortable." She turned away from Sam and moved around to the telescope, running her hand over the cool metal to comfort herself. "But it's not because you asked. It's just that it's hard to talk about."

"You don't have to if you don't want to, Lucy. I don't want to do anything to hurt you. I'm just curious about her life. She's such a vibrant kid, and it just makes me wonder what her life was like before."

Lucy stopped moving, and turned to face Sam. "To be honest, Shiloh's life was pretty confusing before the accident, when her mom stopped visiting. Before that, Jennifer would pop in and out on us. We never knew when she would show up or how long she would stay, which is hard on a child. My sister had some problems growing up, but she never really shared them with me until later, and my parents and I didn't ever talk about it. She always seemed fine to me when we were growing up. She always seemed happy, okay, and of the two of us, she was always the outgoing one, the one most comfortable meeting new people and having new experiences. That doesn't mean that things were always perfect. She had dark days sometimes, days where she became the complete opposite of her normal self. It was like she would turn in, just fold up inside herself and not let anyone in.

"My parents didn't tell me until much later that she had been struggling with bipolar disorder. It made sense to me then, when I looked back. Her manic days, once I knew that's what they were, were almost scary bright. On those days, she wanted to be and do everything in the world, and there wasn't anything anyone could say or do to stop her. She would come home from school completely on fire, and drag me away from my homework, and we would have whatever adventure was running through her mind that day."

When she stopped talking, Lucy noticed that Sam had moved to sit at one of the computer desk chairs. His hands were folded in his lap and what could only be described as empathy washed softly over his features. That was another thing she could add to the list of things she liked about Sam—he had a way of making her feel as if he was inside her brain, going through her emotions as she spoke about them, but sympathy or pity were never present.

Over the years, Lucy had got used to those looks from people—the ones that told her when passersby felt sorry for her, or worse, felt sorry for Shiloh. Sam seemed much more interested in knowing her heart, rather than deconstructing her challenges. She continued, becoming more and more at ease by the moment as she shared with him.

"But when Jennifer got older, her adventures grew more and more dangerous. They started to involve other people—boys especially. Sometimes Jennifer would just feel so much, and not know what to do with it, so she would unleash all her emotions on anyone who paid an ounce of attention to her. And because she was so pretty, still is so pretty, often those people were men. Needless to say, her behavior in such a small town didn't go under the radar for long. My parents did the best they could to get her the therapy that she needed, but Jennifer had trouble sticking to her medication regimen, and even though they did their best to get her to take her pills, sometimes Jennifer would pretend to swallow them and spit them out. She said they made her feel weird—she didn't like the brain fog they caused.

"They started to fight about it, and, added up with their other differences, I think they just felt completely helpless, and turning to each other didn't seem to offer answers. It got to be too much for my mom, and one day…she just left."

Sam raised his chin and his eyes met Lucy's, their warmth almost palpable. "Where did your mom go?"

Lucy shrugged her shoulders. "Your guess is as good as mine," she said. "She never called, never wrote and never came back." Lucy rubbed the back of her neck to ease some of the tension that had built there over the workweek. "It was almost as if she completely disappeared, and, without her, I think my dad felt even more powerless when it came to Jennifer."

Lucy walked around the telescope, working to even out her breathing and to control the emotion that was welling up inside her. She hadn't talked about these things in years, not since she had told Tessa what happened with Jennifer, and that was different because her best friend knew her sister—knew the history and didn't need to hear context to understand. Talking about it to someone new was an odd challenge. But when she thought about it, it was also sort of comforting in a way. Maybe her policy of holding everything inside wasn't such a great idea after all.

But then again, she wouldn't have shared this with just anyone. She had chosen to share it with Sam, partly because he'd asked, but also because, wise or not, she was beginning to trust him.

She came out from behind the telescope and slowly walked over to where Sam was sitting, pulling out a chair and setting it straight across from him. To her surprise, he reached out and set a hand on top of her hand, squeezing it briefly before letting go. The touch struck her like a splash of cold water, rousing the sleepy nerves under her skin until they stood on edge.

He didn't say anything, just offered her an encouraging smile, so she went on.

"Despite never applying herself, Jennifer was a bright kid. She aced her SATs. When she got accepted to a small college in New York, she and my dad both agreed that it would be a good thing for her to get away from home and have a chance to start a new life. And it was. She did great at first. She was taking her meds, going to class, studying even—" Lucy laughed, remembering how much she'd always had to push to get Jennifer to crack open her books "—then out of the blue, she just stopped. Because she was away from home, it took my dad a long time to figure out what was going on. But then he started getting letters from the college, notifying him that Jennifer was failing her classes. He tried talking to her, of course, but sometimes Jennifer would disappear for days, and no one knew where she was."

Sam shifted in his seat, and when Lucy looked up she found lines etched across his forehead that looked to her as if they indicated discomfort, but he just nodded, letting her know it was okay to keep talking.

"Then one day, Jennifer just showed up at home, pale and weary-looking. She refused to talk about school, telling my dad and me that she just needed a break, but it was too much for her the first semester and that she would go back when she was ready. She told us that she had applied for a deferral, and that she wouldn't have any problem getting back into school when she wanted to. It wasn't until a couple of months later that I put two and two together, and I realized that she was pregnant. I begged her to tell me who the father was, or at least to tell him, so that he could have a chance to support her, so that they could support each other through the situation. For the longest time she wouldn't tell me anything, wouldn't let me know whether she had spoken to him or not, but one day I pushed her more than I had previously and she said that she had told him. Everything."

Lucy put her head in her hands and released a deep breath. She looked straight into Sam's eyes. "She said he didn't care—he didn't want to know the baby, and he wanted Jen to forget she'd ever met him. He wanted nothing to do with either of them, the bastard. I pressed her to get a lawyer, to try to force some responsibility from the guy, but Jennifer demanded that I just let it go. I was livid for a long time, but then I realized something that changed the way I thought about it. If Shiloh's father wanted nothing to do with her, then he didn't deserve to know her, and God, he's missed out. He is the one who lost."

Lucy looked up at the ceiling and breathed another heavy sigh. She hadn't noticed it until now, but relief swept through her, replacing some of the pain that had knitted into her heart over the years. Every word she spoke, each heartache she shared, released more and more tension from her tired body.

Sam's silence was thick, permeating the space between them, but she'd gone too far in the story to turn back. She needed to finish telling him.

"When the baby was born, Jennifer went back on her meds and was actually doing fine for a while. She had moved back to New York into an apartment across the hall from a sweet older lady who watched Shiloh while Jennifer took just two classes and worked the rest of the time. When she called to talk to me, I could tell it was hard on her, but she loved the baby and she was trying as hard as she could, or at least she made it seem that way."

Lucy folded her fingers together in her lap.

"She should have been honest with me, she should have told me that she was having a really hard time, and I would've taken a break from school to come up there and help her. But she never opened up to me about that, and I think it was because she was afraid to fail again. I think she felt like she had failed so many times growing up that if she did it once more, it would destroy our dad. But she kept it to herself, and that spring when I came home for break, the doorbell rang one day. When Dad opened it, there was Shiloh, a little note pinned to her clothes, and all we could see of Jennifer was a taxi flying off into the distance. It was years before I heard from her again."

Sam's hands had moved to rest under his chin, and his expression was closed to her—entirely unreadable.

"Sam, if you want me to, I can stop talking about this. I don't know why I've been going on and on anyway. You're just…you're just easy to talk to, I guess."

Easy to talk to. Easy for Jennifer to lie to.

Chapter Six

Sam's blood boiled, searing through his veins, firing off adrenaline and anger. Why hadn't Jennifer told him all of this? Why hadn't she let him in? And why on earth had she lied to Lucy and allowed her to believe she'd told him about the baby? He would have helped her, would have raised Shiloh on his own if she hadn't been able to. Yeah, he had been young and stupid and reckless and made his share of bad choices when it came to women. But none of that changed Sam's right to know his own kid. She was his daughter, too.

He'd been robbed of so many instances, so many moments filled with experiences he could never get back. Shiloh's first smile, her first words, her first steps. His heart twisted in pain at the thought of those precious pieces of a life he hadn't been allowed to share.

Even as fury surged through him, Sam had a sudden urge to touch Lucy, to ground himself in her gentle stillness.

He reached over and this time took both of her hands in his. "No, no. It's okay. I just feel terrible that this happened to you, that you were so young and suddenly had to take on so much responsibility."

Responsibility that should have been mine.

Lucy's eyebrows knitted above the deep, dark green of her eyes in the increasingly limited light that filtered through the walls of the control room. "It's fine for you to feel that way," she said, "but don't you think for one second that I regret taking care of her. Shiloh might've changed my life, but she also gave me new meaning, a stronger purpose than I'd ever had before her. She's taught me so much about moving forward and accepting change, even when it seems impossible to adjust." Lucy shook her head. "Even if I could go back, I wouldn't change a thing. She is not what I had planned, but she's still the best thing that's ever happened to me."

Sam's chest filled with an itchy tightness at the thought that he might have upset her, but he needed to know more, even if it was hard on Lucy. He forced himself to ask the question, the one question that he knew he shouldn't ask, but he couldn't help it—he had to know.

"Lucy?"

"Mmm-hmm," she mumbled, probably lost in private memories, seeing images from her past with the daughter he'd been denied. He didn't want to hurt Lucy, but he reminded himself that he did have a right to know.

"What happened to Shiloh? I mean, why is she in a wheelchair? Why don't her legs work?"

Lucy was silent for a moment and Sam gave her the space she needed. He would wait for her, but he wasn't going to let her walk out of that room until she gave him the answer that he craved. She stood from her chair, bumping his knees with her own as she squeezed out of the small space between them and went to wander around the telescope again. He watched as she walked over to the equipment, touching it again as she had before. He could tell that the smooth metal offered her a sense of peace, some steady footing like a worry stone.

When he grew impatient, unable to let her move around the room anymore without looking at her face, he stood up as well and walked toward her until he was only inches from Lucy's back. He could see her shoulders rise and fall as breath entered and left her lungs. His fingers burned to touch her, to run through the coppery spirals of her hair, and his body fought opposing surges of emotion. Part of him wanted her to keep talking, to force her to keep sharing information with him about his daughter. But another side of him wanted nothing more than to give in to his urge to be next to her, to pull her into his arms and do things that would distract both of them from their hearts and heads.

He wanted desperately to feel her skin against his, to wrap his mouth around her lips, and give in to the hunger that was building up inside.

His fist balled at his sides. He would not touch her and set off events he might be unable to stop—he wouldn't. Not when he was so close to finding out what had happened to his beautiful daughter. Whatever it was would be unforgivable to him, and he wished that it didn't have anything to do with Lucy.

"Lucy," he said. "What happened?"

She turned to face him suddenly, her expression full of new suspicion. "Why is this so important to you?" she asked, sending Sam's heart straight into his gut.

How could he answer such a question without giving himself away? Maybe he should just go ahead and tell her who he was. But…how could he, after hearing how angry she had been when she'd found out that Shiloh's father supposedly wanted nothing to do with her? He had a new challenge now, convincing Lucy that what her sister told her about the mystery man was as far from the truth as it could be. He would have to work twice as hard to prove himself to her. And there was no longer a question of whether proving himself mattered. He was beginning to care about Lucy as much as he did his own daughter. The two of them were entwined with or without him, and he was the one who had everything to lose.

It was more than that, though, wasn't it? Lucy mattered to him independent of his daughter. The realization struck him like a jolt of electricity, and he quickly tossed it aside before it threatened to take over. There were more pressing issues to deal with at the moment. He didn't have time for…whatever *that* was. For now he would just have to be honest with her and hope it was enough.

"It just is," he said, praying she would accept his lack of an explanation.

Her eyes narrowed and she scrutinized his features. He silently thanked the stars when she opened her mouth again.

"What happened to Shiloh was because of Jennifer. There was a terrible accident."

She turned away from him again, and he resisted the urge to put his hands on her shoulders and force her to face him. He wanted to make sure that she didn't hold anything back. He wanted to see her eyes, to know that what she told him was the whole truth rather than a version invented to keep him from feeling pain. He deserved to feel pain. Even if what happened to his daughter wasn't directly his fault, he should have been there. He should have been there to protect her.

"Jennifer was off her meds," Lucy continued, her voice breaking slightly before she cleared her throat and found her strength again. "Jennifer had come into town to visit Shiloh for a couple of weeks when Shiloh was about seven, and one night she went out drinking. She came home completely wasted and we got into a fight. I yelled at her, told her she was irresponsible—" Lucy put a hand to her forehead. "I told her she was a bad mother, and all sorts of other horrible things that I shouldn't have said. She went into her old room and slammed the door. I could hear her in there, crying, and I was worried about her, but she'd locked me out. I stood outside for the longest time, just to make sure she didn't do anything... harmful. When I thought Jen had fallen asleep I checked on Shiloh and everything was normal, so I went to bed."

Lucy's head lowered and Sam couldn't see her face—only the vulnerable, milky skin on the back of her neck. "I must've been so tired...in such a deep sleep, because I didn't hear them until the car started. Jennifer had grabbed the keys from my purse and taken Shiloh. By the time I got out to the front of the house, she was already driving away with the baby. I swear, Sam, there was nothing I could do to stop her. If only I had gone back to check. If only I had woken up and heard the sounds, it might never have happened the way it did."

Sam could hear the tears welling up beneath Lucy's words and the sound broke something inside of him.

It killed him to think that Lucy blamed herself for what was actually his fault. If only he had been there. If only he hadn't been such a selfish asshole back in college, thinking he could sleep with anybody that showed interest—no emotions, no attachments, those were his rules—whenever he wanted, with no consequences. He had treated women like disposable toys, thinking that he could use them, play with them and then discard them. It was the only real example he'd grown up with. Promises of love and fidelity didn't seem to mean much, so what purpose was there in making them? He'd been careful of course, making sure to use protection, but how stupid of him to think that would always be enough! How stupid of him to think that there would never be a price for the way he behaved! It had seemed the only way to live at the time, the alternative absurd.

He'd seen what became of people who fell in love, got married and swore vows to each other. Look what those promises had got his mom—a broken heart and a mountain of bills, and a son she could barely feed and clothe.

He should have called Jennifer the next day, should have checked in on her to see if she was okay.

Thinking back, he had known there was something different about that girl, something more vulnerable than most of the women he'd been with. It could be said that she had seduced Sam—she had certainly made it clear what she wanted—but behind her bravado he had noticed a hint of defenselessness that he should have paid attention to. He'd chosen to ignore the signs, and it served him right that he had finally accrued a debt.

He couldn't stand that Lucy thought it was hers to pay.

"There's nothing you could have done," he offered, willing his words to sink into that deep disparity he knew she felt, because it matched his own. "You couldn't have stopped Jennifer, and you've done nothing but be a great parent to Shiloh—" he paused "—as far as I can tell."

The drive to hold her was too strong to ignore any longer. He stepped toward Lucy, not missing the sharp intake of her breath as he wrapped his arms underneath hers and around her waist. He'd done it mostly for himself, for the comfort he needed and couldn't ask for, but the way Lucy's warm hands grasped his forearms before she turned and buried her head in his chest told him she needed the contact just as much as he did. It didn't escape him that she had no idea she was consoling him, and the thought caused an ache that radiated through his body.

He opened his lips to tell her the truth. It might not be the right time, and he knew she would probably hate him instantly and want him out of her sight, but he had to do it.

A loud ring shattered the silence, and they looked at each other, momentarily confused, before realizing that it came from Lucy's pocket. She pulled out of Sam's arms and reached to grab the increasingly insistent phone.

"Hi, sweetie," Lucy said, her voice filled with false strength. "Yes, Sam and I are here—" She covered the mouthpiece and whispered to him that Shiloh was on the other end. "We're up at the Rigsby but we're leaving now for the café. Meet us there?"

Sam walked out of the control room, desperate for some fresh air and a second to himself to go over what had just happened. He'd rolled into town less than a week ago, determined to find his daughter, armed with only a vague plan and a single suitcase. Now what the hell was he doing, lusting after the girl's aunt? Under normal circumstances, he wouldn't blame himself.

After all, Lucy was beautiful, smart, kind and the best mom he could ever have wished for his daughter, so it made sense that he would be attracted to her. And he was no stranger to being drawn to a pretty woman, but this was so much different. What he was beginning to feel for Lucy was unlike anything he'd ever experienced before. It was something deep and wide and terrifying, something he didn't want, and something he sure as hell didn't deserve.

He shouldn't have let her invite him into her house, should have said no when she offered to take him on a walk around the grounds. He'd been well aware of the risks, and he decided to ignore them anyway, just as he had done with Jennifer.

What he needed to do now was to take a deep breath, get some distance from Lucy and regroup, to remember why he'd come here in the first place. Any steps he took from here on out would be for Shiloh. Everything he did from that day on would be in her best interest.

There was no room in the equation for Sam to be selfish, which meant, of course, that there was no room for Lucy.

Lucy exited the control room, stopping briefly to lock up behind her, taking a moment to center herself before she joined Sam. Her heart was kicking against the inside of her chest, even as she was relieved for the interruption of Shiloh's phone call.

What had happened back there?

It was as if within the space of an hour she'd let everything out that she had been holding in the past few years, or really her entire life. What was it about Sam that made her feel as if she could do that without judgment? He'd opened up something inside her, allowing her to expose all the raw spaces that previously she'd felt were too tender to let anyone see, for fear they might start bleeding again. She had shared things with him that she hadn't ever shared with anyone, not even Tessa.

Even though she knew it probably wasn't wise, it had felt incredibly good to talk about all those things. Once she'd got past the pain when she first opened her mouth and the words had started spilling out, a strange calm had come over her, and she knew what it was. It was healing.

She tucked the keys back into her pocket and went to find Sam.

He was wandering along the edge of the hill that the telescope sat on, leaning against the orange rail, staring out into the distance. When he turned to look at her, his face was pale, and realization hit her that even though it might have felt good for her to say so much, maybe it wasn't good for Sam. Maybe he had just been polite and he didn't really want to hear all of the things about her past, about Shiloh and Jennifer.

Her heart sank.

She shouldn't have been so open with him—it was completely selfish of her. She was just starting to really like him, to enjoy his company, not just for the way he opened her up but because of the way he just let her be herself. He didn't ask much of her in the time they spent together. And now she was afraid she was going to scare him away. She looked down at her toes, worried he might see the blush that was rising up in her neck.

Then he surprised her for the millionth time that day by taking her hand in his. He didn't say anything, just led her away from the railing and down the trail.

"Hey, you two," said Shiloh, who was sitting at the edge of the trail when they returned from the telescope.

"Hi, sweetie," Lucy answered, suddenly pulling her hand away from Sam's. Shiloh caught her eye though, and Lucy knew her niece had seen. A slow, mischievous grin spread across Shiloh's face, but thankfully she didn't say anything. She just headed over to Sam, and the two of them started chatting wildly about her day.

Lucy thought again how incredibly strange it was that the two of them had bonded so quickly. Especially when Shiloh normally took so long to warm up to people. It wasn't that she was shy; it was more as if she knew what she was looking for in a person and she was careful to only spend time and invest in people whom she thought were genuine and true. Lucy realized suddenly that that was one of the reasons that she was starting to trust him so much, even without knowing him for that long. Shiloh was an incredible barometer of people. She knew instinctively whether or not someone was good at heart, and Lucy had learned to trust her niece's intuition even more than she trusted her own.

The three of them moved companionably down the trail in comfortable silence. Lucy walked behind

Sam and Shiloh, noticing how sweet they looked together.

But something prickled in her chest.

She had done everything she could to be a good mother figure for Shiloh, and it wasn't often that she thought about Shiloh's father. Who he was, where he might be, why he had chosen not to be involved in his daughter's life. It wasn't something that Lucy saw a lot of value in spending time on. At the same time, though, she had loved her dad so much, had spent so many good hours with him, and sometimes she wished the same for Shiloh.

It was one thing to have lost a father, it was another to have never known one.

"I'm thirsty, Aunt Lu," Shiloh said, turning around to make a circle around her and Sam.

"If Lucy has the keys to the café," Sam said, "I think I know just the thing to fix that."

"Awesome," Shiloh said, speeding ahead of the two of them. Lucy feigned a cough as dust rose around them. The color had come back to Sam's face, and Lucy wondered if it was okay to bring up what had happened. She didn't want to see him so pale again, so distressed about the things she had chosen to share with him.

"Look, Sam. I'm really sorry about what happened back there. I know I shouldn't have told you all those things. You're just trying to be nice and I said too much and I hope it doesn't affect your decision to work at the café. I know I'm not your boss, at least not directly, but I really shouldn't have been so open with you."

Sam stopped talking and turned to face her. "You didn't do anything wrong, Lucy. It was my fault. I asked you about Shiloh and her past, and you were just being kind by answering my questions. I'm sorry I brought up so many things that caused you pain to rehash. It wasn't my intention to hurt you."

She wanted him to hold her hand again, to feel his warm skin against hers. When he'd done it before, it had been more comforting than anything he might've said. But at the same time, she didn't want to concern Shiloh. She didn't want her niece to get attached to someone who hadn't made any sort of commitment to them. And she still didn't know that much about Sam. She didn't know if he was just a drifter, passing through town along with his incredible culinary skills, or if he was running from something more dangerous…something she should be worried about. She wanted to ask him again why he was here, to see if this time he might share more. But it wasn't the time. Enough nerves had been exposed for the day.

They reached the Lonestar Café, and Shiloh headed up the ramp to the outdoor deck, stopping to leave room for Lucy to open the door. The sunlight was fading, painting the sky brilliant hues of red and orange and yellow. Soon the vibrant colors would be replaced by Lucy's favorite sight—the Milky Way, stars and the spring moon.

Thinking about that reminded her of the upcoming fund-raiser gala for the observatory. She had done most of the planning already, but there were a few more things to set in place. The annual dinner was something that most people enjoyed, but for Lucy it was just a reminder that the observatory was hanging on by a thread. It was a reminder that they needed the generosity of the Peach Leaf community, and other donating guests in order to survive, to keep teaching about things that mattered so much to her and to the scientists. She knew that if things got any worse, they would be in trouble. It was almost impossible to imagine the observatory folding, ceasing to exist. But she knew it could happen at some point.

Once inside the café, Sam headed straight to the kitchen, leaving her to talk to Shiloh. Lucy pulled up a chair at one of the tables, and Shiloh drove over to join her. Her niece's long beautiful hair was pulled up into a ponytail, and her cheeks were pink with the effort of pushing her chair around the grounds.

She looked just like her mother, whom they both missed so much but never talked about with each other. Lucy had always been open with her about Jennifer. They had come to an unspoken agreement long ago that they wouldn't obsess over the reasons why Jennifer left. For a kid her age, Shiloh was incredibly mature, and seemed to have an understanding that it wasn't her fault that her mother had been unable to care for her. Jennifer had been in and out of their lives over the years until the accident, when Shiloh was just seven years old, so her niece was aware that Lucy wasn't her real mother, but she treated Lucy like one.

"How did it go with Paige today, sweetie?" Lucy asked. Shiloh reached up a hand to brush back her bangs, rolling her eyes. She smiled and Lucy let out a laugh. "That bad, huh?"

Shiloh shook her head. "No, no. It was great. It's just that Owen and Winnie can be a handful sometimes."

Lucy nodded. "All kids can be."

"Except for me," Shiloh said, grinning at Lucy.

They both laughed, but it wasn't too far from the truth. They had their ups and downs, but Shiloh was a wonderful kid. Even when Shiloh gave her grief, not a day went by that Lucy wasn't aware of how lucky she was to have her.

They both looked up then as Sam came toward them, carrying a tray of what looked like fresh lemonade. Sam set the tray down on the table, and began serving them. He set a tall glass in front of each of them and poured the sunshine-colored liquid.

When Sam wasn't paying attention, Shiloh looked over at him and then back at Lucy, as if the two of them shared a secret. Lucy opened her eyes wide, silently praying that her niece wouldn't say anything to embarrass either of them. If Lucy were honest though, she enjoyed Sam's efforts. Most of the guys Lucy had dated in the past hadn't shown any interest in her niece, and Shiloh had given them the same treatment. With Sam, it was different. Shiloh and Sam seemed perfectly fine to talk to each other with or without Lucy.

Lucy realized that the two of them were developing their own relationship, regardless of whatever mysterious thing was happening between her and Sam. That's why she needed to be careful. Lucy had never been spectacular at reading other people's body language, but she knew that there was a connection between her and Sam. And she was almost certain that he had nearly kissed her more than once that day. More than that, she knew that she had wanted him to.

Once Sam finished pouring the lemonade, he sat down across from them and took a sip from his own glass. Lucy noticed that Shiloh was nervously drawing circles in the condensation that had begun to develop on her lemonade cup. Lucy wanted to ask what was wrong, but she knew that if she held out for a few moments, Shiloh would talk about it on her own.

"So, I have some news," Shiloh said, her voice quiet. She still didn't look up from her glass.

"What is it, Shi?" Lucy asked, trying to keep her tone casual.

"Well, remember how I told you about the dance coming up at school?"

"Yeah, I remember," Lucy said, a worried tingle going up her spine.

"And remember, how I told you a while back about that guy I sort of like?"

Lucy opened her mouth wide, unable to hide her surprise that Shiloh had decided to share something so personal with her with Sam present. She shot a glance over at him, but he was avoiding her eyes, purposefully it seemed.

It was sudden and strange to have him share this moment with the two of them, but wasn't she the one who had just been mourning the lack of a father figure in Shiloh's life? Plus, it didn't escape Lucy how much the three of them sitting at the table, talking and hanging out, felt like family. She sat back in her chair, letting herself pretend that that's what they were, enjoying the image while it lasted.

Shiloh stopped fiddling with her lemonade glass and looked at both of them, her eyes wide and filled with sorrow. "Well, it turns out that even though I wanted to go with him to the dance, he definitely didn't want to go with me."

Shiloh's words pierced through Lucy like an arrow, and she resisted the urge to take her niece in her arms and tell her that everything was going to be okay. It was funny how often in her time as a parent that she had that feeling. It was a constant battle to try to decide whether or not she should tell Shiloh the truth, or to let her figure out on her own that sometimes the world was a painful place. Sometimes everything was not going to be okay. Lucy knew that most parents battled with that, but with Shiloh, who had experienced so much pain already in her young life, it was even harder for Lucy to see her suffer any more..

Lucy opened her mouth to console her niece but Sam spoke first.

"Obviously the guy's an idiot," Sam said. "So it's a good thing he didn't ask you to the dance. Because we—" he glanced at Lucy as if to ask permission to use the word, and even though its intimacy jolted her a little, it seemed right, so she nodded and he went on "—definitely don't want you going with someone like that."

Lucy couldn't have said it better herself. Shiloh seem to agree, because despite the sadness that had been in her eyes only seconds ago, a wide grin now spread across her face.

"Thanks, Sam." She looked up at their new friend with blatant admiration on her face, and Lucy's heart suddenly felt as if it was too big to remain inside her chest.

"Sam's completely right."

Sam caught Lucy's eyes across the table, and Lucy had a brief understanding of how it must feel to raise a child with another person. To have someone to look to when you weren't sure whether or not you were doing the right thing. It was an amazing feeling, and she wished she could bottle it and keep it on her shelf for when Sam eventually went away and she was alone again. All the time, since she'd quit dating, Lucy had convinced herself that she was fine on her own, that she knew what she was doing and that she alone was the best person for the job of parenting Shiloh. She didn't need any help from anyone else. But sitting there with Sam, who seemed to know his place while also offering guidance when Shiloh sought it out, made Lucy wonder if it wouldn't be worth getting back out there again. The problem was, now that she had been around Sam, no one else would be good enough.

"So, now that this guy's out of the way—and good riddance, if you ask me—who are you going to take with you?" Sam asked.

Shiloh looked down into her lap, suddenly very interested in the fabric of her jeans. "I…I don't think I want to go anymore."

Sam was silent for a moment, giving Shiloh her space. Lucy admired his patience.

"Why in the world not, honey?" she asked. Shiloh looked up at her from her jeans, as if Lucy had just sprouted a bean stalk from her forehead.

"Geez, Aunt Lu," Shiloh spat out.

"I'm sorry, sweetie. Just trying to be helpful. I don't want you to miss out on this dance. Even though you're not going with this boy, I don't think you should let that keep you from being there with your friends. Don't let a boy stop you from having a good time."

Shiloh rolled her eyes. "It's just not the same. I wanted to go with *him*, and since I don't get to do that, I just don't want to go at all. End of story."

Lucy didn't want to say it, because she knew Shiloh would deny it, but she truly did know exactly how her niece felt. She remembered back in high school when prom came around, and she had a similar experience. It was wrong to project her own feelings onto Shiloh, but she couldn't help it. That kind of teenage heartbreak hurt very deeply, and she didn't want her niece going through the same thing, let alone shying away from an experience just because of a guy. Lucy wanted her niece to be all the things she had not been at her age—independent, confident, brave. Most of the time Shiloh was all of those things and more, so Lucy hated the fact that the lack of attention from a boy was causing Shiloh to build a shell around herself.

Lucy raised her shoulders, preparing herself for the fallout that she knew was going to come. She would push through anyway, because she knew it was the right thing to do. "I know you disagree with me here, but I really think that you should still go to the dance."

Shiloh pushed her chair back from the table quickly, and without a word she headed over to stare out the window.

Great.

"What did I say this time?" Lucy asked Sam. He

met her eyes, and all she saw there was compassion, no judgment.

"It's not really anything that you said," Sam offered, his voice low and soothing. "I think sometimes teenagers just want us to understand what they're thinking without having to say it. I know it's not the same, and I'm not comparing your situation to mine, but I had the same sort of issues with my mom when I was growing up. Near that age, you have all these emotions flooding through you all the time, plus the hormones, the peer pressure and the stress, and I think sometimes it just builds up. There were a lot of times when I wished that my mom could just intuit what I was thinking, so I didn't have to try to find a way to explain it to her, but of course that was almost impossible. I wanted her to be a mind reader."

"How do you know so much about raising a kid?" Lucy asked. "How can you be so smart about all these things, when I'm so clueless about them? Maybe we should trade places." Lucy let out a sad little giggle, but when she looked at Sam again, the expression on his face was startlingly serious. Before she had a chance to ask him what he was thinking, what had put that look there, he gave her another warm smile.

"Do you mind if I ask you something?"

"Of course not," Lucy answered "Anything."

"Okay, why does it matter so much to you that she goes to this silly dance? She's only in middle school—there will be other dances. Why is it so important to you that she go to this specific one?"

"It's not that this dance is important—it's just that...I'm worried that if she doesn't go to this one, that she won't go to the next one, and eventually she'll stop going to anything that presents a challenge for her. She's at an impressionable age, and I'm worried that if she doesn't go, because it makes her uncomfortable, then she'll learn to avoid things that might stretch her."

Sam's features were filled with understanding, and he nodded his head. "I can totally get that," he said, "but at the same time, if it hurts her to go, then maybe it's best if she just sits out on this game, and goes to the next onc."

"I know. I know," Lucy said. "Sometimes it's so hard knowing what the right thing is. Sometimes I don't know what to say to her. She has...challenges...that other kids don't. Most of the time we just go through life, she and I, pretending that everything is fine. And just because she's in a wheelchair doesn't mean that she's not a regular kid. But then when something like this happens, I know what she's thinking. I know she's wondering whether or not that boy not asking her to the dance has anything to do with her physical condition."

"What makes you think that? That might not have even crossed her mind. And actually, because of the way you've raised her, I think it would be just as safe to assume that it hasn't." Sam leaned over, placing his elbows on the table. His eyes bored into hers with a passion that she hadn't seen there before. "You're doing an amazing job with her, Lucy. But she's at an age where she needs to start feeling out life on her own. She needs to start making her own decisions, and if that includes deciding not to go to something, then maybe you should leave that up to her, and just be there to support her."

Every fiber of her being bristled at Sam's words. On some level, she knew he was exactly right, but at the same time, what right did he have to interfere, to tell her how she should parent Shiloh? Yeah, they had grown close over the past few days, but he had just crossed a line.

"I do nothing but support her," Lucy said. "My entire life is supporting her."

Sam moved his hands toward hers and Lucy knew he was going to touch her. Before, she would have welcomed his skin on hers. Earlier that day, she had felt so close to him—as if they were building, if not something romantic, then at least an important bond. It broke her heart that the words he'd spoken now had almost completely shattered the way she had felt that morning.

As Sam's hand moved to close the open space between them, Lucy pulled hers away fast, unable to stand the thought of such intimate contact after what he'd said.

"I'm so sorry, Lucy. I shouldn't have implied that you're not supportive of Shiloh," Sam said. "And it's not what I meant. Anyone can see that you're doing an amazing job."

Lucy knew he meant the words as comfort, but she'd already heard the omitted accusation in them, and it was too late for him to take them back. "Yeah, it's just that the best I can do is not good enough."

"That's not it, Lucy. I—"

Lucy stood up from the table, the confusing emotions bubbling around in her chest too much for her to manage. She composed herself and made her face as neutral as possible. "It's fine," she said. "I think it's best if Shiloh and I go on and head home for the night. You can let yourself out."

Sam's eyes were filled with questions, but he didn't say anything. Lucy grabbed her keys from the table and walked away to tell Shiloh it was time to go, leaving the lemonade—and her heart—behind with Sam.

A half hour later, Sam still sat at the table where Lucy had left him, staring out the window at the now-dark sky.

Why couldn't he have just kept his mouth shut?

He must've confused the hell out of her when he busted in and interfered with Shiloh. She had no idea how much the girl's life meant to him, and it was his own damn fault. He needed to stop being such a coward and just tell her who he was. He needed to stop thinking about whether or not it would prevent any kind of relationship between him and Lucy and focus instead on his own daughter. Putting himself first was what had got him into the situation in the first place. Being hardheaded and selfish had stopped him from checking on Jennifer, and ultimately stopped him from getting to be a part of the first twelve years of his daughter's life. All he could do now was try to pick up the pieces and avoid missing out on anything more.

Chapter Seven

"What's up with you, girl? The nerds are over there going on again about Earth 2.0 and you haven't even batted an eye." Tessa pointed a thumb in the direction of some researchers chatting over a cup of coffee across from the reception desk where she and Lucy had been going over the summer tour schedule.

Lucy laughed, Tessa's comment interrupting her thoughts. She'd been so stressed out about what had happened between her and Sam, about the way she'd overreacted when he was just trying to help yesterday. Tessa was right, of course. Normally she would've loved to listen in on the conversation, to hear about the latest research, but today Sam was the only thing occupying her mind.

"I told you not to call them nerds anymore," Lucy said, jabbing Tess in the side with her elbow. "You know I almost was one of them." Lucy gave her glare.

"You *are* one of them. But you're a lot cuter. Plus, you know how to function in the normal world."

Lucy squinted at her best friend. "What are you talking about?"

"This morning I asked Dr. Gleason what happened to his shirt, and he told me that he accidentally washed it with windshield wiper fluid rather than his wife's laundry detergent. I swear, sometimes I can't figure out how those smarties get their own heads on straight every morning."

The two of them burst into a fit of giggles. It was good to laugh with her friend.

"Speaking of men," Tessa said, "how's everything going with our hot new chef?"

Lucy felt heat flow instantly into her cheeks. She could tell Tessa noticed almost immediately after it happened, as her friend's eyes widened.

"I see," Tessa said, her voice full of suggestion.

"You see nothing. Nothing like that's going on."

"Tell that to the grin on your face."

Lucy had so much to say about the past few days with Sam, but for some reason, rather than sharing with her best friend, she'd kept it under wraps. Normally her bad dates in the past had been fodder for almost every conversation with Tessa, but Sam was different. She wanted to keep him to herself for now, out of the line of scrutiny. Besides, she'd been doing enough of that for the both of them, reading too much into everything that Sam said or did. That had led to her reaction the day before, and she needed to ease up on him, or he would end up running like the others.

She hadn't given much thought to Jeremy in a long time, but suddenly there he was on her mind. It was only a year ago that she had pressed him for answers on where their relationship had been going. They had dated for two years at that point, and he seemed to be a decent guy, but he never got close to Shiloh. The two of them had never bonded the way that she and Sam had just in the past few days. When Lucy had brought up the possibility of Jeremy moving in with her, he had completely freaked out, saying that he wasn't ready for something that deep.

But how could he not have been when they had spent two years of their lives together? When she had eventually pressed him to say more, he admitted that he was uncomfortable being a father figure to her niece. Lucy had never communicated that to Shiloh, of course, but it had been a huge blow. She hadn't dated anybody since, afraid of getting her heart broken again.

She didn't even know why she was comparing the two, because she certainly wasn't *dating* Sam.

The problem was she really wanted to.

But inside she knew that if she was going to let someone into both of their lives, to have the serious relationship that she wanted, to have the family that she wanted, she was going to have to learn to let someone coparent with her. Was she really ready for such a huge step?

"He is pretty amazing," she said.

Tessa beamed.

"But don't start thinking too far into this. You know how I feel about dating these days."

"I know, sweetie, but Sam really does seem different than the others. And he's a far cry from Jeremy the jerk-off."

"Yes, he is. And he's fantastic with Shiloh, which is the most important thing."

"Lucy, a guy being great with Shiloh is wonderful, but you need to give yourself some credit, as well. You need to find somebody who's fantastic with *you*, not just your kid."

Lucy nodded at Tess's words, soaking them up.

"So have you found out if he's going to be staying any longer?" Tessa asked.

"No, I actually need to talk to him about that. Somebody came by this morning, someone from one of the restaurants in Austin, and he was interested in applying for the chef position. He said he wanted to move his family to a small town and he was looking for work in the area."

"Well," Tessa said, "you had better hurry, because if you don't snatch Sam up soon, I can guarantee you that someone else will."

That's exactly what Lucy was afraid of.

"Speaking of," Tessa said, nudging Lucy with her shoulder. Lucy looked over and saw Sam coming toward them, looking as handsome as ever in a simple plaid shirt and dark jeans, having forgotten to take off his apron. Just the sight of him gave her heart a little tug. Lucy thought again about those few moments yesterday when he had almost kissed her, and how much she had wanted him to. She found herself hoping that he would try again soon.

"Hey there," Sam said, joining them, setting his elbows on the top of Tessa's reception desk. He nodded at Lucy. "How's it going, Tessa?"

"Oh, it's going. Not too bad for a Tuesday afternoon."

"Good," Sam said, giving her that dazzling smile. "Do you mind if I borrow Lucy here for just a few minutes?" He looked over at her. "I've got something I need to talk to you about."

"No, of course not. I'll see you later, Lu," Tessa said.

"We can talk in my office," Lucy said, and Sam followed her away from the reception desk. They walked together down the hallway, not saying anything. Lucy felt the words balling up inside her chest, and she wanted to apologize, but they got stuck there, refusing to come out. She had said so much yesterday, and it had got her into trouble, so the thought of saying too much again prevented her from being able to speak.

When they got to her door, she opened it and let him walk inside first, closing it after them. She motioned to one of the chairs in front of her desk and Sam sat down. Instead of sitting behind her desk, Lucy opted for the chair next to his.

"Lucy, I just want to apologize for what happened yesterday. It wasn't my place to step in so much when Shiloh was talking about the dance. I'm really sorry that I said something to upset you. If there's anything I can do to make it up to you, please let me know." Sam sat there looking so distraught that Lucy almost laughed.

"No, Sam, don't apologize. I'm the one who was wrong. You were just trying to help, and even though I don't really want to admit it, you were actually right. I was projecting a lot of myself on Shiloh, when we're not the same person." Lucy looked down into her lap. "She is a lot stronger than me, and I know in my heart that if she doesn't want to go to this dance, that won't stop her from doing things in the future. I just got worried, and when you stepped in, it made me uncomfortable. It's just been the two of us for so long that I'm not used to having anyone else's input when it comes to being a parent to Shiloh."

She looked up at Sam and once again found his eyes to be gentle and kind, not judgmental. It occurred to her not for the first time that she could spend hours just soaking in their warmth.

"I appreciate you saying that, but you are right to say that it wasn't my place to step in."

"Can we just agree to forget about that?"

Sam studied her for a long time, his expression unreadable. When he spoke again, his voice was hoarse, sexy and so thick that Lucy wanted to swim in it.

"Deal," he said. "But I can't agree to forget the whole day. It was one of the best I've had in a very long time."

"Me, too, actually."

"There's something else I don't want to forget," he said, leaning over closer to her. "I don't want to forget how beautiful you were in the afternoon sun, or how much I loved hearing you talk about…everything."

His mouth moved closer and closer to hers, and Lucy's temples pounded with her pulse. Suddenly, his lips were on hers in the softest, but also the most amazing kiss she had ever experienced. His mouth was gentle, demanding nothing—a lot like Sam himself. But somehow, in the middle of his gentleness, Lucy could feel a hunger, and it matched her own. She knew instantly that if they ever kissed again it would be more urgent, more heated, that she couldn't wait for that to happen.

The kiss was over almost as suddenly as it had started, and immediately Lucy wanted to pull his face back toward hers and kiss him again. She would have, if only she could breathe. For a moment she was speechless, a thousand questions running through her mind. Finally she sucked in a breath and pushed them all away.

She would not ruin this by questioning his motives. She knew by now she could trust him, and he had kissed her, and it had felt better than anything she'd ever known before. That would have to be sufficient for now. She opened her eyes and sat back in her chair, trying to figure out what to do next despite the spinning room and the tingling sensation traveling up and down her spine in rapid spurts.

"What is it that you wanted to talk to me about?"

Sam chuckled, but he didn't say anything about her obvious attempt to change the subject. "We just talked about it," Sam said, his eyes crinkling around the corners.

"Oh," Lucy said, embarrassed. "I thought maybe it was something to do with the café."

"No," Sam said, "this was much more important."

Lucy let his words sink in beneath her skin, trying not to overanalyze them. She cleared her throat. "Actually, now that the subject of the café has come up, I do have something that I want to talk to you about," Lucy said.

She was nervous to bring it up, afraid that Sam would say that his time in town was only temporary, and that he needed to get back to New York, but she brushed that aside and barreled on.

"Sure," he said. "What is it?"

"Actually," Lucy said, "a guy came by this morning and he wants to interview for your position, or at least the position you're in temporarily. I know that when you got here the other day you weren't expecting to step into the chef job, but you're so fantastic at it that I'm reluctant to put anyone else in your place. Plus, the sales have been fantastic over the past week. It must be word of mouth because, as far as I know, no reviewers have come by recently, but people are raving about your food."

Sam shifted in his seat, and Lucy's pulse, which had just started to calm down, kicked up its pace. He sat still for a moment, his eyebrows knitting in concentration. "I know it's a lot to ask, Lucy, especially since you have somebody interested, but I'd like to stay for another week or so, and think about it more."

Lucy hesitated. Her answer was yes. Of course she would let Sam stay as long as he liked. She would tell the man who had approached her that she would call him back in a few weeks if she wanted to interview him. That wasn't what bothered her. What bothered her was Sam's continued reluctance to tell her what he was really doing in Peach Leaf, and, more than that, her unwillingness to force him. What could he possibly say that she was so afraid of?

"Sam," Lucy said, pausing to choose her words, "you know the answer is yes."

He nodded, but the look of concern in his expression told her that he knew it wasn't that simple.

"Thank you, Lucy," he said. "I'll make arrangements to stay at the bed-and-breakfast for another week, and I'll make some phone calls to my restaurants to let them know that I'll be sticking around here a little longer."

Lucy resisted the urge to breathe a sigh of relief. It wasn't exactly what she wanted to hear, but at least it meant that he would be in her life for another week. But she needed to know for certain that he wasn't going to break Shiloh's heart when he left. The fact that he would break her own was another matter, but she wasn't going to let that happen to her niece.

"And, Sam—"

"Don't worry, Lucy," he said, as if reading her mind. "No matter what happens…with us…I won't hurt Shiloh. That's a promise."

Lucy wasn't a fan of promises, but for some reason she believed this one. There wasn't a doubt in her mind that Sam was telling the truth.

Sam reached over and pressed his fingers across the top of Lucy's hand, setting off a new series of fireworks inside of her. She had to change the subject fast or she would be tempted to pull him close again and do things in her office that she would fire one of her employees for. She turned over her hand

and Sam tickled her palm with his fingers, sending her nerves into a frenzy.

"There's something else, Sam, that I wanted to ask you about." Lucy reluctantly pulled her hand away so that she could regain some of the concentration she'd lost when he'd touched her. "There's this… thing coming up. It's a ball to raise money for the observatory, and I was just wondering if…if you'd—"

"Yes," Sam said, "I'll go with you."

Lucy laughed and glared at him in mock annoyance. "How did you know that's even what I was going ask you?"

"Isn't it?" he asked.

"Well, yeah, but—"

"Then it's settled. I'll take you to the gala, and anywhere else you want me to." His eyes glowed with glorious mischief, and a conga line of inappropriate thoughts started in her head. "There is one problem, though," Sam said. "I didn't exactly roll into town expecting to go to a black-tie function, so I'll need to scrounge up a tuxedo somehow."

Lucy beamed at him. "You mean you don't do this often," she said, "travel around to small towns, sweeping unsuspecting women off their feet and taking them to classy events?"

His face was suddenly serious.

A knock on the door interrupted them and a docent stepped in to inform Lucy that one of the tour guides had gone home ill. The staff needed Lucy to fill in for the afternoon, if she was able. Lucy said she could, so she and Sam got up to head back to work.

As they walked out of her office, he leaned in, his lips tickling the top of her ear. "No," he whispered, "just you."

Lucy finally let go of that breath she'd been holding.

Chapter Eight

"So," Shiloh asked the following evening, "what are you going to wear?"

She and Lucy were standing in front of Lucy's bedroom closet, as so many women had done in their own wardrobes before them, trying to figure out an answer to that age-old question.

Lucy released a huge sigh, disappointed with every piece of fabric in her closet. She really needed to go shopping.

"I have absolutely no idea," she said. Shiloh thumbed through a few pieces, pointing out the more promising ones, but even those were unacceptable. She tugged at one and Lucy pulled it out for her, handing the dress to her niece. Shiloh held out the navy blue cocktail dress, one of the least mediocre things in the bunch.

"How about this?" she asked, spreading it over her lap.

"Nope," Lucy said. "I wore that one last year. Otherwise it wouldn't be too bad."

"You know what this means," Shiloh said.

Lucy let out a huge groan.

"We have to go shopping." Shiloh looked super-excited but there wasn't much that Lucy would enjoy less. She loathed shopping, and often thought that the world would be a much happier place if everyone could just go around in their pajamas all the time. Shiloh didn't share that sentiment though, and she had taken after her mother as far as her fashion sense. For some reason Jennifer and her daughter were able to pull almost anything out of the closet and make it unique, give it that flair of personality that Lucy never seemed able to pull off. Whenever she went shopping, she chose neutrals, preferring them to brighter garments, which came with the risk of making her stand out. She had always walked the path of the wallflower, and with someone like Jennifer in her family, it was a wise choice.

"Fine, fine," Lucy said. "But if I'm going shopping, that means you have to come with me." Lucy winked at her niece, knowing that her comments would cause an eruption of joy.

Besides, bringing Shiloh along would inject a little excitement into the trip, and maybe Lucy would be lucky enough to find something that was both elegant and simple. Shiloh seemed to have a different idea. "I'll agree to that," she said, "but only if you promise not to pick something boring."

"I can't believe you would even suggest such a thing," Lucy said, her voice coated with sarcasm. "I can't promise that, but, if you're nice and don't make fun of me, maybe, just maybe, I'll try on something crazy. But I'm definitely not buying it."

Shiloh seemed satisfied and she nodded.

Lucy gathered up the dresses that they had pulled out, stuffing them one by one back into the closet. While they had been looking for something for Lucy to wear, they had both ignored the elephant in the room, but they would have to talk about it at some point. Now was as good a time as any.

Lucy pulled in a deep breath through her nose, releasing it slowly through her mouth, trying to figure out the best way to phrase her question without upsetting Shiloh.

"You know," she said, "if we're going dress shopping, we might as well pick up something for you, as well."

There. She'd said it.

She braced herself for whatever the consequences might be. She expected Shiloh to either lash out at her or shut down, so when neither of those things happened, she was more than a little surprised.

"I was thinking about what you said, Aunt Lu, and I might go." Shiloh moved over to the side of Lucy's bed and lifted herself up onto it. She met Lucy's eyes, looking a little smug.

"Oh," Lucy said, feigning nonchalance, "whatever you want to do is fine." She stuffed the last dress in and shoved the closet doors closed before stealing a glance at her niece. Two could play at this game. But Shiloh wasn't buying it.

"Oh, come on, Aunt Lu," she said. "You're not fooling anyone. I know you're excited that I decided to go."

Lucy rolled her eyes. "Oh, all right. You win." She sat on the bed next to Shiloh and put her feet up. "Honestly though, Shiloh, I'm just glad that you decided not to let a guy ruin your day. You should be able to go to the dance by yourself or with someone—it doesn't matter. You have every right to go and have a fabulous time, even without a guy."

Shiloh looked so adorable sitting on the bed, and Lucy thought how much her niece still resembled her younger self, how much she still looked like that child that had come into Lucy's life all those years ago. One of these days, she would be old enough to decide for herself what kind of woman she wanted to be. She would turn eighteen, and she'd be able to get the nose ring she'd always wanted, and all the tattoos she'd dreamed up and drawn into her notebooks.

And that was fine with Lucy. None of that bothered her. She wanted Shiloh to be her own person. What worried her wasn't her niece, it was the world that she was going into. Lucy knew that people could be cruel sometimes. She knew her niece had a strong core and she was glad for that. It would get her through so many things. It was other people that Lucy worried about—other people who had the power to break Shiloh's heart. And once Shiloh was out on her own, Lucy wouldn't be around to protect her anymore. The thought terrified her.

But another scary thing weighed on Lucy's mind, replacing some of the worry she felt for her niece.

The gala. It had caught up to her heels, and was coming up that weekend.

She'd been planning it for months, but with Sam's arrival, she had lost track of some of the preparations. Luckily, Tessa had been taking care of things and it looked as if everything was under control. It was something she endured every year, but this time it would be different. This time she would not be alone. And the thought of going with Sam, a thought that earlier had made her want to kick up her heels and dance with joy, felt more like doom with each passing minute.

She hadn't been on a date in so long, and the gala was always such a romantic affair. She didn't know what Sam would expect. Would he want her to dance with him? She was a revolting dancer. To say that she had two left feet would be the understatement of the year. What if he wanted to kiss her again, especially in front of all of those people? What if—what if he wanted more at the end of the night?

The thought sent a rush through her body. The truth was that she wanted more, too. But not just physically. Every moment she spent with him, even the ones that had been difficult, made her realize that he was exactly the sort of man that she would choose to spend the rest of her life with. And what if he didn't see that kind of a future with her? After all, he hadn't even explained to her why he was in town. What if he had more of a life to return to than he'd been honest about?

Lucy's chest tightened and her mouth went dry. Fear and apprehension exploded in her like the death of a star.

She looked over at Shiloh, who had been sitting a little too quietly.

"Can I tell you something?" Lucy asked.

Shiloh nodded.

"I asked Sam to go to the gala with me and he said yes, and I want to know what you think about that."

Shiloh's eyes widened and Lucy stared into their blue depths. "Oh my gosh, Aunt Lu. That's so awesome!"

"You really think so?"

"Totally. He's definitely into you—anyone can see that." Lucy was filled with sudden embarrassment.

"It's not a…date or anything. We're just going together as friends."

Shiloh rolled her eyes—her signature move. "That's total BS, Aunt Lucy. It's definitely a date and you know it."

"Don't say 'BS,'" she warned. "Maybe I shouldn't even go. Maybe it's a stupid idea."

Shiloh twisted on the bed until she was facing her aunt. Her expression contained wisdom far beyond her age. "No offense, Aunt Lu, but stop being such a hypocrite." Shiloh crossed her arms over her chest.

Despite the warning, Lucy *was* offended. Shiloh had never said anything like that to her before.

"What are you talking about?"

"Oh, come on. You know exactly what I'm talking about."

"Actually, I don't. Would you care to enlighten me?"

"I can't believe you're being so dense. You always do this."

"Do what?"

"This. What you're doing right now." When Lucy shook her head, she thought Shiloh would explode with frustration.

"This. You tell me to do something—you tell me to be brave and get out there and conquer the world and all that stuff, but you're too afraid to do what you're telling me to do."

Lucy placed a palm over her chest, stunned at her niece's blatant honesty. They sat quietly for a moment, not saying anything. Tension buzzed between them as if they were two opposing magnets.

"That's not true," Lucy said, her voice filled with defeat.

"It is. It is true. And I'm not saying it to hurt your feelings. I'm saying it because you need to know." Shiloh's voice was soft now, all the frustration gone, replaced with tenderness. "You're asking me to put myself out there, to take a risk by going to the dance, even after Zach asked someone else when he knew I wanted to go with him. It's gonna be hard for me to go to that dance, Aunt Lucy, but I'm going anyway, mostly because of what you said. You were right to tell me that I shouldn't let him get in the way of me having a good time with my friends. Zach doesn't get to have a say in my life. And if I don't go, then I'm just admitting defeat. Then Zach wins. So I'm going. But now you're telling me that you don't think you should go with Sam, just because it might be uncomfortable. Just because maybe…maybe something good will happen, and you're so afraid of that."

Shiloh was right, and her honesty floored Lucy.

"How do you know so much, kiddo? You're too young to be so wise."

Her niece shrugged her shoulders, flashing an adorable grin. "Guess I was just raised that way. But seriously, you have to go with Sam. I saw your other dates, Aunt Lu. I know how crappy they were, and

I know you're lonely. So you have to do this, even if you're afraid."

Lucy sank into her pillows, relishing the feeling of the soft plush against her back.

Shiloh continued. "So here's the deal. I go to the dance, without Zach, and I have an amazing time, and maybe make him jealous that he made the stupid decision not to go with me. And you go with Sam and have a good time, too."

"All right. Sounds like a plan," Lucy said.

"But first—dress shopping!" Shiloh squealed.

Lucy reached behind her and grabbed one of the decorative cushions, then fired the first blow of what became an epic pillow fight.

The night of the gala, Sam pulled his rental truck into Lucy's driveway, switching off the engine. He didn't open the door, knowing that if he did, Thor would jump straight into his lap, ruining his rented tuxedo in a heartbeat. He laughed to himself at the sight of the dog's tail thumping on the ground outside his door. Thor let out a slow whine and Sam shouted to the dog that he would be just a minute.

He pulled down the visor, opening the little mirror there, and took one last look at his tie. He wanted to look perfect for Lucy. He couldn't wait to see her in her dress. Not that he didn't love her normal look, but she was the kind of woman that had an understated beauty. He knew that when she dressed up, she would be absolutely stunning, and he felt his body responding at the mere thought.

He reminded himself that he needed to take it slow, although his actions in the past few hours proved that he was doing anything but. First, he'd made phone calls to all of his restaurant managers, telling them that they would have to fend for themselves for a while. They were used to doing that. Sam only got around to each one every once in a while, but he reassured them that he trusted them, that things were in their hands, and to call him if anything came up that required immediate intervention.

Then, he made an even more dangerous call. This time to a Realtor.

He knew it was a crazy move, that it was risky at this point, but he was growing to love Peach Leaf. As soon as he had a chance, he was going to tell Lucy that he was Shiloh's dad, and he would make sure she knew that he wasn't going anywhere.

Then the ball would be in Lucy's court. He knew what he wanted, but he wasn't going to force her to make any kind of commitment that she wasn't ready for. He knew he was jumping in with both feet, without a thought to how the water would be when he landed in it, but the past week had meant more to him than the entirety of his life up to then. The kiss he'd shared with Lucy just sealed the deal.

He was reluctant to put any labels on it, but he

knew what was happening. He knew it because it was a feeling unlike any other he'd ever had. He'd been with a lot of women, but never, not even once, had he wanted to jump in the way he did with Lucy. He was ready to give her his all and he could only hope that she felt the same way. He knew it was a lot to put stock in, but if that kiss told him anything, it was that she was on the same page. He had felt the hunger in it, had felt her need for him to give her more. And tonight he would.

He ran a hand through his hair one last time, thinking about their shopping trip together that day. He wasn't too interested in shopping most of the time, even for himself, but he'd had so much fun that day that he'd almost forgotten that the three of them were looking for dresses for the girls—something he normally wouldn't be a part of.

His girls, as he was beginning to think of them.

He knew he was throwing caution to the wind, but somehow he no longer cared. It was time to go all in, and he was ready. He opened the truck door holding out a hand filled with biscuits that he picked up for the dog, thanking his lucky stars when Thor took them and carried them over to the porch to eat instead of hurling himself onto Sam's rented tux. Sam took a deep breath and pushed Lucy's doorbell button.

Here goes.

He adjusted his coat as he waited for her to come

to the door, steadying himself, knowing that her beauty was likely to knock him on his ass.

He wasn't wrong.

When she opened the door, it was as if sunshine flooded out. He took her in from head to toe, memorizing every inch, not wanting to miss anything. Her curly red hair was drawn into a simple updo with a few strands falling here and there. From what he could tell, she wore very little makeup, but her eyes shone like emeralds against the backdrop of her ivory skin. The apples of her high cheekbones were pink as though the sun had kissed them. He paused when his gaze wandered over her berry lips, which begged for his mouth, but there was more to be savored, so he kept going, running down the length of her, noticing the way her golden dress hugged every curve to perfection. The dress was somehow modest, but sexy, too. It outlined every inch of her body, leaving plenty to the imagination, but suggesting that what was underneath would be well worth the exploration.

And, oh, did he plan on exploring.

"Hi," she said shyly. Sam pulled his eyes back up to her face, and it was even more beautiful now, covered in her smile.

"Hi, gorgeous." They stood there staring at each other like two teenagers on their first date. Finally, Thor brushed past Sam's legs to get inside the house, and he pulled his head back down from the clouds.

You do have somewhere to be, doofus, Sam reminded himself.

He hated to break the moment, since he was enjoying the way Lucy ogled him as well, but the sooner they got the gala over with, the sooner he could have her all to himself.

He'd asked Tessa a favor, and she'd happily acquiesced, arranging for Lucy's friend Paige to take Shiloh to the school dance after she ran it by Lucy first. Paige was going to chaperone anyway, and then Shiloh was going to go home and spend the night at her best friend's, whose mom was picking up both girls from the dance.

He commended himself on his expert planning, knowing that was what it would take to get Lucy alone. The woman was so selfless that it never would've occurred to her to send her niece away for the night. Sam loved having Shiloh around, had become completely enamored of his daughter, but it was about damn time that he got a little closer to Lucy.

He knew that once he could touch her, run his hands over every inch of her body and make love to her in the way that she deserved, that she would truly understand the way he felt about her. Once she knew that for certain—knew that he was ready to give her all of himself—he could risk telling her the truth. Surely she felt the same way. Surely she was falling for him as hard as he was for her.

"Can I come in?" he asked, and Lucy slapped a hand to her forehead.

"Of course," she said. "I'm so sorry. I don't know what I was thinking, standing here like an idiot."

"It's okay. You can look at me like that as long as you want to."

He was pleased when her cheeks turned a darker shade of pink. She opened the door wider and turned to head down the hallway, giving him a spectacular view of her backside. Whereas the front of the gown was modest, the back was just flat-out stunning, the fabric forming a deep V that opened all the way to the very bottom of her waist. The urge to reach out and run a finger all the way from the nape of her neck to the top of her bottom was almost impossible to bear, so Sam took the safe route and looked down at his feet.

"Let me just grab my bag, and I'll be ready to go."

Sam nearly coughed at her words.

He was ready to go, too. Right now.

It would take everything he had to make it through the evening first.

The Lonestar Observatory's fund-raising gala was an annual event, yet it still had the power to take Lucy's breath away each year when she saw the outdoor patio set up for the party. It was like something out of a dream. The deck was covered in pergolas, each of them draped with strand upon strand of tiny twinkling lights. Tall vases filled with flowers were dotted here and there. And then there was the night sky.

It was the most beautiful decoration of all, unobscured by city lights. Peach Leaf was the closest town, and even it was a few miles away; because it was so small, its lights barely made an impact on the vast darkness, illuminating the starlight against the pitch black. Out here, Lucy could revel in the thousands of stars she could see with her naked eye. In her opinion, not even the finest ballroom could compete.

When they'd arrived, she introduced Sam to her friends, all of the staff that he hadn't yet met during the workday. She had been nervous about how she would introduce them, and he had taken over for her when she stumbled, presenting himself simply as her friend. The word was comfortable, and it seemed the best fit for now, but hearing him say it just affirmed what she had already known.

She did not want to be just Sam's friend. She wanted so much more. If only she could work up the courage to tell him. Maybe tonight was the night. It was a magical setting, and Sam looked thrilled to be on her arm, so maybe she would be able to find the words to let him know she wanted more of those kisses.

She felt him behind her back before she could see him, his presence heating her body from the inside out. When she turned and saw him standing there, holding out a flute of sparkling pink champagne, his appearance took her breath away all over again.

God, he is gorgeous.

"I have to tell you, Lucy, I've been to a lot of events in my time, for the restaurants and everything, but I've never seen anything like this. It is truly amazing."

Lucy took a sip of the champagne, enjoying the sensation of the bubbles that jumped up to tease her nose. "Well, I wish I could take credit, but I didn't do any of this. After the initial planning, and a couple of phone calls, it's all Tessa, so I'll let her know you're a fan."

Sam gently removed the glass of champagne from Lucy's hand and set it on the deck rail, his fingers grazing hers in a way that set off tiny sparks underneath her skin.

A thought interrupted the sensation. If just touching him did that to her, and if just kissing him nearly knocked her off her feet, what would it be like to have his naked body next to hers, to have him all to herself, to have those hands running across every crevice, every curve? She closed her eyes, imagining his hands on her—everywhere. She wished she had her champagne back because her mouth was suddenly devoid of all moisture.

"What I'm a fan of, Lucy…is you. I've been wanting to tell you that for days now."

Lucy couldn't have answered if her life depended

on it. She made an effort to swallow, but it was futile. There was no getting around the lump wedged in her throat—a lump she was fairly certain was her heart.

"I know we've only known each other for a week—"

"Less than a week," Lucy interrupted, holding up a finger to correct him, finally able to form words like a normal person. Unfortunately the ones she'd found sounded ridiculous.

Sam grinned. "Less than a week, then," he said. "But sometimes that's enough."

"Enough for what?" she asked.

"Enough to know when something special is happening." He watched her face as she processed what he was saying. "And something special is definitely happening here, Lucy. I can feel it every time you're around me. I know it's very soon, but…what I'm trying to say is…I really, really enjoy your company."

It was her turn to smile. He was completely adorable—sexy as hell, too—but also insanely adorable. She wanted to wrap her arms around him, to hold him close so that there was no chance of his escape, and she would have…if she'd been able to move. But every muscle in her body was frozen in place, locked in the spell of his eyes, his body, the words coming out of his enticing mouth.

He took both of her hands and tugged her away from the deck's railing, pulling her gently toward the center before she had a chance to protest. As a slow, beautiful song began, Sam started to move expertly across the dance floor, leading her with such confidence that she didn't even have to guess what to do with her own two clumsy feet.

So, he was a dancer, too. Apparently there was nothing that this man couldn't do. As the song continued, he pulled her ever closer to him, and she was lost in the light scent of his cologne, and the masculine-smelling soap underneath. She could feel his heart pounding against his chest, the steady rhythm setting her own pulse on fire. Knowing that he wanted her this way gave Lucy a high like nothing else.

How could someone so handsome, so kind, so generous and so obviously enamored with her niece, be so interested in someone like her? It wasn't that she didn't see her own merit. She knew what she looked like, and she was…kind of cute. She was smart, strong and hardworking, and she could see those things about herself. What surprised her about Sam's interest in her was that she made such a concerted effort to go unnoticed, to blend into the background, so that she never had to be afraid of getting too involved…of getting hurt. Somehow, Sam had noticed her anyway. Of all the people in the world, he had picked her out, had chosen to get to know her. That in itself made her feel more special than she ever had before in her entire lifetime.

Her nerves stood on edge when he lowered his

mouth to her ear, skimming it with his lips. Every time he touched her, it set off a craving for more contact. She was becoming addicted to him, and she wondered if they could ever be close enough to satisfy her. At the same time, though, in the back of her mind was the slightest worry.

If he left now, after she'd sunk so deep into him, would she be able to survive without him? She was beginning to crave him like water, like air, and the more she needed him, the more vulnerable she was to the pain of his absence. But she didn't have a choice.

She was falling in love with him, and that was that.

She had thought she'd been in love with Jeremy, but she had never been certain. Whenever Tessa had asked her, Lucy had skirted the question, never able to come up with a sufficient answer. The truth, she knew now, was that she hadn't. She hadn't loved Jeremy. She had wanted to, but he had never been the right person for her. Thank goodness he had turned her down when she'd asked him to move in with her.

The speed at which she was falling for Sam scared her, but at the same time, she knew exactly what it was, and as long as he was here, there was nothing to be afraid of. How sweet it would be to just let go, to stop worrying so much—to just give herself to him. Maybe, for once in her life, she should just trust her instincts. She should just trust that which she felt about Sam was reliable.

She made a decision then. Whatever happened that night would be up to Sam. She was tired of being the one in charge all the time, tired of being the responsible person. For tonight, she would just let go and let him do all the thinking. If he was going to leave, if he was going to hurt her, then it would be his decision. She didn't want to think about how she would recover from that—not now.

Tonight was for her, and she would take it.

Sam moved away from her ear, and he reached down to kiss her neck. The motion was so soft and so gentle that for a second Lucy thought maybe she imagined it. But in the next second, his mouth was on hers, and he was kissing her, gently but deeply, in front of everyone at the event. Lucy closed her eyes, let herself dive into the feeling of his lips on hers. Time seemed to stop for a long moment and when she opened her eyes again, she noticed that several gazes were trained on her and Sam. For once in her life, though, it didn't bother her, not a single bit. She ran her tongue over her lips, letting the taste of Sam sink in as she smiled to herself.

"If you disagree," Sam said, "feel free to let me know, but I think we've been here long enough to please everyone. What do you say?"

"You're not wrong," Lucy said. "Just let me grab my purse and say goodbye to Tessa and we can get out of here."

"Deal," Sam said, but as she turned to leave he

laid a hand on her elbow. "But don't be too long."
Lucy bit her lip and nodded. Sam tickled the inside of her elbow before releasing her. She could feel his eyes on her back as she walked away, and she loved every second of it.

After she grabbed her purse, she looked around for Tessa and found her best friend chatting up a guy at the open bar. Tessa looked over his shoulder and winked when she saw Lucy.

Some things never change.

Tessa excused herself and she and Lucy walked a few feet away.

"I'm bringing Sam home with me tonight," Lucy said, her statement causing Tessa's eyes to expand as wide as the moon above them.

She reached out and grabbed both of Lucy's hands and squealed like a little girl. "Are you sure you're good with this?" Tessa asked.

Lucy almost choked on her disbelief. "Are you kidding me? Aren't you the one who practically shoved me into this guy's arms? Don't start backtracking on me now."

Tessa shook her head. "Oh, no, girl, I am not backtracking at all. I think this is the best decision you made all year. It's just that I love you, and I want to make sure that you're okay."

Lucy's heart swelled at Tessa's sincerity, and she wrapped her friend in a bear hug, pressing their cheeks together, not caring whether or not she destroyed their makeup.

"Thanks," Lucy said, "but I agree with you. This is definitely the best thing I've done in a while. It's the only thing I've done *for me* in a while. I need this, and I know what I'm doing."

"Well, get the hell out of here, then." Tessa pulled out of the hug and shooed Lucy away. "Go on now."

Lucy reached over and gave Tessa's arm a little squeeze. Before she looked away, even though the idea was crazy, she was pretty sure she saw a tear in her best friend's eye.

Half an hour later, Lucy and Sam were back on her front porch.

Her nerves got the best of her as she fumbled with her keys at the door. When she finally got it unlocked and led him inside, the darkness in the house startled her. It had been so long since she had been in the house alone, much less with a man. The newness of the situation gave her a thrill. She knew she should probably feel nervous, should probably be worrying about how she would look when he removed her clothes. What would he see when he peeled off the layers and got down to the heart of her?

It had been so long since she'd let a man near her bare body that she had forgotten to be self-conscious about it until right then. She expected to feel that way now, but for some reason, all she sensed was a mind-blowing desire to be touched, held, kissed by this man. There wasn't even a trace of trepidation. All she felt was need.

After they let Thor out and then managed to tempt him into his dog bed with a few biscuits, Lucy led Sam down the hallway and into her room.

As she closed the door, she turned and saw everything that she was experiencing reflected in Sam's eyes, along with a heat she hadn't seen there before. She reveled in the fact that he wanted her as badly as she wanted him.

She stood with her back to the door, not knowing exactly what to do next. She was glad when Sam took the lead. He drew near to her, so close she could feel his rapid breathing. He reached up and ran a single finger along the side of her face, drawing it down to her lips. He touched her bottom lip with his thumb, leaving it there as he stepped closer to her.

When his mouth touched hers, it was as warm and sweet as hot caramel, and she melted into it.

His kiss was firmer now than it had been when he'd kissed her before and when he ran his tongue along her upper lip, urging her to let him in, she was more than pleased to say yes. The kiss deepened, and his hands were in her hair, his fingers weaving through her thick curls. At first, her hands remained by her sides, as she was unsure what to do with them. But then she worked up the courage to let them do what they wanted to, and she reached out to settle them on his waist. Her fingers worked his shirttails out of his trousers, and when she was able, she slid them up the sides of his waist and over his firm chest, discovering that the skin there was as hot as his mouth. He kissed her again as his hands wandered away from her hair down to her own waist. He wrapped them around her, pulling her closer still until she could feel exactly how much he wanted her.

He continued kissing her until they were both breathless, and only then did he pull away.

"Lucy…Lucy," Sam panted, "look at me."

She obliged and when she met his eyes, desperation and concern warred in them.

"Lucy," he said again, her name sounding like music on his tongue. "Are you sure this is what you want?" She nodded her head, but Sam shook his in argument. "No, it's not enough. I need to hear you say the words."

Lucy hesitated, her confidence suddenly shaken by his doubt, if that's what it was. "Why? Are you having second thoughts?"

"Absolutely not," Sam said. "It's not that at all, I promise you. I just need to make sure that this is okay with you. I don't want you to do anything that you're not ready for."

Sam's care for her tugged at her heart, but was overridden by her frantic craving to be closer to him. If voicing that kept him from putting a brake on things, then so be it.

"Yes, yes. This is what I want. I'm a grown woman and even though it's been a while, this isn't my first rodeo. Now stop yammering, and kiss me."

"Yes, ma'am," Sam said, clearly enjoying her sudden bossiness. He did as she told him, kissing her again and again, pushing her as far as she could stand. He tugged her dress off over her head and explored her skin, his fingers generous and tender. He touched every part of her, bringing her body back to life one starved inch at a time, and she gave back as much as she received.

When they both tottered on the edge, she led him to the bed, where he showed her exactly how much he adored her body. Each time he let go inside of her, and each time he gave her the release she hadn't known she craved so much, he exposed a little bit more of himself to her. And by the time they collapsed in a happy, exhausted heap in the early hours of morning, the sun peeking in through her bedroom window, Lucy knew without a doubt that she'd fallen in love with Sam Haynes.

Sam awoke the next morning to find Lucy asleep in his arms. Sunlight streamed in through her window, its rays stroking her fiery hair, illuminating strands of gold. Her beauty was ethereal and he wondered if he was still in a dream.

She stirred and stretched out her arms and Sam

leaned on his elbows to watch her, admiring her porcelain skin, fully exposed for his pleasure.

When she showed no signs of joining him in the waking world, he reached over and gently tickled her stomach. Eventually she opened one sleepy eye and caught him, but then she closed it again. He grew impatient staring at her, waiting for her to wake up and join him. He wanted so badly to talk to her, to see if she was as happy as he was about last night.

He tried to ignore the funny feeling in his stomach, the one nagging him to tell her the truth. He would do it today, before he left her house. He knew she might be angry, but the way things had gone last night, he was certain he could convince her that he had no malicious intent in keeping it from her for so long.

She would have to believe him; otherwise he wouldn't know what to do.

As the night had gone on, as they had made love over and over again, the passion growing deeper each time, he became certain of what he had been feeling this whole time.

He knew now that he was in love with her.

All he had to do was work out how to tell her. But first, she needed to know that he was Shiloh's father. He knew what he wanted, but he wouldn't ask her to want the same things. He knew that it might take her some time to decide whether or not she wanted them to be a family. But if there was anything in the world he could give her, it was time. His restaurants were doing fine, according to his most recent check-in phone calls and emails, and he had no pressing need to return to New York anytime soon. At some point he would need to get his things from his apartment there, but for now, he cared only about Lucy and Shiloh.

After he tried again to get her to wake up, Sam gave up and reluctantly dragged himself out of her grasp, tugging on his shorts as he left the room. He headed down to the kitchen and let Thor out the back door to do his morning business. As Sam waited, keeping an eye on the dog out the window, he opened cabinets and found Thor's dog food, and coffee for himself. He turned on Lucy's geriatric coffeemaker and added water and grounds, making a mental note to buy her a Keurig on his next trip into town—that is, if one could be located in Peach Leaf.

Starbucks would be better, but he would settle for baby steps.

As the old coffeemaker sputtered to life, Sam glanced out the window to check on Thor. He scanned the front yard a few times, but the dog was nowhere to be found. A twinge of fear prickled at his neck, but he was sure there was nothing to be alarmed about—the dog had probably got distracted by a strong smell. He set down the coffee cup he had pulled out of the cabinet and opened the front door to whistle for Thor to come back inside. But when he looked out, he found the last thing on earth that he would've ever expected to see.

A woman stepped out from an old beat-up car and tugged a duffel bag out of the backseat. He knew who she was before she even turned around.

Jennifer.

The obvious question was…what in hell was she doing there?

Sam couldn't form a single coherent thought. He just stood there like an idiot as she closed the car door and walked toward the house, covering her eyes with a hand to shade them from the sun. His feet were leaden and he couldn't seem to move at all.

When she stepped onto the porch, she didn't say anything, just stood there reciprocating his moronic stare.

"Well," she said. "This is a surprise."

"Hello, Jennifer," he said, crossing his arms over his chest. He wished he could cross them over other things, as well. He wasn't exactly adequately clothed to be standing on a porch in broad daylight. The fact that he was so exposed irritated the hell out of him. He might be able to manage some dignity if he'd had a few more stitches of fabric within reach.

No such luck.

"You win the prize for the understatement of a lifetime."

Jennifer stopped on the porch and dropped her bag. "I have to tell you…I did not expect this of my shy sister." She looked down and dug her toe into the porch like a nervous child.

"Can I ask what brings you here?" he asked.

"I just came to see my daughter. Our daughter." Her eyes jumped up to his. She looked the same as she had back then, back when he was in college when they had met each other at that fateful party. Her eyes were the same cobalt as Shiloh's, but they were tired—old beyond her age. And she was still an attractive woman, though he wasn't drawn to her as he had been that night, now so far in the past. The evidence of her hard lifestyle was etched into her features. When he looked at her, Sam felt a rush of sadness—a flood of regret at how Jennifer had chosen to handle something that could have turned out so much different, so much better.

"Well," Sam said, "this isn't my house and—"

Jennifer reached down to grab her bag and shoved past Sam into the house. He rushed after her, his brain working to find a way to get her to leave. If he couldn't do it on his own, he'd have to wake Lucy. He didn't want her to find Jennifer here, knowing the grief it would cause the woman he loved.

But another part of him needed to talk to her—there was so much he wanted to know.

"Jennifer," he said, "I should've said this a long time ago, and it's probably strange to say it now, but I'm sorry about the way I treated you that night."

"As far as I recall, you treated me just fine." Her

eyes were filled with pain and regret when she said the words, negating any of their truth.

"That's not what I meant," he said, his stomach churning. "What I meant was, I should have called the next day. I shouldn't have just hooked up with you and then let you walk away. Doing so was a mistake. I made a lot of them back then, all of which I'm sorry for. I just want you to know that I didn't intend to harm you."

Jennifer studied him. "You don't owe me any apology. I was an adult and we made a decision to do an adult thing together. Neither of us is to blame for what happened. Condoms aren't foolproof, and I should've thought about that before I took that risk. I made plenty of mistakes on my own back then."

Under any other circumstances, the words would've hurt, but they were completely and totally true. She was right. They were both to blame. That didn't excuse her decision to block him from Shiloh's life, but it wouldn't do any good to rehash that now. What was done was done, and he had already taken steps toward the future he wanted.

Sam's hands balled into fists of nervous energy. "You've got to go, Jennifer. You'll wake Lucy and I don't want her to find you here. It will hurt her, and I can't allow that."

Jennifer just gave him a sideways glance and moved toward the living room, Sam following quickly behind her. Before he could stop her, she picked up the book that Sam had noticed before on the coffee table and had it open in her lap.

It was a photo album, and as Jennifer flipped through the pages, Sam watched Shiloh's history unfold before his eyes. There she was as a baby, as cute as she could be, and then again on a bicycle with training wheels, and in a swimming pool wearing pink goggles and flotation armbands.

And then the pictures stopped. There was a huge gap after about age six or seven. Then they started again, but this time Shiloh was in a wheelchair. It occurred to Sam that he should be livid beyond belief at the woman sitting next to him on the couch.

She had given birth to his daughter and kept her a secret. Then she had gone out drinking, and put Shiloh in that car, taking their daughter with her, and had forever destroyed the child's ability to walk. He had every reason in the world to be angry at Jennifer, to want to punish her for all the suffering she'd caused, but, looking at her there on Lucy's couch, such a far cry from her sister's vivacity, all he felt was a wave of sorrow. She was sick, and that wasn't her fault. He would not presume to understand what it must be like to struggle with a mental illness. But he couldn't help but wish that she'd chosen a different path—one that involved his and Lucy's help. And it broke his heart that she'd abandoned her daughter.

He was going to be the one to be a permanent fixture in Shiloh's life. He was the one who got to start fresh with his amazing daughter. He planned to be around for everything that happened from here on out. For that he was grateful, and his thankfulness eradicated any anger that he might have otherwise felt for Jennifer. He only had so much room in his future, and he chose to fill it with good things. He could only hope that, at some point, Jennifer would get back on her medicine, and make the same choice. Her daughter deserved that.

They sat quietly for a while, Sam studying the pictures over Jennifer's shoulder as she turned the pages. The photographs were touching, obviously taken by Lucy. The adoration for their subject was evident in each shot.

He sipped his coffee and got lost in the images.

"Does someone want to tell me what in holy hell is going on here?"

Neither he nor Jennifer had heard Lucy pad down the stairs, and they both jumped at the sound of her voice. It was filled with ice, and it splashed across Sam's neck and down his back. He turned and caught her eyes. Every trace of the heat from the night before had completely disappeared. All that filled them now was unmistakable hatred, most of it directed at him.

He opened his mouth to speak but Lucy raised a hand, commanding him not to say another word. "It looks like you two know each other," she said.

Out of the corner of his eye, Sam saw Jennifer look at him before they nodded in unison.

"How?"

Sam would never forget the look on Lucy's face when she asked the loaded question. He had never seen so many warring emotions in one place—confusion, pain, betrayal—and he wanted to punish himself for causing them.

Sam looked over at Jennifer, but she had disconnected and focused on her lap, refusing to engage any further. He knew it would be up to him to explain. Jennifer did not have the strength. And it was his responsibility to pull himself out of this hole. He'd been digging it for a week now, and he deserved whatever came his way. He should have told Lucy everything sooner, but it was too late for that now.

"It's a long story," Sam said, rubbing his hands over his face.

"Well," Lucy said. "I've got time."

"Jennifer and I…we met a long time ago, in college. There was a party one night and we…I…"

"We slept together," Jennifer said, her voice low and difficult to interpret.

Lucy crossed her arms over her chest, and Sam noticed even from a distance that she was shivering in the shorts and T-shirt she had thrown on. He wanted to pick her up and wrap her in his arms to warm her against his chest. He wanted to tell her how desperately sorry he was, and that everything was going to be okay. Up until that moment, he had believed that it would be, but now the look in her eyes brought back every doubt he'd had about them before last night.

"I see," Lucy said. A brief hint of jealousy crossed her features before she headed away. Sam realized that she still didn't understand the extent of his and Jennifer's relationship.

"That's not it," Sam said. He closed his eyes, squeezing them shut until he felt pain. He opened them again and forced himself to look Lucy straight in the eyes, sending up a silent prayer that what he was about to say wouldn't change her feelings about him.

He knew that was a lot to ask, but after last night, it didn't matter. He would do everything in his power to make her understand that he loved her. No matter how long it took, no matter what he had to do, no matter how hard he had to work, he would make her understand that she and Shiloh meant more to him than anything in the world, and that he would be there for them from here on out.

He wasn't leaving unless she told him to. He ran through a string of words in his mind, all the possible ways he could phrase the facts, but none of them were good enough. None of them would express everything that he was feeling, so he decided to go for the simplest.

"I'm Shiloh's father," he said.

Lucy's face was instantly stripped of its color, and she grabbed the banister next to her for support. Sam shot up from the couch and went over to her, but when he reached out a hand to touch her she batted him away. He expected her to cry, to scream at him and to be angry, but none of that came. What happened instead scared and unnerved him.

Her face was devoid of any emotion, and he had no idea at all what she was thinking.

"Say something, Lucy. Please say something," Sam said as he knelt on the step in front of her.

Lucy opened her eyes and they burned into his. "I have nothing to say to you—either of you."

Finally, Jennifer spoke up. "I came here to see Shiloh," she said as if it was the most reasonable thing in the world.

Lucy turned her attention to her sister. "You've got to be kidding me," Lucy snapped. "How dare you walk in here after all these years, after what you did the last time you were here? Don't you think you've caused enough damage for a lifetime?"

Jennifer rose from her position on the couch and stood at the bottom of the stairs. "That's not fair, Lucy."

Lucy's eyes shot daggers at Jennifer. "Not fair? You want to talk about what's fair? What's not fair, what's never been fair, is that the two of you made a choice many years ago, and I'm the one who paid the price for that choice." Lucy stabbed a finger into her chest. “I’m the one who never got to make a choice. All of your choices fell on me. I’m the one who raised your daughter—the daughter that the two of you abandoned. I love her more than anything on this earth, and I wouldn’t trade her for the world, but I should’ve had a say in the matter.”

Jennifer looked down at her feet in shame.

“I can’t believe that the two of you think you have the right to come into my home and disrupt the life that I’ve made for me and Shiloh. After all you’ve done, you think you can just show up all of a sudden and be a part of her life? It doesn’t work like that. I’ve made a home for her, I’ve given her stability, and I don’t want her to have to go through any more loss.”

“I have a right to see my daughter,” Jennifer said.

Lucy winced at the words. “You have a right to see her when I say you can see her. You know I have full custody of Shiloh. That was the deal. I let you visit back then because I thought that she needed to know her mother, but that was before the accident. You can’t just show up here whenever you want, without calling, and expect me to just let you in. It’s confusing for Shiloh. We’ve built a life here, and it’s a good one. If you want to be a part of it, you’re going to have to start seeing a doctor and taking your medications again.” Lucy sighed and rubbed her temple. “If you need my help to do that, Jennifer, just ask.”

Jennifer seemed to consider Lucy’s words for a long moment before she hesitated. The sudden spark of hope was gone and she looked away from Lucy, turning toward the living room to pick up her duffel bag.

Lucy sat back down on the step, but her body didn't relax. Her spine was stiff and she held her shoulders high, even as deep sadness and disappointment filled her eyes. Her voice and demeanor challenged either of them to say anything in contest. Sam tried again to touch her, but she slapped his hand away.

This is what happens when you love someone. You have the power to cause that person pain.

Before he met Lucy, he would have said that love wasn't worth it. But she had changed his mind. He knew she loved him too; he knew she wanted a family for Shiloh. Even though she had a right to, he wasn't going to let her throw that away.

But right now, what she needed was space.

"Get out," Lucy said, her voice soft and deflated. "Right now. Both of you, get out. I want you out of my sight and out of my house—" Lucy covered her eyes with her hands, and Sam saw tears begin to flow down her cheeks "—and out of my life."

Without a word, Jennifer picked up her bag and walked out, slamming the front door behind her. Sam lingered for a moment, wondering if there was anything in the world he could possibly say to change Lucy's mind. There was only one thing he could try. "Lucy, I…I didn't know until—"

She held up a hand and he could see that she'd blocked him out completely. She wouldn't be able to hear him until she had some time to think.

"Please, Sam. I can't listen to another word right now."

In the space of twenty-four hours, he had both fallen in love and had his heart shattered into a thousand pieces.

And if that was how he felt, he couldn't begin to imagine what Lucy must be experiencing.

She needed time, and he would give her that.

He would be back—there was nothing in the world that could stop him. But for now, he had to let her go.

Chapter Nine

A few days later, Lucy tried her best to listen as Dr. Blake droned on and on about an upcoming project with a group of kids from a nearby school, but for the life of her, she couldn't make herself concentrate on a single word he was saying.

All she could think about was Sam…and Jennifer…and Sam and Jennifer, and all the things they had kept from her. She expected such a thing from Jennifer, but Sam…Sam was another story altogether. She loved Jennifer, and understood her sister's illness. She knew that Jennifer's daily life consisted of a kind of pain that Lucy would never be able to fully understand. And even though she knew that maybe she shouldn't, she gave Jennifer allowances that she wouldn't afford other people, because Jennifer was her family, and that was just what you did for family.

But Sam was different. Lucy had trusted Sam with her heart, with her body, with everything that she had to offer. She never would've expected what had happened. She had truly begun to believe that they could have a life together, the three of them—they could be a real family.

She would probably never see Sam again.

After what had happened, she hadn't been surprised when he had turned in his resignation. In his favor, he had done the right thing and delivered it to her by hand, rather than by email like a coward.

She scoffed. Even when she wanted to hate him, she couldn't.

And even though she wanted to forget about him, to erase him from her mind so that she could begin to fill it with other things, she couldn't. He filled her every waking thought from the moment she got up in the morning to when she went to bed at night. And no matter what she did to prevent it, she wondered where he was, and whether or not he had gone back to New York.

After the eruption of chaos the other day, she had gone round and round with herself wondering whether or not it was the right thing to tell Shiloh who her father was. Eventually she had decided that she would. She had had enough secrets for a lifetime, and even though Sam wasn't going to be a part of their lives, she genuinely believed that Shiloh had a right to know. Her niece was old enough now to handle such a delicate piece of information. She sure as hell was smart enough, so Lucy had given it to her.

Shiloh had taken the news with her usual maturity. She had been upset, of course, not because of the information, but because of what had happened with Sam. She blamed Lucy at first for not trying to get him to stay, but then she had come around and forgiven her aunt. There wasn't any point in keeping secrets anymore. The thing that they needed to do now was to pick up the pieces and get on with their lives, just the two of them.

There was a knock on her office door, and Lucy was relieved when Tessa poked her head around the corner. Dr. Blake looked at his watch and excused himself, letting the two women get to their lunch plans.

"I thought he was never going to go," Lucy said. Tessa nodded. Dr. Blake had a reputation for being a little bit long-winded, which was normally okay, but became a little less tolerable when lunchtime rolled around.

"I'm ready for some lunch," Tessa said. "How about you, lady?"

"Definitely," Lucy said, grabbing her purse out of her bottom desk drawer. "What are you feeling today? It's your turn."

"I know you may hate me for this, and you can definitely say no, but I really, really want to eat at the café."

"No," Lucy said, "it's fine."

"You sure?"

"Yeah, it's not like he's still there."

"I know," Tessa said. "But I would understand if you didn't want to go back there yet. The only reason I brought it up is because everybody keeps raving about the new menu and I can't stand to hear another word about it without knowing for myself if it's really worth all the hype."

"It really is okay," Lucy said. "You don't have to explain. Besides, I need to go down there and check on things with the new guy. I met with him several times, and he's getting rave reviews from customers and the staff. He seems to be doing just fine on his own, but I really should drop in and see for myself."

That settled, the two women headed to the café and grabbed a table. Lucy went into the kitchen and chatted with the new chef for a while. She had called him back for that interview and he was a perfect fit for the small restaurant. His repertoire included a mix of classic, home-style dishes, but with enough flair to keep things interesting—much like Sam, but, if Lucy was honest, a little less creative.

She rejoined Tess at the table just as their orders arrived. They tucked into their food. After several moments of quiet, Lucy noticed that her best friend wasn't her usual chatty self.

"What's up with you? Why are you so quiet today?" She eyed Tess across the table.

Tessa poked at her food, stirring it around into little mountains. Lucy noticed that she had barely taken a bite since they'd arrived. Tessa finally put down her fork.

"Okay," Tessa said. "I have something to tell you and it's going to sound strange. It happened yesterday and I wanted to come and talk to you right away, but you were busy leading that tour, and I didn't have a chance. That's why I wanted to have lunch with you today."

Lucy gave Tessa a funny look. "We have lunch every day."

Tessa rolled her eyes. "You know what I mean. Just listen."

Lucy set her own fork on the edge of her plate and folded her napkin in her lap, focusing her attention on her best friend.

"Okay, what is it?"

Tessa stared down into her food. "When I got home last night, I found Jennifer sitting on my doorstep."

"Oh," Lucy said. "What in the world was she doing at your house?"

Tessa's shoulders bobbed up and down and she tilted her head to the side. "At first I didn't want to let her in, knowing what happened to you the other day. But she insisted, and she looked so…downtrodden… so finally I did. I remember how she could be sometimes, and I didn't want to leave her outside. She was acting so weird, different from even one of her manic states. She just seemed so sad and lonely."

Lucy didn't like where this was going. Jennifer had spent many a night at Tessa's home when she'd run away from her own after a fight with their parents. Lucy hated the thought of Tessa having to be involved in their family problems again. But she wanted to hear what her best friend had to say. Even if Jennifer couldn't be a part of Lucy's life, Lucy would always care about her sister's well-being.

"Lucy, she told me something that I really think you should know. It pretty much changes everything."

"You have my attention," Lucy said.

"Do you remember back when Jennifer first brought Shiloh home to you?"

"Of course. How could I forget?"

"Well, remember what she said about the father? About how he didn't want to have anything to do with the baby? She said that she had talked to him, and that he had refused to be part of Shiloh's life."

"Yes, I remember like it was yesterday, and now I know that the father was…Sam. What's the point?"

"The thing is…when Jennifer spoke to me yesterday, she said that was all a lie. She said she told you that so that you wouldn't look into it any further."

Lucy looked down into her lap and noticed for the first time that she had shredded her napkin into several tiny pieces. A chill flooded through her as she remembered a moment from their argument. Just before Sam had left, he'd said something about not knowing, but she'd been too hurt to listen. She'd told him to leave, and he had done as she'd asked.

"Lucy, do you understand what I'm saying?"

Lucy nodded, her stomach queasy. Her brain felt as if it was going to explode with all of the information that it had taken in over the past few days.

"It wasn't Sam's fault, was it?"

Tessa nodded, focusing her wide eyes on Lucy. "Sam didn't find out that he had a daughter until recently—just before he came here, in fact."

Understanding hit Lucy like a rocket barreling into earth's atmosphere.

Everything that hadn't made sense about Sam's sudden arrival in town now became crystal clear.

That was why he had come to Peach Leaf. That was why he had pressed so hard when it came to how she parented Shiloh. He had told her the other day that he was Shiloh's father, but she'd refused to listen when he tried to tell her the whole truth.

It seemed that Jennifer had lied to both of them, and they had both been operating under assumptions that had no basis in fact.

But Sam had still chosen to withhold his identity from her before then.

"Why didn't he tell me earlier that he was Shiloh's father? We spent all this time together, getting to know each other, and…falling in love…or at least it felt that way, and the whole time he kept that from me. Why would he have done such a thing? I really thought I could trust him. If it wasn't his fault, if he really only did just find out before he came here, then why did he keep that from me for so long? It would have been so easy for him to just tell me that the first day he showed up."

Tessa reached a hand across the table and looped her fingers around Lucy's. "I wish I could answer that, honey. But I can't. I can only tell you what Jennifer shared with me—that she hadn't told you the truth because she always felt like you were the better kid, the more perfect one. She was so ashamed that she'd got pregnant so young, and that she wasn't able to care for Shiloh that she couldn't tell you she'd left the father out of it. She thought you would sympathize with her more if you believed he'd turned her away. But I can't speak for Sam. There's only one person who can."

It made a lot of sense, actually. Jennifer had always been so much like their mother. She'd been the passionate, vivacious one who had worn her heart on her sleeve, and let herself be vulnerable to having it broken by almost anyone who paid attention to her. Lucy's father had been so involved in his work that he hadn't noticed their mother's cries for attention—or her multiple affairs. It wasn't that he hadn't loved his girls—he just wasn't the type to display affection like their mother. He had difficulty relating to people. Honestly, Lucy couldn't figure out how their parents had ever got together, much less fallen in love. They were polar opposites, and they never should have been drawn to each other.

She didn't want to be like her father, though. She didn't want to lose someone she loved by shutting him out.

Lucy sighed and dropped her head onto the table. She let out a groan. "That figures, because he's the last person that I want to talk to right now."

Tessa squeezed her hand. "I know, but don't you think you owe it to him to at least find out his side of the story?"

Lucy wiped her bangs out of her eyes and tugged her glasses back up her nose. "Ugh. I really freaking hate it when you're right."

Lucy looked up and Tessa was sporting a self-righteous face. "I know you do, but what you hate even more, honey, is that it happens so dadgum often."

Chapter Ten

Sam loaded the last of his bags into the back of his rental truck, the hot Texas sun sending beads of sweat trickling down his neck. Mrs. Frederickson came up beside him and he turned to hug her one last time. The poor older woman had tears in her eyes, and Sam didn't know whether to laugh or to join her.

"I promise I'll visit," Sam said. "The apartment I'm leasing for a while is just up the road. And I promise next time, I'll cook for you instead of the other way around."

Mrs. Frederickson hugged him tight before releasing him. "And make sure you let me know what happens with your girls," she said, shaking a finger at him.

Sam grimaced. He should've known better than to share such things with the woman who, he was slowly figuring out, was a notorious town gossip.

"All right, then," he said. "That's everything."

He took a last look around and hopped into the rental truck that would take him to the apartment he'd leased until he could convince Lucy to let him back into her heart.

He'd made a few phone calls to handle things in New York until he could go back and make more permanent arrangements.

Funny, he thought, but New York didn't really feel like home anymore.

The realization that he would never have a home without Lucy and Shiloh sank like a bag of sand to the bottom of his stomach. They were his family. They were his home. If only he could find a way to convince Lucy of that. He had tried calling her probably one hundred times since their terrible fight, but she had refused to answer the phone. The truth was, he didn't blame her. He and Jennifer had really given her a load of awfulness to deal with, and he knew it would probably take time for her to get used to that information. That was okay. He had plenty of time.

If only he had a little more patience to go along with it.

He started up the engine and drove out of the bed-and-breakfast parking lot onto Main Street, taking in all the shops and the restaurants he had grown to love, despite his initial reaction to the small town's food selection.

Still, though, the place needed a respectable coffee shop. Not to mention a decent pizza joint. Both were things he planned to address once things were right with Lucy.

As he drove toward the apartment, he wondered what she was doing at that very moment, as he had done every second of every day since they'd met. He had thought multiple times about just going over to her house, demanding that she see him, to listen to reason. She didn't even know his side of the story yet.

Part of him knew that that would just make things worse. Wouldn't it? He wasn't going to force her to love him. She had to come to that on her own.

But what if she never did?

Lucy was a woman who gave everything of herself to others. She wasn't the type to ask for something, even if she wanted it.

What if Sam had the power to change her mind? What if he just needed to fight for her? From what he knew of her, no one had ever fought for Lucy. People had used Lucy, had taken advantage of Lucy, abused the privilege of her love and her selflessness, but no one had ever stood up for her.

Sam slammed his foot on to the brake pedal and his truck screeched to a stop at the side of the road.

Calling and texting her just wasn't enough. She needed him to be stronger than that for her. And he needed to show her that she was worth fighting for. He knew what he had to do.

He couldn't go another minute without seeing her again, without making her understand that he hadn't intended to deceive her. All he had wanted, all he had been working for since they met, was her and Shiloh's happiness. He kicked himself for not realizing it sooner. All of this that he'd been trying to do, leaving her alone, giving her time to herself, was really not helping anything. It was all due to the shameful fact that he was afraid. He was afraid that if he confronted her she might say no to a family with him, and it would destroy his life. He needed her in it, and the thought of her deciding not to be was something he couldn't handle.

But he had to try.

He put his foot on the gas and turned the truck in the other direction, heading toward her house.

This was his last chance.

This was *their* last chance at real love, hope and happiness…at family.

Lucy and Shiloh were tossing the ball to Thor in the front yard when she saw his truck pull up. The sight of it made her catch her breath as a mix of emotions welled up into a dark cloud inside of her. She couldn't tell if she was angry, sad or…hopeful.

Ever since their fight the other day, she had imagined and daydreamed about this very moment. She had wanted Sam to come back so that she could ask him how he felt. Eventually, she had convinced herself that if he loved her, he would try harder to let her know. She had been evading his texts and calls for a week now, knowing that anything they had to say to each other would be completely inadequate through an electronic device.

She needed to see him. She wanted to see him, even if it was one last time. She had so many things that she needed to ask him, so many things that she needed to understand, before he walked out of her life forever.

She wasn't ready to let him go.

But when she saw that truck pull up, her pulse went off on its own.

She couldn't seem to control her feelings when it came to Sam. She loved him and that was it.

And if it was just her, she would have confronted him a lot sooner, and forced him to tell her why he had been so secretive about being Shiloh's dad. But it wasn't just her that she had to think about. She had to consider how this new development would affect Shiloh, as well. And until she had some answers, until she knew whether or not she could really trust Sam, she had to be fierce about protecting her niece. Shiloh had always come first, and even though now Lucy was more open to allowing herself to love a man, her niece remained her first priority, as she always would. Lucy had dedicated herself to

Shiloh all those years ago, promising she would do her very best to be a parent, to put her niece's needs above her own. She had kept her promise, and even though she wanted to love Sam, her commitment to Shiloh hadn't changed.

But the fact remained that if she could have chosen any man in the world, could have put together all of the finest qualities in a father, she could have searched a lifetime and never have found anyone better than Sam. He was kind, generous and loving.

How much it must hurt him to have missed so much of his daughter's life. Even if he was guilty of deception, hadn't he paid a high enough price already? Wasn't the worst sort of punishment the one that Jennifer had doled out to him?

Lucy didn't want to inflict any more pain.

Sam pulled the truck to a stop and stepped out of the cab and immediately found himself covered in Thor's slobber as the dog bounced up into his arms.

Shiloh seemed to know instinctively that Lucy and Sam needed some space, so she called Thor to follow her into the house. Before she closed the front door, she nodded to Lucy and gave her a thumbs-up. Despite the rapid sound of her heartbeat, the beads of perspiration forming, and the hairs standing up on her neck, Lucy smiled at her niece's gesture

She pulled her shoulders up, straightening her posture, and raised her chin, ready to face whatever

Sam had to say. Regardless of what happened, she only needed him to know one thing.

She would tell him that she loved him, and let him make his own decision about that information. Of course she hoped that he would stay. Of course she hoped that he wanted to be a permanent part of her and Shiloh's lives, but she wouldn't demand such a thing from him. She would let him know that he was welcome whenever he wanted to see his daughter, and the rest was up to him.

Instead of walking toward her, Sam moved to the back of his truck and lowered the gate. He jumped up into the bed and patted the space next to him, inviting her to join him.

Lucy's heart swelled at his gesture, recalling that day when she came home to find him building Shiloh's wheelchair ramp and they had sat in the afternoon sun enjoying each other's company, before things got complicated.

It was an afternoon that she would cherish for the rest of her life. It was when she had first noticed how comfortable, and yet how alive and on fire she felt in Sam's presence. She wondered now if that was the moment when she had first started to love him.

Had he felt the same way? Even if he did decide to stay, how would she ever know if it was for her, for Shiloh, or for both?

There was only one way to find out. She walked over and took Sam's hand as he held it out to help her up into the truck. Neither of them said a word, just like before. But unlike then, when they had sat together in total peace, this time the air crackled with an unpleasant sort of tension.

It seemed as if all the words they wanted to say to each other were stuck inside their hearts. Lucy couldn't tell how much time passed before Sam spoke, but it felt like forever. A mix of relief and bittersweet hope hit her when he opened his mouth.

"Lucy, I came to tell you that I'm not leaving."

Rather than its usual calm, soothing tone, his voice was filled with determination.

Paralyzed, she sat in silence.

She didn't know what she'd expected him to say, but his words were exactly what she wanted to hear, and they further softened her already tender heart. Lucy felt the prickle of tears behind her eyes, and she removed her glasses to rub them.

"Sam, I—"

"Hang on, Lucy. I'm not finished. I have some things that I want to say to you."

This time his words were even more firm, and even though they weren't exactly the "I love you" that she'd hoped he would say next, it seemed like a little more life was injected into them.

"I'm listening."

She fiddled with a hole that had sprouted in her jeans, nervous and jittery, but Sam just sat there as calm and steady as the oak tree that had been in Lucy's front yard since before she was born. Even in this moment of terrible tension, he had the capacity to soothe her.

She wondered if she would ever find anyone like that again, but even before the thought fully landed in her mind, she knew the answer. There was no one else in the world like Sam, no one else she would ever want the way she did him. He was the only man who had ever come into her and Shiloh's lives and shown interest and passion for both of them. Lucy knew now the reason, because he was her niece's father. But a spark of hope inside of her clung to the possibility that maybe what they had was real, independent of Shiloh.

"You have every right to despise me," Sam said. "It was wrong of me to come into your life without any explanation, to take so much time from you and Shiloh, without giving you any reason. It was stupid as hell of me to withhold the truth from you for so long. And I'm not saying any of this to excuse myself, or to give you reason to forgive me. I'm not asking anything like that of you. I just want you to know that when I came here, it was only for Shiloh."

His words sliced through her so sharply that she wondered if he also had the power to remove the stars from the sky. It felt as if he had reached inside and grabbed her heart, pulling it out of her chest and leaving it on the floor.

She had been wrong. Her instincts had misled her.

He had come for Shiloh alone, and he didn't want anything to do with her. She thought for sure that the tears would come, fast and relentless, but it seemed that she was dried up, hollow inside.

"Sam, please don't say any more. I don't think I can take it."

He turned to her and for the first time he looked uncertain as his hands fidgeted in his lap. So many emotions covered his face, and she couldn't make sense of any of them.

"No, Lucy, that's not it at all. You don't understand. Even though I came for her—when I met you…everything changed."

"Thanks for that, Captain Obvious. Everything changed for me, as well. That tends to happen when a new person walks in and turns your world upside down."

In the midst of what would probably be the most important conversation of her life, a hint of humor flashed across Sam's eyes at her statement and she wished so hard that things were different. She wanted to go back to a few days ago when they had laughed together, got lost in each other's bodies, when they had been happy for that brief stint of time. She would do anything to get that back.

Sam's face turned instantly serious. "Lucy, listen to me. Stop being so stubborn. I'm trying to tell you that everything changed in a good way. I didn't expect you. Up until I met you, I would've told anyone with certainty that I didn't have room for that kind of love in my life. Up until I met you, I didn't even believe that that kind of love existed. I would've told you that it was just a joke, something sold in movies, but that didn't exist in real life."

Something inside of her shifted as she slowly began to understand his meaning. She wanted to latch on to that tiny inkling of hope that was starting to bubble up inside of her. She dared to look into his eyes, and when she did, they spoke of his love more clearly than any words he might have said. All the same, she wanted to hear it from his lips.

"Sam, are you saying that—"

He interrupted her with his mouth, but it wasn't by speaking. In the space of half a second, he had moved in, wrapped his palms around her face and he was kissing her. The kiss was both harder and tenderer than any they had shared so far. As it grew deeper, Lucy struggled to maintain control, afraid that if she didn't stop she might get lost in it.

She pulled away, biting her lip.

"What I'm saying, Lucy, is that I want to be a part of Shiloh's life. But that's not all I want. I want to be a part of your life, as well. I didn't expect any of this, and I know you didn't, either, but it would be a damn shame if we let something like this go. Lucy, you're the most beautiful, smart and interesting person I've ever met, and I'm not going to let you go without a fight. You're a damn fine woman—and I love you."

Lucy was glad she was sitting in the truck bed because if she hadn't been, she was pretty sure her legs would have given out beneath her. When Sam's truck had pulled into her driveway, she thought that she was about to lose one of the best things that had ever happened to her. But Sam had just said all of the things she wanted to hear, and it was going to take a minute for her mind to catch up. She resisted the urge to pinch herself to see if this was really happening.

When she looked at him again, his eyes begged her to say something back. The truth of everything he had just told her was reflected there. Now it was her turn to make his dreams come true the way he had for her.

"Sam—" She paused, trying to find adequate words to express the immense, mind-blowing joy that was thundering through her heart like wild horses. When they didn't come, she decided it was best to do what she always did, and stick with the facts.

"I love you, too, Sam. You're welcome in Shiloh's life, and you're exactly the kind of father that she deserves. I couldn't wish for a better one for her. But I want you in *my* life, as well. I want all of you, and even though I want to know you more, I don't care what happened in the past. I'm not going to judge you based on the person you were before. I only want the person you are now—the person I've fallen in love with in the past few days."

When Lucy finished speaking, Sam wrapped his arms around her and pulled her in for another kiss. This time it was uncomplicated, passionate and filled with hope for a future that they would share together.

When Sam pulled away, his eyes shone. “Let’s go tell our girl the good news,” he said, jumping down from the truck and lifting Lucy into his arms.

She wrapped her hands around his neck, and let him carry her off into their new life.

Epilogue

One year later
Lonestar Observatory Annual Starry Night Gala

Lucy couldn't have been happier as she watched the two of them dancing, Shiloh spinning her chair around as Sam twirled her on the dance floor. They were a sight beyond beauty—father and daughter—and Lucy was the luckiest woman in the world for having two such special people love her.

The stars overhead seemed to have been hung there just for her, and Lucy smiled, remembering the way her father's face had lit up when he'd taught her about each of the constellations, naming them for her one by one, as if handing over a gift for her to treasure. Looking at the two people she loved most in the world, she knew she had more riches than she could ever have hoped for.

Sam had come crashing into the Lonestar Café kitchen, and into her life, a year ago and changed her world forever. He spent time with Shiloh every day and had proven himself an amazing father. The two of them were inseparable. And Lucy still had to catch her breath each time he looked at her, touched her or held her in his arms. It was all unbelievably amazing—yet it was real.

And it belonged to her.

Lucy turned to Tessa and started to say something, but her best friend held up a finger. "I know," Tessa said. "I know. You are…so lucky. And I am so very, very happy for you. I love you to pieces and I'm so glad you finally stopped being so darn stubborn and let that man love you."

Lucy laughed and the sip of champagne she'd just taken nearly shot out of her nose.

"Oh, come on now," Lucy joked, "tell me how you really feel."

Tessa wrapped an arm around her shoulders and they watched Sam and Shiloh finish their dance. Sam took a bow in front of his daughter and kissed her small hand.

Lucy reached into the sleeve of her dress for a tissue to rub away the happy tears that had formed, but Tessa nudged her.

"Oh!" Tessa shook Lucy's elbow, nearly causing the champagne to jump out of her glass as she pointed furiously toward Sam and Shiloh. "Will you just look at that?"

They both stared, speechless, as a boy about Shiloh's age walked over and tapped Sam on the arm. Though the two women couldn't hear what he said, they both held their breath as Sam nodded at him, and the boy took Shiloh's hand in his, leading her back onto the dance floor.

Lucy watched as her niece's face filled with starlight, her green eyes twinkling at the cute kid's attention. Lucy laid a hand over her heart and looked at Tessa.

"I know," her best friend said. "She deserves that. Just make sure you send that kid my way if he breaks her sweet heart. I don't care how young he is, I'll kick his little ass to Timbuktu."

"Tessa!"

"What? You know it's true."

They both burst into giggles, eventually forgetting what set it off and just enjoying the laughter. By the time Sam joined them, holding out two fresh glasses of champagne, they were in hysterics and unable to take the drinks.

"What's got you two so riled up?" he asked, setting off a fresh round. "Never mind. Forget I asked." It wasn't long before Sam was laughing with them.

When they finally calmed down enough to watch

Shiloh's second dance with her new guy, Sam took Lucy's hand. His warm skin was familiar to her now, but the contact never failed to set off magic. She knew it would be that way forever, and that was how long she planned to belong to Sam.

Sam leaned over and kissed Lucy's head before tickling the top of her ear with his lips. He squeezed her hand and then led her away from where they had been standing, nodding at Tessa as they left.

"Where are we going?" Lucy asked, the speed of her pulse increasing.

"You'll see," Sam said. He led her away from the deck, away from the dance floor and farther into the dark night. When they were far enough away from the building to be alone but still bathed in the light from the party, Sam stopped and leaned down, lifting up each of Lucy's feet to remove her shoes. He hooked his thumbs into the straps, before grabbing her hand and leading her over the soft ground toward the Rigsby telescope.

"What are you doing, crazy man?" she asked, chuckling.

"For a woman who claims to trust me, you sure do ask a lot of questions," Sam said, his voice lighthearted and filled with boyish mischief.

"I'm a scientist at heart. It's what I do."

"I know. You can't help yourself, and I love that about you."

Lucy's breath was heavy by the time they reached the top of the hill.

The view from up there was even more astonishingly beautiful now than the first time they had seen it together. This time, Lucy knew Sam loved her, and she knew she didn't have to wonder about that ever again. Her heart was secure, and in that security she found a freedom that allowed her to say yes when the chance for adventure came her way.

She felt as if she'd been sleeping for most of her life, and Sam had come along and woken her up. Each day with him, new light found its way further and further into her heart, into the dark places that had formed—when she'd lost her mother, then Jennifer, then her father.

Sam hadn't erased the pain—that was impossible—but he had poured sunlight over all of it, exposing the ugliness that she'd hidden away, bringing it into the day so she could see it for what it was, and then slowly start to let it go.

She could never thank him enough.

When they got to the telescope, Sam reached into his pocket and pulled out a key. He unlocked the door to the control room and grabbed Lucy's hand with urgency, leading her inside. He closed the door, and the place was dark except a few rays of moonlight, which gleamed and bounced off Sam's sandy hair, pouring over his gorgeous face and casting shadows over his tawny eyes. He moved her to the middle of the room, letting the light splash over both of them so they could see each other.

As her eyes adjusted and his face became clear, Lucy noticed that Sam's hands were shaking.

She would play the next few moments over and over in her mind for the rest of her life, never tiring of it, like a favorite film. Time seemed to stop for the two of them as Sam dropped down to one knee, holding her gaze firmly in his the whole time.

Everything on Lucy's mind vanished in an instant, leaving only the scene in front of her. Her jaw fell as Sam's fingers disappeared into his pocket only to return with a diamond ring. It was beautiful, the moonlight glinting off it rivaling the shimmer in Sam's eyes as he said the words she'd never expected to hear, but that she realized she'd been waiting for her whole life.

"Lucy, I love you with all of my heart, and I need you more than the earth needs the sun. I refuse to live a life that doesn't have you at the center of it."

Tears escaped and were sliding down Lucy's cheeks in great waves as she anticipated Sam's next words. When they came, Lucy thought she might explode like a supernova.

Sam slid the band on her finger before he even asked the question.

"Lucy Monroe, you're the best thing that's ever happened to me. Please say you'll be my wife."

She composed herself enough to finally speak.

"Well, you better hope so, don't you, because I'm not taking this thing off my finger—" she held up her hand and marveled at the rainbows cutting through the center of the gem *"—ever."*

Sam laughed and picked Lucy up, spinning her in circles as she wrapped her arms around his neck and kissed him with everything she had. He put her down and walked over to the control room door, checking the lock, then he reached into a drawer and pulled out a blanket, winking at her as he spread it across the floor before joining her again.

When she thought back to those precious moments, alone with Sam in the telescope's bubble, what she would remember most was the way he looked at her, the way his eyes shone with love, a light stronger than anything in the cosmos. She would remember the exact second that everything she could ever have wished for fell right into her hands.

Sam belonged to her, and she was his. It was that simple, and that complex, and nothing would ever make it untrue.

Lucy didn't know if she would ever get the chance to go to space—though she'd learned enough recently not to discount the idea—but she could say now with certainty that she knew what it felt like to be over the moon.

* * * * *